During his career as a noveli writer and dissident Yuri D thing from a 'traitor to the Russia'.

He is the internationally recognized author of a diverse body of work that includes *Informer 001*, the provocative *Contemporary Russian Myths: A Skeptical View of the Literary Past* and the psychobiography of Alexander Pushkin, *Prisoner of Russia*. He has sold over 250,000 copies in Russia and is considered by many European authors (including Alexandr Solzhenitsyn) to be one of the most important Russian writers of modern times.

His satirical novel *Angels on the Head of a Pin* – published in English by Peter Owen – was named as one of the ten best Russian novels of the twentieth century by the University of Warsaw and received the Dostoevsky Prize. The novels *Passport to Yesterday* and *Madonna from Russia* have also recently been published by Peter Owen.

Blacklisted in his homeland for fifteen years, Yuri Druzhnikov survived Stalinism and endured censorship and KGB harassment before emigrating to the USA in 1988. Now he teaches literature at the University of California and lives with his wife Valerie in Davis. They have two adult children.

PUSHKIN'S SECOND WIFE
AND
OTHER MICRONOVELS

PUSHKIN'S SECOND WIFE
AND
OTHER MICRONOVELS

YURI DRUZHNIKOV

Translated from the Russian by
Thomas Moore

PETER OWEN
LONDON AND CHESTER SPRINGS, PA, USA

PETER OWEN PUBLISHERS
73 Kenway Road, London SW5 0RE

Peter Owen books are distributed in the USA by
Dufour Editions Inc., Chester Springs, PA 19425-0007

Translated from the Russian *Microromany* by Thomas Moore

First published in Great Britain 2007 by
Peter Owen Publishers

ISBN 978 0 7206 1300 1

Printed and bound in the UK by
CPI Bookmarque, Croydon, CR0 4TD

CONTENTS

Pushkin's Second Wife   11
The Man Who Read Me First   91
The Death of Tsar Fyodor   115
Cracked Pink Lampshade   141
The *Kaif* at the End of the Business Trip   168
Money Goes Round   190
Valedictory   220
30 February   244
Musical Comedy with One Part Too Many   274
Honeymooning at Great-Grandma's, *or*
    The Adventures of a *Genatsvále* from Sacramento   300
Postscript: On the Micronovel   339

PUSHKIN'S SECOND WIFE

> Allusions are forbidden.
> *Department of Censorship, State of California*

> Claims for allusion entertained daily from 8 a.m. to 5 p.m.
> Lunch break from 12 a.m. to 1 p.m. except Saturdays and Sundays
> *Legal Office, Kopper & Son*

I

Things started bustling around noon on Friday. Lectures had finished the day before, and exams were still ahead – the ideal time for a quick bash in this narrow interval. In search of an excuse for a party, one of the group of friends latched on to the fact that Todd Dankey's birthday was today. The bum was trying to keep it quiet. To hell with his inhibitions!

Everyone who could afford it chipped in on the spot. Two of them went to the nearest supermarket for some food and drink. They stuffed the car boot and the back seat full of grocery bags, and when they got back the guys started doing what girls would be doing in other countries, that is, getting the food ready and putting it out on coloured paper plates on tables in the living-room and the garden. They set up a keg of beer and a box of paper cups on the porch, then they pulled out the stopper and plugged in the pump. It wheezed gloriously, serving out the foaming, heady liquid.

The five of them were renting a three-bedroomed house on Monroe Street, with a spacious common living-room and two bathrooms, twenty minutes by bicycle from the university campus. The owner wasn't around to keep an eye on the property: he'd left California for the other end of the USA, the state of Maine, and required only that they pay the rent on a regular basis. The house was never locked. Sometimes other people – anyone who didn't have a place to spend the night – would sleep in their living-room; nobody was bothered by that. Because the old house was insured the landlord wasn't afraid of fire, and those scatterbrains could have started one easily enough.

Four of the five permanent tenants had permanent girl-friends on hand. I knew the house on Monroe Street very well because my son was one of the four. The couple that didn't have a separate bedroom built themselves a nest in the attic, right under the roof. In other words, the total population of 440 Monroe Street was nine people. The birthday boy, Todd Dankey, lived by himself in the garage.

Todd was six years older than the rest. He'd already passed umpteen examinations, had long ago finished his master's thesis and was now preparing for his doctorate, but in all other ways he was still a student. He'd made his garage rather comfortable: he slept on a saggy couch that he'd dragged over from the neighbouring hotel's rubbish bin, covering himself with a warm tartan rug. For cold nights there were two holes cut in the rug: one for him to see out of and one for a single hand, to hold books and turn out the light. He also had an armchair with traces of the original gilding, thrown out of some rich family's house and passed down from owner to numberless owner. And Todd had dragged home a written-off bookcase from the university dump. In addition to his door to the outside world, set into the former garage gates, he'd sawn out a rectangular hole in the wall, through which he could crawl like a snake from the garage into the living-room without setting foot outside.

The news that there was going to be a party on Monroe Street spread by e-mail over the entire Stanford University campus in the wink of an eye. People who had been planning to head for the coast with their aqualungs, or go horseback riding, immediately changed their plans because the Pacific Ocean wouldn't be going anywhere in the foreseeable future whereas the party was going to be today. A crowd, friends and acquaintances plus other people who just happened by, flocked to Monroe Street in cars, on bicycles, motor cycles, roller skates or just on foot. The well-off brought with them snacks and six-packs of Coke or a bottle of wine, while the penniless were looking forward to refreshments on the house. You couldn't even park your car any closer than two blocks away. Somebody came rolling up on an electrified wheel-chair, borrowed from a neighbour, and immediately demanded an extension cord to recharge it for the trip back.

Even non-drinkers on that marvellous June evening found themselves a little tipsy. Somebody explained the situation like this: 'We have to hurry up and drink as much as we can! Alcohol's been banned from campuses for a long time. Now there's a rumour going around that they're going to prohibit alcohol for students altogether, just like they're not letting doctors smoke. If a doctor lights up they take away his licence to practise, which is fair enough, but if a student has a drink – so what? He'll get his picture taken with the bottle of beer and get kicked out of the university. Now's the time to fight against totalitarianism!'

This piece of oratory was laughed at, but no one had a clue how things were going to turn out. The USA is a free country, which is to say there's freedom here to impose prohibition as well. But it also means that there is still freedom of opportunity. I forgot to mention that the city of Palo Alto, where the revelry was brewing, is the most expensive in Silicon Valley. For the crummiest nook in an old building there you have to shell out a sum that would get you a palace in other parts of the country. Here in the computer Mecca of California brains are turned inside out looking for the improbable ideas that feed the progress of computer technology in the whole sublunary world and further, on up to black holes in the universe. Here as nowhere else everyone lives in a hurry because the nice little computer you just bought becomes obsolete as soon as you leave the shop.

Smart kids – if they're lucky as well – get rich quick soon after they leave university. But they have to slave away for several years, without sleep or holidays, and consequently without any personal life either. This is why, in the computer firms of Silicon Valley, there is a definite oversupply of lonely thirty-something men who could buy an airplane each but don't even own an extra spoon. They dream of having a family, even though women don't have access to them: an affair at work today is fraught with serious unpleasantness, and the involuntary bachelors don't have any leisure time. Maybe that's why the quartet of students at the house on Monroe Street had acquired girlfriends in advance and were hurrying to make hay while the sun shone.

The fifth, Todd, in contrast to his housemates and innumerable other computerhead friends, was a liberal arts major. He did possess a spare spoon, but he would never stand a chance of getting well to do. Young people with literature and art dissertations are ten a penny, and the university arts departments are tiny and packed full. These young Californians are sustained by hope for a while, but in the end they have to go to work behind a bank cashier's window, grill hamburgers at McDonald's or deliver pizzas. This would be an uncomfortable subject on which to dwell on your birthday, since life is wonderful as long as you're a student. As they used to say generations ago, 'You're in the pink.' Once, while I was still in Moscow, I proudly used this phrase in a conversation with a US journalist; he burst out laughing, because nobody had used the phrase since the thirties. But I'd picked up 'to be in the pink' from a Soviet textbook called *Contemporary English*, published in the seventies.

Some among the growing crowd only found out whose birthday it was after the party had already heated up and Todd was being honoured in strict conformity with American tradition. They tied him to a pine tree in the garden, and everyone had the chance to express their love for him on his thirtieth birthday.

At first they just stuffed his mouth with food and drink, since the pine tree had hold of his hands. But then they started autographing his shirt and jeans with ketchup, cake icing and ice cream. Then the birthday boy got vitaminized: they squeezed the juice from tomatoes, oranges, grapefruits and lemons over his head and down his neck. They poured beer on him to help him grow and made epaulettes for him out of éclairs. Things ended with the remains of a cake being upturned over his head, the chocolate lava sliding slowly down his face and beyond. Notes of ironic congratulation were read aloud amid raucous laughter and then stuck to Todd with mustard or teriyaki sauce. He soon looked like the kind of cylindrical pillar used for sticking up personal ads. The remains of a salad slid down through his beard, and pink whipped cream hung from his eyebrows. Now, of course, Todd was literally 'in the pink'. Figuratively, the whole crowd was.

Then people started dancing around the figure tied to the pine tree. Then they started doing a circle-dance. Eventually the girls decided to call a halt to the outrage. One of them unrolled the hose they used to wash their cars and played a strong stream of water over Todd.

They carried on until four in the morning, and then the crowd of people just as merrily went their various ways. Anyone who lived too far away, or was afraid to drive in such a state of intoxication, settled down on the rag rugs in the living-room or made off with a blanket and a bundle of old newspapers and found themselves a place on the grass under the trees. Three people contrived to drive off in the wheelchair, which had had a thorough recharge by this time. For a long while the house continued to hum like a hive with all the bees at home. Here and there you could hear sleepy sounds in the darkness, snatches of phrases, singing and moans of love. Most likely their neighbours had called the police, more than once, to ask if they could come and quieten the idiots down.

I myself once had to call the police when there was a student bash going on next door, and I had to give a lecture the next morning. You couldn't just go and ask them to tone down the racket: that's an intrusion into someone's private life. The police just knock on the door and politely request them to turn down the decibels, but they're the representatives of the law and have the right to ask after ten o'clock at night. So when I phoned them the duty policewoman answered, 'I'll pass this on to a patrol car now. We'll try to help, but it *is* the end of the semester, as you know. Yours is complaint number one hundred and thirty-nine, and there's only the one patrol car for the whole town.'

They did come, but only when everything had already died down on its own.

So, in a word, nobody interfered with the bash on Monroe Street. And everything came to an end through natural fatigue. Todd had to take a hot shower to remove all the butter, icing and cream, using plenty of shampoo to get the chocolate out of his hair and wash off the sticky teriyaki sauce. Now he lay in his garage for a long time, staring dully at the ceiling and listening to the various sounds coming from his friends' rooms. As I already said, he was the only one who didn't sleep with a girlfriend.

Everyone loved Dankey the Postgrad. He was an open and smiling sort of dude, tow-headed, with a beard that was red even when it wasn't covered with ketchup, a little taller than medium height and fairly well built. He loved to swim and now and then would even drive over to the ocean, put on his wetsuit when the water was cold and go surfing. He had only one weak spot: everyone in the group had already had several girlfriends, getting together with the opposite sex and splitting up just as easily, whether painfully or just by accident, whereas it was suspected that Todd was still a virgin at his newly achieved age of thirty. In any case, it seemed that Todd's friends suffered over his chastity more than he did himself.

More than once they had tried slipping promising girl students into his life. Todd would first take the girl to Lake Tahoe up in the mountains (or she would take him), five hours knee-to-knee; they'd stroll along the shore admiring the bottomless blue of the water, then casually squander a few dollars at the casino for fun. He would take her to a restaurant for dinner (according to American custom a woman's consent, especially a young one's, to go to a restaurant often signifies that, even though she would doubtless be paying for herself, she *is* prepared for things to go further). But then, instead of just renting a room at the first available motel like anyone else, on the principle of striking while the iron was hot, Todd would suggest renting a four-wheel bike for a ride around the park or he'd take her to the movies, driving for five hours through the night back to Palo Alto. He would drive her to her home (or she to his). Back at her place, or here, in front of his garage, after a pregnant pause, she would give him a peck on the cheek and disappear.

His friends began to suspect a certain limp-wristedness (California is famous for it, after all), but there was no reek of that on him at all. He liked women, and they liked him, although Todd seemed to approach them the wrong way. Maybe he would get embarrassed, or say the wrong thing, get his timing wrong, or overdo it, or his hands would suffer from paralysis at the wrong moment as though gripped by some devilish force. What could be easier in this super-emancipated age of ours? But, every opportunity he got, he blew it, and this had turned into a complex.

Besides, Todd had a secret that he'd never told anyone: he'd been married once before, although it hadn't worked out. Why Todd kept his marriage a secret is an important question, and we'll come to that. The short answer is that he concealed it from his friends because he was too ashamed to admit it.

On the Sunday morning after the party everyone sloped around the house on Monroe Street as sleepy as sheep on a hot day. They should have been chasing after some hair of the dog, but this custom hasn't really taken root in the USA yet. Finally, when the guests who'd crashed out had gone their separate ways, their hosts, in bathrobes, bathing-suits or shorts, gradually assembled around the kitchen table to get some coffee. They ate up the leftovers from the night before which had been shoved into the fridge anyhow or scattered around the living-room or the garden. When Todd snaked his way into the room through the hole in the garage wall, everyone suddenly fell silent. He paid no attention but opened the lid of the washing-machine and threw in his clothes, stained with dried icing, juice and chocolate, and poured in some soap. But the other exchanged looks that seemed to say they hadn't yet had enough of their practical jokes and were preparing another surprise for him.

Pouring himself some coffee and grabbing a chunk of cheese off the table, without paying attention to any of the conversation, Todd pressed the button and the old washing-machine began to rumble, unhappy at the clothes being so filthy.

'Listen, Dankey,' Brian said to him, twisting a long braid of hair around one finger as Todd joined them at the table. 'We've just sort of thunk up a kind of really tempting little project . . . Kind of like a present for you.'

Brian had come to study at Stanford from South Africa; he'd just got his master's degree in computer science and had rustled himself up a spot with a small company in San José.

Either everyone back home in Pretoria was devoted to jokes, practical and otherwise, or else he was a unique specimen, I don't know, but he was drawn to the pursuit more than he was to studying or working.

'So, any luck with your morning-after brainstorm?' Todd enquired, rocking back in his squeaky armchair. He put his coffee mug down on the floor.

'The morning after is a hard row to hoe, indeed, but we've been brainstorming in spirals. We're going off in search of a tenth member for our little collective. What about you – are you in?'

'Yeah, but it's already crowded here,' Todd muttered, getting the hint right away, and started spreading peanut butter on a slice of bread.

'Massa doan' undastan'.' Brian exchanged looks with his snub-nosed girlfriend, Leslie. 'We're the ones who are crowded, and you've got all the room you want. We're going to advertise on the internet that we're looking for a young lady with particular attributes – which we're going to discuss with you right now. You, old man – what kind of girl, in principle, do you like the best: big or small, fat or skinny? You just specify, and we –'.

Todd waved him down. 'Here you go foisting some broad off on me again. But I've decided finish my dissertation first.'

The company was indignant and grew noisy. 'Come off it!' Brian pouted. 'You're too serious, old man, that's your problem. Where's the play of that lively and inquisitive mind of yours? We'll get as many ads out as possible. Maybe at least someone will suit you and, if not you, maybe us. It's time we got an update as well – right, girls?'

The girls considered this a bit rude, but it would have been ridiculous to get indignant, so they just giggled.

'Just kidding.' Brian winked at Leslie. 'Polygamy's still prohibited in America.'

'And you really do want to waste your time,' Todd grumbled.

'The important thing is to have fun. Life without games is

like a robot-controlled conveyor belt churning out tooth-brushes.'

'If you want to have your fun, go ahead. What's it got to do with me?'

'You just have to let us know your requirements. That's all.'

'Why bust a gut?' Todd opened the Sunday supplement to the *San Francisco Chronicle*. 'Here they've got all the phraseology and all the numbers. "Real man with empty heart . . ." Or "Athletic and cheerful guy wants to meet charming girl . . ." Will that do? Or this, "Looking for girlfriend, with whom I can –"'

'Can what?' everybody cackled.

'What size bust do you want?' Brian elucidated. 'Large, medium or small?'

'Well, let's say the bigger the better.'

'OK! That's what we'll say . . . Candidates from around the world are going to be writing you. We're all somewhat occupied, at present, and you're as free as a bird. I was just looking at a Filipino marriage magazine: there they usually give their height and the size of their hips, waist and bust. But that's boring. What if we add a spiritual dimension? Suggest that the candidates do some sort of . . . ? Think, Socrates, think! You're the only philosophy major around here.'

'Have them write a poem and send that,' Todd suggested. He made the suggestion because he enjoyed writing verse, although he seldom showed it to anybody; you weren't going to impress the world today with poetry.

'Hey, there's an idea! A sort of exam. Are they worthy of our intellectual friend, Todd? Make them pass a test.'

'Besides, we haven't got any women poets here, have we?' Leslie came to life. 'And you can add: "Wants to get acquainted with a view to a stable relationship." That always gets them.'

Brian stuck to his own tack. 'It'd be better to put "an unstable relationship".'

'No, we have to attract them with something.' Leslie patted Todd, as if accustoming him to the thought. 'And to make it look respectable, add the words "and possible marriage".'

'What, are you serious? You can all go to hell!' Todd burst out. 'I don't need any talk of marriage! I'm fed up to here with it. There's nothing good about it, just bad news.'

'Really? You've never given us an inkling . . .'

'I've never said anything because I've been hoping to forget about it.'

If someone isn't going to show his hand, you can't force him to. Todd didn't finish his coffee. He jumped up in a temper, pulled his clothes out of the machine, threw them into the dryer and dragged his once-gilded armchair across the garden to his place in the garage.

When Todd had gone, after a silence Brian said, 'It's a brilliant idea, but he's against it. But why do we have to do what he says? It's a free country . . . Let's send off the ad without his consent, and he can sort it out. What kind of girl does he like best? Let's put "blonde".'

Brian pulled his laptop out of his bag, the little computer that never left his side, connected it up to the phone line and sent the ad out over the world wide web.

2

They had installed a computer at the Pushkin Apartment Museum at 12 Moyka Street in the city of St Petersburg. Why they had installed it no one could understand. Pushkin didn't seem to need one, and the cashier even less so: she had her splendid, ageless abacus – little balls on wires. But how could they not take the computer if their sponsors had bought themselves a new one and were now making a grand gesture by giving the museum their old one?

Tamara the tour guide had proved herself to be the most advanced in this sphere. Anton, her husband, worked as a programmer for the steamship company. Tamara brought computer games to work with her, and now, taking a break between tours, with the director nowhere to be seen, she was playing a card game against the computer. Diana Morgalkina exuded indignation; playing games in the apartment where Pushkin died was blasphemous.

'What's wrong with it?' Tamara protested. 'Pushkin loved to play cards, and he bequeathed that to us.'

'Lolling around in this place is shameful!' Diana growled.

'You get the work you pay for,' was the reply.

Incidentally, before the computer age, Diana had become indignant whenever anyone in the place had told a joke. Nobody loved Diana, but they tolerated her, because she was a born tour guide and worked willingly for herself and for others.

Diana was a strange creature but not bad at all. She wasn't very tall, but she wasn't short either, not young but not old, thin but not badly built. Her face was regular, without noticeable defects, just not looked after. Her skin knew no creams, her hair no do, her eyelashes no mascara. Her teeth were all hers. They could have been whiter and more even; that wasn't her fault, though, just the underdevelopment of Russian dentistry. Diana's weak point was something else entirely. For her profession, she was not very – or, more precisely, she was very *un* – sociable. Her outer coolness, her aloofness from the people around her, put them off.

She didn't share her womanly secrets with anyone. No one had ever been to her place. She never did anyone any harm, never even saying a bad word about anyone, but inflexible as she was, unable to adapt like other people to the constant vicissitudes of life, she was always a loser. Diana had taken languages at university because she loved reading books; she said she wanted to become a journalist but had never written a single article in her life, persuading herself that all her energy was going into the spoken word. She'd got a job at the Pushkin Museum, and Pushkin didn't just feed her, however miserly her salary was; he was her buttress – in him alone lay the reason for her existence. She kept a diary, day after day, at home. The only thing she was ever candid with was her notebook. And, through this notebook, candid with Pushkin.

Eight years earlier a romance had developed between Diana and the Pushkin scholar Konvoysky, a man well known in that small circle. Unfortunately she soon came to understand that, he loved neither her nor even Pushkin but only his own compositions on the subject and never spoke about anything else. He would walk around the room and read his academic compilations out loud to her. Their intimate relations were strange, without intimacy, which Konvoysky didn't need for some reason. With his slipperiness and tediousness he'd turned her off other men, and once he'd left her Diana had concentrated her adoration more and more upon Pushkin. The incorporeality of this devotion was also somewhat disconcerting, but its advantages were indisputable. Pushkin, in contrast to Konvoysky, loved her devotedly, and, what was even more important, their relationship always depended upon *her* mood and not in the least on Pushkin's.

In contrast to her colleagues, Diana took things seriously. Even though they all worked in the same institution, the others were servants of the government, while her master was Pushkin. They worked for money, while she, even though she received the same 'slave ration', as Pushkin put it, laboured out of love. Finishing their tours as quickly as they could, they would try to sit that little bit longer in their crowded staff cubbyhole drinking green tea out of the little handleless cups that somebody had brought back from Samarkand. They would blather away about any old thing as long as it didn't concern work; at lunchtime they would sneak off down Nevsky Prospect to hit all the shops (not to buy anything – their wages were too paltry for that – just for window-shopping). Diana didn't even go home for lunch, even though she lived near by, on Millionnaya Street. Whenever she uttered the last words of her tour in the poet's study, she would weep, because the poet dies in the end. As she conducted eight identical tours per day, eight times she would weep at the end.

Diana's parents had passed away long before, and her brother, who had his own family, had gone abroad to make his living. Nobody at work except Tamara had ever made friends with Diana, and even Tamara was only nominally a friend. Life had not dealt Tamara any trumps, but she still had a non-drinker for a husband and an almost healthy little girl at school and had no complexes of her own; Tamara remained a cockeyed optimist. She wanted to know about everything, be everywhere, laugh at everyone.

'Look around you, girls,' Tamara said. 'If you take everything seriously, you'd be better off hanging yourselves straight away.' She provided a third of Petersburg with its tales and gossip, and she always knew which artists and writers had split up with whom and who else they'd taken up with.

Her husband had taught Tamara how to surf the internet, but even there her curiosity was insatiable. She had frequently run across marriage advertisements. Naturally enough, notions about the lonely Diana came into her mind. Several times Tamara had suggested to her, 'Come on, Morgalkina, let's answer one of these ads. He might be interested. You'll go nuts without a man . . .' But Diana didn't even want to hear about it, never mind getting caught up in that game.

Once, when the weather was awful and they weren't about to let anyone go home early, even though the number of evening tours had tailed sharply off, Tamara was fiddling with the mouse, surfing from one internet site to another. Suddenly, reading an ad, she said, 'Hmmph', and decided to have a go at teasing Diana. A devil had got into Tamara and was guiding her hand. The imp scribbled off a coquettish reply to the get-acquainted proposal, filling in details matching the man's requirements, indeed exceeding them. The ad included a request to compose a poem. The devil flicked its tail, smoothed down the forelock between its horns and added a poem.

Nobody ever says anything but good about themselves, and fewer still read this wordy crap, the imp prompted Tamara. *Sign the e-mail 'Two-Faced Diana'. Maybe the guy will ask 'Why two-faced?' out of curiosity.* The outcome wouldn't bother Tamara at all, since she never did anything seriously. Pressing the return key, she sent the e-mail on its way and turned off the computer. The imp sitting on the monitor clapped its hands in glee.

3

On Monroe Street in Palo Alto, Brian, the student who'd signed himself Todd Dankey, received proposals to get acquainted from sixty-two candidates from all over the world. They had all added poems of varying degrees of romanticism. Some of the letters had been lifted whole from handbooks published for the purpose in countries where there's an over-supply of marriageable girls.

When Brian flung the batch of printed-out hard copies of the e-mails on to his desk, Todd got angry. But everybody had already had a laugh at his expense, and it would have been stupid to make a big deal out of this prank. Todd dragged his aristocratic armchair out of the garage and back into the living-room, sat down in it, and together with his friends set about studying the e-mails that had arrived. As he went along he marked little pluses and minuses alongside the bust sizes and other attractions indicated.

Nobody bothered reading most of the poems, written in Japanese, Chinese, Hindi and some other language unknown to anyone there, although among their fellow students it wouldn't have been hard to find any kind of interpreter. One poem caught Todd's attention, however, and he read it simply because the text turned out to be Russian, and Russian was going to be Todd's future profession. The untitled poem appeared to describe a certain hypothetical sexual situation.

> She approaches, he reclines
> And dozes in voluptuary comfort;
> The covering slips from off his couch
> And his brow's encauled in hot down.
> The silent maid before him
> Stands unmoving, breathless,
> Like two-faced Diana
> Before her darling shepherd.
> And now she, upon the khan's bed
> Lowering down on to a single knee,
> Sighs, her face inclines to him
> With languor, with a keen trembling,
> And sunders sleep for the lucky man
> With a mute and passionate kiss . . .

Todd's Russian was good but not enough to catch all the nuances, the old-fashioned style of it or to detect the hoax. He translated the poem for his friends as best he could. Two of the more obsolete words he had to look up in his dictionary, and a couple of others he guessed from their context.

'In your mangy garage,' Brian retold the story, 'her face inclines to yours and . . . what happens? A *ki-i-i-ssssss*. And what a kiss! A mute and passionate one. Can you imagine? The ideal woman: on the one hand passionate, on the other – mute . . . And her vital statistics are perfect!'

Todd showed the poem to his academic adviser, Professor Josef Verstakyan, a man of Russian origin with Armenian antecedents. He looked at it and chuckled, 'These lines are good, wonderful even. But do you know who the author is?'

'Of course,' Todd nodded. 'A girl I know.'

'Your friend has quite a gift!' Verstakyan said. 'A really talented visionary. But this *is* a poem by Pushkin, after all.'

Todd was astounded and didn't believe him. He dragged himself off to the library and spent half the day looking through volume after volume of the collected works of

Pushkin. Professor Verstakyan turned out to be right. Todd explained away the plagiarism in his own way. His correspondent clearly had a sense of humour, since she had made the joke, and that was already something.

Todd Dankey was writing his dissertation, albeit slowly, on a wholly appropriate subject: 'Feminist tendencies in the works of Alexander Pushkin'. Verstakyan, who had suggested the splendid subject to his graduate student, understood full well that if there were any such tendencies in Pushkin's works, from the point of view of, let's say, an educated American woman nowadays they would be considered wholly anti-feminist. Pushkin, according to the feminists, was by every possible measure a typical male chauvinist pig. But Verstakyan also understood full well the speculative tendency in US comparative literature. Feminism was trendy, these days money was going – with alacrity – on research into it, and it was easy to score a hit.

For me, writing these lines, as it surely was for Professor Verstakyan, it's somewhat sad and shameful that on this liberated American continent the expression 'Right now, you have to write about such-and-such . . .' sounds just as peremptory as it did on one-sixth of the earth's land mass under any of the old Communist leaders. In truth, irony knows no bounds. What was in store for doctoral candidate Todd Dankey was the scribbling of over three hundred pages of academic reasoning for the case that Pushkin was the first feminist in Russia, developed women's literature, fought for the emancipation of Russian women, their equal rights with men in politics and, of course, in the sphere of sex and in general facilitated the progress of society with respect to its feminine half. To collect his material, Todd had to go to Russia and spend time there in libraries and archives.

Todd wasn't exactly getting excited about the e-mail from St Petersburg, but he wasn't completely indifferent to it either. In any case, after some hesitation, he decided to answer it. Now he was sending off an e-mail himself.

Tamara was now getting drawn into composing of flir-
tatious letters, too. She didn't conceal this from her husband;
on the contrary, she consulted him about the psychology of
the stud, and how to turn someone on, to hook a live one.

'What do you want to do that for?' Anton asked.

'Life's a bore, that's what for!' she explained.

But she always signed her letters 'Diana', and at first she
told her everything about the correspondence as well. But then
she stopped, because Margalkina showed no enthusiasm for it.

Todd said he needed to correspond with this girl from St
Petersburg to practise the language. Maybe that was true, but
he was getting hooked. Todd's friends started trying to convince him to visit the Russian bear to check out the results of
Pushkin's hard work for emancipation, as well as to see Two-
Faced Diana with his own two eyes. Todd resisted, at first
actively then just from inertia. At this point his friends all
chipped in and put a ticket on his pillow in the garage. He paid
for the visa himself. Ostensibly he was going there for
research, so the department paid for it, and Todd paid his
friends back. But the correspondence added a sharp cayenne-
pepper piquancy to the trip.

When he told them in St Petersburg that he was coming,
Todd received an intriguing answer, hinting at great pleasure,
with the same signature, 'Two-Faced Diana'.

4

Tamara firmly decided to say nothing to Diana, since it would
have been useless trying to talk her into it. She was as stubborn
as a mule. But the day before Todd was to arrive, in a break
between two guided tours, she glanced at the uncombed and
manicureless Morgalkina, the sloven, and could suddenly no
longer hold back.

'Just look at your hair: no colour, no styling. Let me take
you to Kostya's.'

'What do I need a hairdo for?'

'The director isn't happy. What do our visitors think about you, and about our whole museum, when they see you?'

'The most important thing here is the spiritual nourishment –'

'What the hell kind of spiritual nourishment can you get from a scarecrow?' She pulled Diana over to the mirror and opened a French magazine. 'Compare these beauties with yourself. If you don't want to look decent, you don't have to. But the director's going to fire you and hire somebody who *does* look better than you.'

Diana didn't say a word. She couldn't come up with an answer.

'Here, my dear,' Tamara said, not giving her a chance to recover herself. 'Let's go to Kostya's together. I have to get a hairdo as well. Today, straight after work!'

Tamara waited until nobody was in the staffroom and telephoned Kostya, the hair stylist. She'd had quite a close relationship with Kostya in the past, although now there was only a practical friendship between them.

'I'm bringing one of my girlfriends to you. You have to turn her into a blonde by accident.'

'What?' asked Kostya. 'There's never a dull moment with you, Tamara.'

'Lord, what a dimwit you are! All you have to do is muddle up the dyes, and that's it.'

'But what if she sues me for it?'

'Don't worry, she won't.'

'Or she might scratch my eyes out . . .'

'Do what you're told, Kostya. You'll be all right, I guarantee. She'll even thank you for it. Somebody from America is coming to marry her, and he was told that she's a blonde. Geddit? Just don't warn her in advance!'

Tamara and Diana left the museum together. They sat in

line at the hairdressers' for two hours. Diana was about to get up and leave when Kostya sat her down in his chair.

'It's been some time since the hand of a real master has touched you, girl,' he purred into her ear. 'We're going to make you beautiful. Trust me?'

'Do it, Kostya,' Tamara urged him on. 'Do it, quick!'

'Or maybe we should give her a shaggy look,' he continued, accidentally on purpose trailing his fingers down the back of her neck.

'Knock off your stupid jokes,' Tamara cut him short.

Kostya wrapped a plastic cloak around Diana and pushed her head down into the basin under the tap.

'The water's really hot,' Diana gurgled, indistinctly.

'Keep quiet, or you'll choke.' Kostya was already lathering her up.

An hour later, when she went back to the mirror and Kostya took off her cowl, a gloomy blonde looked back at Diana.

'What have you done?' Diana yelped. 'Who told you to do that?'

Kostya pointed the finger at Tamara right away. 'What do you mean, who? She did! But, you know, it suits you. I'm telling you that as an expert. Just like a real bride!'

'Smile,' Tamara ordered her, 'and keep on smiling until you get married.'

'I don't want to get married!' Diana yelled, and the women in the queue laughed.

Her eyes opened wide, and a cold conjecture congealed within them. Her scruffy appearance had always been her defence against the problems of the outside world, which was full of dangers. But it was too late to fight it: she was already a blonde.

'What – is he on his way?' Diana asked.

'Who?' Tamara pretended not to understand, but she was delighted at the question.

'Don't pretend, I'm not a child. The guy . . . from California . . .'

'Congratulations!' said Kostya, sitting Tamara down in his chair and starting to work his magic on her.

Diana, meanwhile, was having quiet hysterics. Neither of them could calm her down.

'Stupid twit!'Tamara baldly announced as she paid Kostya. 'You're howling like someone's sold you into a Persian shah's harem. Who the hell needs you? And happiness was *this* possible for you, *this* close . . .'

Diana was forced to shell out for her transformation into a blonde, even though it was a blatant outrage. On their way home she announced that she didn't think she would go ahead and meet him.

'Whatever,' was Tamara's answer. 'But at least the goods now bear some relationship to the customer's requirements. You're a blonde.Your bust is the right size. I thought you were a grown woman, but you're a zombie. My social conscience is clear. I've done what I could, and you can just go ahead and win the Hero of Russia award for your chastity!'

Diana just kept sobbing.They parted on that note.

5

Todd flew into St Petersburg towards evening. Friends that he'd made before, when he was an exchange student for a semester at Leningrad State University, met him at Pulkovo airport with open arms. They took the sleepy traveller home for a party.

On the plane he'd sworn to himself that he wasn't going to let a drop of liquor pass his lips, and he kept repeating the oath to himself in the car on the way to the city. Being a Slavic languages graduate student was harder than being any other kind. Not because you had to read a lot every day. If you wanted to have anything to do with Russian culture, you had to learn how to drink. And Todd had attained some mastery of this part of the culture. When he was in the city before, his Petersburg buddies had put on a farewell party for him – at his expense, of course. On the way back to his place he'd collapsed on the pavement and came to his senses in a drunk tank. When he woke up, all of his money and his return ticket had disappeared, his jeans had been exchanged for some ripped cotton workman's pants, and he was warned that if he so much as hinted at it he'd never get to leave the country. In a word, the alkie-Slavicist had undergone a sort of specialist training.

When Todd had got back to Palo Alto on that occasion, he'd remained an adherent of the principle of daily alcohol use in accordance with the well-known adage 'Drunk in the morning, free all day'. His housemates decided to kick him out, since one souse among sober people is irritating. He would now and then borrow money for something to drink but never had any money to pay it back. On top of that, Todd couldn't pay his share of the rent. So they evicted him from the garage, giving his place to a newly arrived grad student on an exchange programme from the Sorbonne. But then they felt sorry for him and let him hang around, so Todd took to sleeping wherever he could, rolling out his sleeping-bag on the floor at night and in the mornings hiding it in the fireplace which nobody ever had the energy to light. Things went on like that for nearly a year and a half. Then his friends found him a job, pressured him on a daily basis to give up his drinking, and, when the garage came free again, he moved back in.

But from the very first day of his present visit to Russia, a bottle of vodka was set on the table in every Petersburg apartment as soon as he appeared at the threshold. And he had a whole notebook full of addresses, not just of his own bottle-buddies but of acquaintances of his Stanford friends who had been to Petersburg before, so he sloshed from one place to another. For a week Todd never dried out, rolling from one party to the next, with everyone explaining to him how alcohol truly facilitated the progress of mankind in every sphere and in the development of the science of philology in particular. The more vodka, the quicker the progress. To the delight of his hosts, he took to toasting them with a particular banality that he'd learned from a teacher of German and Russian at his San Francisco college, a great admirer of elbow-bending and an expert in alcoholic folklore: 'Anyone not drinking is a sneak.'

One day Todd went visit a friend who worked in the offices of *Pitersky Bomond* magazine. There they were hitting the bottle because they'd just got some money from a sponsor. When they parted a fine rain was drizzling down, although Todd had left his cap and umbrella at his hostel that morning. It was the end of October, and dusk was setting in early. He walked along the Moyka in the direction of Nevsky Prospekt and suddenly came to a halt. The door of the Pushkin Museum was closed, and there was an 'Open' sign hanging on it. Todd had already taken in the museum of the famous Russian feminist – a quality obvious even to a hedgehog – on his last trip to St Petersburg. He was now in a state of severe inebriation, otherwise no one would have been able to drag him into the museum again except in handcuffs with a gag over his mouth so he couldn't resist and couldn't shout. But he remembered something about his silly correspondence with a certain Two-Faced Diana, who was supposed to be working here as a tour guide.

While he was trying to decide whether to go in, the rain came down heavier. Todd tumbled in and stopped indecisively inside the door.

'Come on in, sonny.' The elderly ticket-seller waved him in. 'A tour has just started.'

'Er, what's the name of the tour g—' Todd stumbled, not knowing how to say it.

He'd learned Russian well, but he spoke it worse than he did French or Spanish, especially in his cups. The ticket-seller understood.

'Her name's Diana. But what difference does that make to you? They're all great; they know their business.'

'What should I give you?' he asked. 'Dollars or roubles?'

'Dollars,' the ticket-seller swiftly replied.

Todd held out a five-dollar bill.

'Will that do?'

'Of course it will. God bless you! This way, up those stairs. And slippers – tie those slippers over your shoes . . .'

The ticket lady indicated where he had to go with one hand, while she quickly hid the five-dollar bill in her bra with the other.

He had to tie the dirty slippers on over his dirty boots. Stomping into the group of tourists and looking around, Todd hiccupped from time to time. His head was swimming. Now and again he'd bump into someone or step on someone's feet and apologize in a loud whisper. The tour guide, a pretty blonde, as it seemed to him from a distance, held her pointer horizontally, sticking the sharp end into the tourist closest to her. Now and again she would pass her gaze over the group of twenty or so people and in a husky voice say something about this house that Pushkin had lived in for all of four months.

Todd made an attempt to get to one side, to check out her legs. But she was wearing a long dress, as it turned out. *That means*, he thought, *either that it's fashionable here, or she hasn't got anything to brag about under her dress.*

In Pushkin's cramped study the tour guide stopped in front of a little couch and waited for the visitors to arrange themselves, to fill up the empty spaces and quieten down. In a sepulchral voice she pronounced the part of the presentation that always brought a quiver to her throat: 'It was on this sofa that the mortally wounded poet lay. Pushkin asked for some cloudberries, something he dearly loved. On the twenty-ninth of February of the year one thousand eight hundred and thirty-seven, at two forty-five in the afternoon, his pulse stopped and his hands grew cold. Pushkin, unable to bear his torments, pass . . . passed away . . .'

Tears glistened in her eyes. She tried to hold them back; she pulled out a handkerchief, dabbed at her eyelids. Her imagining of the moment of his death was so vivid that her tears would always flow, involuntarily. But today she actually burst into sobs. Her nerves were probably under strain.

'Here, now, there's no need for that . . . Why are you carrying on like that, my girl?' an elderly woman, a teacher by her appearance, tried to soothe her. 'It was such a long while ago, anyway . . .'

'For you it was a long time ago,' the tour guide objected sharply, her voice catching. 'But for me it's as though it's right now.'

The tourists stood in embarrassment, holding up the following group. Somebody from the back walked to the exit. Their guide finally calmed down. She wiped her reddened eyes with her dainty little handkerchief.

'If you have any questions,' she said, 'I'll answer them with pleasure.'

'Any questions at all?' asked Todd with a smile, trying to look her in the eye and concealing his accent. He was just asking out of boredom. He didn't expect an answer. Diana worked out straight away who he was. She pressed her lips together so as not to give anything away, but her cheeks flushed.

'What exactly interests you?'

'Well, where's the bed?'

'What do you want a bed for, young man?' she riposted, losing it.

'Not for me! I just meant that the poet needed a bed for himself and his wife. Maybe I'm wrong . . .'

The tourists smiled. Someone laughed.

With anyone who spoke not just disrespectfully of Pushkin but even without the proper pathos, Diana would refuse to associate ever again. She would walk past them, suppressing her anger, and turn her face away. But this was a foreigner, after all. *Maybe he doesn't understand what Pushkin means to us.* None the less, after a brief pause, she pronounced sternly, 'This is a museum, young man, and not . . .'

'Not what?' He failed to understand.

'Nothing! Your exit is on the right.' Diana regarded him with hostility. 'And you should drink less, too!' Turning sharply, she walked into the tour guides' room.

Their work day at an end, her fellow-workers ran off to their homes. Tamara, of course, divined from a distance who this person of the masculine gender was, conversing with her friend. Glancing at him as he walked off, she whispered to Diana, 'You idiot! There's no way he's a local, or even an émigré. A classy guy, and a real American, to boot . . .'

Diana didn't answer. Wrapping herself in her raincoat she stopped for an instant in front of the exit to get her umbrella ready so that she could open it right away on the other side of the door, and then she dived out into the street slush and was swallowed up by the dark.

The rain stopped, but the damp hung in the air and swollen drops were falling from the trees. Diana strode along quite determinedly, as usual. She didn't look around, but after a while she began to feel that she was being followed. At the metro station she slowed down and turned sharply around. Todd nearly ran into her.

'What do you want from me?'

He recalled that he'd flown to St Petersburg to find this Two-Faced Diana, and aboard the plane he'd dreamed in detail of what they were going to do and how. But now he was standing almost right up against this blonde and no sort of electric spark was springing up in his vodka-soaked body.

'As a matter of fact, I have some more questions.' Todd looked at her with the utmost seriousness. 'For instance, why are there so many Pushkin museums in Russia?'

'Well, he's Pushkin, after all!'

'OK. Let's say he lived in a hundred different places. Are you going to have museums everywhere? Isn't one enough? After all, it's the taxpayers' money, and life is hard here. Look how many Lenin museums there were, and now you're tearing them all down. Maybe it'd be better to spend the money on public toilets than on Pushkin.'

'What do you mean? How dare you!'

Todd realized that it had been a mistake to mention toilets. It wasn't a romantic topic.

'Pardon the expression.' He remembered this phrase, long ago dinned into him.

'I won't pardon you!'

'But look at Ireland, Dublin. I was there last summer. My ancestors come from there. It's a small country and poor. They've opened a single museum for all their writers. And they don't charge writers any taxes at all, and the government supports magazines and publishers. But your taxes all go on dead writers, while the living, as far as I can see, have no life at all!'

He reached out amicably and grasped a button of hers that had been badly sewn on. She steered his hand away, but she didn't know what to answer, so she said, 'You don't understand anything!'

Turning sharply on her heel, she strode determinedly away from him. Todd wanted to carry on the conversation, but he was left all alone in the middle of the pavement. He looked after her, turning over the button in his fingers. His stupor had passed, but the jet lag was still making itself felt. Todd wanted only to tumble into bed and go to sleep.

6

It was an ordinary day at the museum. The museum director was arguing with the ticket-seller, who had been pocketing the money without tearing up the tickets. The ticket-seller didn't give a damn about the director or the museum; she had retired long before, and she was earning extra money there but not a whole lot. The corridor was crowded with milling visitors, waiting for a tour guide to come out to them. The tour guides themselves were all cooped up in their cubbyhole. The usual female palaver was under way. At the table payslips were being filled in. Sandwiches were being eaten, makeup being put on, and two ladies were smoking a single Marlboro cigarette, dragging on it in turn. Tamara was playing a card game on the computer. Diana was putting a plaster on a finger that she had scratched on a nail that stuck out of her old couch when the telephone rang.

'Diana,' someone yelled from the far corner of the room, 'it's for you. A pleasant, masculine baritone, by the way, and what seems like a foreign accent.'

Sighing, Diana got up from her chair and took the phone.

'Who is it?'

'Todd.'

'Todd who?' she pretended not to know who he was.

'The guy who wanted to see you home last night. Maybe we can get together?'

'What for?'

'Hmmmm. So I can give you your button back.'

'What button?'

'It came off in my hand. I want to beg your pardon for depriving you of your button. But if you agree, we can have dinner together . . .'

'I'm busy.'

'Then can I call again? You might be free, all of a sudden?'

'Anyone has the right to telephone the museum.'

The cubbyhole had grown silent. Everyone was curious about who it was who'd shown up for Diana out of the blue and was calling her in the middle of the day to invite her somewhere and her just mucking him about. Evidently the voice on the telephone was insistent, because she answered, 'I don't know. Maybe. If I can . . . If I have any free time . . . But only to get my button back!'

And she hung up the phone.

'Don't be stupid, Diana,' Tamara observed, not taking her eyes off her computer.

'What do I need him for?'

'What if he's got serious intentions?'

'I don't need any of his intentions, serious or otherwise. I don't want to know him.'

'The blonde starts getting tough on guys in her old age,' commented someone, and everyone guffawed.

'Let's go, girls!' another voice rang out. 'These are personal matters, but we have to go to work. The director's in the corridor – can't you hear him fuming out there?'

Tamara hung on, trying to beat the computer, but again without success.

'Listen, friend, don't try to be a clever clogs.' Diana was back on her favourite hobbyhorse. 'I don't need anybody! And, anyway, Diana is a symbol of virginity.'

'What, you want to preserve your virginity to the grave, do you? But you'll be lying there all alone, you know.'

Shrugging her shoulders, Tamara switched off her computer, got up and went out, slamming the door. Arguing with her was hard; Tamara was never at a loss for a choice word. So Diana sulked, as usual.

Left on her own, Diana thought about it a little longer and convinced herself to go on a date with the man – but only to get her coat button back from that wretched American alcoholic. You couldn't get buttons like that at any price nowadays.

Todd did call back again. She went to meet him after work. He was stone cold sober and terribly courteous. He'd pored over a map of St Petersburg and found a nice place to have dinner. Half an hour later they were sitting at a table at the Belye Nochi restaurant. Todd studied Diana, which she could feel, not without a certain curiosity.

'Why are you smiling all the time?' she asked.

'That's what I was taught to do.'

'Where?'

'I was working as an inspector for the Safeway super-market chain to earn some money for my education. Everyone they hire has to undergo special training, where they're taught to smile.'

'It wouldn't hurt me to go to a school like that,' she said, suddenly lightening up.

'Maybe in Russia it's normal to be sad and serious all the time. But where I come from you can be fired for a facial expression like that. You have to be pleasant to customers when they're in the store. I had to put on clothes that made me look worse off and go to the Safeways in other towns as an ordinary customer, best of all at night, during rush-hour, when the checkout clerks were tired and everyone was in a hurry. I'd pick up any old thing in the store, for instance, a box of cookies or a can of beans, put it down in front of the checkout clerk and say, "Oh, I forgot to get some instant coffee."'

'But what about the clerk? Wouldn't there be a queue?'

'The clerk would wait, because she'd already started to ring up my stuff, and I would stroll off for the coffee. I'd bring it back and see that my checkout clerk now had a queue of five people or so, but she would be smiling away at me, like before. I'd come back up to her and say, "Get me a French bread baguette." She'd send for the bread and smile at me and say, "It'll be right here, sir. Would there be anything else you need?" But God forbid if she got mad at me for jerking her around for so long. Then I'd call for the manager and identify myself as an inspector. The clerk would be fired in five minutes.'

'Todd, you're a terrible man!'

'Terrible to who? To the bad employee? The customer's always sure he's going to be served to the very highest standards so he won't take his custom to another store. And the employees are afraid that any simple customer will turn out to be an inspector. You always have to smile and keep up the store's reputation.'

Todd was leaving one detail out of his little tale about himself: he'd been taught how to smile, all right, but he'd soon been fired for drinking, and that was the start of his misfortunes. Right now he was looking at Two-Faced Diana and thinking: *Will it work today, or not?* He decided that it was going to be today. Come hell or high water, he would reach his goal. Just why today he couldn't have said. He'd taken off, and now he was going on about everything under the sun. And she was listening, so he was certain she was interested in him. From a distance it would have looked like full-on seduction. Maybe that was what it was.

What *was* surprising was that the food was good, and they drank two bottles of a Georgian wine, Tsinandali. Diana softened up a bit, while his confidence increased that what he intended would come to pass.

Outside it had stopped raining, but it was overcast. They walked slowly past shop windows shuttered with iron grilles.

'Let's go to my place,' he suggested.

'And where's that?' Her ears pricked up.

'I have a room in a university hostel.'

'What do you want me to come for?' she asked, and it would have been hard to come up with a sillier question.

'I'll show you my dissertation,' Todd proposed. 'After all, it's a subject close to your heart: Pushkin's feminism.'

'Really?' She was politely surprised. 'But surely it's in English.'

'Then we'll drink some coffee . . .'

'Tamara and I drink seven cups of coffee each per day – between tours.'

'Who's Tamara?'

'My girlfriend. You didn't know? She sent you those e-mails.'

'You mean that wasn't you?' Todd stopped and took her by the elbow.

'Of course not. I would never do anything like that! Well, it's time for me to go home.'

A typical frosty one . . . But in her coldness and constant dismissiveness there was a kind of mystery, a certain motive force that was beyond him. When he asked her for a second time, it sounded plaintive. He shouldn't have said it, but it burst out of him. 'Maybe we can go to my place anyway?'

'Oh, no. I'm married. I belong to another man, and I'll be faithful to him for ever.'

'And who's your husband?'

'Pushkin.'

'Brilliant. He died ages ago.'

'He's dead for everyone else, but he's alive for me.'

He looked at her cautiously. 'Fine,' he said, coming to a halt. 'But Pushkin already had a wife.'

'Had,' she agreed. 'She died. I'm his second wife. You're the first person I've ever told that I'm married to Pushkin. I've never revealed this secret to anyone.'

'Got you. I'll be quiet as a mouse,' he said seriously and only then smiled.

'It's time to go.'

'I'll see you home.'

'You don't have to, I live only a little way from here.'

He tried to pull her to him and kiss her, but Two-Faced Diana's back arched and she pulled away in fright.

The doors of a passing bus opened. Diana, avoiding a discarded Coca-Cola bottle, climbed on. Todd stepped towards her, holding out the button in his palm. She grabbed the button, and the doors slammed. To hell with her, that two-faced blonde! She wouldn't let him kiss her or hug her, to say nothing of what he needed, and what she didn't need at all, apparently. And her sense of humour was more than a bit morbid. He turned up his collar, thrust his freezing hands into his pockets and set off to look for a metro station.

7

Diana was in love with Pushkin, selflessly. If he had walked on snow before her, she would have gathered up the snow from under the soles of his shoes and eaten it. She was absolutely certain that Pushkin belonged to her personally and she to him as well, of course. Her love for him and devotion to him brought energy to her life and gave her the happiness of always being with him – day and night. But here in the real world she stepped into her communal flat, unlocked the door to her room and was all alone.

An acquaintance of hers was an artist by the name of Dasyuk, in his own estimation a genius of the highest degree. Dasyuk was a drunkard who worked as a carpenter for the Bolshoi Drama Theatre. There was something wrong with his skin caused by his alcoholism: blue-tinged red spots covered his face, neck and hands. The winter before, Diana had spun him a long yarn about some exhibition or other. Dasyuk had promised to sculpt a life-sized Pushkin from a drawing they'd picked out together.

'To hell with you. I'll cut it out of plywood.'

'Plywood?' she said in distress. 'But I thought . . .'

'I'll find some good plywood, thick, aviation-quality. He'll look better than life.'

A week later Diana went to Dasyuk's after work. In his rubbish-filled studio, leaning against a band-saw on the other side of a dais, stood her own dear Pushkin, right in front of her, only with no clothes on. Dasyuk had painted his face and body and glued on a wig – curly natural hair – not omitting to cut out and paste on everything else that normally gets hidden beneath one's clothes. Diana blushed when she caught sight of that, and her heart beat faster. She demanded that he tear off the abomination instantly, but Dasyuk made a noise that sounded more like a hen cackling than laughter.

'Why "abomination"? What's wrong with you? You want me to castrate him? I won't do it! I won't let you commit an outrage like that, on our cultural heritage! He's going to have what everybody has. Like the Almighty ordained it. I modelled it on myself, from life. If you don't believe me, want me to show you?'

'No, no, for heaven's sake! You need yours, but what does he need one for?'

'What, he's not a guy? Just shut up! Or do it yourself, as you like! Here's a knife, a brush, my palette – paint over it. Stick on a fig leaf, or get rid of the whole thing you don't like! Disfigure a work of fine art!' The blue-highlighted red spots on Dasyuk's cheeks and forehead were turning brown from the nervous tension, and his eyes were bloodshot.

Diana picked up the knife but couldn't bring herself to touch that place.

'Can you put some clothes on him then?' she asked timidly.

'Buy a suit and put it on him.'

'Are you joking? He's supposed to wear a full-dress uniform. Where am I going to get something like that?'

'What was he?' Dasyuk cackled again. 'A Gentleman of the Bedchamber, right?'

Diana was offended. 'A Gentleman of the Bedchamber was, I'll have you know, on a par with a Councillor of State!'

'Don't confuse me! And are you going to get me a bottle for this? They're going to fleece me for it in our costume department, for sure.'

'I have some money. My brother sent me some.'

'From where?'

'From Mexico.'

'What's he doing there?'

'He's working. Russian geodesists are flocking there because there they pay you real money.'

'Maybe I could get to Mexico, too. Am I any worse than Siqueiros? I could knock them dead, slapping on paint like that!'

The pigeon-toed Dasyuk waddled across his studio, kicked open the door and disappeared. Clutching her throat in a panic, Diana was left in private with the naked Pushkin.

'You see how it's turned out, Pushkin,' said Diana, trying to keep her eyes away from the nude carving. 'I understand how cold you must be. Just put up with it a bit longer.'

Pushkin smelled of linseed oil.

Diana pulled her coat off and draped it over Pushkin, tying the belt around his waist. Now, although the poet looked a little weird, it was easier to look at him. Diana pulled a bottle of Climat cologne out of her handbag and sprayed some over Pushkin's carelessly dishevelled chestnut locks. Pushkin made a wry face; he probably didn't like the fact that it was women's perfume.

Dasyuk came back, dragging a plastic bag behind him.

'The women turned the whole costume department upside down. They managed to find it somehow. They *had* put on a play about Pushkin, they said, but it was a long time ago. And nobody remembered where the costume had got to. Maybe, they said, it'd already been stolen way back when. And then they found it after all. We're going to have to pay them . . .'

Diana opened her purse and took out the money, keeping some back for a taxi.

She pushed aside the empty bottles and old crusts of bread on the table, and carefully spread out the dark-green full-dress frock coat with its red cuffs and super-high collar. The tasselled, gold-embroidered epaulettes gave it an air of solemnity. Along with the coat came white woollen breeches, slightly worn and very wrinkled. Dasyuk threw a pair of shoes on to the floor and pulled some white stockings out of his pocket. Diana found a crushed hat in the bag, also embroidered with gold costume jewellery. Along with the hat, in a plastic bag tied on to it, came a white plume.

'The plume isn't necessary. That's a decoration for a horse,' Dasyuk cackled and tore the plume off the hat.

Laying Pushkin down on the table, Diana pulled the white breeches on to his legs, and then, standing him up, she put the coat on him.

'That's something else entirely!' she said, feasting her eyes on him.

Pushkin was standing barefoot.

'Don't forget his boots,' Dasyuk reminded her. 'Take them with you.'

'Right, he'll freeze. It's cold outside.'

Dasyuk looked carefully at Diana but didn't comment. She pulled Pushkin's stockings on to him and then his boots. He didn't resist; on the contrary, she felt he was trying to help her.

'Your Pushkin is a good-looker,' said Dasyuk, tilting his head to one side and looking at them. 'But in real life he was ugly.'

'You're the ugly one!'

'Listen.' Dasyuk scanned her happy face suspiciously. 'Tell the truth. What is he to you? Don't you have a guy of your own? I could do better than this plywood dummy . . . Let's have a go right now, eh?'

He put a hairy hand on his belt-buckle.

'Don't talk nonsense!' Diana drily cut him off, without getting angry and without taking it as a compliment either. 'I've already told you this is for an exhibition. You only ever have one thing on your mind.'

'Get lost!' snorted Dasyuk. 'I want to drink all the time, too.'

He helped her carry his work of art out to the street and hailed a taxi.

'Where you going to put the doll?' the driver asked. 'In the boot? Does it fold in half?'

'Are you mad?' Diana said indignantly. 'We'll fit nicely on the back seat together.'

Pushkin wouldn't bend, so they had to squeeze him in diagonally. Diana held on to him with one hand under his arm, and waggled the fingers of the other at Dasyuk.

'When are you bringing me my bottle?' Dasyuk yelled, slamming the door.

She didn't answer.

'That for a parade, is it?' the taxi driver asked without looking around, steering into the stream of cars.

Nothing would surprise a city cabbie. He wasn't asking out of curiosity but just to make conversation. Instead of answering the question she drily gave him the name of her street, and he didn't say a word after that.

Pushkin and Diana stood shoulder to shoulder in her lift. She was worried about what he'd think of her room, since she hadn't tidied it up for some time. Fortunately it was late in the evening and no neighbours appeared in the corridor. She didn't really get along with them and tried to have as little to do with them as possible.

Leaning the Gentleman of the Bedchamber against her cupboard, Diana put a hand on his shoulder.

'Well, now, here we are at home, Pushkin. Do you like it here? Would you like something to eat? I'll fix something up right away. Problems with the servants, sorry about that . . .'

Only now she did she notice how hungry she was: nothing had passed her lips since morning except coffee. She peeked into her refrigerator. There was yesterday's soup, so she got out the pot and ran into the kitchen. She returned, quickly set out two bowls, one for him and one for her, sliced some bread, moved Pushkin over to the table, and started to eat. He stood right by her and looked at her unwaveringly.

47

'If you don't want to eat with me, well – you don't have to.' Her mouth twisted, for she was hurt. 'I understand, you're used to being spoiled. But you'll just have to adapt. You won't be taking me out to any restaurants. Do you know what prices are like now? It'd be better if you became a couch potato. After all, you've always dreamed of me, and now here I am before you:

> '. . . Pale Diana
> Stared long at the girl in the window
> (Without this not a single novel
> gets by; that's the custom!),'

she declaimed. 'You won't turn down some champagne, I hope?'

She pulled a bottle out of the refrigerator, bought in advance for this very occasion, set out two goblets, opened the bottle with some difficulty – the cork hit the ceiling – and awkwardly poured some out. The champagne fizzed, the foam overflowing the brim on to the oilcloth.

'Excuse me, it's just cheap stuff. But it is imported, from Hungary. Let's have a drink, Pushkin! We'll drink us being together just like normal people!'

He nodded. Diana drank down her goblet, looked Pushkin in the eye, coughed and, since the second goblet remained full, drank that, too. The bubbles tickled her nose. Everything became light and grand. She put the soup pot back into the refrigerator. She stepped up to Pushkin, wrapped her arms around his neck, pressed herself against him and kissed his cheek.

'Phew, you smell of paint! And mothballs . . . Do you mind if I perfume you a little more? Wonderful perfume, a different one but French, too. My brother sent it from Mexico. Only it's women's again. Do you know what time it is?' she remembered suddenly. 'It's midnight. For you, of course, it would have been just the start of one of your bouts, whereas we have to be in bed by this time. Back to work tomorrow . . .'

She gently stroked his hair, and he tenderly leaned against her.

'Do you want me? I know, I know, you're all the same . . . Be patient for a while. Now we're going to lie down.'

She hurriedly opened out the sofabed, spread a clean sheet over it and got a pillow and blanket out of the cupboard.

'Now, Pushkin, look away. I'm taking off *my* clothes.'

But he didn't look away. She took her clothes off, and he watched her. Diana threw off her clothes, hopping around to take her tights off, and now she stood in front of him. She surprised herself that she wasn't the least bit shy of him. She felt like a bit of coquetry, so she decided to shame him. 'You're a man, you're supposed to take off my clothes. But it looks like I'm going to take off *yours*.'

Pushkin waited obediently while she took off his coat, his boots and his breeches. She took him, undressed, by the arm and slowly led him to the sofabed, trying not to look at that place – fashioned so strikingly by Dasyuk – which boasted the same kind of curly hair as his head. Laying Pushkin down facing her side of the bed, she turned out the light and darted back to him.

'I've never been with anybody before,' she confessed to him. 'And couldn't have been. I fell in love with you while I was still at school. I kissed your portrait in our textbook. You're my first love, you're my last. I'm a one-man woman. All my life I've loved only you! I've saved myself for you, only for you . . . You've finally realized that and come to me! That means you, too . . .'

Turning her face to him, she stroked his head and back. Smiling slightly, he nodded and stretched out his arms to her.

'You'll strangle me,' she whispered. 'I'm ready to die from happiness. Do you want me? Here I am. Take me!'

A lump formed in her throat. A shudder enveloped her

body. She moaned, pressing herself to him, covering his face, hair, neck, shoulders and chest with kisses.

That was the first wedding night of her life.

8

Diana carefully concealed from her neighbours the fact that a man had moved into her room. They wouldn't understand. They would laugh and, of course, envy her. They would report to the building committee that he wasn't registered there.

Since they were sleeping together, it didn't make sense to be on formal terms with Pushkin. It happened so naturally that she didn't even notice. And he did the same.

At night she would undress him and put him in bed with her and in the morning set him upright and dress him. He would watch while she drank her coffee, but he himself never had any breakfast, saying that it was still too early for him. She would kiss him on the lips and run off to work. Looking at the buses stuffed to bursting, she thought: *It's a shame that people ride around so fast, while he had to travel around on horseback. And now he doesn't get out at all. But that's just a detail. The important thing is that we love each other.*

She knew a lot about him, but it seemed to her that it wasn't enough. She tried to memorize more. And she discussed with him everything she read, particularly the stupid things the Pushkin specialist Konvoysky wrote about him.

'He doesn't understand you at all. No, and nobody else does, either. Only I do . . .'

She'd loved reading – Pushkin, in particular – since childhood. Now she read only Pushkin, considering it a betrayal of him to read any other authors.

'"Here is where I spied, too, the fabled ruins of Diana's temple,"' she read, after opening a volume. 'And you, Pushkin, did you pray in my temple while you were in the Crimea?'

'Of course, my dear,' he answered, not taking his eyes off her.

'Now you're back in my temple, and I'll never let you out of here.'

He agreed, joyfully.

Leading her tours, Diana caught herself not only speaking his verses aloud but thinking them as well. It was a genuine melding of the spirit, a penetration, a catharsis. Embarrassed by it, she explained to the tourists, 'I'm supposed to know the whole of Pushkin's work by heart, but I know only a third of it.'

All day in the museum she couldn't wait to get home and fall into his embrace. Whenever she was in a bad mood (and she often suffered changes of mood for a number of reasons), she would get angry at him. 'Pushkin, how dare you write that I'm two-faced? I, who *adore* you! Everyone else in the world gets all hypocritical about you, and only I love you more than anyone else in the world, more than myself! I'm prepared to scratch the eyes out of anyone who doesn't idolize you. I want to die for you. You're mine! mine! mine!'

And she would sob, unable to calm down until he kissed her.

She fantasized more and more, exaggerating the role of Diana in his life. Who was that unknown love of Pushkin's, a mystery to this very day? The answer was clear: it was the goddess Diana. *He wrote only a single verse about his first wife, Natalya, and called her a fool, while he wrote about me eight times, in both verse and prose. Pushkin had a collosal sense of fore-knowledge. He knew that he was going to meet me. Natalya was a Madonna only among brides, while I am a real goddess, he said it himself. A fundamental difference!* Sometimes she would travel through time and say to him, 'You have to divorce Natalya, then we can . . .' Or 'You and I have decided that the duel has to take place. You can't die, after all. You've searched for the ideal woman all your life, Pushkin. She has appeared before you in different guises, but finally you found me. I've turned out to be better than you could have dreamed. Your life was sundered because of that other wife, but you've continued to search for your ideal. You couldn't come to me straight after your death because I still hadn't been born. Now you're mine. Natalya didn't understand you. But I do! And I'll be your last wife. This is your eternal bond!'

Pushkin was in complete agreement with Diana.

'And what about those sluts you went with after you got married?' she asked him. And answered herself, 'They were just casual liaisons, because you fell out of love with Natalya so quickly. There was no joy to be had in your family – so you looked for it on the side. I forgive you.'

This subject disturbed her whenever she left her flat.

'You're not going to love anyone else!' she would say to him sternly, while he lay and looked at her. 'Got that? Don't even think about it. Because there's nobody better than me. Sure, our apartment's just a room in a communal flat. But all the same, here I am – the light of your life.'

He would agree with this, too.

But still, every time she came home she'd be anxious: what if he suddenly started cheating on her? There were women everywhere, and a lot of them dressed splendidly in tiny skirts. It felt to her like he was sneaking out on her all the time. However much she would try during her tours not to recall all of those so-called 'addressees of the Pushkin lyric', they figured in his life, the tourists asked about them – there was no way she could separate herself from his other women.

To fight them and win, Diana decided to find out more about them, to find their weak spots in their memoirs. She compared them with herself and found patent advantages in her own self. She rewrote the Don Juan list that he'd left in an album of Ushakov's and added herself on to it at the end. She knew Pushkin's handwriting – she'd taught herself, and you wouldn't be able to tell the difference – in other words, it was Pushkin himself who wrote her name as the last on the list. Now she was his woman, and justice had triumphed. He had written that Natalya was his 113th love, and Diana ignored all the others, becoming his 114th and last.

All the same a certain discord remained in her heart. The Pushkin that she'd known all her life was a sociable *bon vivant*, while now he was taciturn with her. *Maybe my company doesn't mean that much to him?* She tried being jollier, which took a lot out of her. She was not well attuned to the usual female games.

'Why are you stretched out so indifferently next to me? You playboy! You need something fresher. Go on, I don't object, go! Right now Nevsky is full of prostitutes, even more than in your day. Go and meet only them, if you have to. Don't see anyone home, and don't kiss anyone goodnight, please.'

Pushkin came back to her in the middle of the night. She was already asleep, and he woke her with a touch.

'Finally!' she said. 'You've had enough. Now you're mine again!'

The smell of someone else's perfume roused her indignation, but, after all, she herself had let him go. Diana got up, threw on her housecoat, undressed him, lay him down in her clean bed, leaning his back against the wall so that he could watch her, hung up his Gentleman of the Bedchamber uniform coat and breeches. Pushkin suddenly drew himself up slightly, raised his arms and recited her some poetry. Or maybe it wasn't he who was reciting to her, but she to him – but what was the difference, essentially?

> 'Diana's breast, or Flora's cheeks,
> Are marvellous, dear friends!
> Though either leg of Terpsichore's
> Is marvel more than I can ken.'

She threw off her housecoat and clambered under the covers next to him. Wagging a finger at him, she chuckled,

'What kind of rhyme is that, Pushkin? "Friends – ken"? For shame! God was punishing you for trying to do too much at once, you sinner: you like my breast, Flora's cheeks and Terpsichore's legs. You wretched ladies' man! OK, I forgive you yet again . . . But you're not working very hard. This way you'll lose the art of writing poetry.'

Diana upbraided him for absenting himself and for being lazy. He kneeled down in front of her and begged forgiveness, and after some feigned growling she let him press against her. Somehow she turned to putty straight away, and he could do whatever he wanted with her. Thereafter the other women receded into the shadows, losing all significance for her.

They lay side by side; he recited verses in her ear, verses that she had long known by heart but pretended were incredibly interesting to her. She even clapped her hands, although quietly so the neighbours wouldn't hear.

'What-ho, wifey – why don't we take ourselves off to the theatre?' he enquired of Diana. 'It's frightfully boring here.'

'Are you trying to say you're bored with me, Pushkin? Do you intend to offend me?'

'Sitting at home drives me off my rocker, Dianakins. What's in the offing at the opera?'

Diana handed him a copy of *Vecherny Petersburg*.

'My goodness,' he exclaimed, 'how the theatres have multiplied! I'm dazzled! And are they all good?'

'There's all kinds. You want to go to the opera? Look here: today *Queen of Spades* is on.'

'There's something familiar there,' he tried to recollect.

'I should say so!'

'Let's go!' he hopped off the bed. 'I'll send for the brown filly to be harnessed at once.'

'We'd better go by bus,' Diana suggested.

With a shudder she tried to remember if she had enough money for tickets. She thrust her hand into the bookshelf, where she had hidden money inside a book for a rainy day.

This time Pushkin dressed himself. It was long past time to buy him a new suit, from Finland or even Bulgaria. He creaked from the unaccustomed effort, pulling on his boots all by himself. She was spoiling him, dressing and undressing him. It was cold, though, and he didn't have an overcoat.

'Never fear, m'dear,' said Pushkin. 'I'm accustomed to the frost.'

Diana put on her best – actually, her only – evening dress, a raspberry one with lace trim. They left. There was a crush in the bus, but in the throng and the gloom nobody paid attention to Pushkin. The opera tickets cost an insane amount of money, and there weren't even any left on sale for roubles, so they had to buy them for dollars.

The lights were already going down in the foyer. Pushkin strode along swiftly, and Diana in her long dress was scarcely able to keep up with him. The doors flew open. The theatre was full, the loges sparkling, the parterre and armchairs – everything was buzzing. The house lights began to come down. Pushkin walked between the armchair rows, and she followed behind.

'Pushkin – look, it's Pushkin!' voices rang out.

He was being recognized, greeted. He obviously liked it, and she did, too.

'But who's that with him? That's not his wife, anyway! How could that be?'

'Surely you've heard? All St Petersburg is talking about it. That's his new girlfriend.'

'Diana? What a poetic name! And, you know, she's something else . . .'

'And how! He's crazy about her . . .'

They seated themselves in the parterre. Their neighbours bowed, whispering among themselves. The entire theatre was talking only of them. Pushkin rummaged in his pockets, trying to find his lorgnette so that he could train it on an unfamiliar lady seated near by, but it had disappeared somewhere. Diana had deliberately taken it out of Pushkin's pocket at home, so that he wouldn't peek at unfamiliar women. Just then the conductor appeared, and the overture burst out. But the theatre wasn't listening to the music: everyone just continued whispering about them.

The lights had scarcely come up at intermission when Pushkin appeared to have forgotten all about Diana. There was such a profusion of beautiful women dressed like he'd never even dreamed that he didn't know where to look first: half naked, giving off the sorts of smells that made his head swim. They went out to the foyer for a stroll. Diana held him firmly by the elbow.

'Are you the real Pushkin or an actor made up like him?' asked a nymphette in amazement, walking towards him on long legs that went all the way up to her armpits.

Catching sight of this heavenly creature, Pushkin lost his head. '*Mademoiselle!*' he cried. 'Of course I'm the real one. If you allow me but to kiss your hand, I shall convince you of it. You are charming, a purest angel.'

'Why my hand?' The nymphette batted her eyes at him. 'Who kisses hands any more? Better kiss me on the lips.' And, without giving Pushkin time to think about it, she threw herself around his neck. Pushkin embraced her around her slender waist and whispered something into her ear. The nymphette went limp in his arms, as if she were ready to fall to the ground with him there and then.

Colour flooded into Diana's face. *Lord, why did I bring him here? Why did he come back to life? Now I'm losing him! When he was dead he was mine and mine alone. His wooden body belonged only to me. And now this …*

A crowd was gathering around them. Outraged, Diana tore Pushkin from the embrace of the nymphette and slapped him in the face. Her hand hurt; she'd just struck a piece of wood. Tears gushed from her eyes and ran down to her mouth, where she could taste their saltiness on her tongue.

It was morning, and a tram was screeching around the corner outside her window. Pushkin lay beside her, gazing at his girlfriend. She had to get up and run to work.

9

There was no doubt about it. He loved only her, Diana; he belonged only to her. But that wasn't enough for her greedy imagination, which demanded logic, historical accuracy and, as they say, legitimacy. Since the details of Pushkin's life were unavoidable, it was impossible to contradict them: Natalya was his wife, and Diana wasn't. She had to obtain her own legal right to be by his side. It bothered her not at all that he'd lived then, and she was living now, when he was already long dead. It was the other thing that was important: how to become his legal wife?

On Palm Sunday Diana went to six o'clock mass at the church, to see Father Yevlampy. They had met at university; they'd gone out together on the same potato harvest, and he'd given Diana some of his *samizdat* literature. He was the one who had baptized her, when it became safe to do so. In the secular world Yevlampy had been Yevgeny, a Soviet economist in the employ of the Leningrad Directorate of Trade, who was busted for taking bribes. The Lord enlightened him, found him sanctuary in a monastery and then sent him to a seminary.

After standing through the Sunday service, Diana went up to Father Yevlampy and said she wanted to speak to him in confidence. He took her to one side and inclined an ear towards her. She glanced around to see if anyone was listening, and whispered, 'I need to marry a man, but in secret, at home, like our ancestors sometimes did.'

Yevlampy was just as aware of history as she was, but now he promptly cautioned her, after making the sign of the cross. 'It has to be done in church, by law, with a certificate from the Register Office.'

'What kind of laws do we have now?' she objected. 'Above all else we want to receive God's blessing . . . And it has to be done quickly. I'll pay you whatever you ask. No one will know about it. It's right near here.'

It took her a long time to talk him into it, but he finally agreed, for the sake of their old friendship.

'When?'

'Right now.'

'Then let's hurry,' he said, 'because I still have midday mass ahead of me, and the head of my diocese has threatened to turn up.'

Father Yevlampy was silent on the journey, only now and then glancing at his watch or lifting his cassock up above the puddles with both hands. Diana led him to her home. She knew that her neighbours had all gone to their allotments.

Walking into her room, Yevlampy asked, 'Well, where's this bridegroom of yours who's in such a hurry?'

A heavy green curtain was blocking the light from the window. Diana first silently lit two candles, as if she hadn't heard the question. Then, shifting aside some books, she took an envelope out of the bookcase, pulled out two $100 bills and held them out to Yevlampy. He dropped the money into the pocket of his cassock.

'And what about the groom?' he asked again.

She could only point to Pushkin, leaning back against the bookcase. 'There he is.'

A finger popped into Father Yevlampy's mouth in amazement, and he nearly bit it off. He screwed up his eyes and then opened them again, blinked a little to clear his vision, crossed himself, grunted, and squeezed out, 'You're joking, girl! It can't be that you're seriously . . .'

Diana had already put on the bridal veil that she'd obtained beforehand and stood silently alongside Pushkin, her eyes lowered to the floor. She waited.

Father Yevlampy thrust his hand into his pocket, ready to throw the money away and run. When the banknotes rustled together, he huffed, thinking about it. Money wasn't the issue. He could always give the money back. She was off her rocker, this miserable servant of God. Of course, at this juncture she wasn't in her right mind, but, after all, the Lord, unlike human beings, was always tolerant and forbearing towards human weaknesses.

'I'm afraid,' Father Yevlampy pronounced aloud, and again made the sign of the cross on himself, 'this is quite a situation, may Our Father in heaven forgive me.'

'Get on with it. What's the matter with you?'

'What's the matter? You, Diana, swear on the cross, not a word of this to anyone! Not to a single soul on earth!'

Diana nodded. He held his crucifix in front of her in the palm of his hand. She kissed it.

Father Yevlampy, still uncertain, overruled the protest inside him and began reciting the prayers, trying not to look at Pushkin. He made the sign of the cross over both of them and asked if she agreed to become a wife (he didn't say whose) and pronounced them husband and wife.

'What about the rings?' Diana asked, when he turned to go.

His eyes grew wide. Fear congealed in them, or embarrassment, or maybe the two together.

'Exchange rings,' he hurriedly muttered. 'Exchange them . . . Exchange them . . . Forgive us, O Lord, your sinful children.'

Diana opened up a yellowed box, took out her father's wedding ring and put it on Pushkin's plywood ring-finger. Then she took out a second, her mother's, and put it on her own finger.

'Well, good luck! I'm off.' At the door Father Yevlampy glanced back. 'Just remember what you swore to me, my daughter. Not a word to anyone! Life these days is so complex . . .'

Thus Diana Morgalkina became the legal second wife of Alexander Pushkin – Diana Pushkina.

He was a first-class lover, heavenly, the best in the world, although Madame Pushkina had no previous experience for comparison. Now she became almost happy. Almost – for there remained a singular defect in their relations, despite the hot nights when she would embrace him, that was in no way surmountable: she remained a virgin, no matter what.

The following Sunday morning she again went to the church, to ask the Lord to make an exception just this one time, and return His servant to life. *Turn his wooden body into a normal one, so he can breathe, so he can embrace me himself. Bring him back to life, if only for a short while. If just once it could be not me talking to him, but him to me, so he could confess how much he loves me. Now it's always just me doing the talking for both of us. He's so alive for me, of course; everything we have together is marvellous. It's just that for some reason conception can't happen at all – immaculate or otherwise. Bring my husband back to life, dear God, so he can show me how he loves me. And so that I can feel a child within me.*

She had already begun to pray when, taking fright, she thought better of it. *God won't want to bring just one back to life, lest every other mortal desireth the same. And what would happen if God did take pity on me and brought Pushkin back to life, that is, turned him into a corporeal man? Then I wouldn't have any kind of control over him at all. I mean, his character is well known to everyone. Like every other man alive, he'll go chasing after the first skirt he meets. And he'll start lying to me or disappear from home altogether – I'll just be waiting and waiting. No way. Let him stay made out of plywood but true to me to the grave. And I can embrace him myself; it's not going to kill me.*

She left the church without finishing her prayer. Because of this, Pushkin never came to life.

At times it seemed to Diana that she had somehow got pregnant by him or was already heavily pregnant, her belly already showing; someone was kicking inside her, she would soon be giving birth, and there a boy was, going to school – her and Pushkin's son. But however much she tried to convince herself, she never really got pregnant.

'Tamara,' Diana said in a whisper when the two of them were left alone between tour groups. 'Swear on your mother that you won't tell anyone!'

'What are you on about?' Tamara said in surprise, and looked at her with suspicion. 'You going to rob a bank?'

'Worse,' Diana lowered her voice still further. 'I have to get pregnant right away.'

'That's just great! Have you flipped your lid? Everyone's terrified that they're going to get into trouble, but you're just the opposite. It's straight from the words of your favourite poet:

> 'Beware – it could be
> This is some new Diana
> Hiding tender passion –
> And with shameful eyes
> Searching timidly among you
> For someone's help to fall.'

'And who *can* help me?' Diana latched on to the line.

'What do you take me for, a matchmaker? Out there – all around you – there's all kinds of men.'

'Are those really men? They've no energy, no spirit. They can neither build a house nor seduce a woman.'

'What can you expect? Life is like that, and men are that way, too . . .'

'That's what I mean! He's the only real personality there is.'

'Who?'

'Pushkin.'

'Oh, hell, I can't take this any more,' Tamara yelled, although there wasn't anybody else in the room with them. 'Then go and get Pushkin to make you pregnant.'

Tears welled up in Diana's eyes. Tamara patted her hands, took her by the shoulders and shook her.

'Are playing the fool or what, Morgalkina? If you're serious, go and get anybody you want.'

'Anybody? Maybe you could talk to your Anton? Would he agree? Just the once.'

Tamara pressed her lips together. 'No, you're crazy! Imagine it! Where would I go? Jump down the rubbish chute?'

'Calm down. I'm only asking.' Diana flapped her hands at her.

'Besides, my guy is too lazy,' Tamara added in a conciliatory tone. 'I myself barely managed to conceive Svetlana in our third year together.'

'Who can help me?' Diana couldn't see the way forward. 'I'm very serious . . .'

'All right, but you can't do it in the street anyway! And why are you wasting that Todd of yours? Good, bad or indifferent, he's still an American. And, besides, you already know him.'

'I got rid of him.'

'Well, so what? Get him back again. That's the ideal solution! Just don't be a complete idiot – don't blurt out that you're desperate to get pregnant. Any normal guy will disappear the instant he hears about your Shining Future – he'll be gone in a flash. Screw him, and then he'll go back to that America of his, and that'll be the end of the matter. And if he resists, get him drunk.'

'Why?'

'A drunk guy is always as ready for it as a Young Pioneer. Call him . . .'

'It's scary . . .'

'It's scary when you're getting raped. But this . . . Listen.' Tamara squeezed her shoulder. 'What if he takes you away to America? You'd be a fool to turn that down.'

'How could I leave Pushkin behind?'

'Ah, my dear, there's a psycho ward somewhere just for you. I'll have to keep my distance from you.'

Diana easily found out the telephone number of the hostel through some acquaintances at the university, and she left a message asking Todd to ring the Pushkin Museum. He called back. But before she could bring him home she had to discuss the matter with Pushkin. It had always been easy for him to bed women – why couldn't she do it just once?

That evening she asked him as soon as she got home. Pushkin stayed silent, just looking at her. He was probably freaking out. Thinking about it and not knowing what to answer.

'You yourself slept around, after all!' insisted Diana. 'And now there's full emancipation. Todd says that you were always a feminist. I love you; he's just a donor, don't you understand? Do-nor – that's *le donneur* in French . . .'

Pushkin thought about it a little longer and then gave in. Diana kissed his cheek and ran out.

10

'Finally you've brought a guy home!' said her neighbour loudly to no one in particular, on her way to the kitchen. 'Maybe he'll make you normal . . .'

Diana held her tongue. Todd was standing behind her and evidently hadn't entirely got the gist of what was said. She groped around in her handbag, looking for her key, and unlocked her room. She let Todd in and immediately turned the key in the lock.

Todd had been surprised to hear her voice when Diana called him. She was businesslike, didn't even ask him if he wanted to see her again, just proposed a meeting right off, and he'd had no choice. He didn't even ask her where she was taking him, he felt so awkward. Now it seemed to Todd that there was someone else in the darkened room, and he said hello. No one answered. Diana turned on her table lamp:

Pushkin stood there in the semi-darkness. Todd stretched out a hand to him, but it remained unshaken. Then Todd bowed politely and said, 'Hi there, Pushkin!'

Pushkin didn't answer.

'This is why you were joking about being married –'

'I wasn't joking,' Diana cut in, to stop Todd taking any further liberties.

She swiftly made their dinner, pulling a bottle of vodka out of her freezer. Todd sat at the table and followed her with his eyes as she ran around the room.

'You've got a nice place here. Very cosy. And lots of books,' he said out of politeness, looking at the mess around him which was almost as bad as his own garage back in Palo Alto. 'If I ever get married again, it'll definitely be cosy at my place.'

'Again?' Diana latched on to the word and stopped setting the table for an instant. 'Are you married?'

'Not really . . .'

The conundrum puzzled her. 'How is that?'

'It's just that I was married and got divorced, but my wife keeps on suing me. All I have to do is buy something – like a car, for instance – and she hires lawyers, saying that I was concealing yet another stash of money from her at the time of our divorce. She's just taking her revenge on me, but I don't understand what for.'

Five years earlier, the undergraduate Todd had flown off to Hong Kong on holiday and met a Vietnamese girl who fell in love with him. She was an orphan; her parents had died aboard the boat in which they were trying to escape Vietnam, and the little girl had been saved by the coastguard. Todd had been deeply moved by her story and had decided to take her to the USA. They got married there and then in Hong Kong. After a little while she came to join him in California and got her resident's status in the USA. She refused to live with Todd, though, coming up with various reasons why not.

He soon discovered that she had a fiancé in Los Angeles, and it had been him that she was coming over to be with; Todd was just the means of transport. She talked Todd into not divorcing her until she had got her US citizenship, otherwise she would have been kicked out of the country. When she did get it, she sued him for everything possible and impossible, making a scene over every penny, and continued to do so to this very day, even though Todd the grad student had practically nothing to give, aside from his old armchair and his sleeping-bag. Lawyers in California have more teeth than crocodiles and know how to gobble up clients better than they do anywhere else.

Todd had let her have everything, but he wanted to keep a silver-framed picture of his mother for himself, out of principle. The silver frame wasn't really important to him, but, as far as he could recall, it had hung in his mother's house alongside an icon. So, out of some sort of stupid principle, he wanted to keep the frame. His wife dug her heels in: she wasn't going to give it to him because she liked it, and that was that. As soon as the judge – who had been grumbling at him from time to time about how these male chauvinist pigs would get divorced and kick out their innocent wives and so on – realized that Todd's wife was demanding his mother's picture, she whacked her hammer down and pronounced an altogether unjudicial verdict. 'This just can't happen, madam! Where's your conscience?'

'But now I don't really know whether you should have a conscience or not,' Todd said sadly.

It was also funny that they had never had any kind of connubial bed. Well, *he* didn't have a marriage bed, anyway; *she* was living with her Vietnamese lover. That was why Todd avoided talking about it to his friends. Who would want to spill his guts about having such a unique form of family life? Oh, blessed were the days of our Soviet divorces! Without any property there was nothing to divide, aside from the room in the communal apartment, and that belonged to the state anyway. Bank account? There was never enough money to last until the next pay day, anyway. In the worst case in a divorce, as a lawyer friend of mine put it, you'd have to saw a chandelier in half. It's not that way in California. By law a man is supposed to support his wife to the end of her days after the divorce in the manner he did while they were married. It's a death-defying act when you get married – you're risking falling into a trap.

Then there was another hearing at which his symbolic wife was planning to get some real alimony from Todd for her maintenance in the future, since she hadn't come to the USA to work, after all. Todd was also going to have to feed her fiancé, whom she wasn't in any hurry to marry for that very reason. California laws are sometimes quite useful for dishonest people.

'I came out of the court into the open air,' said Todd, 'and swore never to get married again.'

Diana sat quietly and listened without interrupting.

'Pour us something,' she asked finally. 'Here in Russia the men are supposed to do the pouring. We'll drink to your divorce . . .' And straight away, without waiting for Todd, she drank hers down.

'We'll pour him something, too,' Todd said, walking up to Pushkin with the bottle. 'Otherwise it would be unfair, somehow.'

Wedging a shot-glass between the plywood fingers, he filled it up. Pushkin was holding the glass aslant, and half the vodka ran down on to the carpet. Todd clinked glasses first with him and then with Diana. He wolfed down all the food that had been set out on the table, one thing after another. After half an hour they were both flying. Pushkin alone was still sober.

'Let's do the *bruderschaft* toast,' said Diana, slipping a little quickly into the informal mode of speech, out of the

66

fullness of her heart. 'But we'll have to kiss. You've no objection to that?'

No, Todd didn't mind that. He leaned across the table, and she offered up her lips. And it somehow happened that they found themselves on the couch, clinging to one another. Diana suddenly shook her head from side to side, pushed his hands away, jumped up and smoothed her dress back down.

'Have I done something wrong again?' Todd asked, at a loss.

'Wait. Not here – this isn't the place!'

'Why not?'

'He's watching us. Let's go somewhere else.'

'Where else?'

Diana didn't answer. She had suddenly realized: she had to conceive hers and Pushkin's son somewhere other than this. Why hadn't she thought of that before? It had to be in that other place, not in just any other apartment!

'Let's go!' she whispered, pulling on her raincoat.

Todd reluctantly obeyed. The lift wouldn't respond to the button. Stumbling, Todd followed Diana down the stairs. Leaving the building, she took him by the arm and steered him on to the riverside walk. The wind had blown away the storm clouds, and in the sky there hung a half-moon. Their footsteps resonantly echoed back through the alleyway.

The policeman on guard at the museum at 12 Moyka Street was asleep, but when Diana rang the bell of the main entrance he glanced up through the glass, recognized her and just asked, 'What do you want?'

'Open up, Vasily,' she requested. 'I have some work to do.'

He didn't ask about her companion, gathering that they were together. He turned off the alarm, and Diana and Todd went in. Flabby and getting on in years, Vasily sat back down on his chair, pulled his cap down over his eyes and tuned out.

Diana walked through the museum in the dark as if she were in her own home, leading Todd by the hand. She came to a halt in Pushkin's study. Light, either from the moon or from street lamps, was coming in through a crack between the curtains.

Todd's head was foggy. He had stopped being surprised at Diana's whims. 'Here?' he asked in a whisper.

'Here . . .'

Diana took off her raincoat and threw it on to a chair, sat down on the couch next to the bookshelf and squeezed her knees tight together, waiting.

'He died here?' Todd whispered.

She nodded.

Todd took several steps around the room and then came back. Something was worrying him. 'I have a request for you,' he suddenly decided. 'If it's not too much trouble for you . . . Just in case . . . Write me out a statement that you wanted to do this.'

'*What?*' She covered her face with her hands. 'Jesus! Is there no end to this shame?'

'Don't take offence. It's just that in America everyone's gone crazy and particularly about sexual harassment. I'd rather not get put in gaol for rape if you change your mind tomorrow morning and go to the police.'

'The militia,' she corrected him.

'Right, of course, the militia.'

'I'm not going to go to any militia.'

'I know that! But, please . . . Just in case.'

Diana harrumphed and then strode decisively over to the light switch. The light went on. She bent over the writing table with its piccaninny figure and the little chest that the poet kept his manuscripts in. Now every sort of office rubbish ended up in it. She pulled a sheet of paper out of the chest.

'What should I write?' she asked, her voice suddenly hoarse.

Todd was silent, not knowing how to phrase an official document in Russian. He'd never seen a document like that in English, for that matter.

'Write . . . uh . . . that you voluntarily . . .'

'Couldn't I do it afterwards?'

'No, before.'

Her face suddenly lit up with humour. '"I, Diana Mor-galkina, citizen of the Russian Federation,"' she began pronouncing slowly in a formal voice, writing it down, '"have entered into intimate . . ." What would be better, "intimate" or "sexual"?'

'Better say "sexual",' Todd advised her. '"Intimate" could mean anything.'

'So, "have entered into sexual relations with US citizen Todd Dankey at my own desire. I have no judicial or material claims on Mr Dankey of any sort." Will that do? Signature . . . Just as if the whole thing had already happened between us, right?'

She signed it. Todd folded the paper up and tucked it into his jacket pocket.

'We're not going to get undressed,' she said severely. 'Turn away, I'm going to take off my tights. We'll just get together, and that'll be all.'

He didn't understand. 'What do you mean, get together?'

'You know better than I do how to do this.'

'What about your boyfriend Pushkin?' Todd wasn't really joking; it just came out.

'He's given me permission.'

Diana again sat down on the couch and waited. Todd kept on dragging his feet.

'Look!' She undid two of the buttons on her blouse and offered up her breasts with her hands. 'Not bad in the moon-light, right? Well, why are you standing there like a statue? Do something!'

He didn't know the word she used for statue, *istukan*. 'What does that mean?'

That chilled her a bit, and she didn't answer. Lifting her hands, she placed her palms over his ears and held them there until he'd come to life and decide to do something.

'What about you?' he asked after a while, touching her ear with his lips. 'You've never done it?'

'Never.'

'Oh, and you the ancient Roman goddess of love!'

'What? Diana's the symbol of virginity.'

'Why preserve your virginity for two thousand years?'

'You asshole! Are all Americans like you? Don't you understand? It's a symbol.'

'OK, a symbol. But why, really?'

Diana closed her eyes and didn't answer for a long time. Then she whispered, 'It just happened that way . . .'

The couch turned out to be squeaky. It's incredible how Pushkin could have taken his ease on such an uncomfortable thing. Diana felt nothing, aside from Todd's heavy breathing in her ear.

'What, can't you do it?' Diana said in surprise.

'Don't know. I've never tried it,' Todd muttered.

'Men like that don't exist.'

'Well, here I am.'

'So it just happened that way for you, too?'

What happened was quick, uncomfortable, awkward, clumsy, stupid, disgusting, dirty, loathsome, altogether repulsive. But it wasn't him, after all, it wasn't her Pushkin, she consoled herself, but just his transient deputy. She quickly pulled on her tights and smoothed down her dress.

'Do you have five dollars?' she asked.

Her donor smiled, pulled the money out of his wallet and handed it to her.

Diana turned out the light, took Todd by the hand and, holding the five-dollar bill out in front of her in her other hand, led him to the exit through the half-dark. The militiaman was asleep, so she whacked the bill against his cap. He roused himself, turned off the alarm and unlocked the door. She shoved the money into his hand.

'I'll take you to the metro.' Diana slipped her hand under Todd's arm, but then, remembering Pushkin, she pulled it out again. 'Stay with me, otherwise you'll get lost.'

They walked silently down the pavement, at a certain distance from one another. At the square in front of Kazan Cathedral Diana stopped, looked up at the sky and started muttering something.

'What are you doing? Praying?'

'Do you see how big the moon is? That's me talking to myself; after all, Diana is the moon goddess. I am Selena.'

At this late hour there were few passers-by hurrying through the Nevsky Prospekt metro station. Sobered up by the cold and the rain, shivering, Todd looked at Diana guardedly. *What a waste, getting mixed up with her: she's a strange creature. Not two-faced, though – just different, somehow . . .*

'I'm sorry,' said Todd.

'No, I'm the one who should be sorry,' Diana objected, looking to one side. 'I shouldn't be telling you this . . . I wanted you to help me have a baby.'

'What do you mean?' He took fright.

'God, you are slow-witted. I mean, literally, I wanted to get pregnant by you. I'm probably a repulsive lover and altogether good for nothing. How can the world put up with people like me?'

She turned sharply and ran off. Todd stood there for another minute, staring dumbly after her and then, at a loss, shrugged his shoulders and went into the lobby of the metro.

The next morning he took an Aeroflot flight back to San Francisco.

II

Diana went back to her flat in a complete panic, but why she couldn't understand. After all, everything had come out the way she'd wanted. It was just that her inner harmony had been destroyed. A worm had penetrated her soul, eating away at her, but even aside from that she was being torn by doubts. Pushkin met her silently, looking at her with disapproval. But he was the guilty one! He himself had forced the issue, had urged her on to this step. She didn't feel like justifying herself or even talking to him at all. This was the first time she felt no joy when she was alone with Pushkin. She decided she would go to bed alone. She made her bed, undressed and turned down the blanket, while he, dressed in his green Gentleman of the Bedchamber uniform with its red trim, just stood and watched. Then she took pity on him. She got up, undressed him and put him into bed.

'I hate you,' she said.

She turned him so that his face was to the wall and lay with her own back to him.

Something in her happy marriage with Pushkin went wrong that night. But he didn't care. Diana no longer spoke for him and for herself. She just remained silent. She'd got angry, and now she no longer wept when, conducting her tours, she spoke of his death. Things went on that way for a month and a half, until the day she finally realized she was pregnant.

Everything went back into its groove. She had turned over a new leaf. She came to life, hurried home as before to her Pushkin. She assured herself and reassured him that he and nobody else was the father of her child. *Soon I'll have a living little Pushkin. He'll definitely become a great poet, too! That's the way I want it!*

'Are you happy?' she asked her husband.

Pushkin replied that he was delighted.

'You had four,' she said to him, 'and this is your fifth, another boy.'

'How do you know it's a boy?' asked Pushkin.

'I just know it! We'll call him Sasha, OK?'

'But I already have a son called Sasha,' Pushkin said.

'So what? After all, that Sasha is dead.'

So he agreed that it would be Sasha. Diana merely had to carry him to term and give birth to him.

The women in the museum gossiped about her somewhat. Among themselves they would laugh, but they would ask her, 'Come on, tell us who the guy is.'

'Pushkin,' she would answer. And that was her truth.

But her fellow-workers just kept teasing her about it: everyone knew without her saying so that it was the American.

With her belly, it became more difficult for her to guide her tours, but she felt a special pride when it became more pronounced. She stopped being a blonde and didn't even notice it. But the important mystery became a reality. If you forgot about one little detail, then there was just this fact: she was carrying his baby, the man who was the master in her room, the most intelligent and the greatest man in Russia, she was carrying the new Pushkin.

Her pregnancy progressed with difficulty. Twice Diana had to go to hospital to save the baby. But it was even worse in the hospital than it was at home: starvation rations, no one looking after her and no medicines unless she managed to get hold of something herself through friends. She worked to the very end, leading her tours despite the stuffy summer heat, and feared only that some bustling tourist would knock her off her feet.

Diana woke up one morning when it was still dark, feeling that she had to go, since she couldn't manage at home on her own; she had no hope of relying on her husband for help. He just lay or stood, leaning against the table, staring at a single spot.

'Oh, Pushkin, Pushkin,' was the only thing she could say. 'Wait for me, and see you don't bring anybody here!'

Diana went on foot herself down the deserted streets to the maternity hospital, shivering from the morning damp. They didn't want to take her, since it was already full, and they advised her to go to another maternity hospital. Her legs gave way, and she sat down on the floor of the reception hall. They called for the duty physician, who screamed at Diana that she should stop pretending; she wasn't the first or the last person to ask to have their baby there. 'And how am I supposed to find places for every one of you? You're all having litters like cats.' But after cursing at her and abusing her, for some reason she grew afraid to kick her out, and an orderly threw Diana a shift and some slippers.

In the ward they were all talking about nothing but the fact that everything was infected with staphylococcus, the mothers had it and it was being passed on to their babies, but it was all right, since healthy babies were sometimes born as well. Diana didn't get to participate in the conversation for very long. They put her up on the table, and after that she remembered everything only dimly, except for the pain.

And the obstetrician-midwife was surprised, too. 'What is this – are you a virgin? As if you're Holy Mary . . . Who knocked you up like this just messing around?'

'Pushkin,' Diana muttered again, half delirious.

'You're being rude, girl!' The obstetrician was offended and didn't ask any more questions.

Diana hadn't even known herself that she'd remained a virgin. Her gynaecologist told her afterwards that such pregnancies occur when people come together in casual encounters. And he gave her a significant look.

Diana was unlucky. The birth dragged on and on. Although I've never had occasion to have a baby, even at its best the procedure seems to me to be an enormous torment and an unacknowledged act of heroism on behalf of humankind – more serious, honourable and probably for the greater good of humankind than the majority of male acts of heroism, for which the so-called stronger sex gets trinkets pinned to their breast. And in difficult births it's probably like being tortured in an Inquisition dungeon – even the instruments are similar.

American fathers, who videotape the whole process of their wives giving birth for their family archives, simply amaze me. I understand that it's fashionable, and that you'll have something to show your descendants about the lives of their mothers and grandmothers, but husbands with video cameras who tape suffering for entertainment should be spoken to sternly.

Nobody videotaped Diana. No videotape would have been long enough, anyway, given that she laboured without giving birth. The obstetrician left several times to help other people and came back carrying her instruments with her. Diana raved in delirium, bit her lips bloody, lost consciousness. The obstetrician shoved smelling salts under her nose and slapped her cheeks to bring her back to her senses.

'A boy!' she suddenly screamed over Diana's noise. 'You've worn me out. I could scarcely pull him out . . .'

Four days later Diana, pale as a ghost, walked quietly out of the maternity hospital with her infant in her arms. No one accompanied her, and no one met her with flowers. Cute, blue-eyed, snub-nosed, with a whitish down on the crown of his head, Sasha slept in her arms, infrequently smacking his lips. She brought him home.

Her husband stood by the bookcase in the same pose that she'd left him in five days before. He didn't take his son in his arms, although she proudly showed their boy to him. He said nothing, simply looked at him. Diana suddenly took offence, even though nothing seemed to have changed in him since they'd started living together and got married.

Pushkin remained the same, but Diana's existence was transformed. She took long-term leave from the museum. Her fellow-workers chipped in and bought her some nappies, packing them into a pram that had belonged to somebody else and which they were giving to her for free even though it could have been sold for money. Tamara called and wanted to come by during her lunch break, but Diana resisted as usual, saying it would be better for them to meet in the square. They got together there.

Tamara rolled the pram up to Diana and said, 'Telepathy exists, because I have little surprise for you, too!'

Opening her handbag, she took out a striped airmail letter from the USA that had arrived at the museum. On the envelope it said 'Ms Diana Morgalkin'. Diana tore open the envelope. In it was the document that she'd written out in her own hand, about the lack of any claim on her part, to which had been appended the following note:

> Pardon me for the not-giving back to you of this paper earlier. I was a fool to ask for it. Now I have made of myself a little more intelligent. Hello.
>
> Todd Dankey

His spoken Russian was a lot better than his written Russian. And any language will get worse without practice, anyway; the learned correctness slips away.

Tamara was interested. 'What did he write?'

'Just nonsense . . .'

Diana tore up the letter into little pieces without re-reading it and chucked it into a waste-paper basket. Tamara wasn't offended; on the contrary, she looked at Diana sadly and quietly walked off.

Pushing the pram with Sasha in it, Diana set off for the Register Office to get her child's birth recorded: without documents her son was just a bug, but with them he was a citizen of the Russian Federation.

The queue there was short, but it wasn't moving. It turned out that next door they were registering marriages. Sasha was quiet, then he started kicking his legs and screaming, and neither dummy nor breast pacified him.

'He's going to be a real man,' observed the woman sitting

next to Diana, who had come to get her divorce. 'He'll drive you to despair and then calm down.'

They got to her after half an hour. Sasha, the good child, calmed down. The registrar turned out to be an affable lady; she immediately got out a fresh birth certificate and asked for the maternity hospital certificate and Diana's passport.

'What's the name of the newborn going to be?'

'Alexander,' whispered Diana, holding out the certificate and her passport, rocking the pram back and forth so her son wouldn't start crying again.

'Honestly,' said the registrar, 'he's the fourteenth Alexander we've had today. Or the fifteenth – I've lost count.'

Diana didn't react in any way, and the woman slowly filled in his name on the form in her rounded hand. She blotted the ink with a heavy marble paperweight so that it wouldn't smudge and, glancing at the maternity hospital certificate, said as if it were obvious, 'Right . . . Last name – Morgalkin.'

'What do you mean, Morgalkin?' Diana jerked upright. 'His last name is Pushkin.'

'Don't mess around, girl!' The registrar dropped her polite smile. 'If it's not your last name, then I need his father's passport.'

'Where could I get you his father's passport now?' The tears burst quickly from Diana's eyes. 'If you don't put down Pushkin, I won't register him at all!'

'You can't do that,' the woman objected gently. 'If he doesn't have a father, just say so. But to come up right out with Pushkin . . . To bandy around a holy name like that . . .'

Here I have to make a short statement for those of my readers who have already been disposed by the preceding text to accept Diana as a woman who, if you compare her to more ordinary representatives of the populace around us, has certain inclinations in one direction or another, both in everyday life and in the spiritual sphere. In this case, Ms

77

Morgalkina was behaving with absolute propriety and doing what you or I would have done in similar circumstances – you have to keep going, and you can't do that without manoeuvring. Diana had spent more than a day trying to think of some sort of explanation (she didn't live on the moon, after all) and had prepared something in advance and now, not to alarm anybody, came out with some sort of nonsense about her husband's ancestors being from a certain village called Pushkino. She had married her husband only in a church ceremony. The time had now come in Russia when anti-religious remarks in official institutions were not welcomed by the government. The church today, as the progressive newspapers teach us, 'exerts influence and has a role', so to speak.

'Yes.' Without giving her time to object, as if remembering something and getting even more excited, Diana pulled a huge and beautiful cosmetic case out from under an oilcloth in the pram. 'Here are the most important documents . . .'

The registrar glanced fleetingly at the 'documents' that Diana's brother had sent her from Mexico, sighed, got up, opened her safe, put the box on a shelf and carefully locked the steel door. Diana's eyes followed the box with satisfaction and, continuing to rock the pram, she said, 'The name of my child's father is Alexander Sergeyevich Pushkin.'

'Coincidences happen!' the woman said, almost without irony. 'Yesterday I registered Anton Pavlovich Chekhov.'

You could hear her pen scraping as it slid across the thick, watermarked paper. The heavy marble paperweight rocked right and left, after which her stamp firmly kissed the certificate, and it found its way into Diana's hands.

12

What a paradox it was: the goddess Diana, that is, Artemis, the daughter of Zeus himself, really was the protectress of mothers among the Greeks. And she surely tried to aid Diana Morgalkina. But the mythical goddess Diana herself, as distinct from a lot of other goddesses, had never given birth for some reason. It was obviously a spiteful man who composed those ancient myths that have had such a significant influence on mankind. Maybe their creator didn't believe in them himself. The goddess Diana should have had a beautiful baby, instead of roaming around in the woods with her bow and arrows in the hope of skewering a fallow deer. But for some reason the goddess failed to bear a child. Maybe she never decided who to conceive with or feared the wrath of her father or something nasty that had been foretold. The first Diana was the sister of Apollo – it wasn't by chance that on Diana Morgalkina's wall above her couch hung a terribly dusty and fly-spotted reproduction of Bryullov's famous painting *The Meeting of Apollo and Diana*. Pushkin had long gazed at it attentively.

'My brother Apollo is a soothsayer, the god of wisdom, the patron of the arts,' Diana would frequently repeat, closing her eyelids as if in recollection of something connected to her own childhood. 'He's the ideal of masculine beauty and harmony. Just the kind of man that my son and Pushkin's is going to be!'

She breast-fed Sasha for a year, running to the kitchen for bottles of milk and milky curds and whey to augment her own. She washed the boy and changed his nappies, laundered his dirty nappies three times a day, carefully ironing everything as a precaution against germs, heating the iron over the gas stove and running back with it into her room. She sang him songs, patiently awaiting the day when Sasha would stand up and walk. Waiting for when he could point his finger at the figure of Pushkin leaning against bookcase, could start talking, and say 'Pa-pa' the way she'd been teaching him every day. Waiting until he asked to go on the potty. But for some reason everything was delayed. A year passed, but the boy couldn't pronounce a single articulate syllable; he crawled on all fours, didn't want to stand up and walk; he resisted and bit his mother.

Before she could hand Sasha over to the day-nursery and go back to work at the museum, which she was already missing, Diana had to get a health certificate, so she put her son into his pram and set off for the children's outpatient clinic. There the elderly lady doctor made a wry face as she looked the child over and told Diana that he had to have a whole battery of tests. After feeling over Sasha's puny body one more time, she wrote out a referral to a neuropathologist. The neuropathologist likewise didn't explain anything clearly, just knocked on Sasha's legs with her rubber hammer and wrote out an order for an X-ray and a referral to a psychiatrist.

'But why a psychiatrist?' Diana asked in alarm. 'I'm completely normal, and his father is, too.'

The neuropathologist looked at Diana attentively and explained, obscurely, 'The boy's developing slowly. That could mean anything . . . Perhaps an alcoholic conception, or a genetic defect. Where do you work?'

'I'm a museum assistant . . .'

'Have you ever had a dose of radiation?'

'In the museum, you mean?'

'Who knows? Nowadays you can get a dose of radiation anywhere at all, even on a tram. The boy has to go under observation, and then it'll be easier to see . . .'

They put Sasha under observation, and the psychiatrist let drop something that stunned Diana. First, he wrote down a diagnosis of 'oligophrenia of an unspecified aetiology, problematically connected with a birth trauma (forceps)'. Then, at the following visit, the diagnosis got even worse: 'Down's syndrome, of embryogenic pathology'. Finally, the word 'imbecile' appeared in his case record, which almost made Diana pass out when she read it, because during the intervals between visits to the doctors she had already been paging through books where the word was to be found, in black and white, seeming to alternate with the phrase 'idiot child'.

'My God, how can this be?' she lamented aloud on the way home, pushing the pram and carrying Sasha, growing ever heavier, in her arms. 'What a calamity has befallen me, Lord!'

Passers-by craned their necks at her.

Diana's endless visits to the clinic gave her a little hope, but there was no progress of any kind. Some recommended massage, others miracle-working potions from Tibet or sharks' fins, while still others said that the best thing would be to pay cash to defectology specialists who would work on Sasha from morning to night. But where could she find the money for anything like that? Not even her brother in Mexico could help her out with that. Progress, she was told, would only be slight and a long way down the road, or there wouldn't be any at all.

Diana rushed from one place to another. She went to the church and prayed, prayed in a frenzy, but it didn't help. She was living on pure momentum, although it wasn't really living. She cried at night when Sasha was asleep and sat by him, staring fixedly into space. Towards dawn one morning she slipped into a dream. There was a black tunnel, and she was moving down it, unseeing, unhearing. Sasha was in her arms, and Pushkin silently shuffled along next to her. Her footsteps grew faster and faster, someone was getting closer, and then there was lightning and thunder . . . She was woken by Sasha's crying. He was lying there wet. The calendar said it was 29 January – the day of Pushkin's death.

Even though Pushkin was always alive for Diana, for her and for all of her fellow-workers at the museum this day was always a day of mourning. And today in her room mourning had set in – she could feel it. The entire day passed nervously. Diana couldn't settle anywhere. She flew around the room, washed the floor, something she hadn't done in over three years, shifted all the furniture around, almost bringing the bookcase down on top of her, but nothing got better for all of her activity. Sasha was screaming as if he had a splitting headache.

'Come on, quiet him down!' her neighbour yelled from the kitchen. 'Living in this apartment's become unbearable.'

That evening Sasha fell silent and went to sleep, and Diana calmed down a bit. She sat at the table and picked up her diary, the one that she had carefully kept up for these many years, and began leafing through it, trying to grasp the meaning in various places. Then she leaped up resolutely, tore the notebook into little pieces, page by page, and threw them into the rubbish bin. So that nobody would try to get them out and read them, she poured a bottle of sunflower oil over the shreds.

> '. . . Alone, sad beneath the window
> Illumined by Diana's beam,
> Poor Tatyana dares not sleep
> And at the dark field stares . . .'

she mumbled. There was no dark field outside her window, but rather Millionnaya Street, dimly illuminated by its lamps. An empty bus, leaving behind a puff of black smoke, swung into the lane with a roar. The street was covered with snow. Cars left black stripes of wet asphalt behind them. And there was nobody for Diana's beam to illumine.

'Well, say something!' she yelled at Pushkin, in a frenzy. 'You're the father, after all, the head of the family!'

She stood stretching her arms out towards him, beseeching him for help. Why was life doing her out of her fair share like this? Where was there to hide, so that nobody would bother you, not intrude with their dirty boots, not say stupid things about horrible diseases, so as not to see anyone and find, at last, complete happiness with her husband and son?

At first he looked at her silently as was his wont, and then he suddenly smirked. He was waiting for something from her. She had always acted in his interests, but now she understood: he and his son were demanding yet more love, and confluence, penetration into the world of cold woodenness and peace, where he was. She had no other way out. Suddenly she realized what her role and her responsibility were.

The clock was showing nearly eleven when Diana finally understood this. In silence, gritting her teeth, unhurriedly, she neatly dressed the sleepy Sasha and put on his boots – this time he didn't resist. She wrapped herself in her overcoat. Pressing the boy against herself with one arm, with the other she grabbed the plywood silhouette, dressed in its dark-green Gentleman of the Bedchamber uniform. Pushkin obediently buried his head against her shoulder. Diana carefully locked the door to their room, took the lift down and threw her keys into the rubbish bin.

She ran out into the night. She met no passers-by. Sleet flew down to meet her along the dark corridor of the street, blown by a wind from the sea. Almost no light from the street lamps carried through the blizzard.

On Dvortsovaya Embankment it got a bit brighter, because of the spotlights on the roofs, but the wind and the sleet grew stronger. Diana stopped for an instant near the slippery granite steps leading downwards and looked around. No one could see her. She took several uncertain steps along the uneven ice of the Neva, dusted with fresh-fallen snow. Far off, the spire of SS. Peter and Paul fortress shone with yellow lights. She hurried towards it. The ice was hard and bumpy, and she began to run, stumbling now and again, pressing Sasha to her with one arm and Pushkin with the other.

Ahead of her gaped a crack, full of black water.

Two Special Policemen with sub-machine-guns around their necks were stamping heavily along the deserted Dvortsovaya Embankment, when they stopped for a smoke. They shielded the match with all four of their hands against the wind and sleet. After they had lit up, the one of them who was facing the Neva silently pointed with his chin for the benefit of the other. A dark figure was moving across the river in the direction of Peter and Paul. How come it wasn't using the bridge? The bridges hadn't been drawn up, after all. Besides, you couldn't get across there; there was a clear channel in the river – the ice-breaker had opened it up last night.

The lads slung their sub-machine-guns over their shoulders, jumped over the cast-iron railing and ran across the ice. One of them had thrown away his cigarette, but the other one's was stuck to his lower lip. They ran carefully, stepping softly on the ice, at times sinking into holes filled over with snow.

'It's a woman, and she's got a kid,' one of them saw. 'And who else is that with her?'

The second one kept on puffing on his cigarette.

'It's some kind of a board. Maybe she stole it. Hey, girl, come back! Don't be stupid! There's no way across there!' The other man kept quiet.

Hearing their shouts, Diana looked back in panic. Two people were running after her. She dodged from one side to the other, afraid that they were going to stop her, prevent her from reaching her own happiness, then rushed forward, nearly falling down. And they were already right behind her.

A voice carried to her. 'Come back! The ice here's too weak. It won't hold you!'

Chunks of ice floated at the edge, bobbing in the waves. Diana stopped short for a second, her eyes wide. Embracing Pushkin and Sasha she stepped sharply forward, into the black gloom. She felt the icy water. She pressed her lips to the cold lips of her husband and, sinking, she groaned, feeling a complete union with him that she had never experienced before. But Pushkin was looking into the distance, at the two Special Policemen running up.

The first man reached them and snatched the child out of her arms by the collar.

Sliding into the water, Diana looked up and screamed, 'Give him back!'

She waved her free hand in an effort to get back the son

who'd been snatched from her arms but managed only to follow him with her eyes. The second man stretched out his hand, trying to grab her by the sleeve, but the ice underneath him started crumbling and, letting go, he rolled over on to his back so as not to slide under the ice. The water heaved, splashing; the ice floes rocked and tilted, moved apart and then came together again.

The policemen moved back a bit from the crumbling edge and stood there at a loss. They reported the incident to their superiors on their radio and then, with the child in their arms, urged on by the wind and snow at their backs, walked silently back to the shore.

The plywood Pushkin, taken under the ice in Diana's embrace, was hooked and pulled out by fishermen at the mouth of the Neva. The paint had peeled off the wood, and only a dirty wooden silhouette remained. The fishermen decided that it was Lenin, thrown away after a recent protest march by the Reds. They chopped him into pieces and were going to use him for their campfire. But the sodden plywood refused to burn; it just smoked, and water from it dripped on to their dry firewood, so they had to pull the wet pieces out of the fire, which they threw back into the river, and the current bore the fragments out into the gulf.

Diana Morgalkina's body was never found, and there was no funeral.

13

Todd Dankey squeezed out his dissertation on feminist tendencies in the works of Pushkin, and Professor Verstakyan approved it. I, too, had a hand in it, gritting my teeth; the dissertation wasn't worth a damn, but Todd was a nice guy, and my colleague Verstakyan asked me to support it. The prestigious New Academic Press publishing house agreed to bring out the young scholar Todd Dankey's Pushkin book under the title of *The First Russian Feminist*. On the shrinking university labour market, a place was found for this ever-so-promising Slavicist at a small private college in the corn state of Kansas, where Todd was allowed to enter a competition for the position of professor's assistant, so that he would get to teach Russian to beginners. He was about to go on holiday to Greece; his Monroe Street friends had arranged to rent a yacht there to sail around the Greek islands for two weeks. Unexpectedly, Todd changed his mind.

Not saying a word to anyone, Todd paid for a visa at the Russian consulate in San Francisco, got himself a ticket on Delta Airlines and flew to St Petersburg in the middle of July, changing planes three times along the way.

He didn't call his local friends from Pulkovo Airport, fearing that he would again drown in unrestrained drunkenness, and he'd firmly decided to knock that off. A bus brought him to the Moskovsky station. It was ten minutes to two on the station clock. The day was cloudy, so it wasn't hot. Todd dropped his suitcase off at left luggage and went out on to Nevsky Prospekt dressed the way he'd flown in: in jeans and a wrinkled white tank-top. Sleepy after the flight, he set off for a walk around and at the same time to find himself a room in some inexpensive hotel. But within half an hour his legs had carried him to 12 Moyka Street.

History repeats itself, but sometimes the leading characters change. The new, young ticket-seller at the museum said that there was no Diana Morgalkina there.

'Then where is she?'

'She's not here, and that's it!' The ticket-seller wasn't about to expatiate with some unknown foreigner.

'How about Tamara? Is Tamara working here?'

'Tamara is conducting a tour. Wait.'

'I'll find her.'

Todd was about to go inside.

'Get a ticket first.'

Reading the ticket price on the sign, he handed a note to

the ticket-seller. She held it up against the light before putting it into an iron box.

In Pushkin's study Todd found himself behind a large group of schoolchildren. He felt no sentiments now with regard to what had happened to him in this room. He hadn't got married, either, but had had relationships of some sort from time to time – that much couldn't be denied. Tamara was finishing her tour and in rapid-fire speech was informing them of the final hours of the poet, mortally wounded in a duel. Todd had never seen Tamara, but, although she had only caught sight of him once before, and that just a glimpse, she worked out who he was right away by women's intuition, a thing unknown to science, as soon as Todd came close.

After her tour was over, she took Todd to the staff cubby-hole.

'You're looking for Diana? She's dead.'

'Dead?'

'By her own hand. You know she was loopy . . .'

He didn't understand the Russian word *choknutoy*. 'What do you mean, "loopy"?'

'Well, weird. Her mental state was slightly . . . As for the boy . . .'

'What boy?'

'Didn't she write to you? The boy she gave birth to.'

'When?'

'What do you mean, when? Then! The boy was taken to an orphanage. He had no father and was left without a mother. Besides, he's sick.'

'Sick with what?'

'I don't know exactly.'

Tamara looked at him studiously. Todd bit his lip and was silent for a long time. Finally, he asked, 'Can I see him?'

'Sasha? You'll have to wait for half an hour. I'll come back and try to help.'

She ran off to do her tour, and Todd sat in the room, waiting.

The women who came in looked him over and left, conversing in whispers. Someone offered him a handleless cup of tea. Tamara came back, telephoned somebody, finally wrote down an address and held it out to Todd.

'Can you find it?'

'I'll show it to a taxi driver, and he should be able to take me there.'

'*Guud lock*!' Tamara sparkled with erudition, and she patted him on the shoulder and even touched her cheek against his beard.

Todd got out of the taxi on the outskirts of town, in front of a stone wall that was seriously crumbling in places.

'Over there's the entrance, behind those trees.' The taxi driver pointed, backed his car around and drove off.

Rusty iron gates, at one time painted green, seemed to be bound shut with a chain. Todd pushed on a creaky door in the gate – it turned out to be unlocked. He went through and, stepping over puddles, walked up a path overgrown with weeds. The house that appeared out of the luxuriant, dusty greenery was old, approximately the size of their house in Palo Alto, only, judging from the noise, the shouts and the faces looking out of the windows, it had a population ten times its size.

An ageless woman appeared, with an old-fashioned braid tied around her head, dressed in a smock that had once been white. She didn't even look at Todd, didn't want to talk, said that she had no time, that visitors' hours would be tomorrow. On his last visit to the country Todd had gained some experience of dealing with local institutions, and he pulled two twenty-dollar bills out of his wallet and put them down in front of her. She pulled out the desk drawer and swept the money into it.

'And what are you to him – a relative?'

'I'm his biological father.'

'Come on!' said the director. 'Biological ... How did you manage to achieve that all the way from America? By mail?'

Todd was embarrassed. 'Well, you see . . . It just happened that way . . .'

She didn't wait for his answer, didn't say another word, just curled her lips in condemnation of the immorality in the world and left the room, leaving the door ajar.

Todd glanced out the window, befouled with pigeon down and droppings. The narrow piece of sky visible through the branches had cleared, but the sun wasn't getting through to the office because of the trees growing up against the walls. Todd heard steps and turned around.

A tow-headed boy, awkward, with an inordinately large head of irregular shape, looking like a teapot upside down, swayed from side to side and came through the door dragging his feet, holding his arms in front of him like someone leaning against the air so as not to fall down.

'Here's your Alexander Pushkin,' the director introduced him, without a trace of irony. 'As it turns out, even though he's an idiot he's half-American, isn't he?'

'Hello,' Todd said to the child, cheerfully.

The boy didn't answer and looked past him with colourless, watery eyes.

'Your name is Sasha, isn't it?' Todd asked.

Once again Sasha failed to react. The director stood in the doorway and, without showing the least sensitivity, stared fixedly first at one and then the other of them. She walked over to her desk, leaned on it on her two fists and made something distantly resembling a smile.

'Maybe he does look like you, after all. Are you married?'

'What?' Todd said, not hearing or not understanding.

'I'm saying that you need your wife's consent.'

'No, I'm not married. I came to get married to his mother, but she . . .'

'Well, that's all over now. What the hell . . . We'll take care of the adoption papers, do everything by the book. It's going to cost you three thousand dollars. Payable to the state, of course, not to me. But he's not altogether well. He has hydro-cephaly. We can only wait and see – in America you might be able to do something for him. Then maybe he won't die in adolescence.'

The woman was waiting for an answer from Todd, but he just stood there, at a loss. Sasha looked out the window at the flapping wings of a pigeon alighting on the windowsill and raised and lowered his own arms: either doing his exercises or trying to fly off. He uttered something like 'Va-va-va' and fell silent.

'Nyura!' the director shouted. 'Change his pants!'

A fat-bottomed nanny came in, with an expression of utter fatigue on her face. Growling, she pulled the wet pants off the boy with deft movements, threw them on to the floor and put clean ones on him.

Todd remained in silence, and the director, tired of waiting for an answer, spurred him on, drumming her fingers on her desk.

'Well, what about it, my good sir? Are we going to start the paperwork or what?'

THE MAN WHO READ ME FIRST

I

A woman I didn't know phoned me. Judging from her voice she was elderly. Without giving her name, she said that her husband wanted her to meet me. I cautiously enquired exactly who her husband was. She replied that she would tell me later. I invited her over, but she refused; it was better to meet in the street. The following day we met at Revolution Square, Moscow, near the stairs leading to the Central department store.

She was my height, and I'm not small. Her age was indeterminate, her face colourless. She was of that breed of thin old ladies for whom time has stopped. There were bags under her small, colourless eyes: maybe she had trouble with her kidneys.

'Let's move aside to avoid getting jostled,' I suggested.

'No, it's better here,' she replied firmly. 'No one can see us in this crowd.'

Her eyes darted about, and I thought that she might not be quite right mentally. But she seemed to read my mind. 'Don't worry. I'm sane. Actually, very sane.'

'I don't doubt it,' I said, trying to calm her down. 'So what's this all about?'

'My husband told me to give you this.' She looked around to see if anyone was watching and handed me a package. 'Of course, it would be better to get it out of harm's way completely. But this is what he wanted. I'm afraid not to carry out his will.'

I took the package and instinctively looked around. 'Well, who's your husband? And where is he?'

'He died. A week ago.'

'I'm sorry. Did I know him?'

'He said you worked together.'

'Did he say where?'

'Sure! At the newspaper. He was your censor. That is, I mean, he was the Glavlit representative.'

'Tsezar Tsukerman? Oh, my God! He was a wonderful, kind man.' I overruled my conscience without hesitation. 'Everyone loved him.'

Evidently my tone was not sincere enough.

'He was absolutely honest and decent,' she said sharply. 'He just happened to end up in that organization. It wasn't his fault.'

'Of course,' I agreed. 'Basically we all did the same thing. What's in the package?'

'I don't know,' she answered. 'You mean, what am I carrying? I know that it's his – how would you put it? – notes.'

'Memoirs?'

'Not quite. At first it was his personal production diary. Then later . . . later he said he started to look at everything differently and these notes would rehabilitate him in the eyes of . . .' Embarrassed, she stopped speaking.

'Rehabilitate?' I asked.

'Basically so his grandchildren wouldn't think badly of him. He said you should do whatever you want with it. I was against that. After all, we have children, and everything's going well for them. What if something happened? But the children agreed with him. Why are you waving the package around? Hide it in your briefcase!'

I obediently hid it. We did have to move aside after all, because we were being jostled. For several more minutes we stood by the Lenin Museum. Calmly, even somewhat distantly (to her credit), she told me how her husband's life had ended. 'He died well, quickly . . .'

I had never heard anyone speak of a loved one who 'died well'. 'What do you mean, "well"?' I asked.

'Quietly. Without suffering as others do. It was his heart, and that was it. Everyone should go like that. So when are you . . . leaving, for over there?'

'I'd leave today, but they won't let me out.'

'They'll let you out!' she said with conviction.

'May I phone you after I read it?'

'Do you have our telephone number?' She was anxious again.

'No, I don't, but . . .'

'Well,' she hurried, 'there's no call for that. I've handed it all over to you. I hope that everything goes according to your plans.'

She turned quickly and left.

2

Holding on to a strap on the metro carriage, I half closed my eyes, and Tsezar Tsukerman appeared before me. Or Censor Tsezar, as the editorial staff called him. His name was also shortened to Tse-Tse, and there was also the euphemism 'in charge of no-can-do'. Some simply called him Tsunuvabitch. And in private the chief satirist, Avanesyan, called him 'our Soviet Sakharov'.

Tsukerman was corpulent, unhurried and absolutely civil. He looked like a bookkeeper-in-chief. He always wore black oversleeves over his brown suit jacket. His hairy hands held a Thermos from which he poured out little sips of tea. I also remember his irritating habit of tightening his tie under his double chin, as if he was getting ready to walk into a manager's office or step up to the rostrum.

'He wants to choke himself for what he's done,' muttered Avanesyan, who was censored more than anyone else.

The censor was abused at every opportunity but, naturally, behind his back. He was accused of things that he personally was no more guilty of than we and many others were. However, face to face, the entire staff, including the editor-in-chief and

93

the assistant editors (non-staff employees weren't even supposed to talk to him), kept their distance. That, or the censor kept aloof himself.

It wasn't as though he was feared; he was, after all, of the lowest rank. His status didn't let him permit anything. But he could *impede*. Like an oncologist, only unpleasantness could be expected from him.

He was rarely challenged, since the chance of proving your point was precisely zero. A mighty and mysterious organization called the Committee to Safeguard State Secrets in Print stood behind him. This department knew everything that was not allowed and probably even knew what *was* allowed. This absolute authority – wielding a power obtained from God knows where and sanctioned by God knows who – this invisible and omnipotent power over the minds of writers and readers called for its representative to be treated with respect, even trepidation. Or even fear. Or, most likely, all three.

Everything that happened in the world was called 'information' in Tsezar's language, information that he divided into 'oral' and 'written'. He loved the oral kind, including jokes. He laughed loudly and contagiously, shaking with laughter and wiping away tears, which undoubtedly pleased the story-teller and encouraged him to recall something even racier. And he was panic-stricken by anything written or set in type.

If there was some danger that we did not suspect, his mouth would draw tight and his eyes turn chilly and more penetrating. He would noisily sniff air into his nostrils for a long time, as if attempting to stock up on it until the arrival of the Bright Future. Of course, the Bright Future wasn't just over the horizon, but it was a good idea to build up some reserves anyway. It seemed as though he would now get out a special tool, some kind of infrared binoculars to look not only through the text but through us as well. In fact, he would pull out a large magnifying glass, and if a letter in the most crucial words, such as 'Lenin', 'Brezhnev' or 'Politburo', was imperfectly typed he would spin the composition under the magnifier, looking at it this way and that, trying to penetrate the mysterious meaning of the unclear mark.

'Counterrevolutionary danger has been planted in every letter of the alphabet,' he used to say at meetings and, seeing the participants smiling, would add, 'Every letter is a bomb. I say this to you, taking full responsibility as your adviser and friend.'

'But how can one work normally in such explosive conditions?' someone asked. 'After all, we're not bomb-disposal experts.'

'There's no reason to be concerned,' he stated. 'I am the solemn guard of the nation's interests. Since there can't be any conflict between you and the government, I'm protecting even you from misfortune.'

Censor Tsezar ordered our special correspondent to cut from an essay of his that it was 707 kilometres by highway from Moscow to Leningrad. 'So American spies will get lost,' the victim commented.

The length of the earth's equator was also classified. 'This is strategic data,' he explained. If someone countered that this information was available in a Year 4 schoolbook he would answer, 'That means somebody approved it there.' Or: 'Yesterday this could be divulged, today it can't.'

For every figure, fact, name, event and place name, Tsezar demanded one thing: the official stamp of the relevant department. When people patiently tried telling him that this, at least in certain cases, was absurd, Tsezar would answer with a smile, 'Of course I believe you. But later I'll be the one to get the sack.'

They would say to him, 'What are you shivering for?'

He would answer, 'It's better to shiver in a warm office than from cold in the street.'

They tried shaming him, 'Why, you're a coward!'

'According to you, I'm a coward,' he answered calmly. 'But in my bosses' opinion I'm vigilant.'

'Vigilant' became a catchword in the editorial office. His euphemisms spread to other departments.

Once he expounded a thought which, in my opinion, was fraught with fundamental significance for world civilization and perhaps for the universe as well. 'From the censorship point of view,' he declared, 'the ideal newspaper is a sheet of paper with no text.'

'Maybe pictures, at least?' I asked carefully.

'Pictures are already a crime.'

Tricking the censor, pulling the wool over his eyes, was considered a heroic act by the editorial staff. Grave risks were taken: signatures on permits were falsified; others swore that permission had already been obtained, only there was no available means of transport to go and pick up the permit. They convinced him to sign his approval so as not to miss the paper's publication deadline, telling him they would bring it in five minutes. The lines he crossed out would be paraphrased and put in another place in the same article in the expectation that he wouldn't read it a second time.

I did these things, too, but maybe not as often as the others: I was afraid of ending up on the street, too.

Whenever he was reprimanded for lack of vigilance, the joyous news immediately raced through the office. The more brazen among us telephoned and congratulated him – with disguised voices, of course. He would fume and threaten punishment for insulting the honour and virtue of the body that he belonged to, then slam down the receiver. But he would forget the insults quickly, and you had to credit him for not being vengeful. Although he could have been.

Every profession demands natural abilities that facilitate the work. What he really had no trace of was a sense of tempering his vigilance. Therefore he never lowered his guard, seeing dirty tricks everywhere. Once when I was on duty at the department, he called me on the internal line at ten at night. 'Here in this article from your section I read that tomorrow we'll find a robotic horse on the street and not be able to distinguish it from the real thing. Ver-ry interesting. But who's going to design this horse?'

'It's just science fiction.'

'I understand. But where did the author get the idea?'

'Where? From his head.'

'Excellent. And how did this idea happen to get into his head?'

'Oh, Jesus! From the air.'

'Aha!' He'd caught me. 'Exactly! So the author could have heard about this idea.'

'Let's say he could have. Is that really important?'

'What's important,' Tsezar said triumphantly, 'is that the horse is being designed somewhere and he heard about it.'

'So he heard about it. So what?'

'What it means is that the Scientific Research Institute, which is *developing* such a horse, has to issue a permit.'

The devil had made me say 'from the air'. Things weren't looking good. The article flew out of the column right before publication. I should have foreseen it.

'I've just remembered,' I exclaimed boldly. 'The author said he made it up himself. Of course he thought it up himself. He even told me that it had dawned on him one night and he got up and wrote it down.'

'What is he, a sleepwalker? Don't pull my leg, my friend. You and I are materialists. Nothing comes from nothing. I can guarantee that he got a whiff of it somewhere. What if it's not patented and foreigners, excuse my language, snatch it up?'

He used another, more vulgar word which I have decided not to reproduce. 'Let's say he did get a whiff of it,' I conceded. 'What's so terrible about that?'

'What do you mean? What if he got the idea from people working at some secret institute? What if this is a strategic-type invention? Let's say this is a new technology for the Soviet cavalry. Do you know what this could mean? It could undermine the nation's defence capability. Giving away information that is a military and state secret. Oh! Can you see what this means for us?'

'Well, what kind of permit do you want?' I asked, giving in. 'From the Defence Ministry?'

'Well . . . my friend, now you're talking business. We'll ask the leadership right away. Don't hang up, just wait.'

I heard the humming of the city telephone line through the receiver. 'Comrade Varvarova? Tsukerman here. I have an article in front of me giving away the news that tomorrow there'll be an artificial horse out on the street. Yes, I see. I'll find out this instant.'

Then Tsezar spoke on my line. 'What kind of horse is it? Electronic?'

'Who knows? Probably electronic. What else could it be?'

'It's electronic, Comrade Varvarova. Um-hm. I understand. That's just what I assumed.'

'Well, what?' I asked in agitation.

'Dear friend, a permit from the Electronics Industry Ministry is required, stating that they're not developing such a horse.'

'How can I get a permit like that at ten o'clock at night?'

'You don't have to do it today. What's the rush? Why get all panicky and edgy? It's bad for your blood pressure. All this hustle and bustle can lead us to overlook something else that's important. Today we'll just calmly remove this horse. We'll dispatch it to the devil . . . your horse!'

'But tomorrow, with a permit from the Ministry, can we include it in the paper?'

I still had connections with Ministry people who weren't stupid; they could help. Without these connections it would take years to get the necessary approvals.

'What about tomorrow?' The censor pricked up his ears.

'Just this!' I was angry. 'Maybe they make them at the Ministry of Instrument Making and Automation.'

'Hey, young man! That worries me, too. You know what, dear chap, get permits from both ministries, as insurance. Then I'll call the leadership again and they'll tell me who else to go to.'

It was my misfortune that the newspaper published science fiction, and that it was my department that handled it. If the next story featured representatives from another civilization flying to earth, the phone would ring that evening and Tsukerman's hoarse voice would courteously enquire, 'Dear boy, is the General Staff aware that aliens from the constellation Andromeda are coming to see us?'

'Not only are they aware, Tsezar, but they have nothing against it.'

'Isn't that great! That means we'll have no difficulties. Get me a permit from Military Censorship.'

But there was an extensive category of information that required no permits or agreements. Tsezar would wheezily hum some incomprehensible melody and wander into the next room.

'Just as I thought!' He'd appear in the doorway, his index finger upraised. 'Everything's all right. You don't need a permit or an agreement. This, my dear, simply cannot be mentioned in print and that's it. It's easier for you, less bother.'

It was true – after years of working, experience in 'no-can-do' accumulated. It meant fewer trips to the censor.

'Life's unkind when you have to go to His Excellency the Castrator,' Avanesyan complained.

He would return, happy. 'This subject is circumcised, too. I'm becoming a eunuch, boys.'

Science fiction withered. Science became extinct. Thoughts grew stunted. Even innocent news appeared less frequently in the paper. A permit was called for every time, just to publish it. There were times when no one knew which institution these permits had to be obtained from. Then an instructional letter would appear, demanding that approval from the appropriate departments be presented to the censor, for registration in a special magazine and notification to the central management, several days before the proposed publication date.

Tsezar, satisfied, strolled up and down the corridor, Thermos in hand. 'The more permits, the less agitation.'

He didn't take holidays. When high blood pressure forced him into hospital, he was replaced by an attractive young woman of about twenty-five, with short hair and severe clothing but a wonderful face. She'd been sent from Glavlit as a temporary replacement.

'A literary Snow Maiden from Sh-lit,' said Avanesyan. 'As if we couldn't train a censor on our own.'

Avanesyan was forever mentioning, appropriately and inappropriately, that he was an illegitimate descendant of Pushkin. He said that his great-great-grandmother had transgressed when she was in the Caucasus. This could neither be proved nor refuted. But he sported the same kind of sideburns as the illustrious poet and, incidentally, was also named Alexander. Well, Avanesyan decided to go on a reconnaissance mission, taking with him a satire – published long before – that was, in his own opinion, irresistibly funny. Of course it was in manuscript form. What happened next, I know only from the words of our satirist. Of course I believe him, but I can't vouch for the absolute truth.

'Lyuda, darling!' he said in the doorway.

'Lyudmila would be better,' she corrected him. 'What can I do for you?'

'The censor – that is, Tsezar – always held that people need to get acquainted first.' Avanesyan studied her boldly. 'What about you? Are you of the same persuasion? Or maybe with you one doesn't have to get acquainted beforehand? We can just do it right away, huh?'

'No way right away.' She blushed slightly, not with a censor's but a woman's instinct, catching the *double entendre*.

'Okey-dokey! Cast your eagle eye over this then.'

She started to read, and he retreated to the window so that the table she was sitting behind wouldn't block his view of her. From time to time she smoothed her skirt, and from time to time he gazed out at the workers in the courtyard unloading a lorryload of paper.

'Well?' he asked when her eyes had raced to the last line. 'Do you like it?'

It seemed as though Lyudmila was slightly embarrassed. 'We had a special course in satire at university, and the lecturer said that satire is currently very topical but hard to get past the censor. Is that true?'

'So you studied journalism? That means we're *colleagues*! And you, Lyudmila, you're young and look wonderful.'

'Thank you,' she said. 'By the way, in your article it says that alcoholic beverages are consumed during working hours. Where? In the computing centre? Which one? The Academy of Sciences? Are there Party members among the drinkers?'

'What does that have to do with it?' Avanesyan was startled, sensing no good.

'Your average subscriber reads this newspaper. Why should he be led to think that Party members drink at work? I'll call Comrade Varvarova about your satire.'

'There's no need to do that, OK?' Avanesyan pleaded theatrically. 'She'll definitely cut it. Imagine how awkward it would be if our Soviet censorship reacted negatively to Pushkin's great-great-grandson.'

'Are you really . . . ?'

Avanesyan solemnly bowed his head, giving her the chance to take in this fact.

'So what can I do for you?' asked Lyudmila, genuinely surprised.

'You can do everything, if you want to,' he countered just as genuinely.

She thought about it for a little while longer but ended up making the call anyway. Comrade Varvarova asked what the article was about, listened for a moment and said, 'Wait a minute, they've already published that satire! They're just checking up on your vigilance.'

'And then I understood,' remarked Avanesyan, sitting at a table with friends, 'that it would take more than bare hands to break her.'

The satirist's campaign of seduction became the entire editorial department's concern. Certain hopes were placed in it: no one expected miracles, Lord knows, but we did wish for small indulgences and for the nagging to stop. Avanesyan was given advice, presented with an imported tie and offered the key to an empty apartment belonging to someone's aunt.

'Of course I succeeded,' Avanesyan said afterwards, 'without any real difficulty. As a woman, I have to say, she's very tender and understanding. You don't have to believe *me*; you can find out for yourself. But as a censor she's an armoured train. No concessions even for me, despite all those deep and pure feelings. Even being related to Pushkin doesn't help! You could make nails out of those whores!'

Shortly thereafter, after he'd spent enough time in hospital, Tsezar returned to his vigil. Lyudmila was transferred to another publication, disappearing without leaving Avanesyan her telephone number.

On days when every newspaper published the Leader's lengthy speeches, only the TASS teletypists and proofreaders had anything to do around the editorial office. The rest of us would loiter in the corridors with nothing to do and split up into vodka-buying trios (three roubles a half-litre, back then). I bumped into Tsukerman outside the snack bar. He had some black bread in his hands.

'Let's go to my room,' he offered unexpectedly. 'I'll treat you to some tea. Strong. Real Indian tea. Not like what you get in this lousy public swill-locker.'

He opened the lock and ushered me ahead of him into the room with its 'Glavlit Representative. Entry Forbidden.' door plate. I'd been here lots of times. A desk stood by the window; there was nothing on it, but still it managed to be dirty. All four walls were covered from floor to ceiling with shelves filled with thick files that I don't believe anyone ever opened.

'Now I'll go and get the berries,' Tsezar said cheerfully.

'What do you mean?' I didn't understand.

'Here we have the flowers, and over there – the berries. According to regulations, I should make you wait out in the corridor. Well, never mind.'

He began sorting through his keys, unlocked first one and then another lock and vanished into the next room. The door was covered with spots from the putty that had been used to seal it. Tsezar called the secret circulars, orders, instructions and lists stored there 'the berries'. He reappeared, triumphantly carrying a packet of tea. He remembered to use his foot to check if the door had locked behind him.

'Indian,' he said proudly, plugging the kettle into a socket. 'Their country, of course, is backward, but their tea is fit for human consumption. Now for a divine brew!'

'But we're atheists!' I couldn't contain myself.

He studied me carefully, as if verifying his suspicions. 'Listen,' he barked in a kind of frenzy, switching suddenly to the familiar form of address and picking up a proof of a new speech and a somewhat unclear picture of the General Secretary. 'What is this blabbermouth thinking, eh? What are they all thinking? There's poverty in the country, people live worse than cattle, everything's going to hell, and he rattles on about the triumph of progressive ideology . . .'

I pulled my head into my shoulders, not knowing how to react. Just in case, I cast a sidelong look at his telephones.

With loathing Tsezar flung the newspaper column down. 'This is . . . it's all . . .' – he evidently changed his words in mid-flight – 'it's all . . . not right!'

I had never heard so much intellectual energy put into common cursing. Just to be on the safe side, I didn't pursue the conversation. Having unburdened himself, Tsukerman decided not to take it any further either. Silently, he poured the tea leaves into the boiling water. We drank some tea and talked about insignificant things. The unfinished tea he poured back into his Thermos. I quietly made my exit.

My position on the editorial staff had always been tenuous, and now it was getting alarming. Spitsyn, head of the foreign section and a man everyone suspected of being an informer of indeterminate rank, came by and breathed his whisky breath on me. Whisky regularly came his way at foreign embassy press conferences. 'They came to see the boss about you, asking questions.'

'Who?'

'The organization that asks the questions. Incidentally, they were also interested in Tse-Tse. Funny, isn't it? Remember, I haven't told you a thing. And for not telling you anything you owe me a drink.'

Shortly thereafter I left the editorial staff at my own request, having decided just to be a freelance writer. Since that time I had never crossed paths with Tsezar. My prose was hacked up and proscribed in other editorial offices and publications by different representatives of the selfsame Glavlit.

3

Lost in my memories, I almost missed my stop. I ran home from the metro in the light rain and changed into dry clothes. While the tea-kettle was boiling, I opened the package.

A thick student's notebook was rolled up into a tube. The cover, smudged with printer's ink and stained with tea and butter, was testimony to the notebook's long service. The pages were lined, and every line carried firm handwriting, almost without any corrections. It was entitled 'The Diary of a Seasoned Censor'.

Two epigraphs preceded Tsezar Tsukerman's opus: 'The censor is the strict guardian of diffidence and modesty' (Cicero). 'I'm a hundred per cent in agreement. If something's wrong, it's not the censor's fault' (Tsezar Tsukerman).

I made my tea, put my cup on the floor by the couch and snapped off some chunks of sugar. Warming up a bit from the dank Moscow spring weather, I sipped the tea and began to acquaint myself with the diary. 'The censor is the first reader of absolutely everything in the world, and because of this he bears a huge responsibility to all progressive mankind,' Tsukerman wrote in his foreword.

Unfortunately, the lack of departments for the training of censors in universities, coupled with the lack of an independent scientific base for censorship, leads to the conclusion that rationally based limitations are superseded by arbitrariness and personal predilection. As a result, our field lags behind the demands of the time and is full of dilettantes.

This work represents the first attempt in the history of world publishing to give beginner censors the opportunity to familiarize themselves with the mistakes committed by their senior comrades. This will be accomplished not by rumours and gossip but by the direct transfer of experience from their more experienced and battle-scarred colleagues.

Here are gathered both the mistakes that I caught in time and the blunders for which I have suffered, as well as the mistakes made by my colleagues while representing Glavlit in the various organs of the Soviet press, radio and television.

From the words of my mentors who are no longer among the living, I've recorded the errors of censors from the past for the benefit of our heirs. Young censors will be able to learn from the reprimands given to their older comrades, thereby avoiding the unpleasantries that lurk in wait for them in practically every jot and tittle of our Soviet mass media. For as the censors' great friend and poet Alexander Pushkin once said, science shortens for us the experiences of a quickly passing life.

The notebook continued, page after page, with the late Tsukerman's thoughts and facts. From their tiresome abundance, I cite here the more instructive passages in case the reader feels a special urge and intends to choose the honourable profession of Glavlit representative as his life's calling, because of this bequest of Tsezar Tsukerman's. After all, censorship is in dire straits in many countries. The authorities simply have no one they can depend on, and every single letter of the alphabet is fraught with danger from the counter-revolution.

So this is what I read in the diary:

The word 'censor' is of Latin origin. Censorship has existed for 2,400 years, reaching its heyday with us. In ancient Rome the censor's authority was much broader and the material rewards much greater. In Rome censors were solemnly chosen from among honoured citizens for five-year terms. Even in tsarist Russia the censor was, as Dahl wrote, 'entrusted by the government to censor compositions, to approve or forbid'. I am entrusted with the task of vigilance by Comrade Varvarova. I was thinking about this while waiting in the queue at the snack bar, when the publishing-house director's chauffeur carried in a crate of groceries for his boss from the distributor.

The word 'uncensored' means 'obscene, improper'. This means that everything uncensored is amoral and unethical. This should inspire Glavlit representatives to fight for Soviet writers to self-censor their own thoughts, so that they do not depend upon being always corrected, and before their deadlines.

The important thought is that a minor proofing error can turn into a political error. Someone omitting the 'd' from 'redaction' produced 'reaction'. Caught that one just in time.

An instruction was issued forbidding the publication of anything critical of our environmental protection. Only positive statements about our environmental policies are permitted. The reason is that President Nixon called upon Congress to spend the funds left over from the Apollo space programme on preserving the environment. He said, 'America must show the Russians how we care about the future.' Thus far we have no surplus money from our space programme, but newspapers have to show that a great deal is being done.

Horrors! I myself just heard Brezhnev say over the radio, 'We are proud of the fact that there are the five golden letters of the USSR on our banners.' Three times I read that speech in our pages. TASS had changed 'five' to 'four' in time.

At a meeting, Comrade Varvarova told us that the Glavlit leadership had received a phone call from the Central Committee, wanting to know why *Pravda* had so strangely written 'concrete, welding equipment and under-wear are no longer being delivered to the construction site'. So they undertook to find out. It turned out that the text originally read 'welding equipment and consoles'. But a typist decided that this was a mistake and typed in the word 'camisoles'. Then the proofreaders decided that 'camisoles' was a bit obscure and changed it to 'underwear'. I don't know how severe the punishment was, but what has censor-ship got to do with it?

The Banner film theatre in Moscow had been renamed the Illusion, which might cause the reader to smile ironi-cally. It would be better not to mention the old name but simply to report that one of our cinemas is now called the Illusion.

I met a colleague, S, in the corridor at Glavlit. He had travelled with a commission to Kursk to get to the bottom of an issue. A new circus building was being constructed there. The local newspaper concluded its report on the pace of construction with the sentence, 'Let's finish this circus in time for Lenin's centenary!' The comrades were not thinking and, as a result, the censor suffered.

Here are the tragic oral reminiscences of K, a retired Glavlit veteran. This subsequently rehabilitated censor recalled how he met a fellow unfortunate at the Kolyma labour camp. In an article about Central Asia the man had reported that a memorial had been erected to Stalin in the city of Stalinabad. Meanwhile, Stalin was still very much alive. The comrade was also alive but did not survive to the post-Stalin amnesty.

In an article about zoos in America I demanded that the sentence 'Animals previously lived in cages but now they live in open enclosures' be removed. We do not need these allusions to the rights of animals.

There are problems finding qualified censors in the more remote regions. At a management meeting Comrade Varvarova actually turned red. A regional newspaper had printed a statement about substandard performance at an artificial-insemination station. At the end of the article it said, 'The workers on the collective farm sit and wait until sperm comes.'

Readers sent the Party's Central Committee another regional newspaper, which was redirected to Glavlit. It contained an article about a rude saleswoman in a grocery who was hiding scarce items. If she did not like the buyer, she would refuse to sell anything.

Extr. Ord.! Once again I found a proofreader's mistake in an editorial entitled 'Soviet Cosmic Technology'. In the word 'Cosmic' the 's' was missing. I had a meeting with both the proofreader and the head of the newspaper on the subject of vigilance. I told Comrade Varvarova about the editor-in-chief's decision: a severe reprimand for the proofreader in question and an informal warning for the others.

At Central Television and Radio the boss personally ordered that people with beards or without ties should not be allowed to appear on camera. He makes everyone shave and has ties in readiness at the studios. It will be interesting to see how they enforce this mandate on the radio. It's possible that they will apply the same rule to newspaper illustrations. Note to myself: Get a ruling in advance regarding both beards and ties.

V, a fellow-worker in the propaganda department, was sacked. He had conducted an interview with the secretary of an institute's Party organization. It turned out this person was not the secretary but some nonentity who'd just called himself the secretary for a joke. I was only reprimanded for not demanding a permit. But let's think about it in broader terms: Will we get an instruction to check ID cards prior to an interview?

We have been given a special instruction concerning uncontrolled associations. They showed us samples of subtexts. The difficulty is that, in order to discover them, it is necessary to read the same thing several times, weakening vigilance. I came to the conclusion that several known sources can no longer be quoted. Right now the aria from the opera *The Demon* is being broadcast over the radio. Strangely enough, the great singer Shalyapin is singing 'this damned world!' Their Glavlit representative probably wasn't at the briefing.

On the subject of uncontrolled associations, I forbade this line in a report from the Central Forecasting Institute: 'A thaw is moving in from the west.' I told their management about the ambiguity contained in this sentence. They didn't understand. I mentioned it to Comrade Varvarova. She praised me and said that it was essential to include this in the next memorandum. A monetary bonus would have been better.

Again, I wasn't vigilant enough and was reprimanded for my negligence by the supervisor of the art department. A picture of the Minister of Defence was re-photographed from a TASS Agency photo, and the zinc plate turned out to be a mirror image: his medals were on his right side. This was discovered when the Ministry of Defence telephoned in the morning.

From an interview with the director of the Dental Surgery Institute: 'Every country makes its own important contribution to the development of dental surgery. The USA is ahead of us in their treatment of teeth, but we lead in the theory of denture manufacture.' Here everything is right in a political sense, but, subjectively, I suffer from the fact that our theory is so far ahead of our practice.

Attention! Textual abbreviations can be dangerous. A statement reads: 'Thanks to measures recently implemented, KGB-2 takes care of 1,200 more people per month.' I found out that KGB-2 is Krivoy-Rog Gentlemen's City Bathhouse No. 2.

4

The diary ended abruptly at this point.

Tsezar Tsukerman did not finish his God-given work. He did not come to any general conclusions, and he did a good deal of embroidering. For example, ancient Roman censorship was later abolished by the Romans. Censor Tsezar reached no conclusions whatsoever, either on paper or in life. But maybe that was not true. He did, after all, decide to pass on his notebook. But why to me?

We had never socialized much, even when we were working

together. Even then our relationship had – and I'm trying to say this as kindly as possible – a particular nature.

He was conscientious, and because of this (who would have thought it of him?) he wrote everything down on the sly. The newspaper often published my stories, excerpts from my published books and reviews, and he was their first – and most attentive – reader. My uncontrolled associations naturally did not slip past him; I don't know how he reacted to them. If something slipped through, why did it? Now I think maybe he pretended not to notice.

The man who read me first was also the first to learn from a secret memo that my name could no longer appear in print. The blacklisting went on for years. I never met him again, even by chance. And he was careful not to run into me in print.

But let's take a broader view of the deeds of this responsible, and official, reader. What if Censor Tsezar acted for the best?

Only those who agreed to make accommodations in their work were published. I, along with many others, attempted to do this. He never allowed original artists or real literature to see the light of day, thereby ensuring that everything worthwhile was saved in its unadulterated form. Maybe he had given us the chance not to accommodate, to remain pure and not climb into the mousetrap?

By hindering the publication of significant, independent thought, the censor forced the sharp-tongued to retreat into allusion, to hinting between the lines, to making airy associations, which in turn improved the culture of written discourse. By forbidding everything, the censorship generated displeasure and opposition and created a halo of mystery around dissidence. Prohibition promoted a spiritual deficit. The results were the opposite of those intended. Censorship furthered progress!

Did Tsezar understand this? What did he really want? These are questions that will never be answered. Something was evidently going on within him.

For brevity's sake, I at first omitted the conclusion of my conversation with Tsezar's wife. Now I understand that her words were important.

She abruptly walked off in Revolution Square but looked around at me and came back.

'Excuse me,' she said, gasping for breath. 'I'm frightened. Maybe they keep an eye on people like you.'

'Probably not. They can't keep an eye on everyone.'

'Are you sure about that? When I was young I worked at the KGB – just as a typist, of course. Back then they were already trying to keep tabs on everyone. Do you know that Tsezar mentioned you quite often recently? He was interested in various issues.'

'What kind of issues?' I asked, pretending not to understand. I wanted her to explain it herself.

Shrugging her shoulders, she let out a wistful laugh. 'Well, you've practically got one foot over there.'

'But the other one's here, tied to a rope. Did he also want to go "over there"?'

'No,' she cut me off, frightened. Then she added, much more calmly, 'Who would let us out, given his knowledge of secret information? Do you know what he was up to? He sent a proposal to the highest levels that Moscow should open another secret installation – a Scientific Research Institute for Censorship. Later on, he started writing complaints to the government that Glavlit representatives didn't get bonuses for exceeding the plan. And he ended up . . .' Again she looked around, even though no one seemed to be near by, and went on in a whisper, 'He was trying to work out who was worse, Hitler or Stalin.'

'And what did he decide?'

'He said that Stalin was worse. Can you imagine? When he was retired he'd read the papers and say they ought to drop an atom bomb on Glavlit.'

'How did Tsezar manage to end up at Glavlit, being Jewish and all?'

'He was surprised about that himself. He fought through the entire war and ended up a major. Then he worked in army supply until he got discharged under Khrushchev. One of his fellow officers worked for Glavlit; he'd been sent in there by the security service to knock things into shape. Imagine, he was an important officer in the KGB and not at all an anti-Semite.'

'Impossible,' I egged her on.

'Honestly!' She was offended. 'He told Tsezar, "You're an officer, been wounded twice, a Party member with a pile of medals. We'll use this to try to overcome your genetic defect."'

I remembered one Victory Day's eve when Tsezar showed up covered with ribbons and medals. By this time the young people on the editorial staff were laughing at that sort of display. They said you could buy medals at the flea market for five roubles apiece. 'I was the one in the war,' he retorted. 'Me, not some other guy!'

Once, someone at the snack bar who hadn't noticed Tsezar behind him said that the censor's medals were for circumcising literature and art. He had, in fact, continued to do battle for a quarter of a century after the war. As Avanesyan put it, 'under Comrade Varvarova's command'.

'So they managed to overcome his genetic defect successfully?'

'Yes, but then the children grew up. We have a son and a daughter, both registered as Russians through me. The children became ashamed of his profession. My husband was ready to retire. And then . . .' Tears welled up in her eyes.

'He was buried solemnly and with honour,' I said, with feeling.

'How do you know?'

'I heard.' Of course, I hadn't heard anything, but I wanted to say something comforting.

'We wanted to bury him ourselves. But a representative from the editorial department came by right before the funeral and announced that, because of Tsezar's rank and service as a front-line soldier, he was entitled to a civil funeral at his workplace. My husband left a written will saying to bury him in any old cemetery but to play the Israeli national anthem.'

'Israeli?' I choked.

'That was the problem! I whispered this to the comrade from the editorial department. He hemmed and hawed like you just did but promised to inform management. You know, they really did loosen their purse strings and hired an orchestra.'

'And they played the Israeli national anthem?'

'They played the Soviet national anthem. An obituary was written for the newspaper. I was told to come over and check to see if all his medals were listed. It was powerfully worded: "Merciless death has torn a faithful fighter of the glorious Bolshevik press from our ranks." They went on like that.'

'I know, I read it,' I confirmed.

Something like a smile appeared on her face and immediately faded. 'The censors never gave the go-ahead for that obituary for their colleague.'

I kissed the hand of the widow of my most exacting reader, and the woman quietly walked away.

THE DEATH OF TSAR FYODOR *

I

Fyodor Koromyslov, an actor at the Moscow Art Theatre, had always walked to the theatre, but this time he hesitated, wondering whether to take a taxi. Then he decided not to break with tradition.

Some three hours earlier, Koromyslov had been surprised by a telephone call from Yafarov, the theatre's producer, a man who was said to have friends in high places. As if nothing had ever happened between them, Yafarov had started off asking how he was feeling and how he was getting on. Koromyslov had been angry with him ever since Yafarov, while paying lip service to Fyodor, had simultaneously eased him out of the repertory company, without ousting him entirely. And now here he was, calling him up, wanting something from him. Koromyslov had his refusal ready, when Yafarov intoned, 'There's going to be a change in the programme tonight. We're putting on *Fyodor*. With you in it . . .'

'Really? But what about Skakovsky – a young genius, in your very words!'

'My very words . . . But now the arts council has decided

* Tsar Fyodor (reigned 1584–98), the son of Ivan the Terrible, was married to Irina, a sister of Boris Gudonov, who controlled the country from behind the scenes during Fyodor's reign and then contrived to be proclaimed Tsar in his turn. The drama *Tsar Fyodor* by the poet Alexei K. Tolstoy has frequently been perfomed at the Moscow Art Theatre between 1898 and the present day.

in your favour. Look, Fyodor – if there's anything I've said or done, forgive me.'

'What about a rehearsal?' Koromyslov objected, although he was ready to do it even without any of Yafarov's apologies. 'Without a dress rehearsal I won't consider it.'

'What rehearsal, for Pete's sake? You've played that part three hundred times.'

'More than that. But there must be one, all the same.'

'That's simply unreal!'

'OK then, you'll have nobody but yourself to blame if . . .'

'We're not going to have any "ifs",' parried Yafarov. 'Everything has to be just right.'

The sense of his own irreplaceability made Koromyslov forget his grievance. Those youngsters had been a bit hot-headed back then, but now they'd realized their mistake. God would forgive them. *I belong to the theatre*, thought Koromyslov, *not to them. It's the theatre that's calling me back.*

Koromyslov walked the length of the Boulevard Ring and part of the Garden Ring, up to the Red Gates metro station (which he stubbornly refrained from calling Lermontovskaya, which made others uncomfortable) and squinted up at the new monument to the young Lermontov. The statue was barely visible through the clouds of exhaust from the lorries that roared past in a broad stream. Koromyslov had nothing against Lermontov, but this bronze object was repugnant, intended as it was to express the poet's delight at the socialist state's achievements in every sphere.

Every year things got more and more unbearable, and that wasn't just grumbling on Koromyslov's part. Where once this had been a quiet side street, now you could hardly breathe. All the names of the streets had been changed, and there was never any end to the changes. Rename something, just once, and everything was on shaky ground; there was no history any more, just worthless newsprint. What was left of the Moscow of the past century? What remained of Russia?

He was grumbling out of habit, but his mood was cheerful. He loved Moscow and didn't just say so but really believed that he wouldn't trade her for any other city in the world – truth to tell, he'd never been abroad. And it was clear that he would end his days here, where he was born, although he tried not to think about his end. Not because he was frightened of it but simply because it was such a bore to think about.

Coming out of his house, he remembered that in his excitement he hadn't eaten lunch. His housekeeper, Nusha, who had been looking after him like a child for the past thirty-seven years, had left him instructions about what was in which pot while she went off to check that his summer house hadn't been burgled. Nusha idolized him; on occasion they even slept together, when the winters were cold and it was warmer sleeping together in the badly heated apartment. In his youth Koromyslov had long been in love with a woman who had contrived to marry another actor. Their romance stretched on for years. Over and over again she had promised to leave her husband but never got around to it. Because of this expectation, or just his own inertia on the subject of marriage and children, Koromyslov had remained a childless bachelor. Every now and then it bothered him, but he contented himself with frequent clandestine affairs whenever the opportunity arose.

Nusha was right: he should have heated something up and eaten at home. Nusha was practically always right. Maybe that was the reason Koromyslov had never married her.

Not being in any condition to forget his hunger, he began thinking of where he could have some dinner. Public cafeterias, with their pervasive smell of rubbish and long-unwashed dishes, appeared every now and then along his way. The very thought of sticking his head into one of them was enough to put him off the idea of food. You couldn't even hear a civilized word in there, never mind how awful the food was. He started recalling the old restaurants that had disappeared during his youth, vanishing along with the names of the streets, customs and everything else. And the ones that remained were unrecognizable.

Behind these very windows, at tables where revellers from the far north were currently belching, the clientele used to perform gastronomic rites, not just gobble their food down. They weren't just gourmandizing, either, but whiling away their time discussing the fate of Russia – working, as it were. What is there to say? Stanislavsky met Nemirovich-Danchenko in this restaurant. Sitting at these tables, famous journalists dashed off their columns, all the while nibbling chicken giblets. Some actors used to spend hours, between rehearsals and shows, nursing a drink here.

Koromyslov's ruminations ended with him walking into a bakery and paying for a loaf of bread; he broke off the crust and chewed on it, throwing the rest into a rubbish bin. He cursed Nusha, who could have chosen some other day to leave for the dacha.

Autumn, Koromyslov's favourite season, was windy and sunless; all the leaves had blown off the trees, while any snow that fell didn't last.

His hunger dulled and not feeling the cold, Koromyslov passed block after block easily, in pleasant excitement. He felt younger, somehow, completely outside time. Horse-drawn carts overtook him, bourgeois carriages with whooping drivers, landaus, sledges covered with bearskins, lorries full of soldiers, Russian cars from the forties and fifties, Volgas and Chaykas, while he walked in the direction of the theatre, urged on by a breeze at his back. Here, near the Chinese store, he had met Esenin one day, close-shaven and slightly tipsy, in a top hat and striped scarf. Near that corner, there, Mayakovsky had bawled out to him 'Good health to you!' Mayakovsky always measured his steps, robot-like, on the very edge of the pavement. Here, at this very intersection, Marina Tsvetayeva had shaken a finger at Koromyslov from her horse-drawn cab – he couldn't recall why. Maybe she'd just been jealous of him. At the end of his long walk Koromyslov felt tired. He should have caught a taxi, after all.

Opening the door with the sign 'Employees Only', Fyodor nodded to the porter out of habit, and he had already set foot on the stairs when he heard out of the gloom to one side, 'Passport, please!'

Only now did Koromyslov notice that, instead of Maximych, who had been warming this chair for the last half a century, there was a middle-aged man in a grey suit and a tie.

'And who exactly are you?' asked Koromyslov, in surprise.

'Your passport,' repeated his questioner, calmly and firmly.

'This is Koromyslov!' explained Maximych, appearing out of nowhere, and tittered strangely. 'Good health to you, Fyodor. How are you?'

'I don't understand what's going on,' mumbled Koromyslov, feeling his jacket pockets for his documents.

Finally he found them, handed them over and waited, perplexed. The man in grey looked from Koromyslov to his papers and back again for a long time, then finally put a mark on some sort of list and returned the passport.

'Everything's in order. Go ahead,' he said.

Young people on the stairs stepped back into the shadows. Koromyslov merely shrugged his shoulders and started up the stairs.

All kinds of new people were walking in the corridors between the makeup rooms – looking, to the trained eye, like extras from some modern play. Twice, though, old actors embraced him; and the costume designer, Anfisa, sobbing, laid her head against his chest. For a long while he tried to calm her down.

'I . . . I'll bring everything in a second. Get out of your street clothes, for now,' she wailed, backing towards the door and wiping the tears from her cheeks with the back of her hand. 'You look so young, Fyodor, so strong. Haven't you got married yet? You should, you really should . . . I just buried my husband. Damned vodka. Wasn't for that, he'd be alive, like you.'

After changing, he started putting on his makeup, unhurriedly, even before the half-hour warning. He did it calmly, with measured movements, as if he hadn't had any kind of break from the theatre at all. He pressed the beard to his face with his fingers and waited while the glue dried. Voices in the corridor gave Koromyslov the feeling that the tension behind the scenes was higher than usual. Going by how emotional the people he had encountered were, he attributed the atmosphere to his own arrival – not out of immodesty but simply as a fact. The bustle was keeping him from concentrating, from getting into his latest role, into the life of a tsar.

The current scene faded out; a curtain rose: Falkevich, the play's assistant producer, greeted them and warned the company to take special care with their preparations. Then he added, 'Introducing: People's Artiste Koromyslov! The troupe welcomes you cordially. How are things going with you? By the way, Yafarov is going to be dropping in on you any time now.'

Yafarov, the producer, ran towards them, red in the face and short of breath. He rolled up, a balding roly-poly man, and put his hands on Koromyslov's shoulders from behind. They spoke, looking at each other in the mirror. Yafarov looked over Koromyslov attentively, even tenderly.

'Right here,' he said, pointing at the left edge of the beard. Picking up a brush, he reglued the beard and pressed it against Koromyslov's cheek.

'What are you doing fussing over me like I'm some dame?'

'Do your best not to disgrace us, Fyodor!'

'Disgrace you – in front of whom?' exclaimed Koromyslov, and suddenly a thought flitted into his head. 'Tell me, brother! For Christ's sake, have some respect for your elder!'

'I couldn't tell you over the phone,' explained Yafarov, shifting to a half-whisper. 'They warned me not to tell anybody. *Himself* is going to be in the theatre today.'

'*Himself*? Who's that supposed to be?'

'Think about it and you'll get it. See? OK. *Himself* has seen *Tsar Fyodor* six times already. And always with you. Between the two of us, Fyodor, I was against replacing you. But Skakovsky – you know whose protégé *he* is. The Minister of Culture got an order, and he made us do it. We had to. But today we can't risk it. We are counting on you. Save our theatre, dear fellow!'

Koromyslov hesitated, wanting to ask whose protégé Skakovsky was, but restrained himself.

'Never fear, Yafarov,' he said peacefully. 'You know how many *Himselves* I've seen? *Himselves* come and go, but the theatre abides, old fellow. Big deal, *Himself*!'

'Shhhhhh!' Yafarov rolled his eyes to the ceiling and pressed a finger to his lips. 'You know what they think of us in some circles. They say we're losing all tradition bit by bit and any plebeian can play a king . . . I myself firmly disagree with that – we're forging ahead, we're progressing. Not as fast as we'd like, but we are moving. Unfortunately we can't stop them thinking what they want about us. But what if the criticism gets to the very top?'

'Vanity! Art is beyond vanity, brother.'

'That's until you get to be the theatre producer,' Yafarov mumbled cheerlessly. 'Ever since yesterday this whole place has been in a fever. Secret service bodyguards everywhere. "Where do these stairs go? Put a lock on this hatchway . . . And that spotlight – won't it shine right into the balcony? We're going to seal this exit, the audience will have to make do with the other ones . . ." They're right, of course. What if something happened? Well, I'll go and check the balcony. If he's late we'll have to postpone curtain call.'

But the very fact that Yafarov was sucking up to him was

pleasant. *The old guard doesn't give up, and we're still irreplaceable.* Himself *has to see that irreplaceability on stage, so as not to fall prey to dangerous thoughts. That's why they called me.* Himself *has seen the play six times, and the last two times he wept.* The lighting man had afterwards told Koromyslov exactly where. *Himself* had begun to cry because he was getting old, but that was flattering, too. And Koromyslov, usually dissatisfied with everything, felt a twinge of liking for *Himself.* Now, right in front of *Himself*, Koromyslov would show his persecutors what the real Tsar Fyodor was like.

2

The show went on, calmly and measuredly. Cutting himself off from the mundane, the tsar walked solemnly down the hall, adjusting the rings on his fingers and slowly began to climb the spiral staircase. The voice of the stage manager, Falkevich, could be heard in the empty dressing-room, 'Koromyslov, you're on.' Two tall young men in civilian clothes obstructed the iron door to the stage with their massive shoulders. Tsar Fyodor made a regal gesture with his little finger and they jumped out of his way, mumbling, 'Go ahead.'

The audience welcomed Koromyslov with a buzz of recognition, after which came loud applause, and Tsar Fyodor delayed his introductory phrase. Despite this, he tried then to slip into the play unnoticed, with restraint. Only later, warming up to the part of Fyodor, with all its qualms and fears, did he gain depth. The experience of long years had become compressed, like a diamond, and it scintillated now, liberated from his mundane actor's self.

At some point this self reminded him, 'You've gone too far; lower the tone, overact for some humour, slide into parody. Once you've felt it, the others will catch on to it. They'll defer to you, and then the audience will catch on, too.' But Koromyslov couldn't stop. He was now playing himself, the way it would be if he *were* the tsar, and it was like a flash of genius, albeit somewhat inappropriate. Leaving the stage to prolonged applause, he thought contentedly that today he had presented the weak and vacillating tsar as never before, and it must have even got through to *Himself*, unless he was completely senile. Koromyslov wanted the modern tsar to recognize himself on the stage.

In the wings, meanwhile, Yafarov had taken Tsar Fyodor into his arms and whispered tenderly into his ear, '*Himself* applauded twice, and his wife did, too. Both times for you. Of course, I'd given the order in advance for an applause track to be played, to raise the temperature in the audience. But you, Fyodor – good for you. Thank you, my dear old chap! We were too hasty with your retirement. Now I'd go through fire and water for you. I'll even stand up to the minister! Ask for anything, even a full-time job!'

Koromyslov listened to this and silently accepted it as his due.

For him, the second act flashed past in a single breath. The troupe swung behind the old swordsman, his voice vacillating between weakness and strength, between hatred and tenderness. Koromyslov was sure that the audience, as always, was under his spell, too.

Koromyslov had no part in the following scene, and he had just managed to stretch himself out contentedly on the sofa to catch his breath when Yafarov rushed in.

'Trouble, trouble! Oh, Lord!' The words tumbled out of him. 'I checked in the middle of the act, everything was rosy. That is, I didn't see the expression on his face – it was dark, and the balcony's curtained off. Now there's nobody in there – it's empty!'

'Maybe he went to see a man about a dog.'

'And the guards? They've taken away the guards, too!'

'The guards wouldn't leave without him. He left. Things happen. Maybe something came up. Some emergency . . . maybe somebody declared war.'

'Oh, Fyodor, you're such an optimist! Or maybe you don't give a damn as long as you've got your pension? What if he didn't like it?'

'Why wouldn't he "like it"? He probably ate something, got a stomach ache, or maybe it was his kidneys . . . He's a bit older than I am, after all. He probably just got sleepy.'

'Sleepy! Here, in our theatre?' whined Yafarov, deaf to any more arguments. 'Who should we talk to? Who can tell us why he didn't stay until the end? The snitches are going to rat on us to the Minister of Culture in the morning. There goes our tour in West Germany.'

'Cut it out! One tsar didn't like another, that's all there is to it. It isn't as if we aren't used to it. Russia has seen lots of different tsars. Who the hell knows what's going on in those heads of theirs. Screw it!'

'If you've got so much balls, call *Himself*'s son. Remember, some time ago you used to drink vodka with him at that Central Committee resort. Make it sound important, prattle on about the contributions of the theatre. Say, something like, "How should we interpret this?" Let him ask his daddy. Say it's important to the theatre for the sake of creative development. And don't turn up your nose – it's not for me. It's for the people. Okhlopkov, a well-known actor, when he was appointed Minister of Culture said, 'It's easy for me, I've played tsars on the stage.' It should be easy for you, too, to give him a call. Don't put it off! Try your luck, man.'

Then Yafarov ran off at a trot. Apparently he didn't have such great connections at the top, if he was shaking and afraid even to pick up the phone.

For Koromyslov, unlike Okhlopkov, the transformation into a tsar took a concentrated effort of will, and his self-confidence had no business wavering. *Himself* had walked out before the point where he cried. So it had nothing to do with Koromyslov, and it couldn't be his fault. *And what is this danger that's threatening the theatre? Yafarov is right: nothing ventured, nothing gained. If there's nothing to it, great, and if it's something serious, it's important to find out exactly what the problem is. I'll phone him right after the play.*

Koromyslov's entrance was called. He got up, conscious as he made his way to the stage the responsibility that had so suddenly befallen him, and he also felt a kind of triumph: he would prove to Yafarov and his people that he, Koromyslov, was the saviour of the very theatre that they had been destroying, he would use the opportunity that had suddenly arisen. It had been a long time since he had last been anxious before going on stage. It was work. But today he was hard on himself and felt a tension that he could not suppress, not even with all his habitual trained actor's willpower. A sudden fatigue spread throughout his body and did not go away.

Having set scene eight, the stagehands hurried backstage.

'I've stitched up your hem, Fyodor,' whispered Anfisa. 'Don't worry.'

All this time he had not noticed her on her knees behind him.

'I've lost a button, Anfisa,' he told her, pointing at his chest.

'It's your entrance.' The wardrobe mistress took fright. 'Where can I find one now exactly like that? Let me just stitch the lapels together, and I'll fix it later.'

Nodding, he looked at the yellow and red footlights lighting up in pairs, illuminating the vaults of the royal apartments. Anfisa leaned towards him and bit through the thread with her teeth.

'God be with you.' She hastily turned around to make sure no one was looking and made the sign of the cross over him.

The fatigue was gone, but he couldn't get enough air. A ball of fear welled up in his throat. Terror stuck its bony fingers through his ribs and squeezed his heart.

'Too much light,' Koromyslov said. 'It's blinding.'

'Impossible. It's just like it always is. These lights haven't been changed for the last twenty years.'

He let go of the curtain and walked on stage, seating himself on the carved royal throne. His clothing was stifling, even though it was lined with gauze and the furs were not real sable but synthetic.

'Curtain!' Falkevich's command came to him over the loudspeaker, and immediately the motor started purring.

A rush of air reached him from the audience, mixed with the smell of sweat and perfume. The pain was gone, or maybe he had forgotten about it. Then, suddenly, it pressed into him again. Tsar Fyodor wiped the sweat from his face, as the part required, and immersed himself in his state papers. Irina put a hand on his shoulder.

'You ought to rest, Fyodor . . .'

Koromyslov had long been used to the silence that would settle over an audience when he set to work, even before he had thrown out a line. And when he did monologues, he knew how to command the audience. He could throw the audience into fits or move everyone with a single gesture, a single intonation. But today the silence was special. No one coughed or knocked their binoculars against their armrests, as if the pain in Koromyslov's heart had spread to everybody, and they were afraid to take a breath that might cause him pain in his chest.

Sitting on the throne he imperceptibly relaxed his body and squinted slightly. It was easier to speak this way. But already it was time to get up, as Kleshin spoke the words, 'From your sick servant, from Godunov.'

Koromyslov never thought about what he should do at any given moment when he was acting. It all happened of its own accord. The producer's directions automatically took shape in him, became part of his being, and everything would have rolled along, if not for that burning pain.

Subtly he tried to turn his face towards the audience, towards the source of fresh air, to make it easier to breathe. He felt terrible. He finally remembered his nitroglycerin pills. Nusha always carefully put their little phial into a pocket specially sewn to the inside of his undershirt. Take one if something goes wrong, she had always reminded him. To get to the pills he had to unbutton his heavy gown. He tried the buttons but couldn't find the one he needed. Anfisa had used heavy thread to sew one lapel to the other. Koromyslov tried to rip apart the stitches but didn't have enough strength. Why the hell had he told Anfisa about the button?

Meanwhile he went on acting.

3

Koromyslov was almost seventy but not that old in either his build or his health.

'I'm a peasant. Nothing gets to me,' he had always boasted, letting people feel his biceps.

His heart had started giving him trouble in the last year and a half. And for some reason it had suddenly got quite bad.

He never went to doctors – hadn't liked them since childhood – but in the spring the theatre had organized a surprise medical examination for everybody, with no exceptions. He hadn't wanted to seem like a stubborn old man in front of the younger actors, so he'd allowed the doctor from the elite clinic to feel him up. She palpated his stomach, listened a little bit to his heart, patted him on the shoulder and went off to whisper with her colleague. Koromyslov grinned complacently. But they returned together; both of them listened to his heart and made wry faces. Then the second physician took out a piece of paper, wrote down her office number and told him to come and see her the following day at the polyclinic.

'You may be a tsar,' she said, 'but your heart's not. It's like a lamb's. I advise you not to ignore this warning.'

He was absolutely sure that it was all rubbish. But suddenly the ECGs – and the blood, urine and other tests – turned into a thick medical history, which he called a mysterious comedy composed by the doctors, based on his life. The doctors never handed over the script to their patients, everyone knew that, but you had to act out their comedy none the less.

When the examinations at the elite clinic were over, Professor Broder, who was young enough to be Koromyslov's son, got up and put a teacherly hand on his shoulder. 'I have great respect for you. I've seen you on stage many times, and I realize that the theatre will miss you, and you will miss it . . .'

Broder finished by simply looking into Koromyslov's eyes. Koromyslov didn't understand or maybe just refused to understand. He told Professor Broder a story from the life of another actor, Abdulov. He was lying in bed at home alone with an attack of angina. He barely had the strength to get to the telephone and call a doctor. The doctor answered that *he* was too ill to come out. 'Better come,' says Abdulov, 'or you'll have to answer for it.' The doctor came, and collapsed. Abdulov dragged him on to his bed and, following the doctor's directions, gave him some medication. He brought the doctor around, the doctor's heart got better, and he went back home. A few days later, when Abdulov had got better, he again called the doctor to ask how he was doing. He was told, 'The doctor's dead . . .'

Broder heard him out with a condescending smile. 'I can't stop you, but I'm telling you that frequent stress is categorically contraindicated. In your place I would be kinder to myself: no more than one performance a week. More often than that is a risk. Don't shorten your life. Take a tour of the health resorts – no beaches, of course. Walk in the park, go to your dacha. Girls, you can . . . look at. Act otherwise and I won't be held responsible.'

Koromyslov wouldn't have told anyone, but Broder, having recognized his patient's name from his posters, told Yafarov, whom, as it turned out, he knew well. Of course, Yafarov used this as a trump card: in the interest of Koromyslov's health his workload was reduced.

Without false modesty, Koromyslov suggested that, with

his departure, the theatre would lose some of its grandeur, and there was nothing that could compensate for the loss. Yafarov was of a different opinion: the progress of art was unstoppable, and the new, according to the law of the dialectic, should always defeat the old. In fact what Yafarov intended to do was to promote his own people to the starring roles, getting rid of the old actors who, with their grumbling and their references to the classics, stopped him from accepting new plays from the Ministry of Culture.

The only problem was *Tsar Fyodor*. They wouldn't let you shut down a production that dated back to 1896 just like that. The Arts Council had met to find a way out, meaning an alternative to Koromyslov. They came up with a new Fyodor – Skakovsky. By the seventh run-through he had acquired enough polish: the play limped along, and soon the posters were up without Koromyslov's name on them, as if he'd never existed. Other actors who had lived long enough to draw their pensions tried to console him. 'After all, Fyodor, what more do people like us need? Talent, money, glory, medals, the dacha – you've got it all. Put aside your pride! Collect stamps now, like many retired guys do, or buy yourself a tortoise at the pet shop and watch it crawl around. Look back on your former existence: did we ever get to rest? You're fixated, Fyodor. Take a break! Even locomotives need down time.'

He didn't argue, only looked at them as if they were weird museum pieces. What were they trying to talk him into? He didn't need a tortoise, and he wasn't a locomotive.

He was a hybrid of plebeian and noble bloodlines. His father, a hereditary nobleman, had spent two-thirds of his conscious life in Italy, and during one of his infrequent visits to Moscow he had sinned with a servant girl, begetting a People's Actor of the Soviet Union. Before the Revolution Koromyslov had exaggerated the noble branch of his ancestry; afterwards the plebeian one.

As a lad, wet behind the ears, he had always sneaked into the theatre, put aside money kopek by kopek, saved on school lunches. The world war left Koromyslov without a father; the Revolution his mother. Meanwhile he starved and hung around the theatre's rear entrance, looking for any kind of work, just to be behind the scenes. A snack vendor used him as a valet to look after people's coats because to earn a profit from his snacks he had to look after the coats for free.

After hanging up all the audience's coats, Fyodor would bust a gut carrying boxes with cider and champagne up to the second floor, and later, having returned all of the coats, he washed the glasses. He would carry tea to the actors' dressing-rooms during rehearsals. They liked him for not refusing to sneak booze to them and also for his skilful imitations of famous actors. One of his turns caught the eye of Meyerhold, who told Nemirovich-Danchenko about him. As Koromyslov liked to joke, Nemirovich consulted Danchenko and said, 'We can't let this one onstage as an extra. He'd attract far too much attention to himself.'

Nevertheless, Nemirovich-Danchenko gave him one line, wearing an apron and wielding a street-sweeper's broom. 'From that moment,' as Koromyslov recalled at his sixtieth birthday banquet, 'I became a solo bohemian.' However, 'bohemian' was just a label; the rest was sweat. His whole career was about work and sweat, and whatever came before or after or in between seemed like a foreword, some sort of commentary, notes that could easily be thrown away as unessential.

Having taken his body, the theatre demanded his soul.

Since childhood he had been a religious man, but for a long time he had been wary of going to church, and Nusha had moved his icon of the Virgin from his room to hers, just in case. Then came a new trend in the theatre: revolutionary heroes could only be played by Party members, so he adopted that label as well, not understanding very clearly why he needed it. The new plays seemed unfeeling to him. He said that he wasn't acting a part but a text. But he played them anyway. There was even some challenge in it, using his genius to animate insignificant characters. Students asked him once, 'Could you play an editorial from *Pravda*?' He answered, 'You bet I could.'

They gave him the rank of People's Actor and entrusted him with making a speech that contained extensive praise for and thanks to Stalin, the organizer and inspirer of the theatrical arts. With his velvet voice he smoothed out the empty phrases, signifying nothing, that were written especially for the occasion and made them sound impressive. At the honours banquet he was led before Stalin, who personally shook the actor's hand. After that, one Stalin Prize followed another. Once he was told that no one he worked with was being imprisoned, thanks to him. But that was neither Koromyslov's fault nor to his credit: he was just lucky.

After the death of Stalin, Mordvinov, a rehabilitated great actor back from a distant labour camp, told Koromyslov that they had had some great people in their Gulag theatre but that Koromyslov's absence among them had been felt.

In the flood of contemporary plays, Alexey Tolstoy's *Tsar Fyodor* remained in the repertoire for some reason, and Koromyslov stayed with it.

'When you were born they called you Fyodor for a reason,' joked his friends after dinner. 'But why are you working so hard? You know the role, so take it easy. It's just a job.'

He felt that the role preserved him from diminution. Living in a period engulfed in an avalanche of shit, *Tsar Fyodor* was his only bastion, a connection across time, a sign that in his own soul and around him not everything was trampled into the mud yet. Everything else had been pulverized, but this oak still showed green leaves.

Koromyslov always hurried to the theatre as if he were late, even though he always arrived early. He would walk home slowly and aimlessly. He didn't know what was in the shops, how people were coping, why they had children. His own home was no more than a dosshouse for him, a place where he had a bed, surrounded by expensive furniture, the only purpose of which was for Nusha to dust it. He viewed gossip, intrigue, slogans and instructions from on high as ephemeral and vain. The only thing that counted was what happened on stage. That was life. All the rest, real life, was just a game.

After losing *Fyodor*, his only anchor, Koromyslov hadn't slowed up, however; he had sunk into the humiliation of low-grade work, afraid even to lose that. He agreed to appear in children's matinées.

On Sundays the audience would be crowded with kids of all ages. The youngest would finish the sweets they had bought in the foyer, voice their opinions of the plot out loud and walk around the aisles during the play.

'Fyodor, what do you do those piddling matinées for?'

'To keep fit. I work best in the morning, brothers, before I've got tired.'

Fyodor Koromyslov was lying. He was simply bored at home, so bored that he wanted to hang himself. But his life in the theatre was getting harder and harder.

Yafarov offered him a small part in a new play about the proletariat entitled *The Metallurgists*, probably hoping that Koromyslov would be offended. But he took it. Conflict arose but from a different direction. Yafarov was trying to resuscitate plays that were all but dead, looking for something to liven them up. His idea was for an old worker, played by Koromyslov, to ride a bicycle on to the stage.

'I'll do it. I don't care,' Koromyslov agreed. 'But the audience will just keep wondering whether I'm going to fall into the orchestra pit.'

'Don't try to teach me my job!' snapped Yafarov. 'They've put an elephant on stage at the Bolshoi!'

'That's the Bolshoi for you – a big blow-out for foreigners.

And who's going to teach you your job? The *metal-shirkers*?' He was punning on the wing. 'There are only a few people left who remember what real art is like. And even those are leaving. You're our heirs, but you're eager to throw all the mysteries of our craft into the bin. Where are you heading for?'

'Dear heart,' Yafarov had responded in conciliatorily tone, 'the theatre is changing. You have to understand that the scale of production is different now. It's the collective that does the acting now. It isn't my idea. It's the times. Stars just blow the general concept to smithereens. However much we love you, Koromyslov, you're still a man of the past. You can't grasp this.'

Koromyslov gave up. For the past few months he had got used to the idea that he was a burden to the theatre. Hack work, oblivious of his old precepts, was easier and therefore more suitable. The organization replaced its talent entirely. Koromyslov waved goodbye to it and, retiring on health grounds, left for good. They found another person for his role in *The Metallurgists* without much difficulty.

All that spring he would stroll back and forth from the Myasnitsky Gates to the Nikitsky, even though this was unpleasant and silly.

'How are you keeping, Fyodor?' old-timers would ask when they met him.

He would answer with a line from *Tsar Fyodor*, '"The whole world knows that I am mortal; that pain in me is the sign,"' adding, 'I'm not hurt by any of it. To hell with them all. "Am I or am I not a tsar? A tsar or not a tsar?" They felt me up and then concocted some kind of libel, but I'm healthier than all the rest of them put together, healthy as a billygoat in March.'

Once it got warmer, he and Nusha left for his dacha. He would walk around the garden with his cat, talking to him. The depth of the cat's friendship amazed Koromyslov and eased the readjustment of his psyche. Once, in the evening, the cat appeared on the porch, his whole countenance showing that he wanted Fyodor to go with him. His master got up and followed him. The tomcat ran ahead, leading him eventually to two pussycats who were waiting near a fence. That was how generous his friendship was – he'd brought two cats, one for himself and one for Koromyslov. At the end of the summer the tom was killed by a motor cycle – Koromyslov and Nusha buried him in the garden under the plum tree.

In September Fyodor heard that there were photographs documenting his career as a People's Artist on display at the Bakhrushin Theatre Museum. He went to have a look. A young female tour guide was mumbling something to a group of carefree secondary-school students, and he joined them. When he introduced himself at the end of the tour the girl took fright.

'Why . . . you are still alive!'

'I'm the king of this theatre!' he wanted to scream. 'Every-one else is dead and gone! I'm the last mammoth!'

But of course he didn't say anything out loud because he could understand this girl who was sure that museum pieces stayed in their displays and didn't come on tours to look at themselves.

4

His face distorted with the pain, Koromyslov kept on acting. All of a sudden he felt very clearly that he had lost contact with the other actors, that he was acting alone, in a dead theatre. Around him were nothing but shadows, phantoms. Yafarov had destroyed the text with all his additions and cuts; now the castrated play was hard to recognize. He, Koromyslov, was the only person who took it seriously, but his strength was gone. They shouldn't have let Yafarov come within a mile of the theatre. He had raped the muses, dug a grave for the arts. Koromyslov had wanted nothing to do with him. He shouldn't have agreed this time – bowing to his vanity, he had become a shield covering a shameful story with his broad back.

And then a thought – just then, onstage, as simple as a gulp of water – rose to the surface of his consciousness: he alone was the theatre. That was why he'd resisted retirement – they didn't understand that he hadn't resisted for his own sake. Koromyslov felt no malice towards Yafarov, who had three children, a sick wife, two life-long mistresses, one kidney and an apartment he'd just received from the ministry that he still had to prove himself worthy of before he received a state dacha. The theatre was what worried Koromyslov, alarmed him to the point of desperation. The theatre was dying, and Koromyslov was saving it. He was giving his last efforts to support the dying theatre. Or maybe, like the play, the theatre was already dead. *Somehow I'm wandering around on stage, but am I still alive?*

Meanwhile the plot had taken them to the tsaritsa's chambers in the royal tower. For the first time in his life Koromyslov detached himself from the role, playing it automatically, while he stood outside it with his own thoughts, worries and bitterness, and he couldn't bring himself back. He felt pressure on his temples and kept raising his hands to his neck, trying to loosen his collar, to breathe more deeply, but somehow he could not. Every breath produced pain in the left side of his chest. He could hardly see Shakhovsky's entrance and couldn't take the scroll handed to him. *A little longer and it'll be over, this scene will be over. I'm not in the next one, and then it's the interval. Then I'll catch my breath.*

But the scene dragged on, and he was not completely sure whether he was saying the right words or just thought he was. Yafarov and the rest had won, they had got through to him. He was losing that confidence in the correctness of his intonation and gestures that he'd possessed throughout his life. His head was swimming. *They're corpses, but they have managed to kill me, too, and my acting's no good. The audience keeps coughing. It's not because of a flu epidemic. It's me – slow, boring; I'm working without any spark. I came to the theatre in an emotional state, I came to cry, and now I realize I'm not going to. I'm going to go home and get drunk. Why do I feel so bad? This all comes from exhaustion, from pointless fighting . . . I . . . I . . . I . . .*

The thought spun around that single sound, aye-aying, and turned into a series of sparks flying up into the heights of the stage and then extinguishing themselves in an instant. He dug his nails into his palms. Seated on his throne, he trembled, then grew calm and suddenly realized that he was playing his death.

He'd never been handed a role like this before. How could he have been? He was playing his own death, and the role unexpectedly required more strength than he possessed. His soul strained at the effort to vanquish itself.

His royal hand grabbed convulsively for the state seal, all his muscles in spasm. His tongue ran over his dry and burning lips, and Tsar Fyodor spat out the hateful words, 'You – my Irina – you're for the nunnery!'

'This can't happen!' Irina dropped to her knees in front of him, at last hearing the line he had been so long slogging towards.

'It won't happen! No!' Tsar Fyodor rose to his full height, pronouncing the words that his brain no longer understood. 'I'll stand by you! Let them come! Let them come with cannons! Let them try!'

He took a few chaotic, drunken steps towards Prince Ivan Shuisky, waved his hand in a curse and choked. Pain overwhelmed his mind and pierced his body. Prince Shuisky swayed and almost fell on to Koromyslov. Realizing that his body was no longer obeying him, Koromyslov tried to take a step to leave the stage. Another step . . . The curtain sailed towards him like a blue cloud, and he hung on to it, embracing it like the last living thing to which he could give his unspent love. The rotten threads of the curtain started ripping, unable to support his heavy body because, as he embraced it, Koromyslov was already dead.

The costumier Anfisa, realizing what was happening, rushed out to him, for the first time in her life showing herself to the audience. Someone in the stalls laughed. Anfisa could not support the weight of his body, and it sank on to the stage.

Quickly they closed the curtain. Few in the audience noticed or understood what had happened, but a nameless worry spread around the auditorium. The head producer was called from his office.

'Did he make that phone call?' Yafarov asked, struggling through the tight ring of people. 'Was it bad news?'

Nobody answered him; they just let him through. The nurse had already folded Koromyslov's hands on his chest and slowly shut his eyes, holding them closed with her fingers, and then started disassembling her syringe.

Yafarov sank to his knees next to her, holding his temples as if doubting what he was seeing.

'Fyodor,' he mumbled in a dull voice, touching the wrinkled synthetic sable on the gold-embroidered royal robe, 'forgive me, a sinner, beloved comrade, forgive us all. What a tragedy . . . What a . . .'

'Why a tragedy? For the likes of us, it's always been considered great good fortune to die on stage.'

'Not in such an important play, though!' Yafarov rose from his knees. 'What if . . .' He did not finish his sentence, but everybody understood. Yafarov thought that *Himself* was probably a real Solomon: he'd foreseen it, and that was why he'd left early.

'Where's the ambulance? Did anybody call one?' The chief producer started giving orders to get control of himself.

'It'll be here right away.'

'Have you informed his relatives?'

'What relatives? His housekeeper . . . Why would she come here, if they're taking him to the mortuary?'

'Who'll tell the audience?' Falkevich asked.

'Me, of course, who else?' Yafarov answered in a frenzy, dusting off the knees of his trousers.

Falkevich ran to the microphone and ordered, 'White light from both sides on the curtain. Half dimmed.'

After a moment's concentration, Yafarov pulled the curtain aside and walked into the light. The audience maintained a respectful silence. Slowly and carefully choosing his words, Yafarov announced that, owing to an actor's sudden illness, the theatre administration begged forgiveness for not finishing the play. He didn't know if he could tell them about the death without consulting the authorities. He didn't name the actor, either.

The cashiers had already learned the truth through their own channels and had told the secret to their own customers, the people they'd let in for a cash consideration, a modest addition to their meagre salaries; and they, in turn, spread the news to their neighbours. By the time the head producer made his entrance on to the apron, part of the audience already knew the truth and the others had guessed it. The room was abuzz. But since this truth was unofficial, everybody treated the producer's cover-up with understanding.

Yafarov stood for some time with his hands spread in an apologetic gesture, waiting for the audience to start getting up. They in turn waited for him to leave and the lights to be turned up. When that finally happened, they slowly stirred and got to their feet, the usual cloakroom press seizing them in its grasp.

Emerging from the theatre, the spectators hesitated and stopped. A crowd had formed at the entrance, spilling across the street.

'Shuisky dies, and so does Dmitri,' speculated a philosophical-looking young man standing among some pretty girls. 'What the hell, maybe Fyodor had to die, too? Hands up if you studied history at school!'

The theatre-goers talked quietly among themselves, making their way closer to the service entrance, and waited. Young men helped their girlfriends to climb on to old scenery flats lying around. Everybody squirmed and shuffled, shoving one another. Then an ambulance drove out of the gate. It slowed down, flashed its lights, moved forward and flashed them again.

'They're taking him to casualty,' said a voice in the crowd.

'Too late for casualty, he's already dead.'

'What do you mean, dead?' a few people asked simultaneously from various quarters.

'If he wasn't dead they would have turned on the siren. He's in no hurry now.'

'You don't know what you're talking about! Yafarov announced that he'd been taken ill. That means a heart attack. These days people like that get put back on their feet.'

'Put feet-first into a coffin, you mean.'

This last remark was said by a passer-by who'd somehow got into the crowd of theatre-goers. He didn't know who they were talking about. Smelling of alcohol, he expressed his opinion, 'Yeah, they'll put him on his feet all right! I got an aunt, she spent two months in hospital. They told her she could get up. She got up, and fell down stone dead.'

Several people agreed with the stranger.

'Nowadays it's either a stroke or cancer – take your pick.'

'That's crap. You can die of anything – the flu, drink, anything.'

'What a bunch of know-it-alls,' mumbled an old man in a threadbare coat.

'Eh, Natasha ... Everybody's favourite circus act in Russia is the death of a tsar,' said a grey-haired, intelligent-looking man without a hat, quietly making his way out of the crowd and pulling his plump girlfriend behind him. 'They don't even need bread to go with it. They stare their fill and go home happy. Let's go, Natasha ...'

'Cut out the chatter. Let the ambulance get through. He's an actor, after all!'

'An actor, so what? It doesn't matter to him – he'll play a tsar or a fool. It's his job.'

'That's right, but it must be pretty nerve-wracking, playing a tsar – look how he burned out onstage.'

'Don't listen to them, Natasha. Let's get to bed.'

The ambulance finally made it on to the street and quietly, without turning on its siren, rolled down the road past the theatre. Tsar Fyodor was being carried on his last journey through Moscow for the second time, three and a half centuries after the first. This time, however, he was wearing makeup.

CRACKED PINK LAMPSHADE

It had been some time now since Sergei Nikolsky had lost his taste for books. Today, however, he was reading with interest. His interest had been fired by a woman.

Nikolsky hefted his latest stack of volumes, trying to determine by their weight if he could get through them all in a single sitting. The books were solemn as antique furniture. The remnants of gold tooling gleamed on their stained leather bindings. There were brass fastenings on several of the tomes, as if to stop the thoughts inside, lying flattened out until there was a call for them, from flying off on their own.

Nodding to the librarian in charge of the researchers' reading-room, Nikolsky took the stack back to his table and placed the books under an ancient lamp with a pink glass shade that had a rim broken off and a crack running across it. The lamp's appearance was – how to put it exactly? – out of place. It looked as if it had been brought here, to this regional library, from some boudoir or other, where it had previously been witness to a completely different and altogether more intimate aspect of life.

Roza, the rather shabbily attired thirtysomething librarian, watched attentively as the imposing visitor settled himself more comfortably in his chair, rubbed his clean-shaven cheeks and straightened his tie, which was already lying irreproachably between his snow-white collar points. Shaking his handsome head of grey hair, the reader took out some coloured pens of foreign make and a packet of lined notecards. He wiped his fingers with a handkerchief, as if sitting down to breakfast instead of a session with some books.

Sergey Sergeyevich Nikolsky fastidiously turned over the grubby pages, which smelled of mould and mouse droppings. A doctor of historical sciences, a professor and Chairman of the Communist Party History Department at the Central Committee's own Academy of Social Sciences, he had come to Gomel to deliver a closed lecture for regional Party activists. Everyone knew that anything was considered 'closed' that was already common knowledge but which could only be spoken about to higher-ups from the relative security of a lectern. This alone gave the speaker a certain privilege. Nikolsky was long accustomed to this, by the way. He'd had it in mind for a long time to look over the books in the partially preserved private library of General Field-Marshal Count Paskevich. The provincial library was housed, incidentally, in what had formerly been the count's palace.

The director of the library, a lady who had been transferred here from the provincial committee's department of propaganda, had introduced their VIP guest to Roza. The director was plump but quite capable of shifting – Nikolsky could barely keep up with her, despite his relatively athletic build. She whispered in Roza's ear that this *particular* reader (she stressed the word 'particular') should be given everything he requested, including items from special collections. The director apologized to their guest for bringing him to a reading-room intended for researchers and not for academicians and professors.

'We don't have anywhere appropriate to your rank at present. When they put up the new building . . .'

The night before Nikolsky had spent two whole hours filling in forms and a special questionnaire that wanted to know what he was planning to read and why. The questionnaire was then compared to the official letter from the Academy petitioning for access to the books concerned. It was all complete and utter nonsense. The official letter had been typed by Nikolsky's secretary, Nikolsky himself had signed it instead of his friend, the vice-director, and then he'd stuck a false registration number on to it.

Nikolsky had no intention of perusing the books for any specific topic he was working on – he was just looking at them, for his own sake. And the director didn't give a damn who read what. But such were the long-established rules: for many years already the job of a library had been to keep people *from* reading, just in case they might find out something they weren't supposed to know, even something from ancient history. This didn't bother Nikolsky a bit. In order to read, you had to understand why you were reading. People who were just piddling around spoiled books. As for the obstacles to reading, seek and ye shall find. There was no need to labour the issue. A long time ago he'd worked out a principle that he would repeat to himself, and even sometimes out loud, 'Everything's grist to my mill!'

And if he were being reproached for conformity, he had a stock answer for that as well, 'So what else is new? Bother everyone and criticize everything. It's like fashion. Fashion is what everyone's in a hurry to do. Right? But I'm an original! There's no truth on earth, but there's no truth on high either. And so, my friends, optimism with a dose of indifference is the only way to avoid a heart attack.'

Nikolsky had always believed in the great benefit to be found in people not reading old books. If one fine day it came out that everything they thought, spoke and argued about had already been thought up, said and proven, what apathy would then pervade society! But apathy was only for the chosen few, for intellectuals. Forgetfulness – that was the life jacket of mankind. It was as if we were acting out roles in a play written long ago and boldly pretending we were discovering something new, moving forward. But only the rare few actually changed anything, and they didn't lead ordinary lives but lives of hard labour. We weren't numbered among their kind.

Knowledge was divided into two kinds for Nikolsky: the sort for other people and the sort for him. And the dissemination of knowledge for other people was simply – let's get this straight – his business. Sure, the books he wrote were fraudulent and by definition couldn't be otherwise. And of course the reader understood this – in other words, he wasn't deceiving anybody. But what was left for him, aside from this whole process, was the gratification of what remained of his soul – which, fortunately, had not yet been totally degraded.

The books sitting under the pink lampshade in front of Nikolsky the historian were old, meaning they were real. In contrast to modern lies, which were simply fake, the lies of the distant past seemed to take on material form. Losing contact with life, they stopped being lies and became some kind of given, a fact, not an irritant.

The last person to have touched these books – Nikolsky had already been told all about it – was a very old woman, the count's heiress. At that time the books had been thrown into the basement of the local museum they had set up in a wing of the count's palace. Except on church holidays the old woman would come every day to the museum, purchase a ticket and, tapping her cane on the parquet, inspect the remnants of her furniture. Her whole pension went on those tickets. The countess was scruffily dressed, and rumour had it that she ate hardly anything at all for her last several years, only breathing and taking a drink of water. Although not the greatest, at least the air and water in Gomel were free.

Once in the library the countess would sit for a long time without moving, her hands on the books and her eyes shut. It looked as though she was dozing off or taking the pulse of the books. Then she would slowly turn their pages. Whenever she came across an illustration, she would mumble away to herself, gazing at the colours on the page. She would come to life, converse with the people depicted in the illustrations. When she left, her face would grow numb again.

Roza really wanted to talk to the intellectual gentleman from Moscow, and she had already filled him in on the city's unofficial sights the day before. It wasn't that often that guests of such stature from the capital visited the regional library. Talking to him, Roza had blushed; her large dark eyes gleamed and came to life. Their whispering gave an air of mysteriousness to their conversation. Nikolsky sadly admitted to Roza that he and the old woman had something in common: like her, he had now decided to read for himself, without any practical benefit, after many years of reading only for professional reasons.

'Where is she then, this *femme fatale*?' asked Nikolsky, gazing fixedly at Roza.

'The museum gave the books to us, and we put them into this special depository. She wasn't allowed access to them. Who was going to vouch for her? Ludicrous!'

'Ludicrous,' agreed Nikolsky. 'But these are her own books, aren't they?'

Roza nodded sadly, lowering her lashes. Then she thought a bit and added, 'The director said that the books belong to the people.'

'Ah, the people!' He chuckled. 'Of course, I should've seen it right away.'

And that is how a mutual understanding arose between Roza and Nikolsky. This was before they went to look at the books. Roza led him down the spiral iron staircase to the basement, previously a bomb shelter. The light was dim, but it was enough to read the books' titles by. They were just lying around any old how, even though they were being given out to hardly anyone.

'It's damp down here,' he said, shivering. 'You're not cold?'

'I'm used to it.'

They walked between the metal shelves, their bodies

touching now and then, giving them both a pleasant sensation. She had something going for her, he noted, gazing not without satisfaction at her roundness.

'Well, we're not going to look at the nineteenth century,' he muttered. 'It's not as if there're any surprises to be found there. But the eighteenth – look at these big ones – we could take these.'

Several large stacks piled up.

'There's a boy here,' she said. 'He'll bring everything up to you right away.'

Without any embarrassment whatsoever she went up the spiral staircase ahead of him, and the spectacle before his eyes appealed to him even more.

'You don't need to get them now. I only want to reserve them. I'll start on them tomorrow, if you'll permit me.'

Nikolsky smiled thinly. He wondered if he should invite her to dinner, but then he decided it was a little premature, for now.

'Everything will be ready for you tomorrow. We're open from ten until ten.'

'I'll keep that in mind.'

Then she added, slowly, 'And I come on at two.'

2

He arrived at the library around four o'clock. Earlier, at his lecture for the Party activists he was asked a few polite questions – exactly as many as were necessary for the lecturer to be satisfied with himself and his audience. After lunching with the secretary for propaganda and his departmental deputies in a special dining-room off the provincial committee's cafeteria, Nikolsky had been taken back to his hotel. Ordering his driver to pick him up in an hour, he then took a splendid nap.

Roza had neatly arranged the stacks of books fetched up from the basement, ready for his arrival. She had already run over to the central card catalogue and quickly found the works of S.S. Nikolsky himself, including his doctoral dissertation, entitled *The Role of the Communist Party in the Creation of an Abundance of Foodstuffs*, published in a solid monograph. The titles of his two other books were equally as basic: *The Struggle of the Communist Party for Purity of the Leninist Legacy* and *Communists in the Vanguard of the Struggle Against Petit-Bourgeois Ideology*. Roza hadn't bothered checking out this trilogy, but it was interesting nevertheless to know what kind of ideas he was planning to extract from the eighteenth century that would be useful for his line of work. Oh, right – he wasn't going to read them with any practical goal in mind.

'I've read all the books you've written,' she said, handing over his volumes. 'They were . . . interesting.' She lied politely, without enthusiasm or irony.

'We won't go into that,' he frowned. 'Everyone has his cross to bear.'

'Do you mean to say that . . .'

'I don't mean to say anything,' he interrupted rather drily. 'But *your* books are really diverting.'

He picked up the heavy stack of volumes.

Roza wondered if she should tell him how the books had been taken away for safe keeping when the estate came under bombardment. She'd heard the story from her mother, who had worked at the library, too, until the day she died. There were even shrapnel marks on some of the bindings. While the books were in transit soldiers at the stations had snatched half of them from the trains going the other way, for something to roll their tobacco in. The women, weakened by hunger, had been unable to stand up to them. After the books had been brought back from the Urals, half of the remaining volumes had been eaten here in the basement by rats. Was it worth telling him? No, let their guest read the remnants in peace and assume that they were the whole of the count's library.

Nikolsky was in no hurry, meanwhile, to delve into the eighteenth century. He took off his glasses, breathed on them and began slowly wiping their light-bluish lenses. Without his glasses everything took on indefinite shapes. The empty reading-room was veiled in a haze, exactly the kind of haze that he lived in. With his glasses on he lived his other life, which he had to relate to what he could see. Words and reality were all the more difficult to link together. It was better not to even try.

Since early childhood Nikolsky had always read at The Library. Not this provincial one, not even those known to the intellectual world, but The Library in general. A large part of his youth had been spent in one library or another. He loved to sit in them; he called it being in voluntary prison. Not necessarily reading, writing and digging about in the card catalogues, but just sitting, like the elderly countess, looking at strangers sheltering in corners, near the table lamps, trying to guess what had brought them here. Back then any library had seemed like a special closed world, a temple, a religion. Back then he was proud of the fact that he was a historian, creating spiritually valuable goods. He even devised a whole philosophy, dividing people into 'materialists' and 'spiritualists'. He, of course, belonged to the second group.

The material objects of this world would not hold any special significance for our descendants. Cars and rockets would all rust away to nothing. Time would reduce steel and cement to dust. It was still too early to say how reliable computer memory might be. But these feeble lines on scraps of paper that even a child could tear up into little pieces were preserved for the ages. There was even something a bit offensive about this. It was the majority of people who were creating the objects of today, of the here and now. It was only the labour of a minority that was going to last down through the ages. The only consolation was that, without material values, spiritual ones would never have been conceived. Those who created also needed to eat. But which lines were spiritual, and which were not? Maybe all of them were or should be considered so. Both black and white would be important for our descendants.

On his way to the top of his profession, Nikolsky had worked in various libraries and archives. As a student he had suffocated in basements and frozen in churches hastily converted into repositories for documents. He saw how libraries were purged, how books were destroyed, how difficult it was becoming to know what there was to read, what had been written. He could have studied history, but instead he took the bait and opted for ideology. To have regrets about it would be silly and, above all, senseless.

In his youth he had been delighted by the fact that, in a library, honest books stood alongside lying ones. There was a special humanity in this – in the right of a liar to lie, in the impossibility of forbidding a lie, in the right of later generations to work out the truth on their own, without any prompting, to smile at our naïvety or, rarer still, to be amazed at our farsightedness. Say what you would, a library was a repository of time, a vault for thoughts. A vault for thoughts . . . he had probably said that pretty well, once upon a time. Nikolsky loved words. They were something that disoriented him: the truth that he'd long since given up seeking, drowned in words. The truth only got in the way, thwarting such matters as business, success and material comfort. He had stopped reading. Instead, his gaze just slid from word to word.

Nikolsky put his glasses back on. The haze disappeared. Across from him on the other side of the table, on the opposite side of this very same lamp, sat a dark-haired boy of about twelve in a faded, blue-checked shirt. His ears protruded, and he had his nose in the air, propping up his glasses. In fact the child looked like an ungainly calf.

He'd been sitting there yesterday, too. Out of boredom, Nikolsky had decided to take in a film that evening. They were showing a movie dating back to his youth. The boy stayed behind. He was sitting and reading. He was reading a thick book in a featureless brown library binding with calico corners. He read quickly. His lips and cheeks betrayed how keenly he felt what he was reading. At times he lifted his eyes and sat for a few seconds without moving, as if an interval had been called, and then continued, off into the next act. And what was a young boy doing in a reading-room for researchers anyway? This very same building housed a children's library at the other end, where Nikolsky had first looked in by mistake.

The boy raised his head. Nikolsky quickly took the top book from his stack and dove into it. Enough of letting his thoughts wander. *We know how to pull ourselves together, we know how to work. True, this had become increasingly difficult in recent years. Age? Nonsense! Not even sixty yet. Not sick or bald, yet.* Nikolsky began reading a thick biography of the highest-ranking courtiers of the Russian Empire.

It was a sluggish spring. It was getting dark later. The windows of the reading-room were flush against the wall of some institution, in whose windows lamps were burning. Heavy twilight fell in the crack between the buildings from above.

'I'll turn on the light, if you don't mind, colleague,' pronounced Nikolsky gallantly.

The lad started, tore himself away from the page. Realizing he was being spoken to, he blushed and nodded. Nikolsky flicked the switch on and off.

'That's not how you turn it on,' said the boy shyly. 'The wire shorted out last year.'

With both hands he capably removed the pink glass cowl from the lamp. Underneath was a buxom bronze mermaid with a serpentine tail that gradually transformed itself into the lamp base. The boy grabbed the mermaid around the waist with one practised hand and twisted the light bulb in the socket with the other. Nikolsky chuckled. The light struck him in the eyes. There was a smell of burning coming from the lamp. Just as deftly the boy put the cowl back, and a pink circle outlined the books. Only through the crack was the light blinding.

Nikolsky went over to Roza and picked up the second stack of books. She had prepared two cards for him, with the words 'already read' and 'remaining' written on them.

'You look fantastic today,' he remarked in passing.

She wasn't exactly spoiled for compliments, and she smiled, embarrassed and pleased that he'd noticed. She really had put a great deal of effort into her appearance, and it hadn't been in vain. True, the director had also turned her attention to Roza earlier. She said that, in Roza's position, she would dress more conservatively, 'After all, we're a government institution here, not a theatre or . . .' The director hadn't finished. Roza, of course, had said nothing.

She wasn't wearing anything special, only a tight skirt with a slit up the side, not a very long one, of course, but it allowed her legs to be appreciated as an achievement of nature. So what if she'd spent two hours in the queue at the hairdresser's to get her hair done? So what if she'd used rather brighter lipstick than usual? Without any personal modesty, Nikolsky realized that Roza's efforts had been for his benefit. If that were so, he was released from any intervening difficulties. Although . . . he had still not yet made up his mind at all.

Nikolsky worked for a few hours, until he felt burned out. The colour of the lamp began to irritate him. He shivered from the dampness, real or imagined. It would be nice to go somewhere for dinner. Wherever would the best restaurant be around here, with stupid, deafening, tasteless music, dancing and so on? The boy read on, absorbed. Nikolsky had heard that the local theatre was putting on something spicy. *Should I go? They said the troupe was young and straight out of college in Minsk, so there would be cute young actresses. Or maybe I'll accept the invitation from the assistant professor from the Pedagogical Institute who's dreaming of doing his doctorate with me. They promised me that refined local society would be in attendance, and for three hours I'll be the centre of attention.*

The lad's brow was knitted, as happened every time he came to a difficult passage. His long lashes would now blink in perplexity, now hold steady, the latter meaning that he'd understood and would now go on. Nothing held his attention except what was on the pages of the books. *But I'm not moving forward. How many books are there left? Half a stack here, plus two more with Roza. And Roza's bored, too. When a woman is bored, who's to blame? The man, of course.*

Nikolsky agonized a bit more, turning over the unenticing pages. He decided he would read some more tomorrow but had done enough for today. After all, he wasn't going to rot away at his reading like that old woman, the count's heiress. The mind has to get some fresh air. He scooped up his scraps of paper covered in scribbles, picked up the pile of books and headed for the counter. Roza readily leaned over and held out her hands to help him. He involuntarily glanced down her blouse: it was soft and very tempting.

'Tired?' she asked, blushing slightly.

'It's just that I have some more to do.'

Her nails were freshly and painstakingly done. Her perfume was good, not at all crude. He softly squeezed her hand and kissed it. Amazingly, she submitted, but then quickly glanced around to make sure no one was watching. He headed for the exit, then turned and leaned back towards her ear, winking conspiratorially.

'Excuse me, but who's that boy sitting across from me?'

'He helps carry the books. Is he bothering you? I'll send him away.'

'No, no, he's not bothering me. On the contrary, his enthusiasm is infectious. I'm just curious about what he's studying here.'

'He reads everything, one book after another,' she explained. 'Well, maybe more geography and history. He's already read everything you're reading now. Just don't say anything to the director. This is a special archive. He helps take the books down into the repository and picks out the ones he reads there.'

'And is he here often?'

'All the time.'

'All the time?'

'After school. And stays here until we close.'

Roza looked at Nikolsky with a little smile, ready to answer all his questions with complete thoroughness. But he didn't ask anything else. On his way out he looked back. The boy sat under the pink lamp, resting his cheek against his fist.

Nikolsky was not too tired to drop by the theatre. The play was about life on a collective farm. In the first act the short-comings of the drunken chairman were unmasked. Nikolsky already had a pretty good idea how he would straighten things out in the second act. The young actresses from Minsk, about whom he'd heard so much at the provincial committee office, had managed to grow old out here at the edge of the world, apparently. He could barely make himself sit still until the interval and even wondered if he should take a plane back to Moscow right there and then. But no one would be waiting for him there.

At the moment Nikolsky really didn't have any family. His third wife had left him six months ago – not that he was terribly upset by that – and the children from his first two marriages had grown up. His relations with them were polite but dis-tant. In Gomel he had deliberately booked his flight home for the day after tomorrow, just to put off the bustle of Moscow. So leave things be.

He strolled along the banks of the Sozha and stood silently watching the ice drift by. But a strong, wet wind blew from the river. It would be safer to go to bed, so as not to catch a cold.

3

In the morning he felt an urge to get to the library. As he entered the reading-room, he even thought with pride that he, Nikolsky, was a workaholic. As in his youth, he loved to toil from dawn to dusk. In fact, he'd already forgotten how to write, long ago. The books that the various publishing houses ordered from him, the famous Party historian, he would divide up by chapters among his graduate students, who would shamelessly crib material from other authors. Incidentally, this practice guaranteed the correctness of their thoughts.

This morning, though, the eighteenth-century folios had to wait patiently for their reader. Nikolsky was drawn to the library to see Roza, not them. She'd been at her counter all morning and was glad to see him – he could see that. He chatted with her for a while, sharing his impressions of the previous evening's play. She commiserated with him, he told an appropriate joke, then took his books and headed towards the pink lamp with the broken rim.

The books were interesting. Their manner of exposition was unusual for him, a man who thought in prefabricated blocks. He got caught up in his reading: life full of transparent intrigues; modestly licentious prints depicting playful moments; monumental physiognomies of the powerful from that bygone world; clumsy explanations of political adventurism, via boudoir details. Nikolsky tried to draw parallels between the imperial court and the present-day administrations in which he'd made his career. *My God, what a bunch of nursery children they'd been then!* Better not get into the habit of allusions like that.

The minute hand of the antique grandfather clock that stood against the wall between huge portraits of Marx and Engels made several revolutions before Nikolsky tore his eyes from the pages. He almost burst out laughing. The boy in the blue-checked shirt sat in front of him, a book covering half his face. Nikolsky hadn't noticed when the boy had come in and noiselessly taken his seat.

'Young man,' whispered Nikolsky, 'pardon my curiosity. What are you reading now? If it's not a secret, of course.'

The boy didn't immediately understand what he was being asked, but when he did he held the book out to Nikolsky. It was a book from the end of the last century, about Suvorov's military campaigns, with magnificent illustrations. Nikolsky had seen it before.

'Quite a compendious thing,' he said. 'What are you reading it for?'

The lad didn't understand and shrugged his shoulders.

'Well, is it for a school assignment?'

'No-o . . .'

'Then why?'

'I don't know.'

'Maybe it's just interesting?'

'Yeah, interesting.'

'What is interesting, exactly?'

'Everything.'

'In general?'

Nikolsky scratched the end of his nose in amazement and recited a verse for the lad, which he usually reserved for the women:

> 'The riddles of eternity we shall never understand –
>   Not thou, not I.
> We know not how to read the obscure letters –
>   Not thou, not I.
> We dispute before a kind of curtain.
>   But the hour strikes,
>   The curtain falls, and we do not remain alive –
>   Not thou, not I.'

'Did you write that?' the boy asked.

'Not exactly. It's Omar Khayyam. He was an oriental poet from long ago. But tell me, for God's sake, why you're reading that.'

'Do you believe in God?' The boy's eyes narrowed and took on a sheen.

'Well, I said "for God's sake" just . . . conventionally, you know.'

'Oh, conventionally.'

The sheen in his eyes dimmed. He seemed to be wondering what this man wanted from him, this guy who looked like some kind television anchorman.

'So, why *are* you?' persisted Nikolsky.

'I just decided to read all the books, that's all.'

'All?! Did I hear you correctly?'

The boy nodded and went back to his reading. Nikolsky pretended to read, too, but the boy had pushed all his thoughts aside. *Just think: all these books! Oh, sure, they let him read everything. Even I don't get to read everything. But this kid needs it all. A crown prince! Wants to study all sixty-four arts at once. How is he going to learn how to tame elephants? In theory? Or to compose verse, in this godforsaken hole? Let's try to find his weak spot.*

'How come you don't play with the other kids? Like, maybe, hockey or something?'

'Don't want to . . . Am I missing something?'

Nikolsky couldn't think of a response and grew angry. *A snot-nosed twentieth-century wise old man. Everything's interesting to this little idiot, while I, a historic figure, don't give a damn about any of it! The world is going to hell in a handbasket, and this boy sits reading a book. Everything is annihilated, ruined, chopped off at the root, gone to merry hell. Whole libraries get burned to the ground. The best minds get poisoned. The remains are rotting away, and the very existence of Russia is in doubt. Soon there won't be anything left of our civilization. But the boy sits here in this dump and reads.*

Nikolsky suddenly had a revelation, something that he couldn't share with anybody. *Maybe the great historical mission of us Communists was to transform culture into pulp, works of art and literature into fertilizer and the blessings of civilization into dung. The goal of our appearance on this earth was to set the land on fire after the harvest. And then what? Would new cultural growth take root in this soil or just tall weeds? Maybe we have infected even the dung. But the boy reads one book after another. Meaning that there'll be something in his head to pass on to his descendants. Unless, of course, he strays from his path. But of course he will. Of course! There's no way out. A dead end.*

Nikolsky took the books he'd read over to the counter to get the next stack.

'I want to say goodbye to you,' whispered Roza. 'I work until two, and tomorrow you're leaving.'

'Hmm. Well, what about . . .'

'What?'

'What about having dinner together?'

He said it casually, matter-of-factly, so as not to seem offended if she turned him down.

'Now, or . . . ?'

Here he grabbed the bull by the horns.

'Right now!'

'In that case, let's leave the library separately, OK? Wait for me in front of the Gifts of Nature shop, just next door.'

'You're a delight. I guessed it right away,' he said.

'And you're a disgraceful seducer. Turn the books in and I'll stamp you out.'

In the window of Gifts of Nature, which he spotted immediately, stood a shabby stuffed deer with well-preserved antlers. Above the deer hung a bright poster with Lenin's powerful profile and a scarlet ribbon on his chest. The text proclaimed, 'The Party is the mind, honour and conscience of our epoch.' Nikolsky pressed against the window to avoid being jostled by passers-by and looked in the direction of the library. He caught himself behaving like a nervous kid, even worried that she might suddenly change her mind. But here she was, her heels clicking hurriedly on the uneven pavement.

'Did I keep you waiting? I had to put the books away.'

'Madame, where in this city can one get something decent to eat?'

'Believe me, nowhere! I'd invite you back to my place, but I live in a communal apartment and all my neighbours are malicious gossips.'

'Then let's go to my hotel. There must be something decent in the Intourist restaurant, right?' He took a five-rouble note out of his pocket, stopped the first Volga that came along with a peremptory gesture, opened the door and handed the money to the driver.

'Hey, mate, give us a lift to the hotel, just down the road from here.'

'Have you gone crazy, throwing your money around like that?' she whispered into his ear, when they had settled themselves in the back.

He put a finger to her lips. She smelled of quality talcum powder. He inhaled deeply, like an addict ready to enter a different dimension. His eyelids drooped, and he even purred.

The restaurant was packed. Nikolsky learned from the cloakroom attendant where the director's office was and, putting his hand lightly on Roza's waist, asked her to wait a minute. The director was entertaining visitors. Squeezing through them, Nikolsky made his way behind the table and whispered into the director's ear that he was from the Party's Central Committee. This made a certain impression. Then Nikolsky asked, as an exception, to have dinner for two brought to his VIP luxury suite, room 301.

'Send a waiter who's on the ball,' requested Nikolsky. 'We'll find a common language.'

He returned to Roza. She was sitting attractively in an armchair, her legs crossed.

'Shall we go?'

'Let's go,' she answered without hesitation. 'Where to?'

'To my room. We'll eat there.'

'And do you suppose that this is proper for a girl from a good family?'

'Completely.'

On the third floor he unlocked the door and invited her in with an elegant gesture.

'Good Lord, what a suite!' she cried, taking it all in. 'How many rooms are there? Dining-room, office, bedroom. Can I open this door? Ah, the bathroom! And all this luxury is for you alone?'

Still in the doorway, he was smiling magnanimously.

'Our enemies call us the *nomenklatura*, Party function-aries,' he said modestly, coming into the living-room. 'So do we . . . But it would be stupid to turn down the perks that are on offer, wouldn't it? If you're going to be an ascetic, someone else will use it up for you, anyway. Ah, here's the waiter.'

They had a brief discussion of what was tastiest. It made no sense to ask the lady: she was just going to nod her head in agreement. Nikolsky ordered the best of everything.

'And, of course, an ice-cold bottle of Stolichnaya.' He took out two large-denomination notes. 'Keep the change.'

'You won't be sorry,' the waiter said. 'I'll see to the prepar-ation personally.'

Twenty minutes later he and Roza were eating dinner, sitting on the couch in front of a small coffee table. Nikolsky had specially directed that the platter of grilled meat be placed there so they could sit together.

'Have a drink with us,' he proposed to the waiter democ-ratically.

There wasn't a third shot glass, but the waiter poured himself a quarter of a regular glass, not holding back.

'My wife and I are in your city for the first time,' continued

Nikolsky, constructing a story so as not to drag things out. 'It's a fine city, I would say.'

'It's all right,' agreed the waiter obediently.

'Then to your city, and to peace on earth!' Nikolsky looked at Roza. 'Bottoms up!'

She drank it down easily, without wincing, which he liked. The waiter bid them *bon appetit* and disappeared. They polished off another straight shot, without eating anything. And this one went down easily, too. Nikolsky stood up and locked the door.

'You're a real master at this,' she said, wagging her finger at him threateningly, and laughed.

'If you want to know the truth, Roza, I'm simply a block-head,' he said familiarly. 'My friend Kuzin the biologist, who wrote his own epitaph, was right. Would you like to hear it?

> '"Passer-by! Here I lie.
> Have you heard of me?
> Brainlessly I squandered
> The gift of earthly existence.
> To my misfortune, I was
> Fondled by the love of a muse,
> And even spent a spell in gaol,
> Too keen on my own wit.
> Smoked tobacco, loved dogs,
> And they loved me like a father.
> Passer-by! Live not so
> But in another way."'

'Another way?' she asked contemplatively, when they had downed another shot and begun to eat. 'If someone had explained . . .'

'Another way?' He remembered what he had wanted to tell her earlier on, in the library, but had forgotten. 'The old countess you told me about: she lived in another way. Incidentally, I found her.'

'Found her?'

'I couldn't have done it on my own. A KGB colonel approached me at one of my lectures with some question or other, and I asked him to find this woman for me. Unfortunately they didn't find her, but the communal apartment where she lived. I drove over there. Her neighbours had buried the old lady a year ago. There were old papers, letters, books, photographs and other junk, as the neighbours said, in her room. A few trunks, 176 kilograms in all.'

'You even know the weight?'

'Her neighbours had it weighed at the paper-recycling centre. And they said there were a lot of oil portraits rolled up in tubes, without frames. Paper recycling wouldn't take them, so they just threw them away. Funny, isn't it?'

'Absolutely,' agreed Roza. 'And the grave?'

'You're reading my mind. I went to the cemetery. The countess's grave had collapsed, and her cross had fallen over. I gave some money to the gravedigger to set it up again.'

Nikolsky poured himself and her another shot, drank it without any toasts and began silently chewing. Roza also fell silent, suddenly embarrassed. Should she tell him she had gone to see the old woman for several years running? She would give Roza something to read while she was there, and then she would hide her books away again. When Roza came on her last visit the countess had already been buried, and the room had been taken over by the next family on the waiting list. It never even occurred to Roza that this responsible Party man would drag himself around trying to find the countess.

'Everything ends in dust,' he said and drank again.

'Passer-by! Live not so, but in another way,' she repeated pensively. 'I would like to live in another way, somehow. For example, like the old countess.'

'Maybe it'd be better not to.'

'Maybe . . . But what happens is that I'm always hoping

for "not so", and I keep waiting for something. But when I have an opportunity to do something "not so" I don't do it.'

'Never?'

Roza laughed somewhat artificially.

'Almost . . . and I keep on waiting.'

'In general, or for something specific?' He looked searchingly into her eyes. His next move depended upon her answer.

'Right now, something specific.'

She suddenly turned serious, abruptly splashed out her remaining vodka on the floor, stood and paced up and down the room, swaying slightly.

'What is it you're waiting for?' he asked cautiously.

She came right up to him where he was sitting on the couch with the knife and fork still in his hands, and with a sudden movement removed his glasses and looked him over from head to toe.

'Your eyes are a strange colour,' she said, finishing her inspection. 'Actually, it's strange that your eyes *have* no colour. Quickly, please!'

'What?' He didn't understand.

'Idiot! Kiss me quickly before I change my mind.'

Nikolsky was used to obeying orders from above and awkwardly rose from the couch.

The bright crack between the curtains at the window had turned dark when Nikolsky lifted his head from the pillow. Roza was asleep, rolled up into a ball. *A normal woman,* he thought gratefully, *she gives herself body and soul, without any affectations or pretensions. I've heard so much about the devotion of Jewish wives, and never experienced it myself. I'm as Russian as you can be, and all my wives have been pure Russian. So her husband left for the USA. She refused to go, and by the time she changed her mind they were already divorced.*

But what if . . . Suddenly he put his hand on her waist, pulled her closer and kissed her to wake her up. She straightened out and snuggled against him, smiling the happy and carefree smile of a young girl who has been kissed for the first time.

'Listen,' he said. 'What if we were to get married?'

'You're insane!' She addressed him with familiarity now. 'Not for the world!'

'No, I'm serious. Serious! We'll get married and clear out of here to Israel, America, Australia, wherever the hell they'll let us, anywhere where there's no history of the Communist Party of the Soviet Union. Even if you still love your husband, take me with you to him.'

'I haven't loved him for a long time, but what would you do there, you wretched idiot?'

'Anything, as long as it's not what I'm doing here. For example, I'll mow lawns. I'll cut grass!' he proclaimed loudly.

'Grass?' she echoed, waking up.

'What grass?' He didn't understand.

'You just said, "I'll cut grass."' She had gone back to addressing him formally.

Their whole conversation had been in his head, and only the 'I'll cut grass' part had come out.

'I was dreaming,' he said.

'What about?'

'Nonsense.'

'What time is it now?' She was suddenly scared.

'Nine-thirty, children's bedtime.'

'My God, I have to get to the library before it closes at ten.' 'What for?'

'I have to. Turn around. I'm going to get dressed.'

'I won't turn around. I want to watch.'

Gathering up her scattered clothes from the floor, she ran into the bathroom. He got up and dressed, too. Her handbag was on the couch. He glanced at the bathroom door, took an envelope from his pocket, dropped it into her handbag and clicked it shut. Then he finished dressing and sat down in the armchair.

She appeared in the bathroom doorway, fluffing up her hair with her hands. All businesslike now, she said, 'Take a look. Is everything in place? I'm still not in my right mind.'

'You're in great shape. A first-class performance.'

'Really? Thank you. And how about yourself?'

'"He attained the highest happiness on earth – the absence of any desires." That's a quote from the Roman historian Tacitus.'

He didn't have any desires. But he didn't feel any special happiness either.

'Farewell, professor.'

'I'll walk you there.'

'No way! It's close by, ten minutes. I'll walk myself there.'

She quietly closed the door behind her.

He stood for a minute, vacillating about whether to catch up with her or stay, then waved it off. He poured himself a shot of what remained in the bottle and knocked it back. In his jacket, tie and shoes he lay down on the bed and fell into the sleep of the dead.

4

He was awakened by a respectful knock at the door. For a long time Nikolsky didn't hear it, then he tried to figure out what was going on, opening his eyes with difficulty. Outside it was light. He got up shakily, looked at himself in the mirror, ran his fingers through his mane, turned out the light that had burned in the corridor all night and unlocked the door.

'Good morning, Sergey Sergeyevich.'

It was the young instructor from the provincial committee, assigned to accompany the Central Committee lecturer to the airport.

'I didn't wake you?' he jabbered amiably. 'How did you spend the night on our Gomel soil?'

'Just great, thanks.'

'I won't disturb you. I'll be waiting downstairs in the car

while you get ready. Perhaps I should mention that we don't have much time left. Should I phone the provincial committee and tell them to hold your flight until you arrive?'

'No need to, we'll make it.'

I'll have to get downstairs in a hurry. If I can manage it, I'll get some coffee at the airport and wash and shave on the plane. He picked up the bottle of vodka from the carpet. *Just a swallow to keep my head from splitting open.* But there wasn't a single drop left. Nikolsky began throwing belongings into his open suitcase.

He sat silently in the black Volga for Central Committee members, with its two zeroes on the licence plate. They drove quickly to the airport. The instructor turned out to be garrulous, obviously trained to accompany VIPs.

'The provincial committee has a very high opinion of your lecture. You said a lot about things we could only guess at. The prospects are certainly realistic . . .'

Nikolsky nodded, staring absently out of the window.

'Working under these new conditions is becoming more difficult, of course,' the instructor went on.

'More difficult,' Nikolsky nodded.

'More interesting at the same time,' said the instructor.

'More interesting, that's right,' confirmed Nikolsky.

The instructor carried Nikolsky's suitcase to the check-in counter. The flight to Moscow was on schedule. They shook hands firmly.

'Have a good flight. Come and visit us again!'

After checking in, Nikolsky was about to pass through the door where luggage and passengers were screened.

'You can go through without a check,' said the stewardess. 'Over there, through the room for Supreme Soviet deputies.'

This was one more completely insignificant privilege. Then someone tugged at Nikolsky's sleeve.

'Hi. I was asked to give you this.'

Before him stood the boy with the cowlick. Nikolsky

recognized him straight away. The boy held out a package, something wrapped in a newspaper. Nikolsky shrugged his shoulders.

'From whom?'

'From my mum.'

'And who's your mum?'

'She works in the library.'

'Roza?'

'Uh-huh.'

Only now did it hit him.

'What's this?'

'Mum said to look at it later, not now. Well, see you.'

Nikolsky smirked at this provincial sentimentality: a present as a memento.

'OK. Thank you. Say hello to your mum. I hope you get to read *all* the books in the world, just like you want to.'

'I don't want to read all the books. Goodbye.'

The lad looks like her, he thought. *I should have worked it out straight away.*

The package was heavy. As soon as he'd taken his seat in the aircraft, Nikolsky untied the string and unwrapped the newspaper covering.

On his lap were books – three books, the author of which was reputed to be Sergey Nikolsky himself. Cards with numbers and stamps from the Gomel Regional Library were taped inside their covers.

'Nutty woman,' he muttered almost aloud to no one in particular, at a loss. 'What do I need this for? No, she's really out of it.'

An envelope with 'Gomel Communist Party Provincial Committee' printed in the corner fell out of the top book on to his knees. The envelope was already torn open, and Nikolsky recognized it. He took out the two fifty-rouble notes that he'd put in this envelope the night before and stuck in Roza's handbag.

'That fool! Idiot woman! Weirdo! Why the hell did I get involved with a cretin like that? I wanted things to be better. To be better is what I wanted . . .'

A return-date sticker was attached to the inside cover of the book. Nikolsky had never taken his own books out of any library, and now he stared at the sticker that had suddenly appeared before him. The sticker was blank. How could that be? Surely someone had taken the book out to read. Not a single person . . . Yet a second edition was being prepared.

He looked at the two other books in the package. The stickers had 'Reader Number' and 'Date' written neatly on them. And then blanks. During all these years no one had ever asked for his books, had never even opened them – the edges were stuck to one another, as if they were still brand new. Not one single note, not a dog-eared page – nothing! Scandalous!

He abruptly got up and began pushing his way through the passengers with their baggage, taking their seats. As he went he put the money into the pocket of his jacket and stuck the empty envelope inside a book. When he got to the toilet Nikolsky stopped, in a state of extreme irritation, intending to throw all three books into the rubbish bin. There was no bin anywhere.

'Lady,' he said, turning to the middle-aged stewardess, 'where's the goddamned rubbish bin?'

The stewardess looked at him in surprise, realizing that he wasn't an ordinary passenger.

'Give me your rubbish, I'll take it away myself.'

In dismay, he hid the books behind his back.

'Not to worry,' he mumbled. 'I was just curious, you know.'

Nikolsky went back to his seat, where he turned the books over in his hands and, unable to think of what to do with them, frenziedly tried to stuff them into his already-full briefcase.

THE *KAÏF* AT THE END OF
THE BUSINESS TRIP

I

The hotel's lift was out of order, of course, so Poludin had to
drag himself up the stairs on his own two feet. His steps made
no sound: the stairs were covered by a soft, grey, mud-tracked
cloth, put there by the management to preserve the carpet's
invisible splendours.

Poludin was tired and full of pleasurable anticipation of
his *kaïf*, now.

Well, they had all got on one another's nerves, as they
were supposed to, and then calmed down. The project had
been accepted long ago, and the acceptance certificate had
been signed, even if the chief designer was still wanly muttering that they didn't yet know whether the conveyor would
actually function at high temperatures. Poludin had given his
word that all minor customer complaints would be satisfied. It
remained to be seen if any reworking would be needed or not.
That promise wasn't set down on paper. Like many Russians,
he wasn't above pulling a fast one – merely too lazy to do it
thoroughly. For this very same reason, his customers pretended to believe him: the fact was, they couldn't care less.
Tomorrow, he would get signed off and start for home.

Poludin wasn't any worse or better than anyone else at
combining business with pleasure. The secretary responsible
for signing him off on his business trip would be plied with
sweets, and then he would ask her for an undated stamp for
his papers since he couldn't get any tickets and would be
leaving in a couple of days. He could always get a ticket by
using his personal charms and try to leave straight away. If he

didn't have a ticket he would just get on the train and hand a little something over to the conductor.

Then, at home, he would lounge in bed for two days and watch television, and in the evening, before his wife came home, he would take off with his friends, and together they would paint the town red on the few roubles he had lifted from the state, not without personal effort. These weren't his friends from work. When *they* called he wouldn't have got back yet, and he would answer the phone in a squeaky falsetto, saying, 'Daddy's not home right now . . .'

After his holiday, true, Poludin would have to go back to the station and meet the same train coming back and, for a rouble, buy a ticket left with the conductor by some passenger who wasn't on a business trip, for his expenses claim. Poludin would then put the date that he needed on his trip papers. Recently, however, the deputy director for personnel and procedures had made it a habit of checking up on the presence of his employees at their sites by calling up the various factories. An understanding had been reached among personnel departments all over the country that business trips by people from Moscow to the Khimmash factory here were henceforth to be strictly documented, so that freedom was again being restricted.

Now Poludin's freedom had been whittled down to just this evening.

Elbowing his way through the factory's entrance by six o'clock, he took a crowded bus to the city cashier's office to buy a ticket. The only available compartment was first class. He didn't have enough money for that and had to take a seat in economy. A poster for the provincial theatre promised a play about smelting some kind of iron. The city was covered with appeals to give one's all, but that just made you want to hold back something for yourself.

Now he had his freedom, what little there was or none at all, and tomorrow there would be none at all, for sure.

Tomorrow there would be the directive: 'You have to . . .' And freedom is when you don't 'have to'. Freedom is found exclusively at end of a business trip, because you're neither here nor there. You're almost not *here* but still not *quite there*. Now, in order to save money, even business trips had become infrequent. Only the bosses travel, but the men also want to get their papers stamped and gulp down some freedom. So, for tonight, to hell with Khimmash, the rest of the chemical industry, Moscow and the whole socialist camp! Poludin was going to party!

On the way, he was thinking about going to a restaurant. You wouldn't get into one with the five roubles left in his pocket. It was a good thing that hotels charged their customers in advance. They didn't trust you and did the sensible thing. But even just a bottle – that wouldn't be bad, after all. Other people wouldn't even have enough for that.

Poludin soon got hold of a surplus bottle, unsold at the end of a shop's shift, along with half a loaf of black bread. Anything else would have to be bought with a coupon, so there was no need to queue, which was also pleasant. From a kiosk at the hotel he bought a sports magazine and a local newspaper. Generally he wouldn't read that sort of stuff, out of principle, so as not to clutter up his head, but he made an exception this time. And he hadn't bought the local rag to read at all but as a substitute for one of the hotel's more common shortages.

Out of breath, he reached the fifth floor. His window faced the Sura river embankment. From the block around the corner, the neon sign of the Hotel Penza threw a vibrating orange light on to his flowered curtains. The room, a box four metres long by three wide, had been reserved by the factory especially for Senior Engineer Poludin. A chambermaid had cleaned the room, even hiding his dirty socks in the wardrobe.

Taking off his fur hat, he knocked the drops of melting snow off and looked at his watch. It was a quarter to eight.

His *kaïf* had begun.

2

Carefully locking the door from the inside, Poludin drew water for his bath and pulled off his boots. They'd been letting in the wet for two years now. For a long time he'd been saving up to buy a used pair of imported boots at the second-hand shop, but either he couldn't find his size or the money went on something else. When the weather got drier the problem solved itself, but now, though, he had to prop the boots vertically against the radiator so that the toes would drain and dry out before the morning.

Poludin solemnly stripped bare, walked around the room and stood for a while by the window. He took the bottle and the bread out of his briefcase and put his cigarettes and lighter on his chair, the magazine alongside them. Dragging the chair to his bed, he pulled down the blanket and switched on the radio. Local news was being broadcast, endless rubbish about some socialist competition of milkmaids with a burning desire to roll as many zeros as possible behind some number or other. Poludin burned with as much desire as the next man and, like everyone, only in public. Alone, and given the choice, no way – so he pulled the plug on the radio.

When the tub had filled, he checked that the water was warm enough before solemnly submerging himself and lying, eyes closed, thinking about everything and nothing. Occasionally, as if contrasting harsh reality with his present torpor, he would periscope one of his toes into the cold air.

He got out of the tub slowly, without having washed – washing himself would require physical effort, in obedience to some sort of 'you have to'. Towelling himself down slightly, he made for the wardrobe, leaving a trail of wet footprints across the parquet floor, and put on his green-striped pyjamas. His wife had always liked the look of them on the men in French movies, and so for Soviet Army Day (a commemoration legalizing male drunkenness during working hours) she had bought him, in the absence of French-made pyjamas, a pair of Chinese manufacture. He'd never once put them on , but now, six months later, his wife had remembered to put them into his suitcase.

At eight-twenty he was in bed and unstopping the bottle. The cap rolled off in some unnoticed direction. He poured out half a glass of the murky liquid, paused, pleasurably anticipating the blessedness of the inner warmth, exhaled – then threw back the contents of the glass. The vodka passed inside him and spread around his body, nicely, as always. Pausing again, Poludin took a bite out of the black bread's crust.

He opened the magazine out on his blanket and began to read it from the humour column at the back. The jokes weren't funny: a bicyclist stopped just short of the finish line, playing she-loves-me/she-loves-me-not with a daisy. Poludin lazily lowered his eyelids. The warmth was flowing around but not to every part of his body, and he could do with downing another half a glass, which he did, following the same procedure. On the whole Poludin didn't have any special passion for drinking, but he had no intention of being a dissident in this respect.

Half a glass, plus another half-glass, drew him into philosophizing. That cartoon daisy had reminded him of the previous summer. Walking through a meadow one day, he had dropped from tiredness, lying down and crushing a patch of daisies under him. He lay as if dead. *Buzzzzzz-zzz-zzz* – a noise swam over his head, a beetle flitted past his ear. Its space occupied, the beetle didn't know where to land.

Lying on his stomach, Poludin examined the beetle, of unknown identity, as it clambered up the stalk of a daisy. The beetle made its way purposefully to the top and, forcing its way through the white petals on to the yellow eye, waggled its antennae and, straightening its wings and pushing off with its hind legs, launched itself skywards.

The meadow had once again filled with an irksome silence. His holiday was coming to an end. All of a sudden he longed for the blast of car horns, the crush aboard a tram, for a furtive drink during working hours – for all that bedlam that you get sick of but without which you felt as if part of you had been ripped out.

Poludin turned to studying the sky. A rather intricate cloud hung up there. The depth of this sky was almost humiliatingly vast. Why do you always want something that you eventually run away from? The human is an imperfect creature, that's what it is. Everyone understands that, but nobody wants to perfect himself. Perfection was something to push others to achieve.

'Hey, look!'

His son had come running up to show him the beetle. The boy had turned out to be more purposeful than the beetle and had caught it. The feeling of aloofness and freedom vanished utterly. It never lasted long. Worries gnawed away at you, and there was never an end to them.

None the less Poludin had come to the conclusion that, amid all your worries, you can always manage to find time for something – that state when, temporarily, everyone leaves you alone and you don't have to keep your nose to the grindstone, when you owe nothing to anyone, when you aren't obliged in any way: if you want to do something, you do it. If not, you don't. It would be wrong to call this laziness. *Dolce far niente*, in Italian, a wonderful sort of do-nothing-ness – but that, actually, is a doing of something. *Kaïf*, now, there's a wonderful word, which some say is Turkish in origin, others think to be Arabic, and yet others to be from ancient Hebrew, meaning 'feast'.

However un-Russian the word *kaïf* may be, it has made itself quite at home there. Evidently not by accident. When it comes to partying, a Russian can keep up with a Turkish sultan.

Now this whole week in Penza had been a drag. As for the history of problems with the component feed – maybe the chief engineer was right that the conveyor wouldn't hold up for long. Now he could think about it, and he didn't have to think about it. Well, damn them all to hell! Poludin was going to get loaded, to *kaïf* it up.

Just as he'd done that time in the meadow, Poludin rolled on to his stomach in bed and stretched out. The vodka had stimulated his mind. Plumping up the pillow with his fist, he swallowed another slug from the bottle for optimism's sake, bit another mouthful of the bread and pulled the magazine on to the pillow. An entire page was covered with a series of photographs: a layout showing the elements of a pole-vaulter's flight. And an article about it, too. This was the message: a fibreglass pole was capable of launching a man of up to seventy-five kilograms to a height of five metres. The body remained at that height for only a fraction of a second but long enough for one to become a world champion.

He suddenly had a sharp urge to take a run up and throw his weight on to a pole so that it bent resiliently and then, straightening, lifted him, Poludin, above the ground. Before succumbing to his inherent laziness, Poludin had enjoyed track and field in his student days. Now there was no time to discuss sport, much less anyone to discuss it with. What he wouldn't give for a vault at this point! There were professions that involved vaulting, that is to say, pushing yourself to greater and greater heights. And there were others that expected a man to get down on his hands and knees and crawl. To stumble through life. Now, a conveyor belt would even things out nicely! Something to deliver athletes up to the bar, one after another. That was the crux of the matter.

Poludin almost purred, lighting up a cigarette. He felt that he was on the brink of an important new notion about society. Sport and technology had contrary tasks. Sport made you work hard; technology tried to spare you from labour. Although . . . here, in this case, they seemed to have something in common. The conveyor produced by his factory was totally unnecessary. The component could be fed at the rate of one every five minutes, so that the feeding device could quickly clear out of the high-temperature zone. To hell with the conveyor that the team had been designing for a year and a half! They'd designed the damn thing sober, hadn't taken a drink for inspiration – that's why it hadn't worked out. It had to be like pole-vaulting: reach the top, and you're heading down.

It took just a second to grab his briefcase. Poludin pulled out several sheets of blank paper and a pencil and began rapidly sketching a diagram. Strictly speaking, the whole thing was primitive. Alongside the bunker, level with it, a mechanical arm going this way and that: it grabs a component from the bunker and moves away, grabs and moves. Everything was brilliantly simple. He would go to Moscow, get agreement for it from the department, then have a meeting with the chief engineer, get approval from the central directorate, and there would be enough work for the whole team for the next six months. That would be two hours of work for any mid-level engineer like me.

He leaped up, grabbed his slide rule from his briefcase and moved the second chair over to the bed. He slugged down another jolt of vodka and choked (it didn't go down well: those scoundrels were trying to poison people with their hootch!) and, spluttering, set the bottle down out of sight. This was a brilliant idea, no question! Poludin, what a son of a bitch! Tomorrow, he would spring it on the factory's chief designer – he was going to be bowled over.

Nobody distracted him from his work, which was accompanied by a state of complete lack of compulsion. When Poludin glanced at his watch it was five past twelve. Just at that moment a piercing ring sounded. The telephone rang and rang, unabated.

3

He hadn't given his phone number to anyone from the factory – didn't know it himself, in fact. There couldn't be any reason for his wife to seek him out. The floor concierge, that's who it would be. She probably wanted to confirm when he was checking out. Poludin threw the sheets with the diagrams on to the floor, put the slide rule down on top of them and got out of bed, cursing. He picked up the receiver, balancing on his heels on the cold parquet.

'Good evening,' came a mysterious, muffled female voice. 'You're not asleep yet?'

'Who do you want?'

'Aren't you alone?'

Poludin took a quick look around the room, just in case. He rubbed one hairy leg against the other.

'Yeah, I'm alone. So what?'

'What have you been doing tonight?' she continued.

'Nothing, really. Catching some *kaïf*.'

'Who?'

'Not who. What.'

'And did you catch it?'

'You could say so . . .'

'Then talk to me. I'm bored.'

His sleepiness vanished, replaced by a boyish curiosity Poludin hadn't experienced in years. He had simply forgotten that the feeling existed at all. Someone was pulling his leg. He realized that, which was why he could play along in the same spirit.

Hooking with his foot, he pulled first one wet boot and then the other over to him. Ramming his feet into them, he regretted having left his slippers at home. It was his wife's fault. She'd neglected to remind him. Poludin took out a cigarette and lit it.

'What are you smoking?'

'Marlboros,' he said, glancing down at his pack of Prima.

'You aren't very talkative.' A note of surprise was audible over the receiver. 'Don't you want to talk to me?'

'Where are you from?'

'From Kishinev. I brought some wine.'

'Wine?'

'What's so odd about that? W-ine. And who are you?'

'An engineer.'

'From where?'

'Moscow.'

'Do you have a wife?'

'A wife?' He hesitated before completing that item on the questionnaire over the telephone, then eagerly switched to a less formal way of talking. 'Let's say I do. And yourself?'

'He left me. We'd been together a month, and it's been a month since he left. He wasn't a man. A dish-rag. A prick!'

'How old are you?'

'Nineteen already. My name's Inga. What's yours?'

'Vitaly.' He should have used another name, just in case, but it had already tripped off his tongue.

'Vitaly? I was thinking . . .'

'What?'

'I didn't think it was Vitaly. That doesn't suit you.'

'What do you mean, it doesn't suit me?'

'I've seen you.'

Poludin looked at his watch: twelve-fifteen. The restaurant downstairs had probably closed by now. He had no money left, in any case. Like that joke about the station announcement: 'Citizens leaving on business: the restaurant is to your right. Citizens returning: the boiled water's to the left.' A hoary joke, but it still had some life left in it. Something to drink was the important thing. You always had to have a drink with the girl in this sort of situation. You had to get them drunk first; everyone knew that. Fortunately, there was still half a bottle of vodka. Plenty.

She broke in on his ruminations.

'Why are you so quiet?'

'Just thinking.'

'Don't think. Come up to 608.'

'You say you have wine?'

'I gave it away.'

'Who to?'

'To the pricks who unloaded my luggage.'

'Come on. Not everyone can be a prick.'

'You're not. Won't you come up if there isn't any wine?'

'I'm on my way!'

The receiver hit the cradle.

Vitaly started dressing rapidly, as if he might be too late for something.

4

For the thirty-five years of his life, Poludin had had to listen to so many tales about chance romances and to read about things like that, especially in translations of foreign novels. Whenever an authoritative masculine rap on the subject began, he himself was as ready as the next man with an opinion or an exploit of his own. Truth to tell, they belonged to somebody else, and he was just relating them as his own.

He himself was evidently not up for an off-the-cuff love affair, and – embarrassing to admit – he had never experienced one. Poludin was not a born ladykiller, that was for sure.

Poludin had never found in himself any of the flashy attainments that attract women right away, like butterflies. Even in his student days, when couples came together and flew apart in an instant, he'd had little success. It wasn't because he hadn't wanted to. It was just that, in order to interest someone in his persona, he would have had to chase after her for a long time to prove how good he was. In fact he did start appealing to someone after all but only after his own initial feelings had already passed. And then quite a different relationship had arisen, almost familial, and he'd had to get married, which is what he'd done, right away.

At his wedding, they'd sung:

'To the shy one, dear Vitaly,
We give you our Natalya.
Grasp her around the waist,
Blah, blah, blah . . .'

Natalya had turned out to be a steady sort of creature. She complemented him, lived with him in peace, without the sort of strife that shattered other families. He liked to come home at night chewing coffee beans to avoid reeking of vodka, liked to have dinner together, to play with their son, to go to the cinema once a month and once a year to go on holiday.

Whenever he was asked how long he had been married, Poludin the engineer would answer, quite seriously, 'My whole life.'

The telephone call hadn't infringed on any of this. It lured him with its instant accessibility. It offered an opportunity to finally experience something everyone else had already done but for some reason had been forbidden to Poludin. Like travelling abroad: nothing special once you'd tried it.

The face that looked back at him from the mirror on the wardrobe door was too businesslike for a time like this, so he attempted a smile. The result was a shade too insolent, nothing like him. He smoothed his hair back with both his hands and ran a finger down his cheek, since a real man had to be not just a little drunk but clean-shaven to boot.

He had to hurry. He took the bottle with him.

The door of his room creaked, as if in spite. The concierge was asleep with her head on her forearm. She shifted around and looked in the direction he had gone but said nothing.

He went one flight of stairs higher, a slightly tense, middle-sized tiger ready to pounce. He should have brought his pyjamas to change into. After all, pyjamas such as they wore in French films give a certain *cachet*. What should he say, incidentally? He had nothing suitable in reserve. Poludin generally wasn't very well-spoken when he had to speak, and without the necessary words things might not work out.

At 608, he caught his breath. Then, decisively, he raised his finger and tapped, pressing his ear to the door. Footsteps carried through the door, and he stepped back, hiding the bottle behind him. Someone stopped at the other side of the door, very close. He could hear breathing. Then the lock clicked and the door half opened.

A swarthy girl with black hair and large dark eyes stared dumbfounded out at him. She had a long nose with a thick bridge to it, he remembered that for sure. She seemed altogether too short and plump, clearly unpretty. Later, however, he would recall her, although short, as slender and attribute her homeliness to a shyness which was, in retrospect, even attractive.

'Hello,' he said cheerfully, remembering that words were what would bring him closer to his goal. 'Well, here we are . . .'

'Who are you looking for?' she said, her eyes widening in the half-light.

'What's wrong, Inga?'

'You're making some mistake. There's no one here by that name.'

'What do you mean, no one?' He hadn't expected this turn of events. 'But this *is* . . . well . . . room 608?'

'Yes, it's 608. But there's no Inga here.'

The girl was looking at him mockingly, or maybe it only seemed that way to him.

'And what's your name?'

'It's not Inga.'

'Excuse me' was the only thing Poludin could say, his tongue moving with difficulty.

He'd never been distinguished for his resourcefulness, and that was the truth.

The door closed, the lock crunched. Vitaly stood there for a moment, then turned and slouched back to his room, swigging mechanically from the bottle, the whole time not wishing to admit that he'd fallen for such an elementary practical joke. It was a good thing that he hadn't brought his pyjamas along with him. There wasn't a thing he could do about it. There wasn't even anybody to get angry with. Next time he wouldn't be such an ass. And now just forget, forget everything.

The *kaïf* continued!

5

Poludin undressed, got into bed and, pulling the blanket up over his head, was about to fall asleep when the phone rang. There was nothing for it but to get up and pick up the receiver.

'Well, what do you want?' he asked in an offended tone.

'Are you upset with me?' she asked. 'Really upset? I know it was stupid of me. It was terrifying. I was so scared.'

'So why are you calling?'

'Come back up . . .'

'For more of the same?'

'No, come on up. I'm not really scared any more . . . You know what it's like to be alone.'

'If that's so, why don't you come down here?'

She was silent for a while. He could hear her ragged breathing in the receiver.

'I can't be brave for very long. I just can't.'

'Well, OK. Do you want me to meet you halfway?'

'All right . . .'

There was a busy signal.

Poludin, snorting or grumbling or something, got dressed again and glanced around the room. The bed was all a mess, but he didn't know what was better: to tidy it up or to leave it ready for business. He turned off the light. No, it was far too dark that way. He turned on the floor lamp. He'd have time to turn it off – let it stay on, so the little coward wouldn't get scared again. Settling into an armchair, he looked at his watch. It was ten past one. At home he and his wife would always be in bed no later than half past ten, since the alarm would go off at five to seven, time to rise and shine. Here, however, he had his *kaif*.

For some Dutch courage he took another sip of vodka and chewed away at some more of the bread. Looking into the dimly lit corridor through the crack of the half-open door, he waited.

She sashayed up, as the poet puts it, and, waiting for an invitation, leaned her shoulder against the doorjamb.

'Here I am.' She took a step forward towards the bed, unbuttoning the top of her dress, either from the heat or out of a desire to remove it. 'What have you been drawing?'

His papers, covered with diagrams, were lying on the floor beneath the slide rule. He lurched, almost toppling over, and snatched them up, arranged them on his blanket and briefly detailed his idea for the new conveyor system to her.

'You're a genius!' She loosed another button.

Poludin didn't know if she'd understood any of what he had been saying, but his wife had never said that to him. He got up out of the chair as swiftly as he could and grabbed Inga's hand, pulling her to him. She obediently came closer, as if hypnotized. He hugged her around the shoulders and squeezed her so tight her bones crunched. In self-defence she dug her nails into his back.

'You crazy man! Brute! Goddamned superman!' she moaned, short of breath. 'Did you lock the door?'

How could he have forgotten about the door? Poludin unwrapped his arms and ran to the door, hitting his elbow painfully on the wardrode on the way. When he got back, Inga had already sneaked across the bed and switched off the lamp. Her zipper whizzed, her dress fell to the floor, her shoes clunked. He saw her silhouette against the window, heard her breathing, felt her warmth and moved towards it carefully, like a blind man.

Inga placed her cold palms over his ears. The orange light from the Hotel Penza's neon sign shimmered on her hair, giving it an unearthly aspect. She was trembling, either out of love for Poludin or from the cold in the room. He threw himself forward, but she slipped beneath the blanket. Only her eyes and her black hair, spreading over the pillow, were visible. He began peeling off his own clothes, tearing off the buttons in his hurry, thinking that he had forgotten to get Inga drunk first. A cardinal mistake, that's what everyone said.

'Come here, silly! Come on . . .'

No. She wouldn't say 'silly'. She'd simply say 'Come here . . .'

Poludin took his watch off and looked at it. It had stopped. He'd forgotten to wind it yesterday morning. It was impossible to establish how much time had passed while he waited for her, playing out the scene in his head. She'd probably come down the stairs by now. And, if so . . .

His door had been open the whole time. If Inga had walked past he couldn't but have noticed her. Flipping his cigarette butt into the sink, he approached the door indecisively. He was in a ridiculous, suspended state. His glider had left the ground but had failed to find the thermal that would carry him upwards. He had to come to earth on his own before something worse happened.

Poludin slammed the door shut. He kicked at a piece of plaster that fell off the wall and walked back swiftly. He took another hit off the bottle and winced at the dreck they were calling vodka. It had to be close to three. He was so tired he felt like lying down on the floor. Summoning the last of his strength, Poludin, staggering, made it back to the bed.

He hadn't had time to get his trousers off when the telephone rang, loud enough to wake up the entire hotel.

He picked up the receiver and waited. She had dialled his number and was waiting for him to speak first. They were silent, breathing at each other over the line. He gritted his teeth, standing there in one leg of his trousers.

'Are you angry?' she asked finally. 'You see, I wasn't brave enough . . . Say something to me. Anything you want. Please . . .'

He should have given her what for, but his irritation had already passed.

'It's time to get some sleep,' he mumbled, tired and indifferent.

'It is,' she agreed obediently. 'But I don't feel like it.'

'Then what the hell do you . . . ?' He didn't finish. 'Look, how do you know me anyway?'

'I've seen you at the Casa Mare.'

Of course she'd seen him at the Casa Mare, since she'd brought that Moldovan wine. He'd been there, after all, and could work that one out himself..

'Do you remember? You said, "Now that's some wine!"'

'So what? Everyone says, "Now that's some wine!"'

'Of course they do. Only, you were the one who did then. You think I'm stupid, don't you?'

'How should I know?'

'I'm not stupid, honest, I'm not. I just followed you to the hotel. I mean, I didn't exactly follow you, I came back to my room . . .'

'It's almost morning. What are you calling me for?'

'I don't know. I don't have anybody to talk to. Maybe you could come up anyway?'

'No chance! Look, we've been talking long enough. Hang up.'

'You don't want to talk? Maybe you're a prick, too. Hang up yourself!'

'Me? Why, I . . .'

He slammed down the receiver in a fit. His drunken buzz hadn't worn off, but it had turned into rage. He was still a man, after all. As if he couldn't make up his mind for himself what to do, letting some snot-nosed brat lead him on like that! Some girl he'd seen for just five seconds through a half-open door! He had his own view of things. If he'd wanted her badly enough he could have had his way. He'd just been too lazy. Just to talk. Sure!

It must have been three o'clock. Time to sleep. Immediately.

To drop off to sleep, quietly and blissfully, in a comfortable bed, alone: the best sort of *kaïf*.

He'd undressed and was standing barefoot, lifting the blanket to get under it, when the telephone rang yet again.

Poludin resolved not to pick up the receiver, but the phone rang and rang and rang. Vitaly leaped up to get it, stepped on the bottle cap with all his weight and howled from the pain. Standing on one leg and holding the other in a pose Yogis refer to as the Palm Tree, he snatched up the receiver and dialled the first digit he came to. Let her try to get though now!

He knocked back the rest of the vodka and promptly threw up. The nice little rug in the middle of the floor looked a lot less cosy now.

His *kaïf* was coming to a successful end.

Poludin switched off the lamp and stretched out under his blanket, getting warm. His eyes wandered among the shadows on the ceiling. He had a sudden urge to call his wife. To get her out of bed half asleep, the two tubes of her curlers twisted around so that it would be more comfortable to sleep. He would tell her that he missed her, and leave it at that. She would snap back that he was crazy, that she had been asleep for a long time, but then would add that she hoped he would come home soon.

He didn't spend the last of his money on the call: he had to save it for food. Sleep was enveloping his consciousness. Poludin commended himself for behaving so correctly and decisively. Self-satisfaction and vodka were making his body weightless, and our senior engineer fell into the sleep of the just.

6

The chief designer made a wry face, listening to Poludin. The original design had already been included in the plan and approved, and the factory's administration had been promised a bonus by the Ministry. And even Poludin himself, while he was laying it out, found the idea somewhat less brilliant than it had seemed the night before.

'We aren't running a track meeting here,' the chief growled, pushing aside the sketches after hardly glancing at them. 'This is the chemical-machine manufacturing industry.'

'You still have to know how to jump,' Poludin contradicted him intemperately. 'Without that, you'll never get off the ground.'

'Jump?' the man countered, looking suspiciously at his visitor. 'Go and jump on the moon; the gravity's weaker there. Down here you're doing well if you get to crawl as far as your grave. By the way, my secretary said there was a call from your hotel. What did you do to their carpet?'

'Their carpet?'

'Well, not the carpet, a throw rug. My secretary said you'd already left town. So don't be surprised if they've written to your home office.'

Rising from behind his desk, the chief designer let Poludin know that his audience was over.

The throw rug in the hotel that all the fuss was about reminded him of the ridiculousness of everything else. His trip was coming to an end. Why had they summoned Poludin here? The factory wanted to insure themselves with approvals and signatures so that in case of any failure they could lay the fault on the designers at head office. It wasn't even Poludin who had designed the thing but Bashyan, the engineer who developed the project, and she was on maternity leave. 'If she's a designer, I can have babies,' Gurstein, an engineer from the neighbouring team, had said about her. Poludin had to carry the can, and he didn't give a damn about any of them. It was great that he had at least last night's fun under his belt. Generally speaking, if you can have 'cultural' escapades like that, life in Russia can't be nearly as bad as their enemies' slander has it.

After writing 'Departed' on his travel documents and stamping them, the secretary informed him that Deputy Director Khanurov in person had called from Moscow, and when she'd answered she'd told him that Poludin was in the clear. He would have bought her some sweets, but his wallet was empty.

After a cheap meal at the plant's engineering staff cafeteria, and with time to kill before his train, he set out to wander aimlessly around the city.

The dull sun had dried the pavement, but his feet were still wet. The heat had been turned off overnight at the hotel for economy's sake, and his boots hadn't dried. He was looking at the local women, and today he liked them even less than the night before. Yesterday it had seemed that they were all ready to belong to him alone. But today they looked at the end of their tether, frumpy and foreign.

Poludin realized that he was standing in front of Casa Mare. That's what Moldovans called a reception room. This wine-tasting hall for Moldovan wines had been opened in Penza not long before (a bold act on the part of the Regional Committee to propagandize for friendship among nationalities and satisfy their alcoholic curiosity). The regulars from the factory had taken him to the cellar for some hair of the dog on his third day. They even paid for it, hoping he would return their hospitality in Moscow.

Swarthy girls in national costume were serving each customer several tiny glasses at a time from trays. Fine wine sparkled in them. While they drank, a lecture on Soviet wines – the best in the world, of course – blared out over loudspeakers. Then they let you taste them. Bouquet, aroma,

187

flavour . . . But these were actually wines for internal consumption, for roubles. Their only connection with the best wines in the world was in their geographical proximity. Not that any of this troubled Poludin: he personally was only able to distinguish between white and red, dry and fortified, while his preference was for the kind you can get the most of for your money.

There was no queue in the cellar at this time of the day, as it was forbidden to sell wine before two o'clock, and nobody could have a taste of anything but heavily watered-down juices. But even if they had been open for business Poludin wouldn't have had money for wine anyway, so the ban didn't distress him overmuch at that moment. After dallying in front of the Casa Mare for a minute or two, he wandered further along the street. His head hurt, his stomach ached and he was nauseous, but Poludin felt fine, all things considered.

His night-time episode, when he recalled the details now, seemed to have worked out in his favour. He would have something with a bit of gusto to tell the small circle of smokers at the end of his corridor at work. Poludin decided on the spot to transfer the main scene to the balcony of his hotel room, where he and the wanton Inga did it in the middle of the night in plain view of the whole city. Drunk, they wouldn't even have noticed the cold. He'd have gagged her with his hand, to prevent her from screaming out in pleasure, in her *kaïf*. The rest of the details he decided would be made up as he went along. It was said that the Deputy Director of Personnel had ordered a microphone to be installed in the smokers' lounge. But, first, even if that were true, it seemed nobody had yet been sent to prison for talking about babes. And, second, the rumour about the microphone had probably been spread on purpose, so there would be less smoking and more work.

Poludin slowed his pace. He decided to turn back, to go down into the cellar of Casa Mare and say a proud farewell. Inga had to be there – where else could she be? Let her be sorry about how much *kaïf* she was missing out on. Having made his decision, as usual Poludin did just the opposite. He flicked his cigarette butt on to the pavement, stepped on it with his wet boot, spat and headed for the train station.

Instead of Casa Mare, all of a sudden he wanted to go home, to his kitchen. Missing him, his wife would knock off work early to tend to his every need for a few hours, so he wouldn't have to lift a finger for a fork or a cup. She was a good sort. Sitting across the table, she would briefly relate who their son had got into another fight with at nursery school – then fall silent, all ears.

Unhurriedly, he would finish his meal and light a cigarette, then impress upon her the details of the successful approval of his project, how he had heroically shouldered the whole thing, atoning for the sins of the entire department. He would explain to her his terrific idea for the mechanical hand, something that the present-day level of technology had yet to reach. He wouldn't forget to mention Khanurov, the scumbag who had him literally by the throat. How he had been honoured by the men in that foolish Casa Mare at their expense, how he hadn't overdrawn on his expenses or borrowed a single rouble, and he would tell her that grub was even scarcer in Penza than here, and that it was hard to see just where it was all going . . .

He'd tell her everything.

Everything?

Almost everything.

MONEY GOES ROUND

I

Masha was awakened by a strained conversation on the other side of her door.

'I'm tired, I'm so tired! You don't give a damn. You just hang around at the garage and forget about everything. But I've got the kids.'

That was her mum.

'Every time it's the same damned thing. I get paid tomorrow. Tomorrow! Did you just come down from Mars?'

That was her father.

'Tomorrow? And what about the kids? They have to be fed today!'

'If you'd got an abortion like everyone else you wouldn't be moaning now.'

'You said yourself, "OK, go ahead and have them."'

'So what? Have you got no brains of your own? We were in the pits already with just the one. Do you think I can just pull money out of a hat? Why do you keep buying all this junk?'

'These dishes aren't junk. They're not in stock very often, so everyone was buying them.'

'The dishes OK, then, but that green skirt, where did you get that from?'

'It's second-hand. Yevdokia gave it to me. You never give me presents like this. Why is it I'm the only one who has to struggle to make ends meet? Faina, now, her husband is a real man!'

This was her mother again. Yevdokia was a neighbour, a sleeping-car attendant on the Moscow–Berlin train. Faina was another neighbour; her husband worked at the recycling centre where they gave you vouchers to buy *The Count of Monte Cristo* in exchange for old newspapers. 'Faina's old man brings something home every day. *Every* day!'

'He's a thief.'

'And that isn't written all over his money, by the way.'

'He'll get caught soon enough.'

'But in the meantime just think how much he brings his family! And what do you do?'

'Faina herself has a lot of clout there in her sausage shop, much better than what you have. You just get chocolate when people want their papers from you. Why don't you take money for it, since you're such a smart worker? Where's all the stuff they give you for their residence permits?'

'That doesn't happen every day. And then the head of the ID office takes it all for himself, almost, you know that. But I do bring home extra coupons, you know! And you want your dinner every day.'

Masha wanted to run in and tell them she didn't want anything – just don't argue! Because it was her fault, Masha's, that she'd been born. Abortions work like this: first Masha's there, and then suddenly she's not. Her mum had felt sorry for her. But it was better to keep quiet. They'd only say, 'Don't butt in! It's none of your business!' But why wasn't it? After all, she and Sasha were the kids whose fault it was that . . .

Every night, as soon as her father got home, her mother would start going on about money. Their yelling would wake Masha up. She used to think that 'money' meant the coins they'd give her for ice cream. Once, at the height of an argument, she got some coins out of her little box. 'Here, I'll give you some money.'

Her father asked her, 'Don't you have any paper money?'

She ran to her spot behind the sofa and got out the pieces of paper she'd cut up to play grocer with. She'd written '10 roubles', '100 roubles' on the pieces of paper

'Goody!' He acted pleased. 'Give 'em to your mother. Now she can buy everything she's ever dreamed of.'

But now Masha knew perfectly well what money was. You couldn't buy it, you got it in exchange for something. But not everyone got it. Some people got more, some got less. Smart people knew where it was hidden and helped themselves without asking permission. Her father claimed he could do without money; even without it he could dig around and get everything on the black market. But he didn't want to because he was tired. He was tired and wanted to live honestly for a while, without thinking about money from morning to night. But then her mum would ask who needed honesty, there was no point in being honest now! So her father would bring home money anyway and give it to her mother. Her mum would take it, smile and kiss him. When he didn't bring any, no kiss.

Today was Sunday. Sometimes her father worked the day shift, sometimes evenings, sometimes nights, including Sundays. At home he always slept or just lay motionless on the sofa, looking at the ceiling. Sometimes he would say, 'Look, there's a cobweb again. What do you do all day?' Mom worked part time as a passport-registry clerk at the housing administration, sometimes in the morning, sometimes in the afternoon. They didn't see much of each other; otherwise they would have fought even more.

'Dad, let's watch television!'

'All day long I have to watch soap operas – I've had it up to here.'

Masha got out a book, sat down on his belly and looked at the pictures. Her father dozed, Masha shifted around, up and down. Then he got up and, as he was getting ready to leave, said to her mother in a conciliatory tone, 'Don't have a fit now! This is hardly the first time . . . you'll work out how to get by.'

'You're spoiled. You get your room and board,' her mother

stuck to her guns. 'I've had enough! Take half the children and do whatever you like!'

Sasha was one half of the children; Masha was the other. Of course Dad would take Masha. Sasha was a slob and Dad was always freaking out with him. Even though Sasha was almost as tall as his mother, she sometimes spanked him with Dad's belt.

Sasha would cry and mumble, 'I still won't do it!' But he would, of course.

'Let's go, Masha!' urged her father. 'Are you dressed?'

'Can you tie my hair bow?'

'Do you want diamonds in your ears, too? Your bow is going to make me late for relieving my partner!'

They took the packed bus to Savelovsk Station and then trudged on foot all the way to the garage across a public garden and a construction site. Masha could barely keep up, so when they finally got there she was happy about going for a ride. She recognized her father's Volga right off. It was grey with a red top, and the licence plate was easy to remember, 23-43-MMT. There was a streak of paint running down a long dent on one bumper. That had happened when her father ran into a rubbish truck. But absolutely everybody had agreed that it was the lorry-driver's fault.

Her father's partner, Uncle Tikhon, stood there, unshaven, wiping his hands on the sleeve of an old shirt. When Tikhon saw that Masha's father had brought her along, he pushed back his cap and screwed up his eyes. 'Hah! You divorced again?'

'No. I just have her for the day.'

'Well, married or divorced, it's all the same – one big mess. Now the dispatcher will have a go at you for bringing her along.'

'I'll talk him round. What am I supposed to do with her? You can't drop children off at second-hand shops, yet. So how's the clutch?'

'It slips. While your majesty was bickering with your consort, I was messing around with the clutch for half an hour in the pit. It needs a new plate. At the shop they say they'll get one after the first. Hah! The first of which month, that's the question.'

'That plate has been slipping for a long time.'

'It's slipping us a hole in our pockets.'

'Get in, Masha,' commanded her father.

She nimbly opened the door, grabbed the wheel, wiggled across the seat and settled back opposite the meter, putting her hands on her knees. Trying to read the numbers on the meter, she wrinkled her nose, on which there were three huge freckles and an entire marching band of little ones. The meter was showing only doughnuts.

'Hah! By the way, I had a political-instruction session again this morning,' Tikhon said. 'That same boy scout in his leather jacket with the red tie with little flames on it, the squeaky little wheel. He asked our Party organizer to find me and then to leave us alone, you know, so he could talk to me in private.'

'I'd have just given him the slip. Why'd you waste your time?'

'Why irritate the people up top? He thinks he's recruiting me, but perhaps it's me who's . . . Let him talk! I'll listen. What harm can it do? His boots were squeaking, and he kept asking if there's any rumours *circulamating* around our clients, rumours about the top leadership, about the Big Comrade himself. Hah! Who knows? All kinds of rumours, I suppose. He told me to listen and remember what I heard. Well, and to report it to him personally, of course. And he gave me another phone number, too, if there was anything important while he was out. He promised to help me out if I needed it.'

'Help with what, specifically?'

'He hinted but didn't give any particulars. If I'm ever talking to passengers and the chance comes, I'm supposed to tell them that the higher-ups aren't planning any currency reforms, for now. He says that's just a harmful rumour. He says the government's on the workers' side, you see! And, he says, needless panic'll affect production figures. We got to keep the people quiet and not get 'em all worried. Hah!'

'They should keep them quiet themselves!'

'They should, shouldn't they? But then he hinted that they're putting microphones in our taxis, at random. Of course I pretended I wasn't surprised, but for formality's sake I asked, "Is there one in mine?" "I couldn't say," he says. "I've got nothing to do with that. Of course we trust you personally – you're one of us. It's just in case you drive a foreigner around. We're expanding our surveillance of foreigners."'

'Fuck them! Our job's handling the steering wheel and the meter.'

'Hah! Well, there it is. You can take it or leave it!'

Masha's father flopped down behind the wheel, and his elbow gave her a hard knock. For a long time the engine didn't want to turn over, but finally it sneezed and began to roar. He leaned out of the window.

'Damned clutch is slipping.'

'Let it slip. Just get out there and make some money!'

Pulling his cap down over his eyes, her father drove off, but then he suddenly braked and reversed back to Tikhon.

'Do you happen to have any spare change? I'm starting out without a bean.'

'Hah! I'm your banker, am I? Why don't you print your own?'

'We'll settle up tomorrow.'

'You're robbing me blind.' Tikhon dug in his pockets and found two crumpled 25-rouble notes. 'You'll have to pay me interest – the hard stuff. I want you to drop in to Klavka's on your way back and get me five bottles for tonight!'

'Five bottles of what, Dad?' asked Masha, when Tikhon disappeared behind them.

'None of your business!'

Cars swarmed around them in the yard like ants on an anthill, nosing in or backing out on all sides. They seemed sure to hit one, but sitting beside her father she wasn't afraid, even in this confusion.

'Who's the passenger riding with the meter off?' the dispatcher asked sternly through his window, mechanically punching in the time of departure on the trip ticket but holding on to it.

'It's my daughter,' explained her father. 'I'm taking her home now, on my way out.'

'You know that's not allowed.'

'I know, I know – I'll cut you in on any action.'

The dispatcher breathed on his stamp, pressed it on to the pass, and pushed a button. The gate rattled and moved aside and their car rolled out on to the street.

'What do you mean, home, Dad? Mom told us to stay out all day.'

'Hush. I know that.'

2

It was neither sunny nor overcast. A feeble wind dug little craters in the dust and moved rubbish mixed with leaves slowly down the pavement. Lorries flooded the streets with blue smoke that spread out and melted away, leaving behind a smell of burnt food. They passed a vacant site in silence and proceeded a few blocks more. Her father looked lazily to both sides and swore now and again. *The clutch probably isn't working right.* On the pavement in front of a hotel stood a suitcase with a shopping bag tied to it. Beside it a man in a grey raincoat was pacing nervously back and forth. He held a box in one hand and waved the other arm to hail their taxi. Masha's father braked and leaned across her to the window.

'Where to?'

'Kursk Station, as fast as possible.'

'Everyone want to go as fast as possible. But if you cross my palm, I can do it.'

'Cross your palm? What does that mean?'

'That's what they say out east, for "a tip".'

'Oh, a tip. Why didn't you say so? You'll get a tip.'

The passenger opened the front door. 'Oops, it's taken!' So he got in the back with his things.

'This is my daughter,' explained her father. 'Her mother kicked us out of the house. But we'll manage – right, Masha?'

'She didn't really kick us out, Dad!'

'I'm joking, silly!'

Masha felt embarrassed, nodded and started looking at the pedestrians on the pavement.

'I've got a daughter at home in Murom, too. I'm bringing her this doll, here. Want to have a look?'

He put the box on the front seat. Masha looked enquiringly at her father.

'Look at it, then. It's not going to hurt you.'

Masha politely took off the lid. The doll was dazzling. She had blue eyes, black lashes, yellow hair and fashionable clothes, even a bead necklace and a watch on her wrist. Putting the cover back, Masha said indifferently, 'I've got lots of dolls, haven't I, Dad? Twelve.'

'Well, I bet you haven't got one like this,' objected the passenger. 'I work in retail myself and know all the new products. This is a new item, imported from Hungary. You haven't got one, have you?'

'No, not like that one,' conceded Masha.

'Ask your dad to get you one! A shipment's come in just now.'

'If I did get one,' laughed her father, 'your mother would throw a fit.'

'Don't you cabbies make a fortune?'

'You salesmen don't starve either, do you?'

'We do all right,' his customer admitted indifferently. 'You get your wages and a bit off the top. But you know yourself that a rouble isn't worth a kopek.'

'Mum says that a rouble is worth a hundred kopeks.'

'What does your mother know?' muttered her father.

'I don't think you can blame the women,' said the passenger.

'Whose fault is it, then?'

'It's money's fault. It slips and slides around. You get some here, you give it away there. Money's round, like your steering wheel.'

'Dad, why is money round?' Masha was watching how one number was pushing away the other on the meter. The passenger glanced at the meter, then at the girl, then screwed up his eyes.

'Round?' he said. 'Because it goes around, in circles. There, you see, the numbers keep turning around. You can't stop looking; it's mesmerizing. Your father gives money to your mother, she gives it to the salesman in the shop, he gets a taxi, and then it comes back to your father and mother.'

'And Mum gives me some for ice cream.'

'And for ice cream. Children should have some fun, too.'

Her father didn't say anything for a long time.

'Round is right,' he suddenly agreed. 'You turn it around, and it turns on you and jabs at your throat, right at your throat. But I don't think money's really worth all that much.'

The passenger looked interested, leaned over to Masha's father and asked, 'What *is* valuable, then, in your opinion?'

'I don't know. Humans have to be human. Or isn't that true any more?'

'Well,' laughed the customer, 'what are they worth, humans? Experience shows you shouldn't ever give anyone something for nothing. If you do, he'll take it and rub your nose in shit. You only learn what your life is worth when you get sick and have to slip a bit extra to the doctor. Trust people, brother, but don't be a fool! Find out if it's not nailed down! Money doesn't grow on trees.'

'And if it did?' asked Masha's father, looking askance at him.

'If it did, I'd become a famous horticulturist: I'd develop hybrids! I'd be crossing fifty-rouble notes and hundred-rouble notes.' The passenger laughed, amused at his idea. 'That would be quite some horticulture – am I right, girl? In school they teach you all kinds of nonsense, but how to make money, well, there's no such subject. And they call what you get out of school a "certificate of maturity"! What kind of maturity is that?'

He tapped his pocket. Masha wanted to defend school but didn't know how. She'd started year 2 almost a month ago and always wanted go to school because staying at home was even more boring. Sasha was in year 6. He knew all about money and had for a long time. He went shopping by himself, and he went to Dad's depot on paydays so that Mother could get the money at once. Otherwise who knew when Dad would turn up at home? He and Tikhon loved to drop by the grill bar with their pay packets. They liked the shish kebabs there.

Her father made a sharp turn and came to a stop by the glass entrance door of Kursk Station. Their passenger started digging around in his pockets.

'How much does it say there on the meter, little girl?'

Masha quickly read out, 'Nought two seventy-eight.'

The man took out a five-rouble note.

'Is this enough?'

'It's OK,' said her father.

'Five hundred kopeks,' said Masha and started to count on her fingers, moving her lips soundlessly. 'I'll work out the change in a second.'

'Ah, don't bother,' said the passenger quickly. 'Just let me have the doll back. Well, see you later, little girl.'

He got out, pulled out the suitcase with the shopping bag tied on to it, grabbed the box and was lost in the crowd.

'What a nice man.'

' Everyone's nice until . . .'

'Until what?'

'Well, like . . . Let's get over to the taxi stand before they start nagging us here.'

The taxi stand was a crush of suitcases, crying children, bundles, faces of every kind of race, dust, boxes, vendors, swearing. Evidently a train had just arrived. Her father slammed the door and walked around the car.

'Who's next?'

Masha's nose was crushed flat against the glass. With all her might she banged on the window.

'What's the matter?'

'Da-ad! Take Hitler over there, with the bird!'

Her father winked, and while three people with big suit-cases quarrelled over who should go first he grabbed the sleeve of a skinny old man in a faded blue suit and pulled him into the taxi. He had a funny square little moustache that made him look like Hitler. This Hitler held a cage in his hand, and in the cage sat a blue bird on a little perch.

'Well, actually, you know, young man, it wasn't my turn, strictly speaking.'

'I know, but my daughter took a shine to you. Where are you going?'

'Well, the Bird Market. To the Bird Market.'

'OK, Bird Market it is.'

'Put the cage here!' Masha wanted to play with the bird. 'Please! I'll hold on to it tight as anything!'

She hugged the cage and stuck a finger into it. Her finger was thin, and the bird pecked at it, thinking it was a worm, apparently. But it didn't hurt her.

'What kind of bird is it?'

'A parakeet, my dear. A multi-coloured one.'

'Can he sing?'

'He can talk when he isn't nervous, but what he's saying nobody knows.'

They drove for a long time. There were traffic jams at the lights, and when there weren't any lights the jams were even worse. No one wanted to let anyone through, so the traffic stopped altogether. Her father pulled out into the open oncoming lane, past several cars, but then a traffic policeman blew his whistle. He wasn't paying any attention to the traffic jam, just looking for a car to flag down.

'Breaking the rules, are we? Let's have your licence!'

Traffic police, Masha knew, always demanded a tenner even if you hadn't broken any rules. But you couldn't just give them the money; you had to do it without insulting them, otherwise you had to wait while they wrote out a report to your garage. Then, to get it back you had to pay not ten but twenty-five roubles. Dad knew how to sweet-talk them, though, and a tenner was always enough. But this time they were talking for a long time. Since his taxi had been stopped in the middle of the road even more cars were backed up now.

The old man was muttering, nodding and running his finger over his moustache. The girl tried talking to the parakeet. It cocked its head to one side, as if listening. Then, frightened by a screech of brakes, it started flinging itself around the cage. Masha turned around a few times, questioningly, and each time the old man would wink at her or softly whistle bird-calls.

Finally the matter was settled.

'Ten?' asked Masha, knowingly.

'Yes,' replied her father. 'I hope he chokes on it.'

'Sorry, son,' said the old man. 'It's me that brought on this bad luck. Something bad always happens when I'm around.'

'OK, we'll sort it out.'

When they got to the Bird Market Masha stroked the cage and tried to whistle like the old man but couldn't. She put her arms around her father's neck and whispered something to him.

'What, you little fool? Mother'll kill us.' But, pushing her aside, he asked the old man, 'You planning to sell it?'

'Well, actually, yes, you know.'

'How much?'

'Well, it's important who you give it to, actually,' said the old man and looked embarrassed. 'If it's to a good home, it's cheap, including the cage. The old lady has asthma, and we can't keep a bird at home, you know.'

'Right. Would five be enough?'

'Of course it's enough.' The confused old man fumbled with the money. 'But there's a slight problem. I've got no business here at the market now, and the old lady's waiting for me, you know!'

'No problem. Let's drive him back to the station, Masha!' She nodded.

'It'll cost me too much.'

'Hey, I'll take you for nothing. I already added that into what I paid for the parakeet.'

'You're lucky,' said the old man. 'You know how to live.'

'Yes, luckier than most!'

'What's your background?'

'Me? Well, the ruling class, what else could I be?'

'What do you mean?'

'The rulers, you know: the proletariat.'

'The working class? That's fine. My family were rich peasants, your class enemy. So I had to spend my youth in prison.'

'Bad luck!'

All the way to the station the old man held the five-rouble note in his hands, but when they got there he blinked and started fussing about, pulled out a change purse and put away the money, muttering all the while. Then he pulled a little packet of millet seed out of his pocket.

'Here you are, my dear. I almost forgot to give you his birdseed.'

'So the parakeet really is mine, now?' asked Masha.

'Yes, it is,' her father assured her. 'And Sasha's, too, of course.'

'Great! Hitler was sweet.'

'Where did you get "Hitler" from?'

'TV. But this one is better. He probably doesn't have much money.'

Her father wasn't listening, because he'd got out to fetch some bags. An oriental man got in, sun-tanned and self-assured and wearing a cap with an enormous visor. He and her father filled the boot and the back seat with sacks of walnuts, and then they set off for Cheryomushkin Market.

'By the way, what's the situation here as far as cultural services go?' the passenger enquired.

'How do you mean?' Her father looked at him appraisingly.

'Do you have blonde girls to hire for the evening, by any chance?'

'Blondes are a tenner apiece,' her father replied without looking away from the street.

'And brunettes?' interrupted Masha.

'I don't want brunettes,' the passenger cut her short. 'We're brunettes ourselves.'

When they'd unloaded the car at the market he reminded Masha's father, 'Get me a blonde then, but no tricks!'

'Here.' Her father got out a notebook, gave him a pencil and read out a phone number. 'Say it's from Semyon, but don't talk too much over the phone, see? You can settle up with her.'

'Does she respect Azerbaijan?'

'She respects anyone who pays.'

The oriental man paid for the taxi and for the blonde's phone number. Masha and her father drove off.

'What does he need a blonde for, Dad?'

'To go to the cinema with.'

'What about the abortion?'

'What abortion?'

'Isn't she going to have one?'

The girl sat hugging the cage. The parakeet had hidden in a corner of his cage and was dozing while they drove around. They carried hikers with backpacks, an invalid on crutches and a family consisting of mother, father and twins. The twins screamed in unison so loud that everyone in the street could hear them. After dropping them off, her father smoked for a little bit and then drove to an off-licence. There was a crowd by the door, waiting for the end of the lunch break. The taxi rolled into the courtyard.

'Are you going to Klavka's?'

'Where'd you get that idea?'

'Uncle Tikhon.'

'No more chatting, just walk around the car and watch and see if anyone comes into the yard. I'll be right back.'

He vanished through the door, half hidden by stacks of empty boxes on either side. After a while he stuck his head out. 'Did anyone show up?'

'No, nobody.'

He carried a box out through the door, clutching it to his stomach as he walked to the car. It said, 'Gross. Net.'

'Gross and Net, are they brothers, Dad?'

'You keep quiet!'

He set down the box and opened up the boot with a blow from his fist.

'Oh, what a lot of fire extinguishers!' exclaimed Masha. 'Five of them!'

'Hold this!' He handed her one and began to unscrew another. After taking off the top, he put a vodka bottle inside and screwed the top back on. 'This is a secret!' For the first time that day he laughed out loud.

'What secret?' asked Masha in a sensible tone. 'Uncle Tikhon sells five bottles a night. But what does he need the money for? He doesn't have a wife, that's what you said.'

'But he does have women,' he said sternly, 'and that costs even more.'

'Why does it cost more?'

'Because there's lots of them, and only one of him, see?'

'I see.'

Then they parked at a taxi stand, and he proceeded to smoke half his pack of cigarettes. Masha started coughing from the smoke, and she was hungry, but her father was working, after all, and he'd get angry if she asked. It'd be better just to put up with it. So she began to feed the parakeet. Nobody wanted a taxi.

'You sunbathing?' The driver of the next taxi in line came up to her father. 'Give me a light off your cigarette. They all decide to walk, or as a last resort they take the tram and keep the money in their socks.'

'Why in their socks?' asked Masha.

'It doesn't fall out of a sock, unless it has holes in it!'

The driver lit up and walked off.

'Well, move your cage out of my seat,' grumbled her father. 'To hell with them all. Let's get *out* of here!'

3

There was a queue in front of the grill bar on Leningrad Prospekt. Pulling his daughter along, Masha's father pushed his way through the crowd and kicked the door. The gold-braid-capped doorman pulled back the bolt as soon as he saw him.

'Is this Lida's shift?'

'Yeah, she's around here somewhere.'

Masha hung on to the pocket of her father's jacket. Inside, the café stank of cigarette smoke and was as noisy as a bathhouse. If you clapped your hands on and off your ears it sounded like music.

'Stand here, don't move.'

Her father disappeared. When he came back he was at once shown to a table in the corner next to the counter. Without asking, the waitress, Lida, brought two plates of shish kebab and tossed a pack of cigarettes on to the table. She was wearing an old-fashioned lacy headdress on her black hair, like the Snow Maiden. Tired, she half sat on the edge of a chair and asked, 'Why aren't coming by any more?'

'I'm swamped with work.'

'Yeah, work is always swamping us. And it's all dirty. Life flies past like a crow. And there's never any fun.'

'Well, doesn't Tikhon see you all the time?'

'So what? I have to pay him fifty a month for giving me a lift here.'

'And I'm a freebie, is that it?'

'A Hungarian officer doesn't take money off a woman. Maybe I have more fun with you.'

Lida got lipstick and a mirror out of her pocket and looked at herself as she ran the lipstick over her lips. After fixing her face she looked at Masha carefully but without jealousy.

'Cut it up for me!' the girl asked her father. He cut her meat into small bites and broke a piece off a bread roll.

'Uh, don't you eat at home any more? And today is Sunday and everything.'

'We had a quarrel.'

'Why don't you come round tonight? I get off at eight, and Tikhon's busy.'

'Look, I've got nowhere to leave her.' He glanced in Masha's direction.

'What a chicken you are!'

'How's the little boy?'

'Now you remember! He keeps waiting for his daddy, and his daddy's a three-timing bastard!'

'Why three?'

'Because! Why have you been hiding it? Rimka had to tell me all about it.'

'What could she have to gossip about to you?' His head lowered.

'About who her daughter looks like, and where you spend your night shifts. Hey, all right, I'm not the public prosecutor. Go out with whoever you want!'

Customers were calling for Lida. She sighed and got up.

'Take the money!' he called after her.

'You don't believe in money, remember?' she snorted. 'You don't earn any, and I don't need just a little bit.'

'Can you eat here for free?' asked Masha.

'You can't eat for free anywhere. You're my little numbskull. Sasha, now, he understands everything. I'll have to pay for all of this some day, see?'

'Of course I see.'

'Well, then.' He pulled out a 25-rouble note. 'Here, stick this in your pocket for your mother so she won't get cross. Otherwise we'll just spend it.'

His daughter put the note into her pocket, ate a slice of pickle and pushed the metal plate aside. Her father picked up the last piece of cold meat from her plate. It was all fat and gristle, but he chewed it down, put on his cap and headed off. Like a little dog Masha ran after him.

Now they were driving two talkative fishermen with their gear. They, too, asked about Masha, and he had to explain again. They offered to pay with fresh fish.

'It'd go bad before I got off work, otherwise I might.'

Masha didn't notice how a shaven-headed guy managed to jump in; he was wearing a jacket that he'd obviously just bought. He hadn't even taken off the price tag yet.

'What're we sitting here for, huh? Get going, come on!'

'Tell us where and we'll go.'

'Step on it, get out of here,' the man howled as if he'd been stabbed. 'Then I'll tell you.'

He fidgeted nervously in his seat, looking back and forth over his shoulders, and when they drove away he started singing, or rather humming through his nose, but stopped straight away. Suddenly he leaned over her father's shoulder and showed him a pistol.

'Let's do us a job, OK?' He played with the pistol in his hand. 'Wait for me half an hour here, uh, around the corner. You'll get 500 smackers, and then you get lost. It's a clean job, no blood. Five hundred to stick in your boot, huh?'

The shaven-headed guy put the pistol into his pocket, rolled down his window and spat. He hit the car beside them and laughed.

'I'd be glad to,' said Masha's father cautiously, 'but, you see, I've got to take my daughter to the doctor right away – she's sick.'

'Well, that's too bad,' said the man, without taking any particular offence. 'Stop – uh – right here. I'll – uh – take another taxi. Give me a smoke and get out of here before I stick ya!'

The bald guy blew the smoke from his cigarette into Masha's face, got out and slammed the door so hard that it sounded like a shot.

Her father drove off, looking pale and gloomy.

'Funny, wasn't it, Dad?'

Masha was still coughing. She wanted to say something pleasant to her father. He was sad all the time. Probably because something was wrong with the clutch. That was the problem.

'I liked the shish kebab café,' she whispered in his ear. He came back to himself, nodded and winked at her.

'Good, I'm glad.'

'The lady there was pretty, wasn't she? Are we going home to Mum soon?'

Masha's father glanced at her and started looking around.

'OK,' he said decisively. 'Let's go and make some money so today won't be a wash-out.'

He drove up to the taxi stand by the Moskva department store. There were lots of customers but not a single taxi.

'To the airport! Domodedovo airport,' he shouted through the half-open door. 'I'm only taking people to the airport.'

'How convenient. That's just where I'm going!' A man in a wrinkled black suit and black tie agreed at once. On the way out he didn't say a word, but at the airport he paid what was on the meter. He wasn't too lazy to count out every kopek of the fare in small change.

'Is that all?' asked Masha's father in a low voice.

'Why more?'

'I need a little extra, considering the risks of the job . . . Or I'll take you right back, see?'

The passenger looked closely at him and then pulled out a badge identifying him as a member of the police fraud squad. Her father turned pale.

'Well?' The passenger kept on looking at him, enjoying the effect he was having. 'Let's drive round to the police station and write ourselves a little ticket: extortion and with threats. And you drive relatives around for free on government transport. The station's here in Domodedovo, not far away.'

'What threats?' asked her father sullenly. 'It was a joke.'

'Yeah, I know that kind of joke.'

'But aren't we on the same side?'

'Evidently not, since you have a poor eye for who to target.'

'OK, so I was wrong. Let's settle up. When's your birthday?'

'What difference does that make?'

'Maybe it's soon? I have a present for you.'

'That's different. Except that it'd be a bribe. And in front of witnesses.' The cop glanced at Masha, snapped shut his badge and stuck it back in his pocket. 'What kind of present? I'm in a hurry.'

Her father had to get out, open the boot and pull out a couple of bottles of vodka.

'Here, don't break 'em, it's Stolichnaya. I bought it for myself.'

'Storing some up for tonight, were you?' asked the customer, sticking the bottles into the inside pockets of his jacket. 'OK, then, you can go, this time. I'm in a good mood today.'

Her father looked after him and got back behind the wheel.

'Are you bored?' He turned on the engine and patted his daughter on the cheek; his hand smelled of oil. 'He paid what was on the meter, thank you very much, right, Masha?'

She nodded.

At the airport he drove over to the taxi stand, pulled in among the cars, put up an 'Out to Lunch' sign and got out. Masha sat quietly, holding on to the cage, and followed her father with her eyes. He joined the crowd at the terminal exit and scanned it for a suitable fare. He picked one out, brought him to the car, let him in and told him to wait. Then he brought a second customer. Both waited in silence, stealing glances at each other. Masha was silent, too. Then she suddenly saw through the windscreen that her father was getting beaten up.

He was right by the glass doors of the exit. There were three of them against his one. Masha let out a scream and ran to help him. They were all rolling around on the ground; she couldn't tell who was who. There was nowhere for him to run because cars were driving by in a steady stream. Crying, she managed to grab her father's sleeve, but he shook her off, not noticing that he threw her against the wall. A good thing, actually, or she might have been killed without his noticing that, either.

'Stop it, I'm telling you!' 'Hey, now! Break it up!' Two policemen started to break up the fight. They'd been loath to interfere, but when a child got hurt in public they had to. The fight came to a halt. Cursing and threatening to get even, Masha's father took one last hit in the back as he crawled away between the bystanders' legs. Then he caught sight of his daughter, got to his knees and picked her up in his arms.

'Are you hurt?'

'I'm fine, I'm fine,' repeated Masha, sobbing. 'How about you?'

He carried her to the car, put her in and got in himself. He looked in the mirror, got a piece of newspaper and, in silence, set about wiping the blood from his cut lip. Below one eye a bruise was forming.

In the back seat, crowded against their two big suitcases, the customers were waiting submissively.

'Well, what happened?' asked the passenger with a brief-case.

'The bastards!' growled her father. 'They want me to pay them. They want twenty-five roubles from every fare – that is, from you. Pay them for nothing! And if I don't, they said they'll slash my tyres. And the cops are in with them. No, I won't pay them even if they shoot me. How can I live like that?'

'You have to pay up,' declared the passenger with the brief-case, judiciously. 'If you don't pay they really will slash your tyres! And dentures cost more than your own teeth. That's how it is, pay or be killed. Although these days there's not much difference. If you'd given them the twenty-five roubles you could always have taken a third passenger. But they didn't let you do that. Am I right?'

The other passenger, a middle-aged yokel from the country, wheezed quietly, huddled in his corner. Just to be on the safe side, he was going to stay out of the debate.

'Masha, sweetie, are you OK?' Her father had calmed down a little. He turned the ignition key.

'I'm OK,' she whispered uncertainly, still sobbing and examining her scraped knees.

'Then let's go. Don't tell Mum about the fight.'

Her father lit another cigarette and tossed the empty

packet out of the window. Masha followed it with her eyes. The packet soared upwards, fluttering in the air, then plopped down on to the asphalt. At that very moment an oncoming truck lifted it back up into the air. The packet fell again, tumbling and was finally crushed under a wheel.

Yellow, mangy-looking trees flew by on both sides of the road. It started to rain, and one of the windscreen wipers began scraping back and forth. The other seemed to be broken. Masha's father cursed but then, glancing at her, changed to more polite language as he heaped abuse on his partner, Tikhon, for using the car to make money but not taking care of it.

'I suppose he didn't take care of the transmission because he was too stingy to pay the mechanics,' he grumbled. 'Or does he expect me to buy the plate on the black market?'

It grew quite dark on the road to Moscow with their two passengers. Although the rain had stopped, the air remained damp and chilly. Masha began to cough and felt cold, so she curled up and put her hands between her knees. Her father turned on the heater. Hot air blew in from beneath, and it became comfortable, almost like home. The girl blinked and blinked and stared at the meter so as not to fall asleep. The numbers kept jumping, jumping, jumping. People got out, others got in, they were wet, water dripped off them when they came in, and Masha screwed up her eyes. She was holding on to her seat and looking straight ahead at the dirty asphalt flowing beneath the car.

'That's it!' her father exclaimed, so loudly that Masha jumped.

'Hey, man, give us a ride, come on!'

'Not for a hundred roubles, I won't. I'm off to the garage, girls, the garage. My time's up. Can't you see the child is almost asleep?'

One of the girls leaned over and stuck her head through the window, whispering hoarsely, 'You got any white stuff?'

'No, I haven't,' he said nonchalantly, pushing her hand off the car door and starting to move. 'I don't mess around with that stuff. Ask someone else!'

'White stuff? Toothpaste, Dad?' Masha had woken up.

'Of course, toothpaste. What ugly mugs they have! Yuck!'

Masha dozed again but opened her eyes when they reached the garage.

4

It was dark there, and there were lots of cars lined up. The same man checked them in; he stuck his arm out through the window, took the authorization from each driver, and lowered it briefly beneath his desk before stamping it. Her father got out his trip ticket, too, and stuck some money inside it like everyone else so he wouldn't get stamped 'Late'. Then, thinking about Masha, he added some more so there would be no questions about her and folded the document over twice.

They drove into the car wash, and her father pulled out another rouble and stuck it into the smock of the old cleaning woman who turned on the brushes and wiped off the back seat with a rag.

'It's clean. No vomit here,' she said, but took the note just the same.

Once again they squeezed through the labyrinth of cars with green taxi lights. Her father parked alongside the fence, took the notes he had out of various pockets and began putting them into several stacks on the seat, muttering to himself, 'This is for the cashier, this for the repair shop, this for the head driver, this for the boss.'

'What about Grandma?' said Masha.

He didn't answer; he was calculating how much of his pay-off the boss had to give to the manager of the garage and to the Party secretary to split between them. The manager would then give a third of his takings to the head of the district traffic police, while the Party head gave something to the district Party secretary. Who came next and what they got isn't our business. None of them would miss out.

'Hey, wait a minute!' He counted the money again. 'It doesn't come out right!'

He sighed, closed his eyes and rested his head on the wheel, just sitting there for a while.

'Masha!' he yelled. 'There isn't enough money in the proceeds. We drove the old man for free, but what else happened? They must have pulled money out of my pocket in the fight. Give me back the note that I gave you.'

She dug in her dress pocket and found it.

'There. But keep this ten-rouble note, Masha.'

He got out of the car slowly and rubbed his numb back for a long time.

'Dad, the man who told Tikhon to call him – is he nice?'

'What?'

'You know, the one with the squeaks!'

He looked at her, gave a tired sigh and didn't reply. He just slammed the door angrily and disappeared among the cars.

When he got back, Tikhon was already there, sitting in the driver's seat next to Masha.

'Well, your daughter has a sense of humour. I asked her how much you made today. So she shows me the tenner. Ha, ha!'

'It was a bad day, you know!'

'I bet you're just being sneaky! Did you get the stuff from Klavka's? Well, I'm off to make some cash!'

'Goodbye!' said Masha politely and got out into the cold.

'Hah! Goodbye, chickie!'

Masha's father picked her up and carried her like a baby. It was a good thing it had stopped raining. She hugged her father and pushed her nose against his neck. It smelled of shish kebab, petrol and something sweet. They had a long wait for the bus, and then it was at least an hour's ride to where they lived. When they got off the bus, Masha's feet were frozen, and she wasn't sleepy any more.

'Run around a little to get warm!' He put her down in the courtyard and rummaged in his pocket for some change. 'I'll get some cigarettes around the corner, if it's open.'

In the yard the metal swings were creaking. Two girls were swinging in the dark, seeing who could go higher. Masha went over to them.

'I rode around in a taxi all day. You don't think so?' She dug into her pocket. 'Look, I have ten roubles, they're real. Let's play shish kebab café!'

When her father got back to the courtyard Masha was gone. He went upstairs, opened the door with his key and said loudly, 'We're back!'

'And what's that?' His wife saw the cage in his hand.

'It's a parakeet, a multi-coloured one.'

'A parakeet? Am I supposed to be a rubbish collector?'

'It's not rubbish. Masha wanted it.'

'And you were glad to oblige! So where is she, then?'

'Isn't she here?'

He dropped the cage on to the floor and ran downstairs, leaving the door open.

'Where are you rushing off to?'

Masha looked happy as she walked upstairs towards him, licking the wrapper of an ice cream bar.

'You're bringing dirt into the apartment!' Her mother threw up her arms and ran to the bathroom for a rag.

Her father tossed his cap into the corner under the mirror and, with his hand, smoothed down his rumpled hair.

'Give your mother the money, don't forget!'

Masha pulled out a couple of coins.

'Haven't you got any more? Where is it?'

'I bought ice cream for the girls. They really wanted some.'

'What about the change?'

'A man took the change.'

'What man, for God's sake?'

'A big man who needed a shave.'

'So that's it! The man's gone already, of course. But the sales girl? Was it the one with the purple hair? And she didn't say a thing! Let's go, I'm going to pull her hair out!'

'She's closed up already, Dad. She didn't even want to sell any to us.'

'OK, tomorrow I'll let her have it. But don't tell Mum!'

Her mother came in and started to wipe the floor under their feet.

'What are you whispering about?'

'Well, we had brought you some money to tide you over. And tomorrow I'll get my advance at the garage.'

'Finally, you've worked it out!' Mother said, looking pleased. 'You actually can make money when you want to. Everyone else could do it but not you!'

Masha's father dug around in his pockets, winked at her and like a magician he pulled out a couple of crumpled ten-rouble notes. Then he thought for a bit and added a fiver from another pocket. Her mother wiped her hands on her housecoat, smoothed out the notes and looked at him.

'And for this you worked all day?' She wanted to add something more, something insulting, but held back. 'What's that under your eye?'

'Got into a fight.'

'Did you go back to Domodedovo again? Don't go there! You've nearly lost an eye!'

He didn't say anything. Her mother put the money away in her pocket and wiped some drops of rain from his hair. 'You can bring home your pay yourself tomorrow. I won't send Sasha.'

The doorbell rang. It was their neighbour Yevdokia, the attendant on the Moscow–Berlin train. She brought back things that were in short supply, and Masha's mother helped her drop them off at second-hand shops all over the city.

'So did you reap the harvest?' asked Yevdokia. 'Let's have it!'

'But today's Sunday!' said Masha's father, surprised.

'It's the end of the month,' Yevdokia explained. 'They had to stay open today to fulfil their Plan.'

Masha's mother got her bag and counted out 225 roubles. With an ostentatious gesture, Yevdokia returned fifty to her for her trouble.

'Come around later on.' Satisfied, Yevdokia hid the money in her brassière. 'I've got some more stuff. But not now: I've found myself a new boyfriend, and he's coming this evening.'

Winking rather vulgarly at Masha, she disappeared.

'And how much did you pinch from her?' asked her father when the door had shut behind Yevdokia.

'She can check her receipts. But I did sell her old dress to some Uzbeks at the market; that's sixty for me.'

'There, and you still complain.'

'Well, am I supposed to rely on you?'

'Yevdokia has a new boyfriend,' said Masha. 'A policeman, a junior lieutenant. He had a wife, but she upped and left him.'

'How do you know all that?' asked her mother.

'Yevdokia was bragging about it herself downstairs. Guess where Dad and I went? To a shish kebab café! They gave us pickles. It was really good. Is Sasha here?'

'Yes, of course, where else would he be?'

'Has he seen the parakeet?'

Sasha had taken the cage into the kitchen and put it on the table. The parakeet was sleeping, standing on one leg and looking as though he was frowning. Sasha was kneeling in front of a stool, licking stamps and sticking them into an album.

'Look!' He showed her some stamps he'd just taken out of

an envelope. 'I got them today. Grandma gave me some money because I got a B in physics. And I had some money of my own.'

Masha got down on her knees, too. What pretty stamps! Big, bright and with animals on them. Ones you wouldn't even see at the zoo. Sasha collected stamps with animals on them, and Masha did, too.

'Are they foreign?'

'Of course they are! Look, these are the same ones,' Sasha pointed out. 'I tried to sell them at school, but nobody would cough up. Take them if you want!'

She grabbed the three stamps.

'You already owe me for six.' Sasha put the rest in the envelope. 'Now you owe me for nine.'

'But where can I get the money?'

'Where? Save it up and pay me back. Get some money from Mum for ice cream, but don't buy the best kind; get the cheaper kind. Then you'll have money left over. See?'

'Yes, I see. Get money for the best, buy the cheaper kind, and I'll have change left over. And the parakeet will live in the kitchen, won't he?'

Masha's eyelids were drooping. Her father was already lying on the sofa, about to fall asleep. Masha silently went up to her mother and took her hand. Her mother understood. She took her daughter first to the bathroom to wash her face, then to the living-room, undressed her and put a night shirt with pink flowers on her skinny body. She opened the folding bed next to the sideboard, laid Masha down, covered her with a blanket and glanced at her father with a meaningful look.

'You've worn her out completely,' she whispered, this time not angrily at all.

Masha barely heard the words because she was falling asleep. Her father had really been very nice to her all day, driving her around in the car. *The only thing is that he didn't*

let me ride on his belly this evening. That waitress, Lida, is nice;
those pickles she gave us were delicious! Mother's nice, too. And
the parakeet in the cage is wonderful. Sasha's just great. He
bought stamps for himself and sold me three. And money really
does go round. You can get enough for expensive ice cream, then
buy the cheaper kind and have money left over . . .

VALEDICTORY

Gurov, the school principal, didn't know what to do.

There had been no direct orders from above; they had just said, 'Work it out yourself, but be sure the issue is resolved properly by the end of the school year.' Gurov had even gone to the district committee and asked, 'Give me a hint what I should do!' They had replied, 'But we've already told you to make the decision yourself. So do it! If you make the wrong one, we'll correct you.' That was easy to say! If you made a mistake no one would tell you and nobody would remember old favours. That's why Gurov was putting off doing anything at all. But now the school year was coming to an end and he couldn't put the issue off any longer.

A month earlier, commissions from three different government departments had visited the school, one after the other. They had dug around everywhere but had taken care to conceal the actual reason why they had come. Gurov felt in his gut that it had to do with ideology, but with precisely what ideological issue he couldn't ascertain in spite of all his connections. Presumably they hadn't dug up anything very bad, or they wouldn't have left matters up to him. Instead, they would have unravelled the whole affair and made some administrative changes. But now everything had died down, almost.

The situation in his school was no worse than in others and in some respects even better. The teaching staff had stopped feeling flustered as things settled down. But suddenly . . .

'Well, we're glad for your sake that the denunciation was unfounded,' the district committee's head of schools congratulated Gurov.

'Denunciation?' He felt as though he had been struck by lightning.

'You look like you were born yesterday. You know, the anonymous letter, the spark that lit the fire. Claiming that your geography teacher, Pavel Komarik, was praising fascists and American imperialism in class.'

'He did what?' Gurov choked and couldn't stop coughing.

'Don't get so worked up! Perhaps he didn't really mean it. He just let it slip out. He's old and respected, but unfortunately it's a fact that his politics are not in order, so to speak. There's no smoke without fire. If a structure is not permeated with ideology, cracks will appear. Well, there was a draught blowing through one of those cracks. Incidentally, how old is he?'

'Sixty-one.'

'Sixty-one, plus he's not a Party member. You need to do some more work on this. It wouldn't be right for the commissions to have done all this work for nothing! However, the teacher in question is well known all over Moscow, and people will talk. They'll say you're not looking after your staff.'

'Wha . . . what do I do, then?'

'You'll come up with something.'

On his way home Gurov pursed his lips in offence as he recalled a recent teachers' meeting where Komarik had come out with an unsuitable remark. Once a week Gurov held a half-hour session for the entire school at which he read aloud from *Pravda*, but Komarik felt this was rather too premature for the youngest classes and too hard on them to stand to attention.

'You're not keeping up with life, Komarik! They are, after all, the future defenders of our country.' Gurov had been trying to shame him, paying no attention to Komarik's criticism.

Now it turned out that it had been a mistake not to.

Gurov wanted to consult the teachers whom he trusted but was afraid that rumours might start circulating sooner than necessary. He therefore decided to tell nobody except his director of studies, Marina, and to swear her to secrecy. And the only reason he told her was to try to find out who had written the anonymous letter (before they wrote another one about him tomorrow!). But she couldn't guess who it was, either; a lot of teachers could have scribbled the note, to say nothing of offended or malicious parents who were always in abundance.

Gurov didn't hesitate for long. Once he had received instructions he had to carry them out at once. Knowing he could do all the thinking he wanted to later on, Gurov summoned the teachers and instructed them to pay more attention to the Party line, to stress 'our Soviet successes in the sciences'. As for Komarik, Gurov came up with a really brilliant way to deal with him to everybody's satisfaction.

'Mr Komarik,' he said through the door to the teachers' lounge, 'could you come and see me if you have time?'

He walked away quickly, taking a deep breath. People weren't hired for their years but for their politics; morality had nothing to do with it. There was no need to snivel like some member of the intelligentsia. The devil had made Komarik provoke someone badly enough for a complaint to be lodged against him. This was a school, after all, and you had watch what you said. On the other hand, it wasn't so long ago that Gurov had been appointed principal of this school, and he should soon be promoted to the Ministry of Education. If only the teachers wouldn't interpret the action he was now taking as an attempt to curry favour or as love of red tape! They were already calling him 'the colonel' behind his back.

Gurov had, in fact, been mobilized to strengthen the front line of education after leaving the army. But here, as in the army, he always tried to avoid military drills, and whenever possible he allowed people to behave, as it were, not in accordance with regulations. But there were limits! What was he to do if a teacher couldn't cope with his lofty mission? Gurov hadn't invented the practice of getting rid of a man with full honours; that's how it was done everywhere, even at the highest level.

In the meantime Komarik willingly put aside what he was doing, lashed together his old briefcase with its broken lock and propped it up against the wall. He shuffled along the corridor, clearing his throat in anticipation of the conversation, opened the door to the principal's office and stopped in the middle of the room, which was decorated with the obligatory portrait of the Leader. The old teacher remembered that in this old building (itself dating from the beginning of the century when it was still a private school), in this same principal's office, on that same wall, Khrushchev had hung and, before him, a portrait of Stalin and before Stalin, they said, Trotsky and before Trotsky Tsar Nicholas the Last. The portraits of Stalin and Khrushchev (what were you supposed do with them?) were even now stuffed behind the cabinet, covered with dust. Gurov probably didn't even know about them. What if someone needed them again one day?

The principal got up, his stomach brushing the corner of the table as he turned towards the teacher. In theory he'd already made up his mind, but again he hesitated: what if his decision were hasty? But there was no way he could protect the old man. If he did, he'd be guilty himself. Since Gurov was no coward, he wasn't going to retreat now.

'My dear Komarik!' He took the old man by the elbow. 'I hear you were denounced in an anonymous letter. Rubbish! What was it all about?'

'It was serious, not rubbish.' Komarik pulled a fine-toothed comb out of his pocket and combed the moustache that made him look like some foreign nobleman. 'I've used the same example for thirty years, every time we study

Holland, but this is the first time I've had an anonymous letter.'

'What was it you said, specifically?'

'During the war the Germans carried off treasures and technical specialists from other countries. From Holland they took carloads of soil. That's how clever the fascists were.'

'How do you mean?' asked Gurov carefully.

'You see, the Dutch soil is very fertile, everything grows in it even better than in the US state of California.'

'What does California have to do with it?'

'Marina said the same thing: "What does California have to do with it? It would be better to compare it with the Kuban, wouldn't it?" Fine, next year I'll compare it with the Kuban.'

This was the last straw: telling students that the soil in Holland was better than in the Kuban! The old man was completely off his rocker. What had possessed him to make him babble on about all this? And the bit about the wise fascists – that wouldn't do under any circumstances! If he'd kept quiet nobody could have touched him, but now the wheels had started turning, and before it was all over everyone would look like angels except Gurov, who would be the Evil Sorcerer.

'Mr Komarik,' Gurov took the bull by the horns, 'I hear you're getting ready to retire. It's wrong of you to hide the fact from us, yes, very wrong! After all, we're your second family. We, your colleagues, have a counter-proposal: we'll not just see you off, we'll celebrate by inviting the public to your valedictory class. We'll organize the whole thing, that's what we administrators are for.'

Gurov felt awkward as he said this. How could this be a second family, when Komarik had never had a family of his own? What if he thought this was a reference to his long-forgotten affair with the director of studies, Marina, that everyone had been droning on to Gurov about when he arrived at the school?

Komarik hadn't known that he was planning to retire, so he bit his lip and said something like 'Mmm'. He was taken aback, but throughout his life he had never raised any objections to the administration, nor would he do so now. He could object later, to himself, on his way home.

It was as slushy as in the autumn, and yet it was early May. The asphalt on the pavement was broken in places, and puddles, reddish with mud, reflected the fences and the passers-by. The damp got inside him and his briefcase felt heavy, although it was almost empty. All he needed for his classes was inside his head. That colonel, where did he hear that he was retiring? Perhaps he'd had instructions from the district department of public education. It was probably time to get rid of him, useless old codger that he was!

2

In mid-May it got warmer. Komarik opened his window one evening. The kids from the block had gone inside and it was quiet. He sat down at the table, covered with a flower-patterned yellow oilcloth. The table served as both desk and dining table; the line of demarcation went right down the middle.

On the table stood a globe, although it looked more like a watermelon. The blue oceans had faded to yellow blotches. During the war, when there had been no textbooks, the children had made a globe from clay, glued several layers of paper over it, cut it apart, took out the clay, glued together the paper hemispheres and put a wire through the resulting globe. It even turned, crunching and wobbling.

There were lots of mistakes on it: Africa spilled over into Europe, Asia was squeezed down narrower, and both Americas were twisted. Both the globe and the sublunary realm itself were retiring, no longer of any use. In due course, naturally, but in the meantime . . . perhaps he could lodge a complaint somewhere? But who paid attention to complaints nowadays? And they were right: he didn't have much in the way of ideology, and nobody studied geography any more. The main thing was to obey orders, and this had entirely replaced knowledge.

The first time he met the colonel in the hallway after that conversation, he just told him he didn't want any celebration. 'I'll resign quietly and that's it. Why disturb the school and waste the time of busy teachers with this purely personal business?'

'I approve of your modesty and respect it, Komarik,' said Gurov. 'But this is definitely *not* a personal affair. You are, after all, the most senior teacher in the district. You know yourself that the community has a very special relationship with its teachers. I can't really stop people attending your valedictory class. *And* they already know about it at the Department of Education.'

So perhaps the instructions hadn't originated from the Department at all but were initiated from below! The colonel himself had decided that Komarik should retire.

The rhythm of old Komarik's life was broken from that day on. At night he would keep tossing and turning as thoughts crowded into his head, one after the other.

The old man got up from his desk, walked across to the bedside table, pulled out a bundle of photos and untied the ribbon. What year was that? Somewhere near the end of the Second World War. Marina, who was then the botany teacher, was pale and as beautiful as the mother of God.

She lived in the school then, in an annexe that was accessed through a side door. Her father was the school's principal. One year, after the war, Komarik had been called in for questioning; he was asked whether the principal, Marina's father, was distorting the pedagogical direction of the school. They explained to him that the principal had recently borrowed a book by a German pedagogue from a friend. The principal was not distorting anything, but the honest Komarik, who had just come back from the front, hesitated a second before answering and therefore did not sound very convincing. The principal was removed for a reason that had nothing to do with Komarik's hesitation. Nevertheless he couldn't forgive himself for not having been more affirmative and felt guilty later for not asking about the old principal or writing to him.

All this Komarik had explained to Marina, feeling that it would be dishonest to hide it. She interpreted his hesitation as cowardice and told him, with the fervour typical of the young, what she thought of him. Later she forgave him, of course, but their moment had passed. Meanwhile Komarik had married another teacher, who shortly succumbed to a sudden illness that sent her to her grave a few years later. Marina had also married. Komarik never became involved with other women. Things just didn't work out; and Marina, taking pity on him, slept with him from time to time. He'd raised his daughter by himself, and when she married and went away he aged quickly and became a pitiful old man.

Leaving one of the photos on the table, he spun the globe. He thought it would be nice if some of his old students would turn up tomorrow at his last class, but he was not being quite honest with himself. He only thought of his students in general in order to focus on a particular one, Anatoly.

Komarik sat down again, removed his glasses and held the photo up to his eyes. There he was, the third from the right, with the crew cut that was *de rigueur* back then in boys' schools. How many times Komarik used to mention his name at teachers' meetings and district conferences! Not for his own sake, of course, but for the good of the cause.

At Komarik's insistence a large portrait of Academician Anatoly Dorofeyenko, in a black suit with his laureate medals, framed and glassed, was hung in the hall of the senior school on the nail that had earlier supported Academician Lysenko. Now Dorofeyenko was hanging there humbly alongside Darwin, Lomonosov, Mendeleev and other famous scientists, like them without any label with his name on it, stressing his fame.

Komarik occasionally used the academician to admonish his students, claiming that Anatoly had got excellent grades in all subjects. Actually, Anatoly was not so much academically gifted as he was active in the Young Communist League. He got average grades but was involved in everything; that was another way of being gifted. And who could blame Komarik for improving on reality? Perhaps in this particular case the end really did justify the means!

At times it seemed to the old man that Anatoly Dorofeyenko didn't actually exist. He was a plaster cast, a teaching aid. But every so often the legend about the famous student would be documented. The children would bring in newspaper clippings, with lists of people with all their titles and honours, or with interviews where the academician explained the direction of Soviet geography in the light of the latest decrees or how Soviet geography differed from that of the bourgeois West.

Twice, on Komarik's instructions, his students wrote collective letters to Academician Dorofeyenko, and his teacher signed the letters along with the children. Both times the replies were slow in coming, and they were typed and signed by his secretary. The letters said that Dorofeyenko wished everyone success in their studies and work. One of the letters had a handwritten note that said, 'Special greetings to the geography teacher, Pavel Pavlovich Komarik.' The best students recited the letter *con brio* to all the classes.

Actually, if Anatoly did show up for his valedictory it would be very good for the reputation of the school, the district and the city. And the colonel would be sorry that he'd pensioned off the very teacher whose student was bringing glory to the school and to the entire country.

Komarik pulled a heavy silver Pavel Bure watch out of his pocket, twisting the long chain around his finger. This was his secret family pride, all he possessed in memory of his ancestors who had owned a puny little estate near Moscow, burned down during the Revolution just for the sake of it. The old man looked at his watch and went out of his room into the corridor. Three other doors also opened on to it, making up the communal apartment with its common telephone, mounted on the wall, and beside it a pencil hanging on a string.

3

Anatoly Dorofeyenko was regularly woken by calls from Moscow and sometimes even from Paris or Rome as well. He stretched, felt for the light switch, squinted in the bright light and, climbing out of bed, fumbled around on the coffee table for his glasses before answering the telephone.

'From Moscow, a call for you,' said the operator's metallic voice . 'This is Moscow on the line.'

'All right.'

Dorofeyenko yawned, tired. A mooing noise came from the receiver.

'Yes, hello, who is it?'

'Tolik . . . mmm . . . Tolik!'

He yawned again. There were not many people who called him, a greying and distinguished man, by this nick-name. He recognized them easily, but this time he was stumped.

'Tolik, this is Komarik . . .'

'Komarov? Hello, old man. Why are you putting off pub-lishing my monograph? You're getting me angry!'

'No, Tolik, this is Komarik, the geography teacher from your . . . your school, sir.' He changed to the respectful form of address.

'Komarik? Oh yes, yes, I do remember you. How can I help you?'

'You . . . mmm . . . please forgive me, dear boy, for dis-turbing you. I do remember you're in a time zone there.'

'You're in one, too. Everybody is.'

'I meant to say that it's late where you are. Maybe I woke you up?'

'A trifle! What's the problem?'

'What?'

'A trifle, I said.'

'No, it's not a trifle. It's a difference of three hours. But tomorrow I'm giving the last lesson . . . m-m-m . . . of my life. I mean, I'm retiring.'

'Congratulations on a well-deserved rest! I remember how you always used to give me Cs. I admit I deserved them.'

Laughing somewhat insincerely, Dorofeyenko got up and put on his dressing-gown with one arm. Every day he had to talk to all kinds of people, and from the first polite phrases he was usually able to guess what the person wanted. This helped save time. But now, probably because he was sleepy, he couldn't work out why his teacher was calling him.

'Everyone knows, Anatoly, that you're my most talented student.'

'Oh, not at all!'

'Forgive an old man, but they say you're in Moscow almost every day. How about tomorrow? That is, where you are in Novosibirsk, it's today already.'

'Moscow? I have to go there on Thursday for a meeting of the Presidium, then I'll stay to see that French theatre group that's on tour. Today is Wednesday, right?'

'Fly here a day early and stop by your old school! There's going to be a ceremony.'

'A ceremony, you say?'

'Maybe it's hard to get a ticket?'

'Nonsense! When is the lesson?'

'One ten, Moscow time. Everyone here loves you, Anatoly!'

'I can't promise, but I'll try. If you'd only called earlier! I don't belong to myself, you know.'

'Your visit will be a special occasion for the whole school!'

'Well, you've convinced me, old man. You've worn me down, we'll do it your way.' Dorofeyenko didn't notice that he'd slipped into the condescending tone he used to subordinates. 'Goodbye!'

'Have you finished the conversation?' asked the operator. 'I'll disconnect you.'

He cast off his dressing-gown and lay down on his back. His wife pretended not to be awake.

Dorofeyenko slowly took off his glasses and found himself in a projection, a place he had totally forgotten. The old Moscow side street, the school, the entrance with its door ripped off, the war . . . Everything else had probably been razed to the ground, but the school was still standing. Yes, he could get there on the early morning flight. He would be greeted ceremonially, of course. The children in their Pioneer uniforms would salute him, they would give him flowers that he never knew what to do with, and all the rest. How many times had he been honoured like that in other places! It was the same thing every time!

Komarik had already seemed old when Dorofeyenko was at school. *How old would he be now? Why did I follow this path in life? Was it thanks to him or in spite of him? Or did he have nothing to do with it? When I retire, I'll address that question in my memoirs. His valedictory class . . . But, thinking about it, it'll be just the same for me – my last publication, my last televised lecture, my last international congress, my last steps . . . I never had time to write anything for myself; first I wrote for others, and now others write for me!*

Dorofeyenko's arms lay crossed over his chest, and he shifted them to his sides. *As Leo Tolstoy said, don't ask why you live, only ask what you should do! It would be nice to honour my old teacher. One must remain human in every way, at any rank, but vanity gets in the way. We're victims. Swallowed whole by science. Tomorrow it's the district committee meeting; they'll manage without me – I hope Temyakin doesn't defy me and go off to Spain himself! Then there's the reception for the Englishmen, but I can shrug that off on to someone else. What else important is there?*

'Are you going to be flying off?' asked his wife sleepily; she was used to his constant trips.

'Well, as you know. . .'

He didn't complete the sentence but turned out the lamp.

4

In the early morning Komarik went to the laundry for the starched shirt that he didn't like because it scratched his neck. He made some strong tea and drank it, as always, with a piece of cheese but no bread. He stuck his briefcase under his arm and went to the door but turned around, put it down on the chair beside the table and walked out without it.

At his school lessons were proceeding peacefully. The corridors were empty. Steps rang out, but it was only the janitor, Nastya, clanking her bucket. Through the doors teachers' familiar voices could be heard.

'Mr Komarik, my dear, where have you been?' the director of studies called out as she came running towards him, waving her hands dramatically. 'The colonel's worried. Go and see him right away!'

How dressed up Marina was today! She was clearly a happy woman and only pretending to be sad. Her husband was a machine-shop boss at an armaments factory, she had three children and she loved her work, which is a rare thing nowadays.

Komarik entered the principal's office, biting his lip and muttering, 'Mmm, Dorofeyenko might come. It's possible . . .'

'Aha!' Gurov was so surprised he got up. 'Well, good for you, Komarik! As they say, no comment.'

This really was something for Gurov to exclaim about. A Stalin Prize winner, member of the Central Committee, president of some kind of international association for peace and honorary member of several European academies – a man like that and in his school in person! The old man had hit the bull's eye! Of course the guest would have to be ceremonially greeted, as was customary. For his students and teachers this visit would be a major positive factor.

The principal put his fist over his mouth, looked at the teacher and suddenly regretted that he'd thought badly of him.

'You've really made us happy with this information, my dear Komarik,' he said, 'very happy. Go on, get ready for your class. We'll take care of the arrangements. The only thing is, don't forget to maintain your ideology at a high level. We've got no use for Holland and even less for California, you understand! Stress our own nation's achievements more, stress patriotism! Oh, yes, and ask the director of studies to come and see me!'

When the door closed behind the teacher, Gurov opened his safe. It contained several bottles of cognac and a box of chocolate, for special guests. As usual, the visit must conclude in his office. The principal took out a bottle that had already been opened, splashed a small dose into a glass, swallowed it, smacked his lips, ate a piece of chocolate, locked the safe and picked up the telephone. He dialled the number of a friend of his at the newspaper *Vechernyaya Moskva* and told him what was up.

'Do you understand the significance of this? Then send a reporter at once and maybe a photographer!'

Marina ran in, breathless.

'Where on earth have you all been?' the principal asked. 'Is the banner ready?'

'Everything's just rosy.'

'Did you work out what to write?'

'It's very cordial, like you said. We wrote, "Farewell, Dear Teacher, Mr Komarik".'

Gurov made a wry face.

'Is something wrong?' Marina asked anxiously.

The principal rubbed his fingers together, as if he were feeling the banner.

'Uh ... uh ... that could be misunderstood, don't you think? Get the seniors to redo it: not "Farewell" but "Goodbye". This isn't a funeral. And then ... "Dear Teacher". You know there's only one Teacher! And to call Komarik that! We might get in trouble again. Well, that's all, I think. So, "Goodbye, Mr Komarik". And maybe an exclamation mark. That's all.'

Marina nodded and turned to run out. The colonel was right, the text *was* stupid. How come she hadn't seen it herself?

'By the way,' called the principal, after first letting his eyes rest on her curvaceous bottom. 'What about flowers?'

'We've collected the money, and the children have already bought flowers in the market. They aren't very beautiful, but it's the best they could get.'

'I'd like to ask you,' Gurov hesitated, ' please, to divide the flowers into two bouquets.'

'Two?'

'Yes, two. Academician Dorofeyenko is coming.'

'Oh, my goodness!'

'A bit less emotion and more action, please! Track down the senior Pioneer leader. Let her get the Pioneers ready for the reception, suitably dressed – white shirts, dark trousers and red scarves. I don't think we need the bugler and the flag; it isn't that sort of event. Call the Young Communist League secretary and tell him to have all the members wear their badges. Check everything personally!'

Blushing with excitement, Marina was about to ask about something, but Gurov indicated that he didn't want any more discussion. He checked that the safe was locked, closed the office door and set off for the teacher's lounge.

The lounge was crowded and the noise was almost as loud as in the halls during breaks. The teachers of the lower years had dismissed their classes and were putting in an appearance, one and all. The upper-year teachers, including those who wanted to skip the event (they had enough to do as it was, without this) and those who felt that the class would be something like a requiem for the dead but didn't say so out loud – all of them nevertheless came to the lounge, fearing the colonel's ire. Staff members and guests were standing around in groups. The instructor from the district committee stood by himself with an expression of great responsibility on his youthful face, which was pudgy from lack of physical activity.

The guests asked the teachers in whispers where the Academician was, and were answered by shrugs. The correspondent from *Vechernyaya Moskva* was telling the head of the Department of Education about a typographical error that had occurred a few years back. Instead of the phrase 'pioneer in space' they had printed 'pensioner in space', the typesetter's idea of a joke.

'The typesetter should have been pensioned off!' joked the head of the Department of Education in return.

'And the editor should have been sent off into space,' added the correspondent gloomily. 'Incidentally, why does your geography teacher have such a Jewish-sounding name?'

'He's clean and of pure Russian stock, according to his passport,' the Education Department head replied quickly.

'But the readers haven't seen his passport. I don't care, but the editor wants to be on the safe side.'

Again and again newcomers walked up to Komarik, who was holding himself aloof. They shook his hand and slapped him on the back and wished him luck in private life. He nodded with a guilty smile, taken aback by the felicitations.

'Did you put extra chairs in the classroom?' somebody called out.

'Yes, we did.'

'Put in some more,' ordered Gurov. 'Take them from the assembly hall.'

Gurov, clutching his keys in his fist, stood by the door

with one foot in the lounge and the other in the corridor, so as not to miss anything.

At exactly 1.10 the janitor, Nastya, wearing a green flowered dress and a dark blue men's jacket with a 'Victory over Japan' medal, wiped her hands on her hem and, with a military bearing that nobody suspected her capable of assuming, marched up to the bell switch.

'Wait,' the principal stopped her. 'I'll tell you when to ring it.'

'But it's time now!'

'Time can wait.'

He leaned over to Marina. 'Are the Pioneers stationed at the entrance?'

She made a startled gesture. 'Everything is rosy!'

'Hmmm, yes . . .'

'The class is on tenterhooks, and Komarik isn't made of steel either,' she whispered. 'Maybe we should cancel the lesson, uh, put it off for a bit?'

'No chance!' Gurov frowned, looked around the teachers' lounge and lowered his voice. 'People from the district committee are here, from the Department of Education and from other schools. OK. Dorofeyenko is late, but it might be even better that way. He'll come straight to the classroom, escorted by the Pioneer detachment – see what I mean? An excellent moment in education: teacher and student, meeting before the children and the community. The return of the prodigal son. I'm joking, of course, you understand. Anyway, let's get started. I'd like you to stand by the entrance and personally supervise the Academician's greeting.'

'Stay there?' Marina clasped her hands together, bewildered. 'But what about the lesson?'

'Well, we mustn't put our personal wishes before our duty.' He turned to the other woman. 'Nastya, ring away!'

'Ring, Nastya, ring! Keep your wits about you!' Marina took her in hand.

Gurov turned to the group. 'Let's have the class bell! Please, comrades! Dear Mr Komarik, are you ready? Then let's be off, let's go!'

'So where's your honoured guest?' asked the correspondent.

'Don't worry,' Gurov reassured him. 'All in due time.'

Nastya wiped her hands on her dress and raised her arm like someone giving a gun crew the order to open fire. She flicked the switch, but there was no bell.

'Jammed again, damn it! How many times have I asked for it to be repaired, but it never does any good!'

She flicked it from side to side and banged her fist on the side of the switch box. The staff members started to smile.

'The school isn't in a hurry for your last lesson, is it, Komarik?' said the head of the Department of Education.

Komarik had been standing there all pale, but now he suddenly blushed, as if it was his fault that the bell wasn't ringing. 'I'm sorry,' whispered the old man.

Finally Nastya smartly smacked the switch with the flat of her hand, and the bell grated, fell silent and then started clanging like mad, deafening everyone.

Komarik, in a brown suit that smelled of mothballs, moved out of the lounge with uncertain steps, brandishing his pointer not like a lance but like a walking stick. Marina squeezed his elbow and walked a couple of steps with him, and he nodded to her absent-mindedly.

Down the corridor that Nastya had just washed, where the stern face of Academician Dorofeyenko hung beside Darwin, Lomonosov and the rest, the procession followed the geography teacher towards Classroom 9B. At the door, the old man stopped to let the crowd in before him.

The students, exhausted by the wait, banged down their desk tops and craned their necks to see who was coming in. They took malicious delight in how the guests jostled one another to get seats. The Department of Education head squeezed with difficulty into a desk beside the correspondent. There weren't enough extra chairs, so some students got up from the desks at the back and sat down three by three.

When Komarik came in, straight away he caught sight of the red banner with its white letters spelling out 'Goodbye, Mr Komarik!'

'Hello!' he said hoarsely.

Everybody laughed at the witty remark and applauded. The straight-A student Sarycheva, with her Pioneer scarf and a Komsomol badge on the no-longer-childish breast squeezed into her school uniform, raised her hand and asked without waiting for permission, 'Mr Komarik, is it true that Dorofeyenko is coming?'

She was trying to please him, but Komarik mumbled something indistinct, sat down at his desk and buried himself in the class report book. Sarycheva shrugged and looked at the principal, who shook his head and put his finger to his lips.

Komarik's throat tickled and his eyes were watering from the tension. A dread of saying something ideologically incorrect was drilling into his consciousness. As if to spite him, a tooth started to ache – he should have had it pulled long before. He kept adjusting his glasses, an ill-fitting pair that hurt the bridge of his nose. *They're glad I'm leaving*, it suddenly occurred to him, and there was no way he could get rid of that thought, although he didn't really believe it.

With difficulty he noted in the report book who was absent and glanced around to see whether the political world map was in place. Good, it was hanging where it should be. At the back of the room the guests were still finding seats.

Komarik didn't know what a valedictory class should be like. During the day he'd been thinking that he might tell the students about himself and about life. But would it be appropriate now in the presence of official personages – who knew of the anonymous letter – to speak about life in general during a geography lesson? Wouldn't that show a lack of political awareness? He started, as usual, by quizzing the students. It would be inappropriate to call on the weakest ones and embarrassing to call on the best ones: what would be the point of showing off? He quizzed those with average grades. Frightened by their historic mission, the mediocre students gave mediocre answers, even worse than usual.

Looking out at his class, Komarik couldn't forgive himself for haing blabbed to the colonel about Anatoly. He'd started snivelling in his old age. If Anatoly just showed up, it would have been fine, but if he didn't, nobody would have known.

The guests whispered to each other about things that had nothing to do with the lesson. The kids kept looking at the door, waiting for the Academician to arrive. Sitting at a desk alongside a gangly numbskull, Gurov watched the minute hand on the clock and closely observed the head of the Department of Education and the instructor from the district committee. Their faces didn't give anything away.

At first Gurov expected the door to open any minute and admit the bemedalled Academician Dorofeyenko, who would stride into the class accompanied by an escort of Pioneers. That would be the climax of the valedictory. If Komarik didn't think to call his famous student to the blackboard, Gurov would have to suggest it tactfully. Something like that would sound good in *Vechernyaya Moskva*. But now the lesson was already half over. Dorofeyenko hadn't shown up and wouldn't do so; there was no point in nursing any illusions. Maybe Komarik had simply made it all up, hoping for support to avoid being pensioned off.

Komarik now went up to the map and started speaking while he moved the pointer here and there.

The old man could give an interesting lecture, but Gurov was only half listening to him as he looked around the room. The students weren't listening but thinking of other things, yawning, passing around notes and giggling. For them this important event was happening on another wavelength. *Yes, only we, the adults, can understand and respect old age! Maybe the school has acted too harshly? But that's the way of the world. I was just told to push the button. Even from the point of view of human morality – and we're not obliged to adhere to it – there was no other way out. Kids grow up and then elbow aside the old folks. I've found a replacement who seems suitable, a young geography teacher who doesn't seem stupid. She's a Russian, and a Party member to boot. The main thing is, she's good-looking. Something to rest my eyes on and maybe not just my eyes.*

Komarik suddenly fell silent. He was choking. The words were rushing and bubbling on their way out but didn't have the strength to jump off his tongue. All his life he had been oppressed by the fear of saying the wrong thing. This fear had crippled his mind and eaten into his knowledge. He knew he'd become a nonentity, but what could he have done, how could he have survived otherwise? There was an embarrassed silence. He swallowed, started to speak, and swallowed again. Gurov raised his eyebrow and almost thought, *Hey, the old man is getting forgetful, he's senile!* Finally Komarik got a grip on himself, coughed and started speaking again.

His internal clock was running and, just as he uttered his last words, the bell rang. The A-student Sarycheva pulled out a bouquet of flowers wrapped in cellophane from under her desk, adjusted her childishly short dress and gave it to the teacher. The second bouquet remained under her desk.

The classroom started to move and make noise. Everyone was mixed up together – the hosts, the guests and the students from the next class, clustered outside the door, who had heard that a real live Academician had come, the one who was hanging in the corridor.

'Komarik . . . bit the dust,' said the head of the Department of Education into the correspondent's ear.

'Well, how was the lesson? Did you like it?' asked Gurov, just in case.

'Not bad,' answered the correspondent politely, glancing at his watch. He was thinking that he'd wasted two hours; without the Academician he wouldn't get more than ten lines, and he'd only get peanuts for it. A good thing he hadn't dragged a photographer along for nothing.

The district instructor leaned over to the head of the Department of Education. 'That Academician of yours, he's turned into a heavyweight. When he was on our register here he'd come running to the district committee on tiptoe. Between you and me, do you know what he got his prizes and medals and stuff for? For deciphering spy-satellite photographs! He's not allowed abroad on his own; he's a security risk. And he's built himself a summer house, not in Siberia but here in the Moscow suburbs, and it's a lot grander than what our district Party secretary has!'

Standing surrounded by tall children who were happy now because they could yell, the old man was worrying about Anatoly. He couldn't simply have forgotten! He had promised, so something must have prevented him from coming. The lesson had been boring and grey. *It's my own fault that I didn't live up to their expectations. And Gurov is sure to grumble about some ideological level that I forgot. I should have spoken about something topical.*

'Komarik, my dear friend!' It was Marina who came running into the classroom. 'Everything was rosy!'

She hugged Komarik, her arms around his neck, and whispered, 'The colonel, that is, the principal, he had a job for me to do, but in my thoughts I was here with you in your class!'

She looked into the old man's darting and tear-filled eyes and wanted to kiss him but shied off with the principal there.

'Do you know why Dorofeyenko didn't get here?' Komarik finally gathered his wits and addressed the principal. 'Siberia is snowed in. I caught the weather forecast this morning with half an ear. I was thinking it didn't matter, but there's a blizzard there. In a blizzard you can't . . .'

The janitor Nastya came running into the classroom, all out of breath, and looked around for Gurov. She pulled a piece of paper out of a ragged pocket in her jacket, straightened it out across her stomach and handed it to the principal.

'Not now, Nastya. Go away!' Gurov waved her off. 'Can't you see I'm busy?'

'Eek! It's urgent!' Nastya explained. 'I ran and ran to catch you in time.'

Gurov opened the telegram, looked through it and cried out, 'Comrades! Don't leave the room! It's an urgent telegram, I'll read it out . . .'

Everyone stopped and fell silent. A couple of students climbed on top of their desks. Someone slammed a desk top down and was hushed.

'I'll read it,' Gurov announced theatrically. '*Offer sincere apologies in connection with impossibility of being at celebration stop important government business stop heartfelt congratulations to teachers collective comma students comma firm handshake comma hug for Mr Komarik stop signed his faithful student Academician Dorofeyenko.*'

Everyone applauded. Gurov held out the telegram to the old man, who received it with both hands – the way you take bread and salt at a welcoming ceremony – and bowed. Komarik looked at it, but the lines on it were jumping around and he couldn't read a word.

'How wonderful!' exclaimed Marina. 'Isn't that just wonderful?'

'I have a suggestion,' said the principal, retrieving the telegram from Komarik. 'We should read out this telegram in every class, on ceremonial occasions.'

'Maybe not,' Marina whispered in his ear.

'But why not?' Gurov looked at her in surprise.

She leaned towards him and whispered, 'I sent it myself.'

'From Siberia?'

'The mother of a girl in my class works at the telegraph office. I ran there and asked her to help me. She did, and everything was rosy.'

'Hmmm, yes.' Gurov scratched his neck and narrowed his eyes.

The guests, teachers and students were milling in a crowd in the corridor. Adroitly running ahead of them, the principal spread his arms, letting through the students and sieving out his guests. When the visitors were all standing in front of him, he announced, 'I would like to ask my honoured guests to come into my office for a brief discussion of the lesson. You teachers are free to go . . .'

He turned and hurried to his office to uncork the bottles.

Unneeded, as it turned out, the second bouquet was about to be divided up among the long-legged girl students, but Marina noticed and took it away, saying that it should go to the teachers' lounge. Once in the lounge, she thought better of it and took the flowers home with her.

Everyone had forgotten Komarik. He was the last to leave the classroom. He looked back at the red banner above the blackboard and thought, *What if I asked to give one more final class? With nobody but students. Would the colonel allow that, or not?*

30 FEBRUARY

> 'What happens to us in reality is completely unreal.'
> – Oscar Wilde

I

The liquor section of the store was fenced off by a wall of boxes full of empty bottles, so that the winos wouldn't cast their pall over the more conscientious and less drink-prone part of the population. There was a snake of human bodies crawling from it all the way back to the door, as there always was at the end of the working day.

'You last in line?'

'That's right!'

Kravchuk winced but took his place behind a tidy old man carefully clutching four empty quarter-litre bottles to his chest. The snake was getting nervous. Vodka was running low, and the queue was moving slowly, or at least seemed to be moving slowly to Kravchuk because he'd been in a cranky mood all day.

Unlike more fortunate people, Albert Kravchuk got to celebrate his birthday only once every four years, when 29 February came around. He'd been born in just such a year thirty-six years before, and since then he'd waited for every birthday four times longer than most other people.

Naturally, he hadn't said a word about the occasion to anyone at work that morning. But the bookkeeper, Kamilyá – whose friends just simplified her Tatar name into Milya – by some uncanny instinct had taken a look at the chart that was taped on to the bottom of one of her desk drawers. And there it was: under 'Name of Merchandise' it said 'Albert Kravchuk', under 'Type' it said 'Economist' and under 'Delivery Date' '29 February'.

'If anyone asks, I'm out on committee business,' she said.

Everyone knew how Kamilyá operated. She would get the wallet out of her handbag and, as the authorized Birthdays and Funerals rep for the local committee, make the rounds of the offices of the Department for Calculation of the Optimum Reserve of Spare Parts. In actuality, not only was there no reserve but there were no spare parts either. None the less the management of the department regularly received bonuses and even held the Administration's rotating socialist-competition trophy.

Bonuses are bonuses, but collecting money as an authorized representative was no simple business. If you told Sklertsov that everyone was putting in a rouble he'd put in three. But Shubin, his deputy, would take his time digging around in his pockets and finally ask you to come back later. He reckoned Kamilyá would just forget about it this time, but he had the wrong girl.

'Yours is every year and his is only once every four,' she announced bluntly. 'So stop being such a skinflint!'

Shubin, the coward, asked how much Sklertsov had given then suddenly remembered that, yes, maybe he did have something lying around somewhere, reached into his safe and came up with two roubles. The rank and file all put in about fifty kopeks apiece. Kamilyá discreetly passed over Kurintsova, whose husband had just left her; she had two children. Then, for the people away on business trips, she borrowed a bit from petty cash, so they'd be paying back double.

Before lunch Kamilyá told Albert that today was her dieting day and not to save her a place in the queue at the snack bar. 'It doesn't look like you need to diet,' said Kravchuk, looking her over, pretending not to understand what she was up to.

Kamilyá smoothed her skirt. 'I'm twenty-three. And a half. My mother started putting on weight at twenty-five.'

Kamilyá had come back an hour later and placed a package in front of Kravchuk without a word. Now, while the snake was busy soaking up its alcohol, Kravchuk opened his briefcase. In it was the package, with three ties. The ties were wide, which not so long ago had still been in fashion, and each had its matching handkerchief. These ties were enough to last Kravchuk the rest of his life, especially considering that he never wore one. They choked you. He'd worn a tie only three times in his life: for the *viva voce* defence of his thesis, for his marriage at the Register Office and at his father's funeral.

Kamilyá had watched with an ironic smile as he tried them on, which she'd demanded he do straight after giving him the present on everyone's behalf. 'Economically speaking, you were born at a disadvantage,' she said. 'You give four times more than you get.'

'What am I supposed to do – celebrate the day I was conceived?'

'Babies are found in cabbage patches,' she explained, fluttering her eyelashes, which she touched up with mascara twice a day, right in front of Kravchuk. 'Hey, is your wife really Jewish?'

'Why do you ask?'

'Oh, nothing. But I'm sure that's why you never get promoted.'

'Shows how much you know. Molotov's wife is Jewish.'

'But he saw the error of his ways: he went and had her locked up.'

'Well, Kosygin's wife is Jewish, too.'

'No one knows that for sure. Listen, if you'd just join the Party and try to get over it –'

'I snore too loud. I'd never make it through the meetings.'

'How awful! How could anyone love a man who snores? By the way, you've got a job to do . . .'

According to custom, Kravchuk had to go out and get cake and something to drink. Everyone would come with their cups, lock the door and try to get their money's worth, with interest, for what they'd contributed. But Kravchuk had only enough money for just one bottle of dry wine. He'd ignore Kamilyá's hint and just suppress the idea of collective reimbursement at his expense.

He was almost at the counter. The old man handed over his four empty bottles in exchange for a full one. The old man fingered the cork, testing its seal and thrust the small bottle into his pocket. The saleswoman was banging a coin on the counter, urging the snake along.

'Gurdzhaani,' Kravchuk blurted out, now the snake's head.

'Anything else?'

'That'll do.'

'What else, I'm asking you! Where am I supposed to find you Gurdzhaani?'

'You're out of it? But you just had some –'

Kravchuk had seen people leaving with bottles of the good wine.

'Now you see it, now you don't! Come on, I haven't got all day!'

'Then I'll take some . . . Alzhirskoye.' He pointed to a row of bottles of cheap wine with identical red labels.

Kravchuk put the bottle into his briefcase, on top of the ties. He fought his way out of the shop and tramped towards the metro but stopped at the corner to take a look at the classified-ads board. For a long time he and his wife had been talking about swapping their room in a communal apartment for a one-room flat. And although they didn't foresee having the huge amount of money needed for the unofficial payment of the difference any time soon, Yevgenia was persistently searching for other alternatives and Kravchuk checked the classified ads on message boards from time to time.

But he much preferred reading the ads that had nothing to do with him. He would memorize them and quote them. Kamilyá would laugh, 'My God, we've got so many idiots!'

But Yevgenia would get angry, saying, 'Haven't you got anything better to do!' She was practical, and in a woman this was both a great virtue and a major shortcoming.

He read: 'Child needs English- and French-speaking nanny. Will provide accommodation. Address: Tbilisi, Georgia . . .'

Kravchuk didn't know any languages, and he wasn't about to drag himself down to Tbilisi to be a nanny for some aristocrat.

'MosFilm Studios needs monocles, fans, canes, snuff boxes and nineteenth-century costume jewellery.'

Kravchuk didn't have any nineteenth-century costume jewellery either.

'Lost: gold watch with band – memento of deceased husband. If found, please call to receive thanks.'

Kravchuk hadn't found any watches recently, and if he had found one he would have sold it to pay off his debts.

'The clown school of the Moscow State Circus announces a new intake. Applications accepted until 1 March.'

Albert snorted, and something warm stirred in his consciousness. He shifted his briefcase with the bottle of Alzhirskoye, as heavy as a bomb, into his other hand and let his eyes wander around the board some more. For some reason everyone who was looking to exchange things was offering something worse for something better, and he needed it to be the other way around. If he came across something suitable, Yevgenia would exclaim, 'Oh! This is the perfect present for your birthday!'

It was a shame they didn't raffle off flats in the lottery. Although it would be a stupid idea to play games of chance with the government – *After all, we are economists, and we aren't completely clueless about these things* – for even the tiniest hope of getting a private apartment Kravchuk would buy tickets. The government didn't have the faintest idea how to make money, but it could have made lots.

He was already standing, jammed into the metro, on his way home. He was supposed to get off in the centre of town, go to Children's World and buy Zoya a present, but he'd just get shoved around for a solid hour and not buy anything anyway: *Those aren't toys there; they're junk.*

Hunger drove him home. As he was changing trains, there was a jam on the escalator, as there always was during rush-hour. Twelve years before, Kravchuk had read that there would soon be monorails and flying taxis in Moscow. He gulped.

2

His key stuck in the lock, which had long ago needed replacing. Yevgenia ran out into the hallway.

'Slice the bread. Everything's ready!'

Holding her flour-spattered hands in mid-air, she gave him a kiss on the cheek. *That means she remembers. And our flatmates aren't home. They're often not home, thank God.*

Zoya rolled like a biscuit into the corridor.

'Bunny, don't come any closer, I'm cold. Anything new at school?'

Zoya was hopping around on one foot.

'There's good news and there's bad news.'

'What's the bad news?'

'Doing addition in my head. The principal tested us one by one. Mama says that I'm slow, like you!'

'Me? Two economists in the family, and our daughter doesn't know how to count . . .'

Kravchuk handed her the bottle.

'It's heavy. Don't drop it.'

Because their flatmates were away, they were able to drink some of the wine and eat their potatoes in the kitchen. They always ate potatoes, the only difference being the way they were cooked. Then Yevgenia put Zoya to sleep. Albert wanted to pour them more wine.

'You've already got me dead drunk. Last birthday' – her eyes sparkled maliciously – 'you were thirty-two. And now? Are you really thirty-six? Look at all those grey hairs! I'm sick of plucking them out.'

Yevgenia was consoling herself by reproaching Albert for getting older. Although they had graduated from the Institute of Economics in the same year, her birthday was in the autumn. For the next six months she could consider herself younger. With age, her sense of irony had grown. She'd perfected the art of finding signs of ageing in others, thereby diverting attention from herself.

'Thirty-six,' she continued. 'Next time you'll be forty.'

'And the time after that, forty-four.'

'Everyone's getting somewhere in life, but what are *we* doing?'

The 'we' represented a delicate softening of her reproach. But its direction was obvious.

'What makes you think "everyone" is?'

'That's what they write in the newspapers . . .'

'Have more faith!'

He decided that there wouldn't be a better time to give her the good news.

'By the way, tomorrow I'm handing Sklertsov my resignation.'

Yevgenia looked at him suspiciously. 'Is this a joke?'

'I'm serious.'

'Khaimov! So Khaimov really wasn't just babbling then? He's kept his promise and he's taking you on? He takes business trips abroad . . . What did I tell you? Khaimov is a serious guy. He has a real sense of duty.'

'A sense of debt.'

'Don't make fun!'

'He used to chase after you.'

'Nonsense. There was nothing between us. There was only you.'

'Do you regret that?'

'Oh, stop it! Khaimov will carry right on moving up the ladder, until they find out that his father was Khaymovich.'

'How do you know that?'

'Don't pester me! He told all the other Jews that.'

'Somehow *I* never heard.'

'You're a Russian, so you didn't hear. Well, they'll definitely give you one-eighty, maybe even two hundred. We'll buy a vacuum cleaner . . . Oh, just think of it! I could tell you were excited about something.'

'I'm not going to work for Khaimov.'

'You're not?' Her eyes widened.

'Mum!' Zoya shouted from the other room.

'Zoya, go to sleep this instant! I'm busy. Albert, stop torturing me. Where are you going?'

'To clown school.'

'What, are they in charge of the economy now?'

'Our economy would collapse without them. I'm going to study. To be a clown.'

She came around the table, raised her hand to her forehead and clicked her heels, saluting. 'As your faithful wife, I'll go with you.'

'They don't take women.'

'What, are you serious?'

'I'm serious. They don't take women.'

'I'm not talking about that – are you serious? Is the grant going to be more than you're making now?'

'I didn't ask.'

'Oh, you didn't ask! You're making one-fifty now. And you don't have any problems with Jewish connections. You'll get a promotion –'

'But afterwards the salary will be incredible, Yevgenia!

And going on tour abroad . . . Get me my cigarettes from the briefcase. Don't you see, I used to dream of this when I was a kid. Well, once in my life I've got to take a risk. Or we'll go on for ever stuck in a rut like this –'

'A risk?' Her voice came back from the corridor, where she had gone to get his briefcase. 'What's this here?' She returned with the ties dangling from her hands. 'What are these?' she repeated in despair, waving the ties. 'Your props, or whatever they call them? These are Soviet-made! They could have shelled out for Polish ones, at least. They're so tacky, it's disgusting just to hold them!'

Yevgenia flung the ties on to the chair. Her eyes were filled with tears.

'What's the matter?' He was bewildered. 'What is it?'

'Have you forgotten how you used to go and play hockey at night? How much money you spent on equipment? And what did you say? You said you felt you had what it took to make the all-star team. A year and a half, with Zoya in my arms, I helped you try to make it. And the result?'

'You know how good my reflexes are. For a goalkeeper that's an indispensable quality.'

'They never let you any further than the stands!'

'A bit longer and they would have. My plans changed –'

'Changed! You went to the ballet class at that stupid cultural centre. "I have everything it takes. They go straight into the professionals after this." Didn't you keep repeating that for two years?'

'It's not my fault that talentless people make it more easily in the arts. They're more obnoxious, they have nothing to lose. But they know they have everything to gain.'

'So now you have talent!'

'They said it themselves, I'm supple!'

'With your height? A Nureyev, is that it?'

'Listen, Yevgenia, from what I understand, clown school is absolutely serious. Why should I suffocate in that dump with that scum Shubin for one-fifty? Let all those damned spare parts burn in hell. They don't even exist anyway – it's all just a load of crap.'

'And I have to live alone and not be able to count on you – again? And then you'll come up with something else, and again it'll be "absolutely serious". That's what you call a man, a real provider for his family. Look around. Look at Sofia – at least *her* husband finished writing his dissertation.'

'Yeah, he finally sweated it out after nine years.'

'And the Likuts, both of them at the Institute with us, look at what kind of progress they've made – we're no match for them.'

'Their uncle happens to work at Central Planning, you know.'

She stood up in the middle of the kitchen and lifted her skirt up to her thighs, showing him the runs in her tights.

'You don't give a damn what men think about your wife.'

'They've got no business looking there.'

'They can tell anyway. By the way, Sofia gave me these tights, her old ones –'

'Yevgenia, I want to go into the arts. They look after their own. All you have to have is patience.'

'Go wherever you want!'

'You don't trust me?'

'I've had enough! I'm tired of living with a nobody.'

'I'm a nobody? Take a look around. At least I don't drink –'

'Go ahead and drink. Drink, sing, play, dance . . . Zoya and I are moving in with my mother.'

She put a chair in front of the wardrobe, resolutely pulled an empty suitcase from the top shelf and took it into their room. Then she came back out, tossed him an old quilt and slammed the door to their room after her, shooting the bolt.

But Kamilyá would live with this nobody and be happy. Kravchuk wandered around the kitchen absent-mindedly. It wouldn't really be a birthday if he didn't have any tea.

He made some strong tea, pouring what was left of their tea leaves into the pot, took their flatmates' transistor radio from the windowsill and, taking advantage of its owners' absence, began to search the airwaves. There was nothing to be heard except the crackling sound of the jamming devices, which all his friends called 'KGB jazz'. They jammed everything they could, even their own idiotic broadcasts.

Hoping that their flatmates wouldn't come back tonight and he could have the kitchen all to himself, Albert got the folding bed down from the same top shelf and set it up between the stove and the kitchen table. He laid the torn quilt over it and slid under it without undressing. Why bother with sheets when it was simpler without them? That was his last significant thought of the evening.

3

The kitchen window faced east. Light reflecting off the side of the nickel-plated teapot was dazzling, and Albert opened his eyes. The entire kitchen was flooded with sunlight. Yesterday had been winter, but today he had confidence that, from now on, the future held nothing but spring.

No one had woken him up. Their flatmates, God bless them, hadn't come back. Yevgenia and Zoya were gone. Even if the monorail had already been built Kravchuk would still have been late for work. He stretched sweetly on the creaky folding bed, squinting in the sunlight. Then he got up, took an egg out of the refrigerator, cracked it with a knife and poured it raw into his mouth. He put a lump of sugar on to his tongue and began to suck yesterday's cold brew from the teapot.

His breakfast eaten, he went out and stopped the first government car that came along, which took him to work. 'How could you pay that much? We could buy the child almost a kilo of apples for that much,' Yevgenia would always say. But, once again, he could.

'Oh, what are we going to do now?' Kamilyá was all nerves when he arrived at the office. 'Shubin came by. I told him you were at the suppliers' and that you'd be back after lunch. But watch out, he might have called over there and checked up.'

'I don't give a damn about Shubin or any of his crap, Kamilyá!' Kravchuk said, rising up slightly on his toes. 'To hell with Sklertstov, too. Give me a blank sheet of paper.'

She brought him a clean sheet on the palms of her hands, but as he tried to take it she hid it behind her back.

'First tell me why you need it, then you'll get it.'

Involuntarily, he put his arms around her, and their lips touched. Kamilyá was very fond of these sorts of games.

'I'm giving notice,' he said, 'of my resignation.'

She was instantly serious and tried to work out if he was kidding.

'You're leaving? For good?! Well, how do you like that! You're always the lucky one. I never am. I'm still paying for the Tatar-Mongol yoke.'

Perching on the edge of the chair, he wrote out the word 'Notice' in sprawling handwriting and added below, 'At my own desire, I hereby request . . .' Kravchuk carefully wrote out the 'my own' with relish, and signed broadly at the bottom with an elegant zigzag that consisted mainly of the two large letters A and K.

Kamilyá's eyes shone with tenderness, the fear of parting and something else, probably admiration for Kravchuk's daring. He winked at her and walked out with a swagger.

Kravchuk waved the sheet of paper at Sklertsov's secretary, letting her know this was important business. In the office, two people from the research section were leaning over Sklertsov. Smiling, Kravchuk tapped on his fellow-worker's elbow for him to shut up and step aside. Wordlessly and with dignity, Albert stretched his hand out to his boss. The latter was surprised but got up from his seat and shook it.

'Well, now, Sklertsov,' Albert asked familiarly. 'Still pondering those same old norms? That's not quick enough! Those should have been approved ages ago!'

Sklertsov raised his eyebrows in surprise.

'What's up with you, Kravchuk?'

'Why be a coward? It says in the newspapers that supervisors are supposed to be daring. Are you?'

'Are you having a joke? I think it's a bit inappropriate. You know well enough, these are dodgy times.'

Albert didn't answer, but just laid the sheet of paper down.

'Sign it. Time is pressing.'

His boss looked askance at the paper, reluctantly. But, after reading the note, he leaped to his feet and began nervously pacing around the office, bumping into the television set and then into the telephone table.

'What *is* all this? Comrades, just look at this unpleasantness here: Kravchuk is planning to leave us –'

'He's not *planning* to leave; he *is* leaving,' Albert corrected him.

Sklertsov looked over at the two people from the research section as if he was seeing them for the first time.

'Step outside. I'll call you in later.'

He walked over to the table with all the telephones. 'Vasily, how much is Kravchuk getting?'

Kravchuk suddenly thought to himself how bookkeepers and personnel department heads were always named Vasily.

'I can't remember exactly,' Vasily stammered. 'I'll take a look now.'

'What kind of a personnel officer are you if you can't remember?'

'Here we are: Kravchuk . . . One-fifty.'

'What vacancies have we got? Something we were, uh, planning to hold on to . . .'

'I get you. Um, if we really dig around a bit we might find a position at, say . . . uh . . . one-sixty.'

'More. Come on, take your glasses off your forehead!'

'I'm looking, I'm telling you. Here we are . . . One-eighty. But that's the, uh –'

'I know what it is. Make out an order for Kravchuk. And get it all ready for the ministry, we'll ask them to approve it. And grab that cognac you got from Yerevan out of the safe.'

'As you wi— '

Sklertsov hung up on him and got his secretary on the line.

'Where's the driver?'

'He went to the cafeteria for a cup of tea.'

'Run and get him, I'm going to the ministry. Pick up the order for Kravchuk from personnel and type it up for signing.'

'All this fuss is in vain,' Kravchuk remarked, observing Sklertsov's actions with a smile.

'No, not in vain, sir. By all accounts, we are at fault here. I personally and self-critically admit it. How many years have you been with us?'

'Eleven.'

'That's right, eleven. You'd already been here a year when I got here. You have a fine record, you don't drink, you have an understanding of our field, and here we've gone and overlooked you for a pay rise. Forgive us.'

'Consider yourselves forgiven!' Albert kicked the air with his leg. 'But I'm still leaving. I'm changing my line of work.'

'Well, now! Changing your line of work?' Sklertsov suddenly appeared bored. 'In what way, if it's not a secret?'

'It's not a secret, but it is still at the decision stage,' Albert stated significantly, raising his eyes to the ceiling.

'I see, I see.' Sklertsov looked up as well. 'Well, if anything comes up, you won't forget us now, will you, sir?'

Kamilyá wasn't working, she was waiting for him.

'Kravchuk, where are you going to? You know I can keep a secret.'

'To study something.'

'Graduate school?'

'Sort of. Clown school.'

'The circus! No, really?'

'Have I ever lied to you?'

'You may yet. Dogs will have their day. So you don't want to confide in me. And here I was thinking –'

'The circus, I swear!'

Kamilyá's slanting eyes widened and froze.

'So it's genius, then. Talent can appear at any age. I've been counting on that for twenty-three years. And a half.'

'Do you think it's the right thing to do?'

'Do I ever! Why waste your life counting spare parts that don't even exist and never will? But there – it's art. You'll be drinking beer with Nikulin next.'

'Why beer?'

'I like beer.'

'It's time for me to go,' said Albert.

'And what about me?' Kamilyá came right up to him, and he felt excitement emanating from her. 'You know,' she whispered breathlessly, 'you were right. I mean, maybe it's even convenient that you're married. I've been a fool, afraid to do it at lunch, worried someone might suddenly barge in here. But now – if you like, I'll give you a kiss!'

'Some other time,' Kravchuk, the gentleman, replied gallantly.

He was finished with this part of his life. The rest he would spend on something a little more showy.

Kamilyá wiped away her tears and pulled out her wallet. She now had an important public duty before her: to make the rounds of the department to collect money for a present for Albert Kravchuk, economist, on the occasion of his departure.

Meanwhile Albert dashed out into the street, flagged down a taxi, climbed into the back seat and ordered the driver to step on it to the old Moscow circus. He took the package out of his pocket and spread the ties out on the seat. He chose the loudest one, wound it around his neck and knotted it twice. He had no idea how to tie a tie, but it'd be funnier that way.

A jolly-looking type with a red nose and huge shoes looked down at him from the circus poster: 'An evening under the big top with Alberto Kravchuk' – in his mind Kravchuk renamed himself. It sounded enticing. They let him straight in at the door and told him to go right to the circus director. Albert opened the door and took off his mangy old rabbit-fur hat.

'Hello!' Kravchuk trumpeted loudly, as if stepping out into the arena.

Without raising his head, an ageing man in an antique armchair behind an enormous desk extended a finger and pointed at the wall next to the door.

'So sorry,' he said.

The same announcement about clown school openings that Albert had seen recently on the bulletin board hung on the wall. It had been crossed out in blue ink and 'No longer accepting applications' had been written on the bottom in sprawling letters.

'Please, excuse me.' Albert crumpled his hat in his hands. 'Maybe you might need an economist or two?'

The director of the circus cocked his head sideways.

'Wha-a-at?'

'I said, do you need any economists?'

'Hmph. Very funny.'

'I'm serious.'

'That's even funnier. What do you do?'

'I'm in the spare-parts business.'

'And you can get your hands on them?'

'Why, do you need some?'

'Me?' The old man looked himself over. 'Almost everything I have works. What can you do? Juggle? Walk a tightrope? Magic tricks?'

'I can do all that but only in the sphere of economics . . .'

'Hee-hee-hee. Just as I thought.'

The director stood up, looked Albert over, and suddenly shouted, 'Pick up your briefcase! Walk around! Tremendous! A perfect stage entrance for an economist!'

'They've promised me a senior position,' Kravchuk said.

'Even better – the entrance of a senior economist.'

Albert walked towards a mirror and grew in size as he did so. He was smiling nonchalantly. He had glasses with black frames on his pale face. His hair was parted. A glance into his Bright Future.

'Bravo, bravo,' the old man clapped. 'Put on your hat.'

'But it's old. It's probably cat fur –'

'Well, it certainly isn't mink! Well then, a senior economist, right? Ha, ha!'

'What's so funny about that?' Albert grew angry. 'For your information, without economics there wouldn't be anything to eat.'

'As if with economics there's *something* to eat, ha, ha!'

The director shook with laughter and picked up the telephone receiver. 'Hey, I'm taking one more. A new kind of character. Listen to this: the ringmaster comes out: "Under the big top tonight, a senior economist." How do you style yourself?'

'Alberto.'

'What are you, Italian?'

'I'm a Russian.'

'Then Albert would be better, OK? What's your last name?'

'Kravchuk.'

'Did you get that? Uh-huh . . . Al-*bert* Krav-*chuk* comes out and makes jokes about economics. Who are they going to throw in gaol? All of us? What – you think it's my first day at the circus? We'll find something a little safer. Did you get that last name down?'

The old man put the receiver down tenderly. 'Here's how it goes, my dear man. Tomorrow you go to classes. Dances, shmances, girls in tights, all that. My only request is that you listen as little as possible to the rubbish they're going to teach you there. Save yourself for the big top, just the way you are. Not everyone has it in them to be a clown. It's quite possibly the most honourable position in the whole world. My regards to your family!'

Walking along the boulevard, Kravchuk stopped at a pay phone and called Yevgenia at her mother's house.

'Come quick! I'll be at the Pushkin monument.'

'They really took you on? I can't believe it. How can I get off work?'

'Lie. And don't forget to borrow a twenty on your way out!'

He walked on to Pushkin Square. Yevgenia was already there, straining her short-sighted eyes to find him but still not putting her glasses on. She gave him a businesslike hug, took his arm, and they crossed the square over to the VTO Restaurant. The doorman opened the door and bowed. 'They called, they called from the circus,' he said. 'Please do come in.'

Dinner was like something that would be served in the greatest houses in the world. Most of the best-known film stars were boozing away right across from them.

'I'll have to get used to my husband being a famous artist,' Yevgenia said as they raced home in a taxi. 'I'll have to buy a broom to shoo off all your groupies. I hope they make you look less attractive on the posters than you are.'

'I'll have it seen to,' Albert said with a nod.

His mother-in-law was putting on her boots. She'd brought Zoya home from her after-school playgroup and put her to bed, and she was now on her way out.

'Finally!' she exclaimed. 'The child is all by herself and her parents don't care.'

'Bunny!' Yevgenia woke her up. 'Wonderful news: Papa is a clown!'

Zoya jumped out of the bed, her nightdress hanging down to her heels, and threw her arms around Albert's neck.

'Is it true? And you won't be working like before? You'll just be going to the circus every day? Can I go with you? Instead of playgroup after school? I'll do my homework there.'

'On Sundays you can, OK?'

'And can I invite Anna and Lisa?'

'You've all gone completely off your rockers,' said the mother-in-law. 'All of you! If I could only just hurry up and kick the bucket so I wouldn't have to see all this. I'll come around tomorrow, same as usual.'

They went to bed. Afraid she would wake up Zoya, who was lying next to them, Yevgenia whispered her dreams of how their life was going to change. 'Everything has come true, simply everything, if you forget the monorail. To hell with the monorail! We're going to join a co-op and get two separate rooms, a kitchen of our own and no flatmates! We'll buy a car.' Holding him tightly with both arms, pressing her body against him and sniffling, she suddenly felt that she loved him now just the way she used to. After they made love, she fell asleep in relief, weary with happiness. Kravchuk himself was already snoring away.

That was how 30 February ended for Kravchuk.

4

On the morning of 1 March he was awakened by his feet, which were freezing. The blanket had fallen off the narrow bed on to the floor. Although the kitchen window did, in fact, face east, there was no sun. The snow was melting outside, but cheerless clouds covered the sky. Even on a clear day the sun never came into the kitchen: it was blocked off by the twelve-storey concrete box that noisy construction-workers had been trying to get a roof on for well over a year.

Kravchuk put some water on to boil. Usually he would have just drunk the tea cold, without bothering. But Yevgenia always said that it was bad to drink cold tea in the morning. He crumbled some bread into a frying pan and added an egg. 'You're not a tenor,' Yevgenia would say. 'You can fry an egg. Don't be lazy.'

He took the metro to work. It reeked of socks, and people were shoving rudely, but after all it was the most beautiful metro in the world. Kravchuk made it to work almost on time. He dashed up the stairs instead of waiting for the lift, nodded his head at the people from the department next door who were smoking in the corridor and sat down at his desk, pretending he had already been there for some time. He was pushing around folders with papers waiting to be analysed when Kamilyá ran in, her face all flushed.

'Oh, God, I almost didn't make it! I ran into Shubin and he's angry as hell!'

She combed her hair, touched up her eyelashes, slid a drawer out from her desk and began to read a book.

'Kamilyá, why don't you ever work? It's all because of you that we never have enough spare parts.'

'And a good thing, too,' she squinted coquettishly. 'There should never be enough of them, otherwise what are we for? So don't disturb me, I'm trying to finish *Queen Margot*. Shubin says for you to get that report to Sklertsov.'

'Listen, I need to take off for an hour and a half.'

'Go and see him and take off afterwards.'

After finding the right folder in his drawer, Kravchuk headed for Sklertsov's office. In the corridor, next to the office bulletins, which everyone wrote but no one ever read, and the punishment board, which never seemed to cause anybody much distress, two people were smoking, pretending to study last year's mandatory Party education lesson plan.

'You still rushing around?' a fellow-worker stopped Albert.

'Didn't you hear, in old Russia institutions were always known for their attendance. A brilliant piece of phrasing: everyone attended, but no one ever worked. And you? How businesslike you look. Are you trying to get a pay rise or something?'

The secretary wouldn't let him through and told him to wait. Kravchuk pulled at the folder in his hands, furtively glancing at his watch. Finally the buzzer sounded for him to come in.

Sklertsov was writing something. Without looking up he gestured for Kravchuk to sit down. He finished writing, read over what he had written, said something into the telephone – looking straight through Kravchuk – and then lit a cigarette.

'You, Kravchuk,' he began, looking out the window at the roof of the building next door, 'this isn't exactly your first year here. You're no novice.'

'Why? What's happened?'

'And we even gave you a bonus. Why are you so slow? Can't you keep up with the work?'

'What makes you think I can't keep up?'

'Then what the hell is stopping you doing your beancount? Because of you we can't give the central directorate an explanation of the reasons for over-expenditure on gaskets and the outlook for an increase in their production.'

'The real reasons?'

'To hell with the real reasons; the numbers just have to add up, that's all. They're skinning me alive, and you don't give a damn! Kravchuk . . . what's your first name?'

'Albert.'

'So then tell me, Albert, you shithead! What the hell is the problem?'

Albert was silent. He could have said that the suppliers were sending them gaskets that were 90 per cent defective; that the retailers put in requests for three times more than they needed and then sold the surplus on the side. But

Sklertsov knew all that already. He couldn't blame Kravchuk for that.

'All right.' Sklertsov took pity on him. 'I want it on my desk today. Otherwise I'm taking disciplinary action, do you hear me?'

'May I go now?' Albert mumbled with alacrity. Feeling relieved, he moved towards the door.

'Get out of here! No, wait, hold on a second. Bring all the papers you need in here, sit yourself down at that table, and don't get up until it's done.'

Oh, that's just perfect. Kravchuk quietly shuffled out of the office. For the first time in his life he had the chance to take his fate into his own hands, and Sklertsov had to go and pull something like this.

'What did he want?' Kamilyá asked, raising her slanted eyes from her book. 'You should have told him that yesterday was your birthday. I mean, really, doesn't a Soviet citizen have the right not to have his mood spoiled once a year? That is, once every four years. So, Kravchuk, what did your wife give you?'

'Leave me alone!'

'Why have you been so jumpy all day? You and your wife have a fight?'

Kamilyá had a sense for these things. Yevgenia hadn't given him a present. For several years they'd had an agreement not to give each other presents. You could never find anything worth giving, and there was never any money. But it would take too long to explain this to Kamilyá, and since she'd never been married she wouldn't understand it anyway.

Holding his folders like a tray, Kravchuk kicked the door open with his foot and set off for his boss's office with a gloomy face. He sat down at a corner of the spacious conference table and clasped his hands to his head, trying to concentrate. He tried not to listen to the conversations or the telephone calls, to pay no attention to the people coming in.

If he could just have the time to get his application in at the clown school. Today was the last day they were taking them. They probably had a hundred people for each vacancy, maybe even more. But if, somehow . . .! Then, with a wide swoop of his hand, he'd invite Sklertsov and his secretary to his opening night. Or, better yet, Kamilyá would collect money for an office cultural excursion to go and see Kravchuk. Everyone would come, especially if it was during working hours.

Albert shook his head to rid himself of these extraneous thoughts. There wasn't really that much to be done with all the graphs. He just had to play around with the numbers on the gaskets and use the usual formulas to come up with some completely false projection, the one they were all waiting for from Sklertsov over in the ministry, even though no one would remember anything about it later.

Sklertsov had gone out to a conference (after conferences, he always smelled slightly of alcohol, a huge meal and expensive perfume), and the office was quiet. Even the chatter of the secretary two doors down had stopped. Albert went out to go to the toilet. Opening the door of Sklertsov's office on his way back in, he found Shubin sitting behind Sklertsov's desk, looking important and rummaging through the drawers.

'You go out for a stroll?' Shubin tried to hide his embarrassment. 'Get moving on that stuff.'

'All right.'

Shubin left. Albert sat down to finish the work, mumbling obscenities to himself.

It was dark outside when Kravchuk, without turning the lights on, quietly placed the damned report on Sklertsov's desk, the numbers the ministry wanted having been underlined twice. He gathered the rest of the folders in his arms.

'Finally banged it out?' Kamilyá asked. 'I've finished that book, I've got nothing else to read.'

Albert dumped the folders on his desk and started to put on his overcoat. After such a stressful bit of work no one had better try to give him a hard time for leaving early. He stopped next to Kamilyá.

'Kiss me. On the lips.'

'What for?'

'For my birthday.'

'Oh! That was yesterday.'

'Well, then, for good luck.'

'No chance! Spoiling a man is the best way to ruin him. My friend over in the replenishment department does it the right way: if her husband doesn't wash the dishes, no nookie for him –'

'There's a Rousseau for you.'

'Just think about it: why should I kiss you now? And on the lips, too. There's no future in that. A decent girl should only kiss men who at least promise her something.'

'Like what?'

'Marriage, or at least some time together. But you don't promise either.'

She waved to him, pulled open a drawer, took her knitting out of it and began to knit.

Albert successfully slipped down the hallway unnoticed. He took a tram to the circus. It was dark and empty around the entrance. He looked around for the service entrance. A crowd was gathered at the produce market next door, mostly Central Asians. The circus smelled of horse manure.

'Let's see your pass!' the guard wheezed strictly.

'I need to, uh – where are they taking people for the clown school?'

'Personnel department. But you still need a pass!'

Half an hour later he had his pass.

A notice board with tattered edges hung under a light bulb. Kravchuk glanced at the notice for the political aware-ness class for circus employees, at the job transfer orders, at an agreement on a socialist competition where the performers promised an increased socialist obligation to do what they would be doing anyway. 'A five-year plan for the preparation of new acts,' Albert read on. 'Actor So-and-so, for appearing in the arena in an unsober state, shall be deprived of such-and-such and declared so-and-so . . . For smoking in a prohibited area according to a report from the Fire Department, the following sanction is to be taken.' A list of unpaid members' dues to the local committee completed the litany.

Kravchuk winced as though from toothache. All his inspiration withered, separated from his mortal being and flew off in an unknown direction, like the soul from a dead man. *Maybe I ought to just leave*, he thought. Leave, without once treading this carpet worn thin by generations of circus performers. More cowardice. All his life, fear had followed Kravchuk like a shadow. But unlike a shadow it was always trying to get in his way, to bar him from the Bright Future, to trample on him and reduce him, a person of talent, to the level of the common masses.

On his way up the stairs Albert gasped for breath. Was he just getting older? No, the most important thing was not to chicken out. He stopped in the dark corridor and tried to calm himself by counting his breath: inhale – exhale, inhale – exhale.

Summoning what was left of his will, Kravchuk cracked open the door marked 'Personnel Department'. Taking off his hat, he poked his head in. Behind an old-fashioned table an elderly, balding man was sitting between two safes reading *Sovietsky Sport*.

'Excuse me, I'm here about the ad for clown school – am I too late?'

The personnel department official put his newspaper to one side, took off his glasses and looked Albert over. 'Did you fill in an application form?'

'Not yet.'

'Who recommended you?'

'Myself –'

'Ever worked in the field?'

'You see, I –'

'If it's "you see", then don't bother filling it in; there's a paper shortage. Education?'

'I'm an economist.'

'University, then. Age?'

'Thirty-five,' Albert said. He didn't mean to lie, it just came out a year less.

'Well, now! What's the point of teaching you for three years? Just to soak up the retirement fund?'

'Well, I'm sorry to bother you, then . . .' Kravchuk nodded his head somehow clumsily and silently backed out the door into the corridor. What the hell had made him go in there? He had already decided to give it up in the hallway outside.

It smelled like a stable again. A wizened old lady brushed against him with a wet rag tied around a stick and called after him didactically, 'You watch where you're going now.'

Outside, the street lights barely seeped through the damp darkness. Albert felt as though he were moving like a fish in a bowl, not knowing where he was going or why.

'Hey, are you blind or something?'

Something hard crashed into his side, and he was suddenly in a great deal of pain. The brakes of a refuse truck screeched and hissed. The driver jumped down off his cabin steps, leaving the door open. He pulled Kravchuk from under the wheel and felt him all over. Finding him in one piece, with only the back and the sleeve of his overcoat covered with mud, the driver shook his fist in Albert's face.

'I should crush people like you like cockroaches!'

The driver swore, climbed up his steps and slammed the door furiously. Stomping on the accelerator, he covered Kravchuk in wet snow and fumes from the truck's gigantic exhaust pipe.

Pulling himself together, Albert stood at the edge of the pavement, leaning against a street lamp. He caught his breath for a bit, feeling the chill in his lungs from the damp air. A great bloke, that driver, a real prince. He could have flattened Kravchuk without even giving him time to make a sound, let alone say a word. So it hadn't worked out with the clown school, but at least he was alive. Good thing it wasn't the other way around.

Albert cautiously walked the rest of the way home, looking to the right, to the left, and even ahead of him.

He took his time inserting his key into the lock. Yevgenia would be home already; she'd hear the noise and open the door for him, shouting, 'Slice the bread. Everything's ready!'

But no one opened the door. It was dark in the hallway, and there was no sound from their flatmates. Keeping his coat on, and leaving muddy footprints on the floor from the snow-clogged grooved soles of his hiking boots, Albert went into their room and turned on the light. Some of Yevgenia's blouses that she hadn't worn in ages were scattered over the couch, and the floor was covered with crumpled-up newspapers. A huge pile of dirty dishes sat on the table.

He brushed the breadcrumbs off the table into his hand, popped them into his mouth and found a note propped against the empty sugar bowl. He rubbed his fogged-up glasses with a finger and leaned close to read the scrap of paper. 'I'm out of here. I can't put it off any longer. Mother took Zoya. Wash the dishes yourself!'

Without taking off his shoes, he lay down on the couch and closed his eyes.

He'd been expecting this to happen sooner or later. Things had been heading this way for a long time. Now he'd be on his own, and he could bring snow into the house on his wet grooved soles wherever he wanted to. He'd just throw away all the dirty dishes and hang a tightrope from the bedroom into the kitchen to practise on. Tomorrow he'd have

Kamilyá over after work. And then all his mistresses would start to come around in the evenings, and he'd see what they could do on a tightrope. *No one's done it on a tightrope yet.* A sexological breakthrough, of sorts.

He wasn't sure how long he lay there in the darkness. Someone rang the doorbell. Their flatmate, who had mysteriously appeared after a long absence, opened the door.

'Have you gone deaf? Take my bag, I barely got it up the stairs. And grab that suitcase, too.'

Yevgenia took off her knitted hat and shook the snow from it. She had her keys, but she'd wanted Albert to open the door for her.

'There was a hellish line at the dry cleaner's, but self-service is still cheaper. I dry-cleaned everything in the suitcase. Did you wash those dishes? Just as I thought. Aren't you looking for your dinner? What *happened* to your overcoat? You should have rolled in the slush yesterday – I could have cleaned it with the rest of the stuff today.'

Kravchuk carried the dirty dishes into the kitchen. He was thinking, *Will Yevgenia ask about the clown school or not?* She was chattering away non-stop about Zoya, about how her mother had taken her for the night, about her fellow-worker Tatyana who never got lucky, she simply couldn't get pregnant. And another one, Valentina, who had no luck either: she'd got herself pregnant again. Then Yevgenia launched into stories about new signs up about flats for exchange, but there was nothing there that would do; they all had a fat little fee between the lines. She even asked about the over-expenditure on gaskets. But not a word about the clown school.

All the same, Albert came to the conclusion that she really did love him. He remembered an article he'd read recently. A sociologist claimed that the most stable families are those that are on the verge of divorce. So, by rowing with him Yevgenia was instinctively strengthening their marriage.

'Yevgenia,' he said. 'You know what I was thinking?'

'I know. You want the patties to cook faster.'

'That's a given. Do you remember Bronstein? You know, the computer guy? He's started going to the race track a lot.'

'To learn how to ride horses? Princess Anne not giving him a moment's peace? But she's married.'

'He's married, too. That's not the point!'

'What *is* the point then?' Yevgenia eyed him warily, as if expecting something nasty.

'Horseback riding is not the point, Yevgenia! The point is, he's a computer programmer and a damn fine one at that! He's started gathering statistical data on the races, but he's not too sharp when it comes to statistics. He wants me to help out –'

'What for?' Her eyes narrowed and grew cold, and something flashed in them, her suspicions well founded.

'What do you mean, what for? Can't you picture it? The horses are all foaming at the mouth, the jockeys are screaming, thousands of people are going mad, the bets keep going up, the betting machine is about to burst from all the money, and we've got the whole thing sewn up already. We've compiled all the data, fed it into the computer and worked out which horse is going to win.'

He used the English word 'computer', since that had become fashionable. She continued looking at him point blank. 'You wouldn't by chance want to go to Spain?' she said.

'Why would I want to go to Spain?'

'Can't you guess? To try your luck at bull fighting. Or, even better, to America! There they strap up the dicks on horses so that they hop around in pain like they're crazy, and whoever stays on longest get big money. That's in Texas, I read somewhere.'

'Would you stop it, Yevgenia. I'm being serious!'

'So where's this computer?'

'We've got a computer at work just sitting there gathering dust. We could stay late at night and work on it. The government paid good hard currency for it – why should it just rust away? We'll work on it on the side at night. Tomorrow we'll leave work a little earlier and head for the race track . . .'

He waited for a response. But Yevgenia kept silent, bending over the frying pan with the steaming potatoes, which had started to burn a little.

'This is serious,' Albert said and, sensing that she didn't want to believe him, added, 'This time, it's really serious!'

Their flatmate came in, and the conversation faded out by itself.

'Are you going to be out of the kitchen soon?' she asked. 'I can't finish washing the dishes with you in here.' She said it without malice and even smiled.

Yevgenia looked at her husband in dismay, as though she wasn't sure what to do next: to scream or to start crying quietly. But since it would be useless to do either of the two, she grasped the oven knob, briskly turned off the gas under the frying pan and began stirring the slightly burnt potatoes.

MUSICAL COMEDY WITH
ONE PART TOO MANY

I

'Caution-n-n, the door-r-rs are cl-l-losing. Next station-n-n, Bee-yella-rooooss-kah-yah.'

They make announcements on the Moscow metro as solemnly as if these were the very doors to the Bright Future. There's a metal in the voice that dispels all doubt. Where did they pick up their vulgar diction? It's as if they're prophesying from the top of Lenin's Tomb. Or maybe it's just that I've become spoiled and grumpy in my old age.

The curmudgeon was going home from a play at which he was now a spectator, and that was fine with him. We can only dream of peace and quiet, he used to say, but now peace had turned into reality and sleep into anxiety.

The colourful crowd crammed into the car that arrived half empty at Mayakovskaya station, squeezing Ippolit against the more agile passengers who had managed to get a seat. To avoid sprawling over them he had to grab for the overhead handrail with both hands. This wasn't easy, considering his inconsiderable height and the pressure from three sides. People notice each other in the metro when there's room. But if the carriage is packed, then everyone's on their own, as if all alone. That's the paradox. Nevertheless Ippolit sensed someone's gaze fixed on him. However, there was no way to turn around and take a look. His hands were clenched fast, and he couldn't let go.

He tried to unstick his sweaty hat by wrinkling his forehead. But it didn't work. He shifted it against the back of his hand and turned his head, which immediately set off a round of grumbling from the neighbour that he'd accidentally bumped in the ear with his elbow. Finally he managed to get as much of himself turned around as he could. Near the doors, two steps away from him, Ippolit saw a young man in large glasses, with a familiar face.

The latter nodded, as if bowing. His lips moved to say something, but it was lost in the roar of the tunnel. And when his trembling lips parted, the young man's name came instantly to mind: *Radik. Of course, Radik. Only the corners of that man's lips would tremble in such a typically actorish way.*

Mechanically nodding in reply, Ippolit was instantly sorry that he'd done so. This wasn't someone he felt like running into.

The train braked at Byelorusskaya, and he had to start forcing his way through to the doors. Maybe he should pretend he didn't remember him? Or at least turn his back? There was still a chance he could squeeze past and avoid him. But Radik had already got going, diving ahead, and when the doors opened they both tumbled out on to the platform. The press of the crowd would have carried them out together even if they'd had their legs drawn up underneath them. Radik ended up ahead, and hardly had the human wave spilled out than they bumped into each other, face to face. There was no way out. They shook hands and stood for a while, looking at each other. Radik was tall and skinny, a whole head taller.

'Remember me?'

'You used to live near Rechnoy station . . .'

'Well, I got off with you. Are you still living at the same place, Malaya Gruzinskaya? I'm coming from the theatre. Are you, too?'

'Good guess! But why are you alone?'

'Well . . . I like being alone,' Radik cut in, harshly.

'So, since we've run into each other, do you want to sit for a while?'

They found an unoccupied bench off to the side, away from the bustle of people scurrying towards the escalators. The hot air and the human tide flowing past created that special kind of tense comfort that's probably only felt in the Moscow metro. Radik was embarrassed, too, which decreased the hostility Ippolit felt towards him.

'Spring again.' Ippolit made this worthless remark to break the silence.

'It's always spring in the metro.' Radik grinned, stretching out his legs and looking at his dirty shoes. 'They say that some day there'll only be good weather. There won't be any bad. It'd be frightening to spend your whole life in the metro.'

'And it's not frightening outside?' asked Ippolit.

They looked at each other, and a kind of mutual understanding set in. *Radik has become a sceptic, like me. Why do I bear a grudge against him? What did he ever do to me? What's he guilty of?*

Ippolit's professional memory retained roles, dates and names. In his old age he'd begun to resurrect and turn over in his mind entire episodes from his past life, living them anew. And here his memory obligingly served up a ready-made video of what had happened between him and this youth that he'd once treated like a son. Not to mention that he was no longer a youth but a man.

This was . . . wait a minute . . . two years ago. More precisely, two and a half years ago.

2

The street-sweepers were struggling to rake up the leaves. Someone had hung a warning sign for tram drivers on the door of Ippolit's neighbour, Listopad the sculptor, as a pun on his name: 'Caution: Falling Leaves!'

As a completely rank-and-file – let's call a spade a spade – and no longer youngish actor, Ippolit had unexpectedly resigned from the theatre on Malaya Bronnaya. That had been his second departure. The first time had been from the same stage, when the State Jewish Theatre had been forcibly broken up following the murder of the great actor Mikhoels. They had taken Ippolit away in a KGB van and tried him as an accomplice of the 'cosmopolitans', as they were calling Jews in those days. The second time he had grown tired of the theatre, and was cutting himself off from it. It was as if Fate had been lying in ambush for him, though: two months later he lost his wife.

Vera, his spouse, worked in the theatre's accounts department. She would go to the bank to pick up the actors' wages and hand them out. One night, coming home from an opening, she fell down, ill, in the street. How much time elapsed before the ambulance picked her up it was hard to say, only that it was already late. Vera had survived prison camp, after which she and Ippolit had lived together in exile. But on this side of the barbed wire, after their cooperative apartment had been completed and furnished with a few bits and pieces, Vera departed this life.

Compared to others, they had spent a relatively short time in the far north, and it could even be said they were lucky to have survived. Their reserves of youthful health had come in handy. He hadn't spent more than six years on hard labour, and in the evenings he'd amused their fat-faced camp bosses from the stage.

Their theatre in the Vorkuta camps, in accordance with the will of their masters, was better than the theatres out in the real world, from which all the good actors had by that time been sent to prison. There they staged dramas, operettas and even operas – there were enough prisoners for everything. The camp newspapers printed reviews of the performances (without mentioning the prisoners by name, of course). One such paper, miraculously saved by Ippolit, read, 'Vladimir Lensky sang his farewell aria with enthusiasm. As for Eugene Onegin, he still needs to work on himself and try to get time off for good behaviour.'

Thanks to his turned-up nose, average build and soft figure, Ippolit played the role in Soviet plays of anti-heroes who get successfully redeemed later on. He was also a stage-hand. Vera scrubbed floors and sewed in the costume room. The fact that they had found each other in the north helped them to survive until the amnesty, but they hadn't had any children. When they could have had a baby it wasn't permitted. And then Vera miscarried twice and succumbed to illness. The doctors said it was too late. The absence of children made them love the theatre twice as much.

After burying his wife, Ippolit held an awkward wake, howled for a while in his den, and went to church, which didn't help. Something had evidently been knocked out of his consciousness and there was no turning back. Moscow doesn't cry over the misfortunes of others. He began to lead the life of a lonely man. Everything around him was topsy-turvy. But he didn't want to give in to loneliness. He tried going back to his troupe to escape being orphaned in his own kitchen. But holy places are never left empty. His parts were now being yammered out by some kid from the Yaroslav Drama Theatre who had managed to marry fictitiously, obtain a Moscow residency permit and get divorced – all within the same week.

To diminish his sense of loneliness, Ippolit stopped locking his door. He even hammered a screw into the lock to keep it from accidentally snapping shut. *I could fall asleep like Vera, and no one will come into the flat. They'll be thinking I'm alive, while I'll be long-gone Charlie.* Listopad, his neighbour, tried convincing him that he'd pay dearly to live in Moscow without a lock. But Ippolit objected.

'Locks are no hindrance to a thief. Prisoners in camp don't lock their doors, do they? I don't have any money. Except for the classics, I don't keep anything at home. What would a burglar want the classics for?'

After Bogatyrev, the translator, had been fatally struck over the head with a bottle in his entranceway, all Ippolit's acquaintances grew alarmed. They began adding two, even three extra locks.

'Bogatyrev wasn't killed by chance, that's a fact,' reasoned Ippolit. 'This has the handwriting of the valiant KGB all over it. As for thieves, the playwright Alexander Flag in our co-op had seven special locks. When he left for his dacha they took the door off its hinges from the inside. And his locks weren't even touched. Whatever Fate wants to do, it does . . .'

His few friends began dropping in unannounced, hanging up their coats themselves. When he heard their voices he'd hurry to greet them. If they asked, he would rehearse his actor-friends' lines with them whenever they had new parts to learn. But that didn't happen often.

At a loss what to do with himself, he blew what remained of his savings after the funeral on a second-hand billiard table. It was huge – it hadn't been made for a one-room flat, even if you ate and slept on it. The couch he slept on could go in the corner of the room, but the only way to make shots from the side without hitting the wall was to use the stubby cue stick that Ippolit had sawn off himself. He thought his friends might be seduced by the billiard table and come to visit more often. Listopad came once out of courtesy. The rest of the time Ippolit played by himself.

You have to live on something; you can't shoot balls into pockets on an empty stomach. To leave Moscow for some provincial theatre where he might perhaps find employment would have been silly. Instead he took up teaching drama classes at the cultural centre not far from his home. Dry bread and no butter but enough for the starveling to work towards his pension. He chose some of the older students to read through a musical comedy from the last century, and that's when a limping youth in a home-made black-and-red-striped sweater entered his life. One lens of his glasses was cracked, obscuring his vision. The corners of his mouth twitched nervously. Constantly adjusting his spectacles, the newcomer immediately demanded the leading role for himself.

'It's not proper for actors to ask like that,' Ippolit said softly. 'But, anyway, it's a good thing you came. We need a type like you, in fact.'

He said this so that no suspicions would be aroused. But in doing so he'd taken a burden upon himself. *Everyone has defects that stop him from being someone else. Things like, 'I can't become a ballet soloist because I'm too short,' or 'I can only sing when I'm at home by myself.' And there's a lot of other things I can't do. There's no law, of course, that says that a person who limps can't be an actor. But there is an unwritten law.*

This was all true. But it wouldn't do to turn someone away from an amateur dramatics class just because he limped. Ippolit felt with all his intellectual's intuition that not taking him on would be spiritually traumatic for him. *If the boy wants to worship at the sacred fire, how can I be responsible for turning him down?*

Playing billiards that evening, Ippolit consulted aloud with his departed Vera, as he had been wont to do when she was alive. It seemed to him that she would answer him back. And he would either contradict her or agree, tearing himself away only to knock a ball into a pocket or drink some tea. He shared his doubts about this candidate for the part of the French count with her. Her interest piqued, she began asking questions.

'My goodness, this fellow is obstinate! Maybe he's got the gift, Ippolit?'

'You know,' he opined, in his head, 'his lips twitch. He has an actor's delicate nervous system. His schoolmates say he's a mathematician. Maybe he's got some talent.'

'There *is* such a thing as having a bipolar talent.'

'In practice it's impossible,' he objected. 'They'll never let him get on as an actor, anyway. A one-armed person can't be a gymnast, nor a deaf one a Richter. Why lie to him? What if he takes to it seriously and gives up mathematics?'

The departed Vera tried to convince him, gently, as if measuring the rightness of her husband's thoughts. She was even able to find confirmation for her point of view: 'Incidentally, there was a lame actor in Molière's theatre. Bulgakov wrote something about it, remember?'

'Oh Lord, Molière!' he objected. 'Bulgakov could have made it up. OK, Abdulov, a great artist, had a limp. But Stanislavsky couldn't bear having him in his theatre and said that a lame artist has to be a *genius*. If an actor's a genius he can convince the world that all normal people limp. It's people who don't limp who are the invalids! By the way, other actors limped after that in Abdulov's roles, thinking that was the only way to do it. But first you have to prove that you're a genius. Try to get into theatre school like that and the selection committee will just make faces at you. Remember how they didn't want to take Gerdt back after he returned from the front with one leg? He got a job in the puppet theatre, standing behind the screen.'

'There are things in yourself, Ippolit, that you have to get over. You have to become aware of them and give them up. This is especially true of physical shortcomings. Like feminine beauty . . .'

'Is that really a shortcoming?' he asked Vera, who could never have been called beautiful but not a plain Jane either.

'Of course! A woman will get prizes for beauty that she doesn't deserve at all as a person. She assumes the unlawful right to have the best men, men that other women deserve more than she does. And to have more money. But it'll corrupt her. A woman who's wise gets purified by passing through the trial of beauty. And a stupid one becomes a whore.'

'So what I am supposed to do with a crip?' he interrupted.

'Let him join, Ippolit,' said his wife's voice. 'It's not a huge risk.'

It was strange that neither he nor even his clairvoyant wife, who couldn't stop giving him advice after her death, foresaw that the all-unknowing Radik would drag Ippolit into the maelstrom.

All the skilfully planned *mises-en-scène* in the musical had to be reworked so that Radik the cripple could walk around less on stage and be sitting or standing when the curtain rose. It was a directorial experiment, with the precondition that for all intents and purposes one character had to be chair-bound. Everything had to be done so that no one would notice.

Ippolit was afraid of offending the young man with too sharp a word or too severe a demand. He realized that he sometimes had to sacrifice other actors for Radik's sake, but he went ahead with it. The whole troupe became more sensitive. Radik over-reacted to everything, even trivial remarks. He would blush, pout and go through his scene even worse than before. There was no way of breaking him of his habit of excessive emotionalism.

In the evenings the director would discuss the rehearsals with Vera. Radik's acting skills weren't making an appearance. An actor is a someone who speaks other people's words in a voice not his own. But even this requires a gift. Why was someone so *untalented* so fanatical about acting? Even Vera had no answer for that.

3

The crowd in the metro was thinning out as night drew on. Trains were less frequent. Ippolit looked at the young man sitting next to him with the same unfriendly gaze as in the carriage, even though he realized it was unfair to be angry with him. As the French say, *Cherchez la femme*. Look for the woman. Look and ye shall find her.

'How's it going, Radik?'

'You know who's a real bore?' Radik answered with a question of his own. 'Someone who gets asked how it's going and then launches into an explanation. I'm completing my third year in mechanical mathematics.'

'Wait a minute! Aren't you supposed to be in the second?'

'I skipped one. Pity I dropped the acting classes back then.'

'You miss the stage?' Ippolit was dumbfounded. 'But it wasn't the theatre that led you to me!'

Radik's ears turned pink. He lowered his head and fixed his gaze on a crumpled sweet wrapper under his feet.

The image of a young lady with sparkling blue eyes and doll-like eyelashes arose before Ippolit. Full of life she was, light and well proportioned. God had given her grace and a way of walking that took your breath away. Irresistible. Moreover, she was self-assured, stubborn and quarrelsome, with a terrible disposition – in short, a real bitch. And, in accordance with dear departed Vera's theory, she was quarrelsome and obnoxious precisely because she was beautiful. Beautiful enough, you could say, to get away with anything. Moreover her father was an important figure in the import–export trade and was constantly rummaging about in foreign storerooms. His colleagues pampered him and his daughter – naturally – with presents. Her parents dressed her to the envy of everyone. Sweets to the sweet. In the old-time musical they were putting on Malvina was playing a serf girl who's having an affair with a French aristocrat touring Russia. Malvina knew her own worth. She ignored any direction he might give, doing everything her own way instead. Beauty is convinced it can get away with anything.

Radik tried to be funny and therefore came across as pompous and false. She acted seriously and therefore came across as funny. Every step of the way with them was a chore.

'Grab her more confidently! You're a Frenchman, an aristocrat, and she's a serf. Don't ask what to do with her. Look!'

Seizing Malvina by the waist, Ippolit turned her around on his lap so that her skirt flew up and showed Radik how to kiss her.

'The sound of that kiss has to be heard in the last row, got it? And you, my dear, don't resist. On the contrary, your duty is to serve him. He's a *foreigner*, after all! Improvise. You're actors. Swim around onstage like fish in an aquarium. Think of this musical as your very own biography. Let's go!'

The troupe danced forward, advancing towards the proscenium, and sang in chorus:

> 'It won't do for a girl to go
> Boldly strolling all alone.
> What's in store for her after that?
> Curiosity killed the cat!'

The committee that was supposed to approve the play ordered them to cut this out.

'Communism, not cat-killing curiosity,' explained the Party committee secretary, 'is what lies in store for us.'

All the improvisations and allusions that they'd come up with together were also rejected. The cultural centre was attached to a huge armaments factory run by the Ministry of Aviation. They weren't about to permit free access to jokes.

When Radik and Malvina weren't busy onstage he would sit next to her in the empty auditorium. If they were working together on their lines, Radik would get all confused, even though his memory was prodigious: having read something once, he could recall whole scenes and prompt the other actors at rehearsals. The others would make fun of them. Then Ippolit would say – out of earshot of Radik and Malvina – 'Only people who aren't bright enough to understand laugh at that. It's better to envy them in silence. And help them make it.'

'Boy and girl make it, boy leaves girl to fake it,' someone commented.

Ippolit made a wry face. Older than them by a whole era, he had suffered through his gulag university in Vorkuta and was trying to teach them about life, not just acting.

As the dress rehearsal drew closer, it became clear that Radik had failed to master his role. His efforts had been in vain. On opening night, however, Ippolit himself was amazed, and his professional acquaintances who'd come in to give them a cursory look also remarked upon the French aristocrat.

Radik wasn't limping, of course, since he wasn't walking around on stage, for which the director had to be thanked. After warming up, the Frenchman grew more confident, more energetic, even happier. He did a first-class job in the scene with the kiss. *Thanks to me,* observed Ippolit proudly. *Attention and kindness pay off. And the part imbues a person with so much that he becomes even more talented. Look how he's come to life, how he's worshipping at the sacred altar.*

He was overestimating both the theatre and himself. The role had nothing to do with it. Malvina, the beautiful butterfly, had inspired Radik, made him a hero. She'd done it nonchalantly, sprinkling pollen from her wings without even noticing it and getting even more spoiled after she realized her instinctive ability. Spiritually lightweight, she fluttered her wings, seized by the all-engulfing whirlwind of the joyful opening night: the bright colours of the makeup, the mysterious smell of the stage-wings, the sprightly music and the applause. Radik truly flew after her, scenting her mysterious emanations – most likely good Parisian perfume. His feelings seemed to be eternal. But butterflies live for just a day.

After the curtain had fallen, an extremely excited Radik ran up to Ippolit, dragging his leg more heavily than usual. 'They didn't notice my limp!'

'And so what, even if they had? What's important for the audience is the kind of spirit you bring to your acting. A body, son, is a prop. That was a tasty performance!'

He was praising him prematurely. Radik had only enough powder for one fireworks display.

'So it turns out you left because of Malvina, too?' Ippolit

had now established this, without surprise. He half closed his eyes to rest them from the shimmering light of the chandeliers over the metro platform.

Radik pushed his glasses back with a finger. The corners of his mouth trembled.

'She got bored with the class. She said you were running a nursery, remember?'

Did he indeed! Even more than Radik supposed. During rehearsal, while they were going over the mistakes of the opening night, Malvina had suddenly kicked a chair and announced that she wasn't going to act any more.

'What's the matter?'

'I'll tell you *tête-à-tête*.'

He took her elegantly by the elbow and led her out into the foyer.

'What's wrong?'

'You're a clever man. You should be able to work it out for yourself.'

She knew how to be polite and insulting at the same time. He didn't consider himself stupid but still he didn't understand.

'So?'

'Let's say I don't like the part of the serf girl, which the audience finds so amusing.'

'You want to play the part of the countess? But she's not a young woman.'

'What's the countess got to do with it? I don't want to kiss onstage. And that's that!'

'This is the theatre. Kissing onstage is part of the profession.'

'Not with him, I don't want to.'

'But he's not Radik – he's a Frenchman! That's the nature of our craft.'

She didn't grace him with any explanation; she just shrugged her shoulders. Sighing, he submissively agreed. If that's how things stood, then it really was better for her to go. Malvina left in the middle of the rehearsal. He had no way of knowing what would happen next.

With Malvina's departure Radik turned glum. Because of some trivial comment, he climbed down off the stage. They barely finished without them: Ippolit had been giving Malvina's cues, and now he had to do Radik's as well. The lights were turned off, but Radik remained sitting in the auditorium. Putting on his raincoat and hat, the director walked over to him and laid his hand on his shoulder. The shoulder trembled. Radik was sobbing.

'I'll try talking to her,' said Ippolit quietly, not knowing how to help.

The female members of the troupe sensed his softness and usually confided in him. That evening he searched out Malvina's telephone number on his class list. She wasn't at home. He left a message for her to drop by the theatre. A couple of days later Malvina showed up towards the end of rehearsal, all dolled up as if she was heading for a diplomatic reception. She sat down in the darkened auditorium and watched. Radik, noticing her, walked off. When the director was free, she came over to him.

'My grandmother said you called. Well?'

'What if,' he proposed, 'we walk down to the metro?'

He gallantly helped her into her fur jacket, threw on his coat, and they walked out. A light snow was falling, the last that spring.

'Mademoiselle!' he began in a roundabout fashion. 'Human relations are complex.'

'Are you sure about that?' she snorted.

'I'm sure, my child. We're incapable of appreciating something that's not lying in the road in front of us or not for sale in some second-hand shop.'

'What isn't for sale?'

'For example, a liking for somebody, sincere feelings.'

'Are you talking about yourself or . . .' She elegantly circled a finger in the air. 'Or Radik?'

'Radik.' He simultaneously took fright and was amazed at her feminine intuition.

'Whatever happened to real men?' Malvina suddenly stopped flirting. 'He's . . . like, this is hard for me to say . . . he's OK, and he likes me. Naturally enough. But he's *ugly*.'

'What do you mean, ugly?'

'Well, he's a crip . . .'

'What about Byron?' he objected. 'Byron was lame, too. Have you read Byron?'

'I've heard of him,' she replied evasively. 'I admire Asadov more.'

'Your own example contradicts you. Asadov was blind. And Pushkin? Did you know Pushkin was extremely short, but, oh, how the women adored him!'

'You're comparing him to Pushkin! Well, I'm ashamed to be seen with him. And, besides, his mother is just a teacher at our school.'

'So what?'

'Social inequality – that's what. I can't even bring him home. What would my parents say?'

He felt sorry for Radik, ready to exchange mathematics for the theatre and the theatre for anything at all, all for this transparent butterfly.

'Forgive me for bringing up this conversation,' said Ippolit quietly. 'It's pointless.'

'That's right.'

'Maybe you'll come back to the show?'

'No chance!'

'Where are you going after you graduate, my dear?' he asked, changing the subject.

'Don't you worry about me!' She winked at him.

The replacement for the serf girl didn't work out. Radik came to one more rehearsal and then disappeared, too, without saying goodbye. There really was nothing actorly about him, except for his quivering lips. The show, for which the cultural centre had already printed promotional tickets, had to be cancelled. The class was disbanded. The director of the centre, a former well-known Stakhanovite and trade-union leader who'd been eased out because of her age, informed Ippolit that he was no good as an organizer.

But it was neither then, nor because of that, that he and Radik had their falling out. That happened a bit later.

4

Before going to bed Ippolit discussed Radik's departure with Vera. His wife's shade said, 'You see, Ippolit, I was right, as always. There was no reason to take him on. At least it's a good thing that he realized it on his own and you didn't have to explain it to him. That would have been unpleasant.'

He didn't bother reminding her that she'd said just the opposite before.

'No,' he stubbornly and suddenly said aloud, driving a ball into a pocket with a sharp thrust of his short cue. 'I had to! Out of human kindness. "This shall I give unto thee," sayeth the Lord.'

Vera, had she been alive, would have shrugged her shoulders and fallen silent. She always did that. A few days later he would have dropped the subject, too. But now, after losing his pitifully meagre wage, the poor organizer comforted himself with the fact that he wasn't such a bad teacher, after all. Well, maybe he hadn't inculcated a love for the sacred art in his students. On the other hand, Exupèry was probably right: human contact is important for its own sake. The stage taught them feelings, ennobled their souls. That would last.

He lay down and read for a while and then set the book on the side table, turned off the light and slowly started drifting off to sleep. Suddenly he sensed he was not alone in the room. Maybe the kitten from the balcony next door had jumped through the open window? Sometimes he fed her sausage skins. Whoa, no, he heard a rustle of clothing by the door.

'Who's there?' he called out, bewildered.

Whoever it was sniggered but didn't answer. There was nothing for it but to turn on the light, and he immediately screwed up his eyes. Not from the lamp but at the sight: a young woman, completely nude, stood two steps away from him, posing like a statue from the Louvre – a place Ippolit had never been in his life. Resting a finger on the baize of the billiard table, she pursed her lips as if getting ready for a kiss. Some kitten!

'Ma – Malvina,' he whispered in alarm. 'How did you get in here?'

'Through the door.' She shrugged her shoulders in surprise. Her breasts jiggled and settled back again.

'And what do you want?'

'You.'

'In what sense, may I ask?'

'In the literal sense.'

'What are you talking about, child? Get dressed this instant! And go home!'

She took a step forward, and now her knees were right alongside his face. She leaned over, smiling mischievously and confidently. There was a strong scent of perfume mingled with vodka – it was hard to say which was stronger.

'I'll go, but only after . . .'

'After what?'

'It! Or maybe you don't find me pleasing as a woman?'

'You're under age!' he cried indignantly. 'They'll put me in prison again – is that what you want? You're just a child!'

'You're the child.' She bent tenderly over him. 'And I'm almost seventeen. If you resist, I'll scream, and then it'll only be the worse for you.'

There was no denying that she had a sense of humour. But he was in no mood for humour.

'It's not right without love,' he said defensively. 'How can you, without –'

'But I love you very much.' She grinned almost maternally, brushing a nipple against his lips. 'Like that. Anyway, you talk too much, for no reason.'

As if she were mistress of the house, Malvina tossed back the covers.

'My God!' he wheezed, embarrassedly covering up his shameful parts.

'Grab her more confidently! You're a Frenchman, an aristocrat, and she's just a serf girl. You don't need to ask her what to do. Look!'

Mimicking his intonation, she pounced on him, not like a child but like a predatory lioness on a hunted deer. He groaned, while she laughed, and her shadow was cast by the lamp beside the couch to rock on the ceiling above.

'You have a strange name,' she said a little later. She'd metamorphosed anew into a butterfly; she folded her wings and kissed Ippolit on the cheek. 'There's no way to shorten it.'

'My wife called me Polya.'

'But Polya is a girl's name,' she giggled.

'So what?'

'So nothing! I have to get home, or my parents will start screaming. Have you got some dosh for a taxi?'

Malvina grabbed her clothes, which were scattered across the billiard table, and disappeared into the kitchen. She came back with her clothes on, lit a cigarette and, exhaling a cloud of smoke, asked, 'So how was it? Did you like it? Oh, I almost forgot. I'm enrolling in the Shchukin theatrical school, and I need a recommendation.'

'From me?'

'Nah, nobody knows *you*.' Once back in her clothes, she was again addressing him formally. 'From someone famous, someone who can grab the chairman of the selection

291

committee by the throat. You're bosom buddies with all of them. Find somebody suitable, okey-dokey?'

And then she dissolved behind the door, just as suddenly as she had appeared.

From force of habit Ippolit was about to consult Vera right then and there about what had just happened, but he realized it would be somewhat tactless, although she would undoubtedly not just forgive but even encourage him. As he fell asleep, he was thinking that Malvina was much more talented in bed than on stage. *Ah, well, professionalism is indispensable to hetaeras and geishas alike, including Hetaera Sovieticus. Sometimes this talent coincides with the profession of actress and helps to advance their career. It's sad that the best roles of actresses like that are more often than not unseen by a regular audience.*

Life, however, comes up with some strange musical comedies. Without any lyrics, though. You couldn't make up things like that.

Harrumphing, Ippolit reflected on this theme throughout the next few days, while scrutinizing Malvina's image on three opening-night photographs he had hung above his kitchen table. His friends had forgotten him; besides, it wasn't likely that he would have shared his secret with them anyway.

He brewed some strong green tea, tuned in to the Voice of America and, as usual, listened keenly to the news. But in truth he was really waiting the whole time for Malvina to ring and ask about her request. He'd already sought out one friend who, based on their many years' friendship, had promised to ask the right person. But Malvina didn't call.

Of course she's superficial, but basically she's kind and generous. I behaved badly, spinelessly, but I couldn't have turned her down and offended her. She's a child but a woman, too. She could have remembered the insult her whole life. She really did love me at that moment. And her behaviour, if you analyse it, was motivated by concern for me, a desire to remind me that I'm not yet a wreck. She preferred me to a naïve boy, and that's a plus for her as well. Men are judged by the class of women they're with. I underestimated her. After all, someone who is capable of showing concern for another is a real person. Vera wasn't quite right about beauty.

He failed to notice that he was gradually thinking more and more seriously about Malvina. He hadn't had a normal youth; life had gone wrong for him. And now he suddenly had a chance to make up for lost time. Maybe this was his reward for past deprivations, for a lack of happiness?

Borrowing 200 roubles from a friend, he bought a ring with an attractive stone at the jeweller's. But it just sat there with no one to give it to. He began to worry – she wasn't phoning him. Had something happened? After waiting and wavering for a few more days, he decided one evening, when the loneliness was clawing at his heart, to ring her himself. Her grandmother answered.

'She's not here!' she said irritably. 'How should I know when she'll be back? Everybody asks me, but she doesn't tell me.'

Not that evening, but after several more attempts, he finally got hold of Malvina. He immediately became flustered as he spoke.

'Hi!' she answered cheerily, as if speaking to someone her own age, chewing on something and smacking her lips. 'Everything's cool. Umm, today I'm busy. Tomorrow? Tomorrow I have to go down to Actors' House. Nah . . . no . . . some day. How am I supposed to know when? We'll see each other some day, okey-dokey?'

'Come over,' he pleaded. 'When you can . . . the door is open.'

'I know *that*. Bye!'

As might have been expected, the call didn't change anything. She didn't even ask about the recommendation from the People's Artist that he'd pleaded to on her behalf. Maybe she'd found a patron on her own? There was no room in her heart for him, that was certain. He'd played the part of a joker, and now he was discarded. But he immediately thought of a saving consolation. Just for fun, she might easily open the door and brag about her God-given assets.

Ippolit lost interest in billiards. He had no peace, pacing from his room to the kitchen. He looked at the photographs – Malvina was the embodiment of perfection. He wondered only if she was going to come today, or not. Since she hadn't come today, maybe she would look in tomorrow? It was obvious that she was not only not a match for him but not even worth wasting energy on. Yet however much he condemned himself, the more he felt attracted to her. The seed of his unrealized youth, buried in the permafrost, had unexpectedly sprouted in this new soil and was looking for a way out. Age was no factor, time was dimmed. The adolescent pensioner (which is what he liked to call himself now) had lost the thread that he'd been clinging to as he wandered through the labyrinth of life.

Nightmares began to overwhelm him. He was tossed between his deceased Vera, who had been with him constantly, and the living but also-absent Malvina, and back again.

To calm himself, reassure himself that his present life wasn't that awful, his thoughts would return to the camp. To the place where he'd been robbed of his life.

Yet here was a paradox. It had been excruciating to wade hungry each morning through the mud in tattered, wet shoes tied to his feet by string, accompanied by the curses of sadistic guards and the barking of fattened dogs. But in the evenings, as the firewood hissed and burned in the stove, an unreal life unfolded on a warm stage, and the salutary joy of creation drowned out the humiliation and anguish. *They say the art in the camp wasn't real, just a game, playing at theatre. Where is it real, anyway? The fear there made you act well.* There, despite all the horrors of their inhuman existence, in his cubbyhole behind the curtain, a prison trusty, he was happy with Vera. There he had hope. But here life was devoid of aspiration, and he had turned into a recluse, an unloved, mangy tomcat who'd got lucky once with a comely kitten.

During his waking hours he excised Malvina from his consciousness completely and categorically. But at night the butterfly flew to him through the unlocked door, changing her guise, and did with him as she pleased, like an experienced woman with a boy. He would groan, toss and turn, jump up suddenly, take his heart medicine. He stopped sleeping. He began playing billiards at night but soon had to stop as the neighbours complained that it was keeping them up.

He knew Malvina wouldn't come, but he lacked the will to forbid himself to wait for her. There was only one way to get rid of his visions and his defencelessness: he'd have to fence himself in with barbed wire and place an armed guard on duty. Ippolit decided to buy a new lock. The locksmith promised to come the next day and install it. Standard price: a glass of rotgut before and a glass after, plus enough for two bottles more. Ippolit went around the corner and stood in line with the local drunks to buy his vodka.

Everything on earth repeats itself, but sometimes the scenery changes.

Not in the mood to read, Ippolit tossed aside his newspaper and switched off the light. He began counting to himself slowly and with concentration, to help himself fall asleep, when his ear caught a click from the door. His heart started pounding. He thought he'd caught a whiff of scent or a barely audible laugh. He held his breath in anticipation of unwonted joy.

'You're not sleeping?' she asked, giggling.

'Is that you? Finally, you good girl . . .'

'I wanted to give you a buzz from the pay phone, but you're at home anyway.'

'Of course I'm home!'

He didn't rush to turn on the light, confident that everything would happen all at once, just like the last time.

'Where's the switch?'

'Do you want something to eat or drink?'

'No, I've been in a bar. Well, maybe . . . do you have anything?'

'Of course! Cheese, wine. There's vodka, too, if you want some.'

In the darkness he put on his dressing-gown and tied the belt. Looking in her direction, to see the thrilling sight that he had waited so long to see, he turned on the light. Malvina was wearing a leather jacket, jeans and boots, like some female biker out of an ad in a foreign magazine.

'Just a second,' he said mysteriously, remembering something.

With an ostentatious gesture he removed the ring in its box from the sideboard and held it out to her.

'For me?' She pouted in astonishment. 'Aren't you the one! What for?'

'For the charm of youth,' he pronounced, exaggeratedly.

With a giggle she pocketed the box without opening it. 'Please forgive me for waking you.' The polite phraseology sounded odd coming from her lips, since she never used it. '*Pardonnez-moi.*'

'Not at all! I'm so glad. I knew . . . that is, I meant to say I've been waiting for you to come. I've missed you.'

'Me, too,' she burst out in a laugh.

'Really?' He approached her and put his hands on her shoulders.

'I have a favour to ask of you.' Her glance took in the length of the pool table. 'Well . . .'

'Speak! For you – everything.'

'I don't need everything. Could you clear out of here for an hour, an hour and a half?'

'What do you mean, clear out?'

'Don't be alarmed. I have to get together with someone. Just to talk. Got it?'

'Yes, certainly.' The colour rushed to his cheeks, and tears of distress appeared in his eyes.

She didn't pay him any attention. 'Okey-dokey.'

He was rattled. He was angrier at himself for his wishy-washiness than at her. She was shameless. He should have immediately said, 'No, of course not! Absolutely out of the question!' But she'd already leaped out into the hallway and opened the door.

'Come on in. He's getting the hell out.'

Hearing himself referred to in the third person and still not fully comprehending what was going on, Ippolit sat like a man condemned on his couch and waited. Radik appeared in the doorway, pushed from behind by Malvina. She giggled.

'What, you don't know each other?'

'No, we've met . . .'

'You see, he kept calling me and calling me.' She laughed. 'Just haunting me. We have to clarify our relationship. What's the best way to put a man off? Right! Play him at billiards.'

'Forgive me,' Radik finally said, looking at the floor. 'I didn't know where . . .'

'It's no big deal, I understand.' Ippolit began fidgeting. 'This is life, not a musical comedy. Go and sit in the kitchen, I'll . . .'

Grunting, he dressed himself in anything that came to hand. Pulled on a sweater. Then, thinking about it a moment longer, he realized he was heading out for a long walk and grabbed his raincoat, hat and umbrella. The clock on the sideboard showed it was after one in the morning.

'I'm leaving,' he shouted from the hallway.

Malvina stood on the kitchen threshold. 'How do you lock this thing, anyway?' She nodded towards the door.

'You can't,' said Ippolit. 'The lock is broken. Why do you ask?'

'Well, you never know,' she pouted. 'You should have fixed the lock.'

'Of course I should,' he agreed. 'You're right, my girl. I have bought a new one already. The carpenter's coming tomorrow.'

'You haven't got any cigarettes, have you?' He didn't keep cigarettes at home.

About three hours later, when the sky had already brightened and the stars melted away, Ippolit, fed up with walking all the neighbouring streets, made up his mind to return. The door was ajar, the flat empty, and the bottle of wine, too, but there was still a lot of vodka left. He poured himself a half a glassful, drank it down and sat for a long while in the kitchen, staring stupidly at the front door.

That was the last he ever saw of his Melpomene.

5

The metro was completely deserted. Some of the chandeliers had been turned off. Ippolit raised himself heavily from the bench. He still harboured resentment towards Radik but at the same time felt guilty about him. Strange that he hadn't felt this guilt before. These two feelings now cancelled each other out. Only emptiness remained. A triangle, minus the jealousy. He took Radik's hand as they rose from the bench and hesitated: should he ask or not? He looked Radik in the eyes.

'How is . . . Malvina getting on?'

Radik looked away. 'At first some film guy promised to get her into a theatre school. She applied but didn't get in. So then her father hurriedly fixed her up with a job at Intourist.'

So his friend the People's Artist hadn't helped – either he couldn't or he'd been faking it.

'But why the rush?'

'To get medical leave. She went on maternity leave immediately.'

'You mean she got married?'

'Nah, she had a baby. A girl.'

The triangle wasn't holding. One corner was much too sharp.

'Whose was it?' Ippolit's voice was barely audible.

'She said it was like the Virgin Mary, immaculate conception. I rang her. She kept saying she was busy. Once I asked her when she'd be free. "Never," she said.'

'And what's the girl called?'

'Polya. I thought you'd heard.'

'No,' said Ippolit abruptly, feeling a stab in his heart. 'I never had occasion to hear about Malvina.'

They let go their hands. Radik sharply turned and ran off. He wasn't limping.

'Wait!' shouted Ippolit, surprised all over again. 'What about your leg?'

'My leg?' Radik turned. 'I had an operation. I found a surgeon in Tallinn who lengthened it. Now you wouldn't have to torment yourself with me.'

Radik nodded in farewell and jumped on to a train.

'Caution-n-n, the door-r-rs are cl-l-losing. Next station-n-n, Deee-nnnna-muh.'

'Polya,' Ippolit mumbled to himself. 'Polya . . .'

Mechanically raising his hat in a parting gesture, he looked quizzically after Radik as he sped away, and then he made for the exit. His hand dropped into his pocket and felt for the piece of string. These days Ippolit always locked his flat. More than anything else on earth, he was afraid of losing his key.

HONEYMOONING AT GREAT-GRANDMA'S,
OR
THE ADVENTURES OF A *GENATSVÁLE* FROM SACRAMENTO

They announced the wedding all over California and far beyond its bounds. Six hundred guests gathered, police types for the most part, which didn't at all surprise the local fans of large-scale festivities. The former sheriff lent a hand in inviting the former governor, none other than President Reagan and his wife, Nancy. Truth to tell, they couldn't make it, but they sent their congratulations to the newlyweds. There was a life-sized plywood Reagan there, though, to greet the guests. He stood on the lawn with a foaming glass of champagne in his hand.

So there I was, too, quaffing the mead, because the woman who was getting married was a student of mine. But the story here isn't about the wedding proper – there wouldn't be anything in that to surprise the reader: almost everybody has been through one, and there are even some who like to repeat the ritual, over and over. Why not, anyway? Life is short, and it's nice to absorb as many deep feelings as possible. What we're getting into here is the deep feelings after the wedding proper and the delights of the honeymoon.

As everyone knows, no one in this day and age in the USA is in any particular hurry to get married, except foreigners who want to stay, while in Russia everyone gets married except those who contrive to leave – for somewhere they can get naturalization papers. Like lots of other universities, ours has an exchange programme. A group of our students goes to Moscow for half a year, and then students from there come over here. As you might imagine, we pay the university in

Russia very well for every one of the students that we send: for their lodgings, for food, for their studies and their cultural programme. In addition, our students have to take money with them for such sundry purposes as getting hot water out of the shower, obtaining a working lock for the room, buying back a stolen camera or simply to be able to get in the door after eleven at night.

And when students from Russia arrive here, who pays? You guessed it – we do, yet again. They don't have the where-withal. And since it's hard times economically speaking in California, and therefore at the university, we have to clamp down. This last time we sent over twenty students and then accepted in return – you'll have to pardon us – only two: Marina and Lyuba. Our finances just wouldn't stretch any further.

About that return business, now: so far there has never been any instance of a US student staying on over there. On one occasion a lad from California did get left behind, but that was because his Russian friends had organized a farewell bash right before his departure. The American partied heartily with the natives and – since he lacked their special training in the sphere of vodka usage – collapsed on the way back to his dormitory, coming to his senses in the drunk tank. And then he had to spend another month in hospital detoxifying his internal organs.

It usually happens the other way round. Twenty of our students went to Moscow and twenty-three came back – or, more precisely, twenty-three and a half. Three of them had got married: a boy and two of the girls. One of the girls had even succeeded in getting profoundly pregnant in Moscow and soon gave birth back here. But her young Russian husband took off for some other state, a long way off at that, as it happens. In general, lots of them soon get divorced, since Americans, like certain other nationals, are not so much a luxury as a means of transport. And children don't really come into this at all.

But we don't have to be so cynical. There have been positive exceptions, romantic ones. Sometimes even eternal love. Well, maybe not *eternal* (a kind of graveyard chill wafts from the word), so let's call it, more pragmatically, *prolonged* love.

So when students from Russia arrive in the USA, as you might already have guessed, only a certain percentage goes back. Or, as happened with the two aforementioned students of mine from Moscow, nought per cent went back. Clever, freckle-faced Marina married an elderly American, a professor of the Japanese language, a tennis player and vegetarian. Marina immediately asked everyone to call her Mary.

No sooner had the professor got married than it turned out that Mary had left her two children behind in the old country, and she flew home to fetch them. They let her back into the States without any trouble, and that just goes to show that there are no obstacles to true love. Then the professor's youngish mother-in-law arrived for a visit to assess the state of her daughter's happiness. This mother-in-law, it was explained, had worked as a full-time Communist Party secretary in the Moscow Central Directorate of Restaurants before the collapse of the USSR. After the collapse she had lost faith, as she put it, in communism and had made a generous payment to the fellow who selected the most talented students for the trip to the States.

Once here, the professor's mother-in-law soon declared that imperialism as the last stage of capitalism was in no way worse than communism as the last stage of socialism and that a bird in the hand was easily worth two in the bush. She decided to stay here for good and find work in her specialism. Since we have nothing here in the capital of California along the lines of a Sacramento Central Directorate of Restaurants, his mother-in-law said she would be willing to work as the secretary of the Party organization in any restaurant. Her son-in-law asked her, 'What party?'

She answered that one firmly, 'Any. Whatever they want me to do. As long as it's a full-time job.'

Of course she already had a full-time job. Mother-in-law.

'Mama,' Marina–Mary asked her, 'when you come into our house, would you say "Hi!" to my husband?'

After this, whenever the professor arrived home from work his mother-in-law would say to her daughter, 'Mary, say "Hi!" to him.'

'Where did your Mary learn such brilliant English?' I asked her once.

'I taught her from her earliest years,' the mother-in-law said expansively. 'I had a feeling it would come in handy. Not for that alcoholic first husband of hers – I'll still make him pay alimony from there, the bastard! – but just in case communism went bust.'

And then I understood why the professor had got married. He did it to get rich on alimony payments from her former husband in Moscow – in roubles, yet.

I lost contact somewhat with the professor, since he acquired a tenured position at another university soon after this and departed with his young wife, their two frightened daughters and his youngish, full-time mother-in-law. She was insistent about living with them, so the professor had to pull out all the stops. He told his mother-in-law that the police came around at night to check and see if parents were living with their grown children, which was against the law. His mother-in-law looked him right in the face, thought for a moment and answered, 'I get the hint.'

So the professor rented her a separate apartment, not far away.

A colleague told me that the mother-in-law had already had a card printed up that said 'So-and-so, full-time secretary, Professor So-and-so's mother-in-law'. I also heard that the mother-in-law's mother from the city of Tobolsk was getting ready to join the professor. And that half of Siberia were her close relatives and had suddenly taken an interest in the American standard of living.

Leaving aside the mother-in-law, I'd say among other things that children from a former marriage are sometimes an absolute necessity for new wedding contracts with foreigners. Not so long ago an actress from the Bolshoi Dramatic Theatre married an American playwright who was on a tourist trip to St Petersburg and who had fallen in love with her on the spot. Everything was fine, except for the language thing. She didn't speak any English, and he didn't have a word of Russian. But she had a seven-year-old son from her first marriage, who was going to an elite foreign-language primary school, and he became their translator. The playwright made his mama a proposal that she accepted. Then he translated that his mama was agreeable. Now they're in the USA, and her son continues to work conscientiously as a translator between his mama and his new papa from morning till night. Nights, at least, they get by without any interpretation. But, excuse me, I'm digressing a little.

The other student of mine from St Petersburg, Lyuba, married a policeman named Patrick Warren from the same city of Sacramento. He's no ordinary cop, either, but an air-patrolman, the kind who flies helicopters over the highway. And where does a Russian girl make the acquaintance of a policeman? That's obvious: never miss the chance when you're getting a ticket. Lyuba had just got her driver's licence and had borrowed a friend's car to go for a spin. When Patrick stopped Lyuba for breaking the speed limit, it turned out that she didn't even know where the car's speedometer was. He wrote her out a ticket, and then, as soon as he could get her phone number off the police computer, he called her up. It gave Lyuba a fright.

'I'm really worried for you,' Patrick explained to her. 'You already know perfectly well how to drive fast, but now you've got to learn how to drive slowly.' And, right there, God gave her the notion to pronounce the most importance phrase of her life.

'So who's going to teach me?' she asked, coquettishly.

Patrolman Warren's answer is obvious. Their slow-driving lesson went on way past midnight and ended up in Patrick's bed. The next morning he was completely blown away by the aromatic Turkish coffee that Lyuba had made while he was sleeping and brought to him in bed. After breakfast there was nothing left for Warren to do – and him an inveterate bachelor – but to work out how to propose to his guest. This was how he ended up paying the fine for the ticket he'd written out for Lyuba.

Lyuba, I must say, was rather an uncomplicated girl, but attractive, and not at all dumb. Dark eyes, chubby cheeks and a figure somewhat disposed to fullness; Monsieur de Maupassant, that expert in such matters, would have called her 'plump'. And she didn't have any children back home, either, as it turned out.

In short, Lyuba Sydelkina walked into the church and half an hour later came out Mrs Warren. The stream of guests at the wedding looked like an Easter parade. A trolley full of glass vases for floral bouquets was quickly emptied, as everyone had brought flowers with them. The block was surrounded by patrol cars and motor cycles. Some guests arrived on horseback. Holstered pistols, batons and handcuffs hung from the hips of the milling well-wishers. The guests drank and talked, seated at tables set up right on the grass of the meadow that adjoined Patrick's house, holding glasses in one hand and walkie-talkies in the other. The sheriff even gave permission for a rifle-squad salute in honour of the event, and his friend, the city mayor, gave the order for a fireworks display. The city firemen's brass band struck up a tune, and it seemed to me that there could well be an unscheduled earthquake at that moment, from all the crashing of the cymbals gleaming in the spotlights.

Not counting guests from the university, the bride was the best-educated person in this crowd: she'd almost graduated from Moscow State University when she got her six months at the University of California. I ran into the Japanese-language professor at the wedding and his wife Marina–Mary, who had come to congratulate her friend. They had flown in for a few hours, leaving the children with the mother-in-law. The professor let me know, among other things, that he no longer had the time to play tennis and that he had stopped being a vegetarian: his mother-in-law had decided it was bad for him.

'I'm so glad for Lyuba,' Mary whispered to me. 'With her poor English she didn't stand much chance of getting married.'

Just as the wedding party was in full swing, a wind swept over the tables. It was coming from a roaring, hovering dragon-fly – well, a police helicopter – and a stern voice proclaimed from the heavens, 'In the name of the law – you're all under arrest!'

The voice suddenly coughed and, deciding that that was going too far, elaborated, 'Nah, only those who don't like my buddy Patrick Warren and his wife, Looba.'

No one got arrested, and a wave of universal love flowed over the meadow next to the home of Patrolman Warren. Hundreds of little white carnations on tiny parachutes floated down from the helicopter. These were gathered up from the ground and stuck into empty champagne bottles. News of the wedding was broadcast on radio and television, and everyone heard about it. It was rumoured that speeds on the highway grew deadly, without the police helicopter and patrol cars on the job.

At the end of this super-bash, somewhere around midnight, when my wife and I were getting ready to slip away, the happy bridegroom bounced up to us. Enveloping my hand in his enormous palm, as big as the scoop of an excavator, Patrick shook it for a long time, thanking me for coming and pronouncing various polite, dutiful phrases. Finally, he shared his joy with us. Lyuba (he pronounced it 'Looba', too, of course) had told him that she had a great-grandmother, a Georgian, who lived in Sukhumi.

'They've got beaches there better than in southern California, and the hills are prettier than in Italy. Sounds like a wonderland! And I really like shish kebab. Only there they call it *kishlak* . . .'

'*Shashlyk*,' I prompted.

He looked at me with delight.

'It sounds like music! But the main thing,' Warren continued, 'is that I collect tobacco pipes. I've got three hundred and seventy-two.'

'You've smoked every one of them?'

'I don't smoke at all! It's just my hobby. But Looba's great-grandmother in Sukhumi, believe it or not, has a pipe that Stalin himself smoked. Maybe I could buy it or swap something for it, what do you think? I'll take a pipe with me that the chief of one of our Indian tribes here in California used to smoke.'

In a nutshell, he and Lyuba had decided to spend their honeymoon at her great-grandmother's, and travel around Abkhazia. Lyuba, it is true, tried to talk him out of it, but the head of the family stood his ground.

'But there's a civil war going on there,' I remarked, cautiously.

He flexed his muscles and laughed.

'Read about that in the *New York Times*. By the way, I *am* a graduate of the police academy. Granted that it *is* possible Abkhazia's a peculiar place, I'm not planning on renting any airplanes there.'

Once I heard that, I realized that my mission as a consultant was over and done with.

Patrick was, in fact, a first-class hunk. His dark tuxedo seemed to be literally splitting at the seams. His orange-flowered bow tie seemed as if it could scarcely make it around his oak-like neck. A descendant of gold prospectors in the central valley, he seemed to exude robust health. Medicine had never been developed for the likes of him, and he seemed in no need of insurance – it was criminals who needed the insurance when they ran into policemen like him. One of the guests at my table had been relating over his walkie-talkie how this past year the bridegroom had disposed of five criminals, two of whom were professional boxers, all by himself. Using the night-vision device in his helicopter, Warren had noticed some trouble at a roadside Mexican restaurant. Robbers were laying their hands on the day's proceeds. Patrick brought the helicopter down on the restaurant car park. Before his back-up arrived, Patrick had had to rough them up a bit. All five were taken from hospital to their arraignment.

The following day, caught up in my own affairs, I forgot about Patrick and Lyuba. Exams were coming, students were getting nervous, and their tension communicated itself to me. A queue of students stood in the outer office or sat in the corridor, either in need of consultation or eager to demonstrate their profound interest in nineteenth-century Russian literature. A few smart alecs had been clever enough to get themselves a certificate of mental retardation so that they could take four hours instead of two to finish their exam.

Then came the holidays, and I sat down to work on my unfinished book.

2

A month had probably passed since the wedding when my phone gave an innocuous ring. At first I couldn't imagine who it was. Patrick Warren had returned from his wedding trip.

'Well, how was it there on Lake Ritsa, Pitsunda, the ape nursery, Mt Akhun?' I tried to remember some more places, but my store was exhausted.

'Wonderful! I got a whole bunch of impressions,' he said. 'Can I come over and see you?'

I imagined the police helicopter coming down on the roof of the foreign languages department, but it didn't happen that way. Warren simply came in and sat down across from me. He was so big that it suddenly seemed crowded in my office. One of Patrick's eyes and part of his cheek were dark blue. I didn't even have to ask: Warren himself launched into the whole story, in detail.

They had painstakingly got everything together, whole suit-cases full of presents. Lyuba had visited her great-grandmother Maniko in Sukhumi the summer before last. Her two-storey house – built by Maniko's deceased husband, who had served as gardener at the dacha of Comrade Kaganovich, one of Stalin's henchmen – stood on the very shore of the sea, surrounded by a vineyard. There (at great-grandmother's, not only at Kaganovich's) the sea wasn't very far from where they slept: they would just have to wake up, and – sploosh! By the way, the pipe that had excited Patrick so much had been given to Kaganovich by Stalin. But when Kaganovich's dacha had been taken away from him the gardener, Maniko's husband, had found the pipe and claimed it for himself.

The house and the surrounding outbuildings were full of holiday-makers in summer – eighteen families. Great-grandmother herself lived where it was a bit quieter: in a little shed on the edge of the orchard, spreading her bedding out on the floor. Her feet didn't fit inside, so, as the old woman put it, they slept out in the fresh air. In that little shed she kept her money in a big old pot that she'd hidden in a hole in the ground. If she sold any fruit or collected rent from her boarders, Maniko would push aside two of the floorboards in her little shed, lift the lid off the pot and stuff in more roubles, Ukrainian *karbovanetses*, Georgian *kupons*, Kazakh *tenges*, *soms*, *lats*, *zaychiks* and other freely convertible currencies. Maniko never did trust banks. She understood the word 'money', but inflationary problems – that was nonsense that didn't bother her in the least.

Peaches and grapes grew in the orchard. The trees were somewhat stunted from their great age, but the fruit was sweet. Formerly, Great-grandmother Maniko used to trundle the fruit down to the marketplace, but now she was old she would set up a stand on the roundabout near the last stop of the No. 4 bus. The drivers would dig money out of their cash boxes, re-attach the wire seal and buy Maniko's fruit. On the other side of the house, behind the orchard, ran the main road and beyond that the railway; further still were the mountains, whose gentler slopes had once been covered with vineyards. After Gorbachev issued his prohibition law the local administration had uprooted the vineyards entirely. Now, when the wind blows, clouds of dust blew down on to the villages and the beaches.

In the first few days of their marriage Lyuba would tell her bridegroom about all of this when he came home from work in his Thunderbird and sat down to dinner. Patrick devoured it all, along with his dinner. He said he loved exotic things. He'd chuckle now and again and could hardly wait to leave on their honeymoon.

Telephoning Sukhumi turned out to be impossible. They sent letters, but no answer came. So the newlyweds decided to spring a surprise on Great-grandmother. If worst came to worst, Maniko could kick some of the boarders out of one of the rooms for them. That's what Lyuba thought, and she taught her husband what to say. 'Say, "*Zdravstvuite, my iz Ameriki*", and I will add, "Maniko, I want you to meet my husband Patrick. He doesn't speak a word of Russian, or Georgian, or Abkhazian." You say, "*Privet!*" Then of course Great-grandma will answer, "Well, finally! If I knew you were coming I'd have baked a cake!" She always says that, and kindness just shines from her eyes. At this point you astonish her with the Russian phrase "*Ochen priyatno*". And things will take their own course after that . . .'

Looking at the map, Patrick thought they would flying by way of Istanbul or Tehran, but the travel agency sold them tickets to Sukhumi via a transfer to Aeroflot in Moscow. There they could drop in on Lyuba's aunt, her mother's sister. Lyuba's grandmother, Maniko's daughter, had died long ago, and for some reason there had never been a grandfather. Lyuba's parents had died five years before when her father, after buying a Zhiguli car, had run into an oil tanker on the way to the Caucasus. Or the tanker had crashed into them – but the number of victims was the same either way. Her aunt and her aunt's husband both taught at Moscow State University. They had even helped Lyuba get to the USA, and now they were very glad their adopted daughter was no longer running around single.

Before their departure Warren had looked around Sacramento for an appropriate T-shirt. A salesman convinced him that the trendiest thing now would be to wear the two-headed eagle with a Russian inscription that went something like this:

> Happy days they were in Rus'
> When kopeks two would buy a goose.

Even though Lyuba translated it for him, Patrick didn't quite grasp what the text meant, but he liked the eagle a lot. In Moscow Patrick was enraptured by the eternally living Lenin in his tomb. He also wanted to stop at McDonald's, but Lyuba was in no shape for standing in an even longer line.

The airplane from Moscow to Sukhumi didn't take off for a long time, and then when they'd got there they took a long time to land 'due to the weather conditions'. Patrick was quite pleased they weren't fed anything on the flight.

'Russians are better than we are at dieting,' he explained to his wife. 'I like that a lot.'

They landed at night, after the wind had dispersed the clouds. The air smelled fresh on the airfield after the thunderstorm, and the stars shone as brightly as they did in California. Nobody was there to meet Lyuba. It was likely that Maniko hadn't received the telegram they had sent from Moscow. Nor was there a taxi. But the driver of the airport refuse lorry, once he'd learned that these were Americans, agreed to take them. Lyuba conducted negotiations as to how much. The driver asked for five hundred dollars but settled for three dollars, demanding them in advance.

The moon appeared to be resting on the edge of the mountain, quietly illuminating the village. It was doing the job of the street lights, which weren't working. Lyuba found the roundabout where the No. 4 bus ended its journey, and Great-grandmother Maniko's house beside it, and they unloaded their present-filled suitcases from the refuse lorry.

Lyuba had spent every summer holiday here from early childhood on and knew not only every tree and every bush, but all the cracks in the asphalt and every missing knothole in the tall, ramshackle fence. Lyuba had often climbed over that fence with her neighbour Givi, the son of the salesman in the jeweller's, when Maniko wouldn't let her go for a stroll in the evening. Lyuba had something going with this neighbour – and not just in the evening, in the daytime as well, when the jeweller's on the riverbank was open and there was nobody at home but Givi. She didn't want to think about that now, though. She walked along the fence, Patrick behind her, carrying their two enormous suitcases.

There was the crooked gate. Lyuba thrust her hand gropingly through the crack, shifted the bolt and waited for Timur to start barking. He always used to bark at any rustling sound, assuming that mischief-makers were planning to grab the peaches that hung down over the fence.

The hinges creaked, but there was no bark from Timur. Clothes lines stretched the length of the path, but the shorts and swimsuits of the numerous inhabitants that usually hung on them to dry were missing. The outbuildings, usually as full as beehives with wild holiday-makers, were dead. Apart from some birds alarmed in their nest there was a deathly silence.

'Oh, look!' whispered Lyuba.

The black mouths of broken windows gaped from the house. Moonlight fell upon a tile, part of it broken off.

'Maybe they've built a new house and they're tearing this one down,' suggested Patrick.

Without answering, Lyuba hurried to the little shed where Maniko slept during the summer. The door was open, and from inside came the smell of a camp stove and dampness. A buzzing swarm of disturbed flies flew out the door.

'What a disaster . . . I simply can't imagine what's happened or what we can do.' Tears appeared in Lyuba's eyes. 'It's two a.m. The neighbours are asleep, there's nobody to ask . . .'

'Hang on . . .'

Patrick put the suitcases down on the path and took a torch from his pocket. Lighting up the ground at his feet, he went into the house. In a few minutes he came back out.

'Looks like there's been an explosion. Furniture's ruined inside, and kids' toys are all over the floor. Maybe we should call the police.'

'The militia,' Lyuba corrected him. 'The telephone was in the kitchen, but Maniko always had it turned off in the summer so that the lodgers couldn't make calls. I'll go and look.'

Patrick lit her way as they entered through the doorway. The door lay to one side on the grass. A patch of sky with the moon in it was visible through a hole in the roof. There was a gas stove on the left and a kitchen table behind it. Beside that was a nightstand, on which stood a telephone. Lyuba took Patrick's torch, lifted the receiver and listened for the tone – the phone was working. She dialled 02. For a long time nobody answered, then someone, coughing, said something in Abkhazian. Lyuba explained in Russian that she had arrived to visit her great-grandmother but there was no house. Or, rather, there was a house, but it was destroyed. How could she find out where her great-grandmother was, and what was going on?

'Lissen, dear,' the wheezy voice replied, switching to Russian, 'you fink you're de only one? Effrypoddy's house here is wrecked. Nopoddy has no great-grandmovver. What else is new? You call in the middle of the night, you don't let the man on duty sleep – you understand? We'll arres' you if you try calling again!'

Short beeps sounded in the receiver.

Lyuba pressed herself against Warren.

'Maybe we should wake the neighbours? The jeweller used to live on this side, and Grandpa Rezo, Maniko's son, used to live on the other . . .'

'You know what,' Patrick decided, 'it's not long till morning, maybe four or five hours. I'm used to not sleeping at night. It's easy for me. In any case, we still have our whole honeymoon ahead of us. I'll lay these suitcases down flat now, with my coat for a mattress, and you lie down. I'll sit for a while and look at the moon. The moon here is fabulous.'

In the morning voices could be heard in the house where Rezo, Maniko's son – that is, Lyuba's great-uncle – lived, and a sleepy Lyuba jumped up and ran over there. My Lord, what that started! They recognized her straight away and began wailing. Children and women, most of whom she didn't know, milled around Lyuba. Several of them ran to fetch Patrick, who didn't understand anything, and they brought him and the suitcases back.

'*Zdrasvee-ooy-tee, mee iz* America,' said Patrick. '*Oshen pree-atno.*'

'So where is Maniko?' Lyuba asked.

'We'll fetch your great-grandma right now,' Grandpa Rezo answered. 'She ain't gone nowhere.' He was hunch-backed, toothless, grey-haired and long unshaven.

'So she's here? Thank God!'

Rezo went out to a shed and walked slowly back with a grey, dishevelled old crone in a white nightdress that reached to the ground. She was leaning on a crutch as she walked.

'Maniko!' shrieked Lyuba, and flung herself on her neck.

'Who's this?' asked Maniko, and a spasm flicked across her face.

'Why, it's Lyuba,' said Rezo.

'Lyuba who?'

'Your great-granddaughter Lyuba.'

'I don't remember.'

'After the explosion Maniko's memory went,' Rezo explained, turning to Patrick for some reason. 'She's not quite herself. But nobody's themself here. Ain't you seen what's been going on? But you just sit down, *genatsvále*; justice don't stand around on its hind legs.'

Patrick smiled at the warmth of the Georgian word for 'mate' but understood neither it nor the Russian around it and for that reason did nothing.

'What's wrong with him? Is he deaf?' asked Rezo.

'No, he's an American.'

Patrick sat himself down on a bench at a large table under a tree.

'He's a real American?' said a dark-eyed little girl with two slender braids, her curiosity piqued. She walked up to Warren and touched his knee. Patrick patted her on the head.

'A real one, a real one . . .' Lyuba answered for him. 'But where's Timur?'

'A tank squashed the dog,' the little girl answered, 'not very long ago.'

'Never mind Tiiii-muuuur . . .' Rezo stretched it out. 'They killed our neighbour the jeweller and his whole family. They were looking for gold. At least we're alive for the time being . . .'

'They killed Givi?' Lyuba blurted out.

'Givi was the first one they killed. He'd hidden his father from them.'

Lyuba was horrified, and she pressed closer to Maniko.

'Who's this?' her great-grandmother asked again.

'They've told you already, it's Lyuba!' Rezo said angrily.

Lyuba kissed Maniko, sighed and decided to distribute the presents they'd brought with them. She opened a suitcase, only to find it half empty. It was the same with the second one. Both suitcases held a pair of hefty stones to make up the weight. Patrick examined the locks.

'See how they're broken? Somebody at the airport, either in Moscow or in Sukhumi, took away a heap of our things.'

'That happens quite a lot these days,' said Grandpa Rezo. 'Good thing they didn't take the lot. They tore Maniko's money-pot right out of her hands. Lucky she's still got her hands.'

There weren't enough presents for everyone, and tears began to flow. Two little girls started fighting, and one of them said, 'It would've been better if you hadn't brought anything. Then it'd be the same for everyone.'

Lyuba didn't even bother to translate this for Patrick. Noticing that the gate was swaying and about to collapse, he picked an axe up off the ground and, propping up the post with his shoulder, started trying to work out how to make it stronger. Silently Rezo brought him a couple of boards and some nails.

Then they sat down at the table for breakfast. Rezo kept on apologizing for the fact that they had nothing but goat's cheese and bread. There weren't even any peaches from the tree.

'There's a war going on here,' he said. 'Brother against brother . . . A shell dropped on Mama's house. Good thing it happened in the daytime. Everybody was scattered about, only two people were hurt, they were taken to hospital, and Mama, you see . . . she was a bit shell-shocked.'

'Did you see the doctor?' Lyuba asked, trying to hug Maniko, but she just pulled away from Lyuba as if she were a stranger.

'The doctor promised that Maniko might get better,' Rezo continued. 'She's lucky to get off so lightly. The Abkhazian militia was driving Georgians out of their homes into the street. Our boys are worse than the Nazis. They're like animals. God took away their brains. They're ready to kill their own relatives for the right cause. And who the hell knows what that is? Who *is* a Georgian, who's an Abkhazian, who's a Russian, who's an Ossetian – who's half-and-half, who's a quarter something? So there you are – me and two of my brothers are married to Abkhazians. So what are our children? You understand, *genatsvále*?'

Lyuba translated; Patrick nodded.

'So you came here for a holiday? Oh-ho-ho! What kind of a holiday are you going to get round here now? The house is a wreck; there's nothing to eat. The sewage system is ruined, and everything spills out on to the beach. Of course, we're very glad to see you. But I tell you, it'd be better to get out of Sukhumi and go somewhere else.'

'What's her name?' Great-grandmother Maniko asked and shook loose a mass of long-uncombed grey hair.

'Lyuba, this is Lyuba!' Grandpa Rezo flared up, and then repeated, 'Get away from here before they start up again . . .'

'But where to?' Lyuba asked, in dismay.

'I think,' said Rezo, 'it'd be better to go in the direction of Sochi. It's closer to Russia. They're not killing so many people there.'

'Looba,' broke in Patrick interestedly, 'ask them where's the closest place to rent a car. That'll be the most convenient for us now . . .'

When he heard the translation, Rezo smiled sadly.

'Then maybe somebody might sell us a used car?' Warren wasn't going to give up.

'Lyuba, explain to him how complicated all this is,' said Rezo patiently. Then he hesitated and suggested, 'You know what? There's a Moskvich that belongs to my son Otar in the shed. He's in Tbilisi and hardly ever comes home any more. He's been declared an enemy here. The car's just sitting around anyway, no use to anyone. There's no petrol. Besides, they've been saying that they're going to confiscate everyone's car for the army . . . Take it, son. As long as you can get it going. Who knows, they might even give some petrol to an American.'

'But how will we get it back to you?' Patrick asked. 'Come back here?'

'Not on your life! My Otar is married to a Russian; her mother lives in Dagomys, right next to Sochi. Lyuba knows her. You can just leave the car in her orchard when you leave. Lyuba, did you understand?'

The youngsters held a short conference. Patrick laughed and shook Grandpa Rezo's hand for a long time.

The Moskvich was parked in the shed. You couldn't say it was brand new, but you could still make out traces of its light-blue paint job in various spots. Patrick had seen cars like that at antique-car shows, and they were worth a fortune.

'So be it,' Rezo decided. 'I've got half a can of petrol stashed away. You'll leave it with a full tank, OK? If the traffic police ask you for the car's papers, slip them a few dollars: that's even better than papers, understand? Here's a couple of blankets for you, too, in case you can't find a hotel. It's not so bad sleeping in a car, either, especially if you've got a young wife, eh?'

'Thanks, you've been very kind to us,' said Patrick politely, and Lyuba translated. 'I'll never forget this. Come visit us in California, and I'll lend you my T-bird, and you can take it up to Lake Tahoe.'

'Children!' yelled Rezo. 'Bread's rationed, so they won't be able to buy any anywhere. Bring them a loaf of bread from the cellar and a jar of apricot jam . . .'

'Could I get just a glimpse of the water?' Patrick asked cautiously.

When he grasped what the American wanted, Rezo took him by the arm and led him through the bushes to the clifftop. There the blue distance opened out, pure and quiet. Somewhere out on the very horizon a tiny ship floated, trailing smoke from its stack. At the foot of the cliffs the surf swished over the rocks.

'You can take a look.' Standing behind him, Rezo shook his head. 'There's the sea. But there's no way you can go swimming. That water's poisoned with sewage.'

They went back to the orchard.

'Looba, I've got a real important question for Maniko,' said Patrick. 'Could I get to see the pipe that Mr Stalin smoked?'

Her great-grandmother shrugged her shoulders in silence. Grandpa Rezo answered for her, 'Well, now, I know that pipe well. Mama treasures it as a memento of my father. When I was young I used to smoke it in secret, out of her sight, and I used to let some of my friends smoke it, because everybody was curious about it. People even said it was magic.'

'Well, where is it, then?'

'Mama caught me smoking it and hid it somewhere, but just where she did has slipped her memory. I've already looked for it . . . Maybe she'll come to her senses and remember . . . Sorry, *genatsvále!*'

While saying their goodbyes, Patrick, a bit saddened, pulled out his video camera and started taking pictures of everything, one thing after another: the sea, the overgrown, untended orchard, Maniko's wrecked house, the remarkable Moskvich automobile, still unaware of the honeymoon journey in store for it, and all his new relatives, who lined up in a long file along the fence, faces suddenly stony.

The most difficult thing for Patrick turned out to be getting into the car. The door was a bit too small. Once in, he found he took up one and a half of the two front seats, so there was only half a seat left for Lyuba. There was no way he could straighten out his legs, but he could still drive. But the motor didn't want to turn over. Patrick, laughing, lifted the hood, tinkered with the spark-plugs and carburettor for half an hour, and the Moskvich came to life.

Everybody stood up and waved after them. Great-grandmother Maniko was weeping, although she still hadn't recognized Lyuba. They drove out on to the roundabout of the No. 4 bus. At long last their honeymoon had begun. And that honeymoon, as Patrick now described it to me, was like something out of the movies, even though it was just life.

3

Lyuba showed Patrick where to go. The Moskvich screeched and banged, yet boldly rolled along the devastated asphalt road between the desert-like beaches and the mountains. They drove on through the suburbs, past the dachas of people who were well known not just in Sukhumi: Beria, Stalin, Kaganovich, Mikoyan. At the city centre Warren looked in astonishment at the ruined buildings, the tanks in the streets and the crowds of people around the shops.

'Everything's so weird!' Patrick would exclaim every now and then. 'It looks like you and me are the only tourists here.'

They were stopped on the way out of Sukhumi. The road was blocked by two lorries and a police car.

'Patrol!' yelled the mustachioed lieutenant, and ran down the list, 'Weapons? Cartridges? Grenades?'

'These are your colleagues,' Lyuba explained. 'The police.'

They were ordered to open the boot.

'What's in the suitcases?'

The suitcases were almost empty: everything that hadn't been stolen had already been handed over.

'And what's this? It's forbidden to take petrol out of the city.'

A policeman snatched up the fuel can and handed it to another cop, who quickly carried it off somewhere into the bushes.

'What are you doing?' Patrick enquired politely.

He didn't get an answer.

'Get a move on. Hold up the traffic and we'll fine you as well.'

Once again the road wound around above the sea, one wonderful vista after another.

'You know what,' suggested Patrick, 'since there *is* a war on here, Rezo is right: we've got to get ourselves over to Russia and vacation there. Judging from the map, that's another hundred miles or so. Look how beautiful this is. I just love mountains.'

For a long time they dodged along the winding mountain road. Armoured personnel carriers were parked in the villages. Here and there they could hear shooting. If you stopped pedestrians on the street and asked them anything, they looked at you in fear. Shops and restaurants flashed past, their windows boarded up, marketplaces all deserted. In a house not far from the road they bought two empty bottles to get some water from a spring.

The sun had passed its zenith when they turned off the road, parked the car near an abandoned orchard, slid down a little hillock and spread out their picnic under an overhanging apple tree gone wild. There wasn't a soul around. The spring water and the bread and jam Rezo had given them tasted wonderful. Patrick, tired by now, stretched out on the dry grass. Lyuba laid her head on his chest. They had spent the night sitting up, and now they both fell asleep.

Noise from the road woke Patrick up. Three heavy black limousines with dark windows, tyres crunching on the gravel road surface, had rolled slowly down from further up the mountain and come to a stop. Warren shifted his eyes from one car to the other, but for a long while none of them showed any signs of life. Then two groups of youngish bodyguards in black suits and ties spilled out of the first and third limousines and, surveying their surroundings, spread out into a semi-circle. The front door of the second car opened. A baldish general with gold shoulderboards climbed out on to the side of the road, glanced around and opened the rear door, bow-ing obsequiously.

For a long time nobody appeared. Then a brilliantly shiny black boot lowered itself to the ground. After a while another boot stood beside it. Both boots moved slightly, the legs hidden inside them stretching. Out of the darkness came a wheezing sound, and a masculine voice with a Georgian accent cursed and asked, 'No pople aroun'?'

'Not a soul,' the general barked. 'Everything's been checked out.'

Leaning on the door and the supportive general, an old man emerged into the light. He had a pock-marked face and a moustache hanging down around his mouth. He was in a threadbare white service jacket with a high-buttoned collar and two pockets on the chest, and he had a white military-style hat on his head. The old man frowned at the sun and said, 'Son of a bidge, it's hod as an oven today!'

Wheezing and shaking, the old man went around behind the car and, unbuttoning himself beside the rear tyre, began to take care of his needs. Patrick shot a confused look at Lyuba, but she was sleeping sweetly. The old man finished his important mission, breathed a sigh of relief and, buttoning up his fly with arthritic fingers, walked to the edge of the road and pushed his hat to the back of his head. He looked at the mountains, pulled a tobacco pouch out of his pocket, then his pipe, and began to fill it, tamping down the tobacco with his thumb.

His bodyguards were spread out in a wide circle, attentively scanning the surroundings. The general was already holding a lighter in readiness. The old man stuck the pipe into his mouth and smacked his lips as he lit up. At this point Patrick suddenly realized who was in front of him. He leaped up, realizing what a piece of luck this was and that he'd never get another chance. He yelled out, 'Mister Stalin!'

Warren had scarcely moved when the guards flung themselves on him, piling on top of him, grabbing his arms. Of course Patrick could easily have thrown them off in a few moments, but instead he hurriedly thrust his head between two of the youngsters holding him by the shoulders and introduced himself.

'An' thiz is my so-galled perzonal bodyguard?' the old man said to the general, spat furiously and stamped on the spittle with his boot. 'Whad does the Peoble pay you salary for?'

'Guilty, Comrade Stalin!'

'Let's do a swap, Mister Stalin,' Patrick hurriedly shouted. 'I'll trade you an Indian tribal chief's pipe for yours.'

'For me, the chief of all progrezzive mangind, you offer the pibe of the leader of some sord of peddy tribe?'

'Well, according to the legend, this pipe gives not only power but immortality as well!'

'Thad's all nonzenze! We are Margzists – atheists. But sinze you are so eager to have the pibe which Comrade Stalin smogued himself, go on, tague it. Led him go. General, give him my pibe.'

Wheezing, the old man crawled back into the back seat of the limousine.

The guards flung Patrick to the ground and immediately piled into their cars.

'As for those young peoble on the grass . . .' the old man said to the general. 'He's an Amerigan. I have still been thinking a bid, and I have decided: why should the segret servize of the Unided Stades know that Comrade Stalin now lives in a dacha in Abkhazia?'

'Should I give the order to let them have it with a Kalashnikov?'

'Whad for? Led our visitors rezd peazefully. But when they have rezded, let Comrade Beria tague care of them withoud any prejudice. I thing id is not nezezzary they should return to the lair of imberialism. Sudge a physigal and strong Amerigan can do some worgue for socialism. And the pibe will return to its real owner. Led's go!'

The engines squealed to life. Patrick was holding the still-lit pipe in his hands. Then he woke up for the second time, this time for real. When he opened his eyes he saw that he was holding a dry twig in his hand, picked up off the ground. The noise from the road and the smoke really did exist. Their Moskvich had been expeditiously turned around and was rolling off, jam-packed with shaven-headed people.

Patrick jumped up quickly and was on the asphalt in three bounds, but the car was already out of sight. There wasn't a single passer-by on the road; the highway seemed deserted. It would have been stupid to run after them. His hand went instantly into his pocket: his car keys were gone.

'The pipe, Looba!' groaned Patrick.

'What pipe?'

'The Indian chief's pipe that I wanted to trade for Stalin's pipe. It's gone.'

Not just the pipe. Everything that was in the Moskvich's boot – their clothes, Patrick's video camera, the blankets – was gone. The wallet in his back pocket was still there, though, since Patrick had been lying on it.

The reader can rest assured that I'm trying to convey what Patrick told me word for word, without adding anything of my own. And if, as regards his meeting with Comrade Stalin, he exaggerated a bit for the sake of a well-turned phrase, I can hardly be held responsible for that. Not long ago I read in a quite serious journal that even long dreams pass through our consciousness in an instant, so Warren might well have dreamed about the chief's pipe while the thieves were already revving up the motor of his Moskvich. Patrick decided not to say anything to his wife about his strange dream.

Lyuba sobbed and said that she didn't want to spend her honeymoon this way. Patrick comforted her: why, their holiday was only just getting under way. Lyuba thought it was already done for, though. On the grass under the tree lay their jar of apricot jam, bees swarming all over it, and half a loaf of grey bread.

On the path leading down from the mountain into the apple orchard there appeared a little white-bearded old man with a sack slung across his shoulder, looking like a beggar. He stopped and asked for a piece of bread. Lyuba gave him half of what was left. He began to eat it ravenously. When he heard what had happened, the old man said, 'It's those criminals they let out of the prisons. They do as they please now, you see.'

'And where do you live?' Lyuba asked.

'Nowhere, now. I'm a Greek, and the Abkhazians have driven out the Greeks just like they did the Georgians and the Armenians.'

'Where are you going now?'

'Everybody's running away from here. I'm heading for Batumi to try to cross over into Turkey. Maybe things are better in Turkey. They're very bad here.'

'Are we very far from an airport?' Patrick asked all of a sudden, looking at his wife's tear-stained face. She translated for him.

'Airport? Right now you're not far from Gagry, but the only airport around here is near Adler. That would be across the border already, that is, in Russia. The buses aren't running any more. Cars don't pick up hitch-hikers, 'cause they're scared. The only thing for it is to go on foot. You can get there in a day and a half, two days.'

So Patrick and Lyuba set off, clutching the jar with the remains of the jam, their two empty bottles and the piece of bread. Whenever Patrick heard the sound of an approaching car behind them he would try to flag it down, but nobody stopped.

Towards evening they came to the village of Gantiadi. All the while, Patrick had been converting kilometres into miles, and it turned out that it was still another twenty or twenty-five miles to the airport. Lyuba had rubbed both her feet raw and couldn't walk any further. Patrick offered to carry her, but plump Lyuba knew her weight and declined.

In the twilight shooting had started up. Somewhere artillery rumbled. There was a clatter behind them and an armoured personnel carrier pulled up alongside them. Someone inside yelled out something in Georgian.

'Who could this be?' Patrick mused aloud. 'Abkhazians? Georgians? Russians? Well, at least they're not thieves. They couldn't have stolen that tank.'

'They're Georgians,' said Lyuba.

Torches played on Lyuba and Patrick from various directions.

'What do they want?' Patrick asked Lyuba as a couple of dozen soldiers in masks leaped from the vehicle, surrounded them and begun to argue about something in Georgian.

'What do you want, young men?' Lyuba asked. 'Who are you?'

One of them switched to Russian and said, 'Document check, girl. Georgian Popular Forces. Passport, passport!'

The whole unit stared animatedly, realizing that they had a foreigner before them.

'Looba,' said Patrick uncomfortably, 'go ahead and tell them, so they'll let us go.'

Lyuba translated.

'Tell him not to twitch a muscle or we'll arrest him,' another soldier broke in quickly. 'He must hand over dollars, dollars! No dollars and we don't let you through.'

Patrick didn't scare easily, but he looked nervously at Lyuba, not knowing what they might get up to in a tight corner like this, in weird old Abkhazia.

'Give them ten dollars,' ordered Lyuba.

They shone a light on the banknote.

'Ten? Not ten; let's have a hundred. You got lots more over there, and we got none here.'

Patrick handed them several more notes, and they gave him back his passport.

'Hey, *genatsvále*, how about renting us your girl?'

Lyuba wasn't about to translate that question for him.

The soldiers started to laugh, clapped Patrick on the shoulder, but then someone bellowed from the armoured transport. They piled into the vehicle and drove off, waving their machine-guns and shouting.

It was time to find a haven for the night. The Warrens decided to forge ahead until they found something suitable. A lot of homeless people like themselves were walking along the road, both towards them and overtaking them from behind, singly and in droves. Many of them had no idea where they were wandering to or why. Nowhere would anyone let them stay the night. So they plodded on down the side of the road, stumbling and finally settling down on the ground to rest until dawn. The honeymooners passed through the sleepy, leafy little town of Leselidze without meeting any obstacles, and they were told it wasn't far to the Russian border. Patrick and Lyuba took heart and even laughed when they looked at each other: the mosquitoes had bitten both of them so badly that their swollen faces were hardly recognizable.

The next day they had almost made it to the Russian–Abkhazian border, and they were walking now past a copse of trees, now past an ancient park, when suddenly, with a laugh and a whoop, a crowd of young hooligans surrounded them.

'Hey, man, give us some smokes!' the youngsters yelled.

'He doesn't smoke,' said Lyuba.

This swarm of locusts, obviously all escaped from places of detention, bellowing and whining for money, romped around the couple, stoned out of their heads on freedom, drugs and the absence of punishment. They shoved them, knocking Patrick and Lyuba off their feet, and then proceeded to walk right over them. Patrick stood up and grabbed one of them up by the collar and the seat of his trousers, lifting him up to chuck him out of the way, but the brat kicked Patrick in the eye. Patrick crouched down in pain.

The swarm disappeared into the forest as suddenly as it had appeared.

'My wallet!' it occurred to Patrick. 'Our passports, tickets. Our money . . .'

They had also ripped off Lyuba's handbag, with what was left of the apricot jam. Patrick's cheek and eyebrow swelled up, suffused with blood. His eye swelled shut, but, thank God, it was in one piece.

The bridge across the River Psou was blocked off by armoured personnel carriers. The Abkhazians were on one side of the bridge, Russian forces on the other. They were interrogated for a long time by both sides, but now Patrick did all the talking by himself. And even though nobody understood a word he said, his utterances had a hypnotic effect. Finally they were even given water to drink and had directions to the Adler airport explained to them.

They walked slower and slower, sitting down and taking breaks more and more often. Half clothed, and starving by the time it got dark again, the last of their strength fading, they finally made it to the airport.

In the courtyard in front of the terminal a woman was putting a heavy lock on the door of a kiosk above which hung a crooked sign saying *Pelmeni* – meat dumplings, like ravioli. Lyuba rushed up to her.

'My dear woman, please, please give us something to eat. We haven't eaten for two days.'

'Can't you see? We're closed.'

'We're from America – there he is, an American – and hungry.'

'Has he got any dollars?'

'No, he hasn't.' Lyuba hesitated, but suddenly (and where does a Russian woman's wisdom come from?) she remembered. 'I'll give you an American brassière. It's brand new. I've only just put it on.' She undid the front of her dress so that the woman could ascertain the brassière's quality. Patrick, understanding neither the conversation nor the gestures the two women were making, averted his gaze in embarrassment from his wife, who seemed to be performing a striptease for the sake of some *pelmeni*. Lyuba took off the brassière and held it out to the dumpling-lady. The latter turned the brassière over in her hands without any special enthusiasm, skilfully tucked it away in her handbag, took the lock off the door and disappeared inside. She soon emerged, carrying two plates in front of her, loaded with the dumplings, and a piece of bread.

Lyuba and Patrick settled themselves down at a table set into the concrete in front of the door. The *pelmeni* were cold, the fat had congealed, but it made no difference. They wolfed them all down.

'For breakfast I still have my American panties,' said Lyuba happily, 'but what'll we do after that?'

'After that . . . I have underwear, too,' Patrick said modestly.

Patrick and Lyuba weren't exactly greeted with flowers at the airport. Only passengers with tickets were admitted into the waiting-room. It smelled like a stable. People slept on sacks or wandered around, stepping on the sleepers. Long lines of people crowded the ticket-windows. What were they supposed to ask for at the ticket-window, anyway? The cashiers they appealed to didn't want to talk to them. Patrick used his mighty torso icebreaker-style to clear a path through the crowd to a door under the sign saying 'Duty Manager'. Lyuba tried to explain that they were from the USA and had to fly to Moscow right away.

'Everybody has to fly out of here right away,' the elderly manager interrupted her, with a sidewise glance at Patrick's puffy black eye. 'But when they actually will I don't know. They keep postponing the flights. There's no fuel. Passports!'

'They were stolen from us in Abkhazia.'

'Tickets?'

'Them, too.'

'Then there's nothing I can do. Go to the police. Next!'

At the police station they had to start all over again from the beginning, but then somebody high-ranking came out and invited them into his office.

'It's tough, I know . . . Well, OK, since you're American tourists we'll make an exception. We'll try to help, but you'll have to pay. Pay well and in hard currency only.'

'But we were robbed, don't you understand? We were robbed.'

Lyuba burst into tears.

'Then that's your hard luck. Ask your relatives for some money; otherwise there's nothing we can do to help.'

They weren't permitted to stay indoors. They went out to sleep in the meadow next to the fenced-off airfield, bedding down on some mats and leaning their heads against a pillar ringed with barbed wire. The world isn't without good people: a soft-hearted cleaning lady had brought them a couple of the mats that she had, stashed away in the terminal building's second-floor VIP lounge. She did it because her beloved grandson had gone off to the USA.

In the morning, hungry and restless, they again drifted around the terminal and its environs. The elderly cleaning lady fed them when Patrick promised to find her grandson in America and help him. The woman even brought Lyuba a warm jacket from her house.

Meanwhile there was no way out, and no one was going to come to their rescue. On the third day Patrick, unshaven, had somehow managed to wash himself in the dirty gents' toilet and then get Lyuba into a seat that someone had vacated and was wandering around the waiting-room, when suddenly he heard a grand English accent. A grey-haired man in an elegant suit was striding in the direction of the deputies' lounge. Through an interpreter he was talking to a companion in a general's uniform. Their entourage surrounded them.

'Just a moment, sir! Stop a moment, please!'

Patrick ploughed forward but was surrounded by a dozen guards. Quick as lightning, he sized up the forces ranged against him: he might well have been able to dispose of at least four of them in half a minute, but what would be the point? His last hope was slipping away.

'Sir, I'm an American. Can I speak to you?' yelled Patrick, striding after them.

Nobody paid him any attention.

'Hey, this is very important! It's urgent! Wait a minute, damn it! To hell with you and your whole gang!'

The foreigner finally came to a halt, turned, and a faint smile could be seen on his tired face. He turned out to be a diplomat from the British Embassy in Moscow. Patrick explained the situation to him in a few words. The diplomat gestured to let the American through, and the guards, not understanding what was going on, drew aside. Patrick described their ordeal as briefly as possible.

'Good Lord!' exclaimed the diplomat. 'This sort of thing is happening here more and more. Write down your names, address and telephone number for me. By evening I'll be in Moscow, and in the morning I'll call the American consul.'

'But we don't have either an address or a telephone here. Adler airport, that's all. We're sleeping outdoors.'

'Better address them "care of the airport chief",' advised

331

the general. He removed his military hat and wiped his damp bald spot. 'I'll explain the situation to him.'

'No doubt you need some money,' said the diplomat, suddenly thoughtful. 'How much should I give you, and what currency? Pounds, dollars, roubles?'

'If it's not too much trouble, give me three or four hundred bucks and your name,' said Patrick. 'I'll get it back to you as soon as I can call the Bank of America. The good Lord bless you!'

For their dollars they were admitted to the airport hotel, after about an hour and a half's wait. At long last their honeymoon was on an even keel. But they had to be accommodated separately, Lyuba in a women's dormitory with six beds, Patrick in a four-bed men's room. The women's and men's showers and toilets were at the end of the corridor down which, between the many people standing around, the young lovers strolled, surrendering themselves to wedded bliss at last. The next day they heard that Delta Airlines had replaced their tickets home from Moscow. But another three days had to pass before Aeroflot sold them new tickets to Moscow, because, they were informed, whoever had stolen them might use the old ones – which was complete rubbish, of course.

In the face of such a one-sided account, the reader might begin to suspect that the author was mining the genre of American Socialist Realism, that maybe he'd soon start saying that everything is bad over there and here in the USA everything's just great. Well, when they arrived in Moscow and appeared at the US consulate the authorities immediately issued Patrick a new passport. But Lyuba, whose student visa had long since expired, was told she'd have to remain for a few months until the relevant US authorities granted her permission to rejoin her American husband. After all, she didn't even have a Russian passport.

Patrick was pretty sure that he was bound to get a long

assignment, with no breaks, after his honeymoon. A hatred for the US bureaucracy that he defended so unstintingly flared up in Patrolman Warren's heart. At this point an author of fiction might do well to give his plot a twist: at this moment, from God knows where, a clever KGB recruiter should come on to the scene and, who knows, maybe bring Patrick Warren over to the Communists or to some other kind of -*ists*. But, as the reader has already guessed, it's not in my gift to make these things up. In a rage, Patrick just called his sheriff in Sacramento straight from the consulate, the sheriff called the Governor of California, the Governor called Washington and from Washington his wrath echoed back in Moscow in the form of a polite request to make an exception to the rule. From the ambassador's office came a likeable young official of basketball height with an order to the consul to issue an entry visa to the wife of Inspector Warren. When this gentleman suddenly caught sight of Patrick in the reception room he rushed up and grabbed him.

'*Genatsvále!*' he whispered. 'Why did you have to kick up all this fuss? You and I were in school together in Sacramento – we played basketball on the same team! You should've come straight to me and we could've settled this whole thing in five minutes.'

Of course, '*genatsvále*' is just a word I stuck in for effect. What he really said was 'buddy'. But Patrick hadn't had a clue that his pal worked in the embassy. I merely wish to emphasize some negative aspects of American reality. In certain – atypical, to be sure – cases, Americans are just as given to pulling strings as the Russians are.

4

'The diet there is really great,' Patrick now reminisced, sitting in an armchair in my office. 'We hardly ate a thing. The upshot is, I've come to the conclusion that I have never had such a rich and fascinating vacation in my whole life. A whole sea of impressions. Looba and I are going to remember our honeymoon for the rest of our lives.'

'And how!' I agreed.

'After the trip I did have a few more things to worry about. I sent some money for a new car to Great-uncle Rezo by way of a friend of mine. I sent a cheque to London for that diplomat. I found the Adler airport cleaning-lady's grandson through police channels. I'll be sending the boy a small sum every month, and I'll try to help him find a job.'

'OK, Patrick,' I said, stifling the impulse to moralize on this theme. 'But surely you didn't come all the way here to the university just to tell me this story. How can I help you?'

'*Slyushay, genatsvále,*' he said boldly, not even giving me a second to smile before switching over into English. 'I want to take courses in the Russian, Georgian and Abkhazian languages. But in the evening, after work.'

'But we don't offer Georgian or Abkhazian . . .'

He stopped short. 'Then just Russian. They say it's still the common language in all their territories.'

'You might say. But you'd have to talk to the director of the Russian programme, Professor Gallant. In fact, he has office hours right now. But why do you want to learn Georgian and Abkhazian?'

'What do you mean, why?' he said proudly. 'I've got roots there. Do you know what the word *Abkhazia* means? Translated, it means "Land of the Soul"!'

That conversation took place last summer. This winter my wife and I were invited to San Francisco for a concert being given by musicians from Moscow. We were late, there weren't many cars on the highway, and I stepped on it, looking attentively on every side, and especially behind, so as not to miss a patrol car. The speedometer arrow was at over 90. We didn't have much further to go when I heard a polite voice from the sky, 'Driver of the dark-red Toyota, pull over to the side. I'm asking you, sir, please! Just not under the bridge but a little further, in that open spot there, sir . . .'

There weren't any other red cars near us and nowhere for us to take cover. We had to pull over to the side and wait. The black helicopter with its white tail came down on the grass near by.

'Wouldn't it be nice if Patrick Warren was on duty,' I said to my wife. 'Our man! But it's not very likely – there's a lot of patrols along this road.'

And there was Patrick Warren, in his entire immense person, looming at my window, blocking out the light of day.

'I'm sorry, sir. I didn't know it was you, and I've already entered the licence number of your Toyota in the computer. The speed limit on this stretch is 65. You were doing 90, that's . . .' his lips worked as he figured something out, '. . . that's 140 kilometres an hour in Russian, but I'll put you down for 75. That'll be a bit cheaper anyway. The treasury here in California is empty, and speeding fines have gone up past 250 bucks a pop.'

'That's daylight robbery!'

'I'm embarrassed myself, sir. But what can you do? We all have to feed a bunch of greedy bureaucrats. The new speeding law makes it even harder to appeal your fine in court, damned if I say so myself. But I'm asking you – don't speed. There've already been three crashes on this section today, one of them fatal.'

He handed me a ticket.

'Because of you, we're late for a concert, Patrick,' I said in annoyance.

Warren understood this in his own way. 'Sorry, but I can't take you to San Francisco. We're not allowed to fly on that side of the bay. It's not our bailiwick.'

He shook my hand in his excavator scoop. In the rear window I could see the helicopter roiling the dried grass and shooting up over the highway.

That autumn, winter and spring I would run into Patrick on campus. He stood out from the crowd of students with his powerful build and the fact that he was still in police uniform. Apparently he never had time to go home and change before class.

'*Zdrasveeooytee,*' he would always yell in his mangled Russian and then add, somewhat less confidently, a couple of words in the language to the effect that he spikka da Russian real good.

One day he came running into my office, beaming.

'Congratulations!' he said in Russian and continued, 'Looba bore a boy!' Of course, he meant something like 'Congratulate *me*.'

'All right! You guys don't waste any time.'

'You know where we made him? Looba and the doctor figured it out exactly: in Adler, on the field by the airstrip, when we couldn't get a flight out. The smell of milkweed was so strong I couldn't hold myself back. Sure, it stank of aviation fuel, too, and the toilet right next to us, but I decided not to pay it any mind. It happened on that mat from the VIP lounge. Just think what kind of people have walked on that thing! Maybe Stalin and Beria. And Kaganovich. And Gorbachev. And that tyrant, Mikoyan!'

'Stalin was the main tyrant,' I answered with a chuckle. 'Mikoyan was just small fry: he was People's Commissar for the food industry. He made hot dogs.'

'Well, sure,' Patrick agreed. 'They all made hot dogs. "Now for two kopeks you can't buy a goose,"' he said in his execrable Russian. I interpreted this as meaning that, in his view, Russian history clearly showed signs of progress.

When I returned from Europe at the height of the summer I came across a fax from Patrolman Patrick Warren. The text was in Russian and began with the words, 'We bring to the attention of all relatives, friends, and acquaintances', and went on to announce solemnly that Lyuba was again pregnant and expecting their second child. I called to congratulate them.

'Have you been watching the news from Russia?' he asked. 'There's still a lot of trouble there. The Georgians are fighting the Abkhazians. The Moldavians are quarrelling among themselves. The Armenians are in conflict with the Azerbaijanis. The Tajiks and the Afghans are having it out . . . It's a nightmare in Chechnya. It has to be stopped!'

'It's got to,' I agreed, eagerly. 'But how?'

'Didn't I tell you? I'm going back there again.'

'With Lyuba?'

'I'm afraid not, this time. She's expecting another child, after all.'

'And what are you going to be doing there?'

'What do you mean?' exclaimed Warren. 'First of all, Looba learned through her aunt in Moscow that Great-grandmother Maniko has come to her senses after her shell-shock. I'm hoping that she remembers where she hid Stalin's pipe. Second, I know the faces of everybody who robbed us. I'm going to find them. Third, I have a colossal idea. I've decided to pa-ci-fy them all.'

'What are you on about?'

'They've been screwing around long enough! I'd have done it last time, only I wasn't expecting to. I was there as a guest, after all, so when they attacked me I couldn't come up with an adequate response, and didn't make any use at all of my considerable physical capabilities. And then I wasn't in uniform, either, and didn't have my gun or my club or my handcuffs with me or my walkie-talkie. This time it'll be a different story, *genatsvále*!'

At this Georgian word, pronounced with a Californian accent, I was so overcome with laughter that I lost the gift of speech. All that's left is for me to summarize the main points: The Warrens were not only raising a Georgian–Abkhazian–Russian–American boy, but, as you've heard, Lyuba was pregnant again – a fact made known by fax to all of California, in particular President and Nancy Reagan, and, by registered letter, to Great-grandmother Maniko.

But neither Ronald and Nancy, nor Maniko, nor the Georgians, the Abkhazians, the Armenians, the Azerbaijanis, the Moldavians, the Tajiks, the Chechens, the Russian foreign ministry, the CIA or the United Nations as yet know anything about this other plan of his. It hasn't reached the ear of that Russian institution known lovingly to the people until recently as the KGB.

So no one yet knows that *genatsvále* Patrick Warren, in full uniform, flew out this morning from Sacramento to Moscow, and from there he goes to the Caucasus to establish a durable peace. I should add 'first' to the Caucasus, and then . . .

Meanwhile, don't tell a soul about this.

POSTSCRIPT:
ON THE MICRONOVEL

My observations here arose after re-reading G.K. Chesterton, who said that Art is always subject to limitation, and the sense of a painting is contained within its frame. Genre, too, is a framework within which the writer presents the reader with his ideas. The author alone defines the dimensions of the framework signifying his genre. Even if they get the genre wrong, writers, as distinct from theorists of literature, have the right to a certain quota of absurdity, otherwise life – and writing, even more so – is a bore.

Steering clear of political considerations, we'll admit that the selection of a framework for a literary production is difficult even in theory, where valid reservations about the conventions of any genre are encountered at every step. This isn't about some Procrustean bed: the issue is rather the adequateness of content and form. In other words, could we put a little book illustration, for instance, within a frame the size of a large painting or, conversely, fit a canvas like that – one that stretches along an entire wall of the hall in a museum – into a desktop frame?

The novella developed from the anecdote, the essence of which lay in the telling. It was appropriated from Boccaccio. Boccaccio's novella (Chapter 9 of *The Decameron*) about Torello, who tames falcons and has them fly him to his wife's bed, was used as the source of the term 'falcon novella', which was at one time fashionable among German critics. Similarly, Russians can speak of the 'Chekov-style novella', even though Chekhov was more often a true short-story artist and not a writer of novellas, at least by comparison with, say, O. Henry.

Within Russian criticism the short story still sometimes gets mixed up with the sketch. But such oversimplification hides the danger of eroding. *The Oxford English–Russian Dictionary* translates the English word 'novella' into Russian as *povest*, while the American *William Morris Dictionary* defines it as a 'short novel'. It can be agreed that the boundary between the two is shaky, and there's not much we can do about it. But it would be a frivolous error to maintain that there isn't any boundary at all.

In the opinion of Goethe, 'the novella is nothing other than the occurrence of an unprecedented incident'. Skipping ahead, I should note that Morris is right: *the short-novel form* comes most likely from the novella, in which, by the traditions of the genre, the ordinary combines with the extraordinary, even with mystical or fantastic elements – in short, with something that unexpectedly for the reader sharply changes the habitual lifestyle of the protagonists.

In the nineteenth century the novel attained greatness in the persons of Dostoyevsky and Tolstoy. The traditional flaccidity of plots in nineteenth-century literature began to bother authors in the twentieth. The traditional approach, that there has to be a 'triangle' in a novel, is sometimes replaced in American literary theory today by something else: the novel's subject needs a kind of envy that they call 'mimetic desire'.

In principle we can speak of two types of prose (or an author's realization of prose): *dynamic* prose and *static* prose. The prose of O. Henry is dynamic; that of Dostoyevsky static. But in both kinds the novelistic framework remains. Today, though, even that seems not to be obligatory, to a certain extent. William Todd divests the novel of its framework. His formula goes, 'What is a novel? A novel is a theory of human life.' And the distinguished literary critic Lionel Trilling simply annihilates the boundaries of the genre with the generalization, 'The novel . . . is the eternal search for reality.' The demise of the novel was announced, for instance, by Robbe-Grillet and by such later personages as Josef Brodsky, who in conversation with me declared the death of the novel in the twentieth century. The novel's pre-eminence in world literature isn't threatened by anyone now, thank God.

So – what's left at the bottom of the barrel after all this reflection? And wouldn't it be easier just to explain to the reader that the novella and the short story are things that you can read in a single sitting, while the novel is for overnight from Friday through Saturday, to be finished only after breakfast? What remains, though, is this: the desire to read a whole novel in an hour and a half or so.

Among American Slavistics there exists the term 'long short story' – testifying to the demand for a genre that hasn't yet been formulated. Victor Terras separates the large Russian novel from the 'short novel (or romance) or long short story'.

In the woolly formula of Wilfred Sheed, the 'short novel' is 'a form that the great masters find suitable for the greatest effect'. And for examples he adduces Dostoyevsky (*Notes from Underground*), Chekhov (*Ward No. 6*), Thomas Mann (*Mario and the Magician*), Steinbeck (*Tortilla Flat*) and Faulkner (*The Old Man*). I would add Pushkin's *The Queen of Spades*.

Tolstoy never worked in the short novel form, although the dimensions of his *stories* were bigger than many a short novel. Ivan Turgenev is considered – rightly so – an affirmer of the Russian short story. But he's the very man who, under the influence of the French novella, composed the marvellous micronovel *Klara Milich*, without specifying its genre but observing all its canons.

Slavistics in the USA regard Chekhov as an impressionist. In his letters Chekhov time and again mentioned that he was writing a novel, but a large novelistic canvas was never to be seen. Chekhov apparently agonized over never writing a novel in his life. But, especially in his later years, the writer created a short-novel form in parallel with his short-story work. 'The Lady with the Pet Dog' can be considered a micronovel. But in the majority of Chekhov's contemporary publications they were released under the rubric of 'tales and stories'.

My 'micronovel' is the entirely unnecessary 'novella' of former times, which spread far and wide for a time. The history of literature holds instances where an already written and even already published short story gets turned then into a huge canvas, since prose has this telescopic tendency. But the problem of expansion doesn't relate to the micronovel any more than it does to the traditional novel. The short-novel form is neither a digest nor a synopsis of a novel, nor is it a stretched-out novella but is precisely a full and complete micronovel.

Analysis has shown that the micronovel differs from the three traditional and highly flexible genres of prose – the short story, the novella and the novel – and has a right to exist in both literatures. In content the micronovel is wider and socially deeper than the novella, although it has some of its features. The micronovel is distinct from the *povest'* as well.

There is present, in this sort of miniature novel, the entirety of plot that traditional Western and Russian literary schools demand of a novel. *Vorgeschichte* ('forestory') is one of three German terms that showed up in Russian theory in the 1920s. In the capacity of a deviation from the fundamental design of a narration, *Vorgeschichte* offers a description of events happening to the protagonists outside the framework of the basic plot. Certain authors in the 1920s and 1930s, depending on the fact that in a novella or a short story the author or the protagonist alludes to the past, suggested that *Vorgeschichte* was above all characteristic of the novella. The issue here, though, is in the depth of the description of the past and the interference of that past in the changes of destiny affecting the protagonists. This is an indispensable component of the micronovel, both historically and in essence.

The *Nachgeschichte* ('afterstory') traditionally contemplates information about what happens to the participants in the events after the completion of the plot. Once again, tradition keeps this term within the theory of the classical novella. Just like an epilogue, though, the *Nachgeschichte* brings a conclusion to the plot, and this is a characteristic of the micronovel. Finally, the Zwiechengeschichte ('mid-story'), information about what happens between plot events, is also a necessary component of the short-novel form.

With the micronovel, a novelistic plot is packed into a novella-shaped shell. Macrocontents in microform. The micronovel is a novel that is finished, realized – just short. The short genre is important. 'I prefer the short story because only in the short story and not in the novel does the writer achieve perfection,' wrote Isaac Bashevis Singer. 'When you write a novel, especially a large novel, you don't have the power to steer your own text, since in reality you can't make a plan for five hundred pages and stick to it. But on the other hand there's always the possibility of putting together a short story that is genuinely marvellous.' Is it necessary to add that the short-novel form, or micronovel, is that very compromise between the novella (or short story) and the novel – in which the writer, striving towards a perfected novel, keeps the situation under control?

One normally speaks of three forms of prose: small, medium and large. Of those three, to which does the micronovel belong – medium? Or is this a small form with large contents? Or to all three at once? It's not much use being categorical about it: after all, one piece of writing captures an entire life while remaining a short story, while Joyce's novel *Ulysses* takes a single day. Speaking of craftsmanship, a particular capacity is a necessity for packing in the required novelistic contents. The issue, of course, doesn't lie in the word count: Art, according to Chesterton, begins with self-limitation. As the wonderful Jules Renard says, style is without drivel.

Why did I choose 'micronovel' and not 'mininovel'? 'Micro' is the prefix we use that comes from the Greek for 'small' or 'short', while 'mini', coming from the Latin 'minor', has as a prefix the usual meaning of 'the smallest (of a class of things)'. The choice of prefixes isn't that important, but the fact is that the term 'micronovel' has already taken root in literary usage. This term of mine first appeared in Russia in Samizdat, my self-published manuscripts of officially unapproved literature in 1960s.

Micronovels reflect the destiny of the unpublished literature of our era. My micronovels were published in the West. For the first time in the world, a Russian book was released as a 'micronovel' by Word publishing house in New York in 1991. Volumes of my micronovels were released in Russia, Poland, Bulgaria and Turkey. Beginning in 1990, the micronovel was introduced into university courses on nineteenth- and twentieth-century prose as a rightful genre on equal terms with the rest.

Individual micronovels of mine have long been printed in the bigger magazines of post-Soviet Russia, but they were regarded somewhat as stepchildren. The first thing the editors would do was to strike out the word 'micronovel' and insert 'short story'. Then they began to get used to it, apparently.

The reality today is that it is a compact genre, in keeping with our fast-flowing times. Fiction with flights of imagination, elastic plots, new subjects. The internet has taken to the micronovel as a genre appropriate to reading on the computer. Readers listen to my 'automobile micronovel' on compact disk on the way to work and back. Whatever the sceptics may predict, no genre dies out. As we have seen, in the twenty-first century this new genre has acquired legitimacy, filling a niche for a genre in which large-novel ideas accumulate energy in the space of a mere thirty pages.

Yuri Druzhnikov
Davis, California

Also by Yuri Druzhnikov

Angels on the Head of a Pin

978 0 7206 1170 0 • cased • 566pp • £17.95
Translated from the Russian by Thomas Moore

'A very important book. This is the way, gradually, that at least most Soviet lies will be revealed.' – Aleksandr Solzhenitsyn

'This stunning work of genius . . . as scathingly funny as it is unrelentingly deadly' – *Review of Contemporary Fiction*

'Combines a sense of humour with a fantastic ability to write between the lines'– Isaac Bashevis Singer

Angels on the Head of a Pin is set in late 1960s' Moscow when liberalization of the Communist regime is threatened by the return to personality cult and repression following the Soviet intervention in Czechoslovakia. The Editor of the Communist Party newspaper collapses with a heart attack partly brought on by the appearance of an explosive *samizdat* manuscript on his desk that fills him with dread at the malevolence its content may unleash. The solution lies with Yakov Rappoport, an ageing and cynical Jewish veteran of the war and two spells in the Gulag, who is the author of not only every obnoxious campaign sponsored by the newspaper (and all its letters to the editor) but every speech made in public by the principals of the regime. His efforts to help his stricken editor, as well as the novel's star-crossed lovers, lead to a hallucinatory climax.

www.peterowen.com

Also by Yuri Druzhnikov

Madonna from Russia

978 0 7206 11255 4 • cased • 224pp • £15.95
Translated from the Russian by Thomas Moore

'*Madonna from Russia* is Druznhikov's
gutsy response to the challenge of his
precursors . . . His writing is at times
reminiscent of Solzhenitsyn, but
Druzhnikov has a lot more humour and
even offers a whiff of magical realism.'
– Tibor Fischer, *Guardian*

'Druznhikov's sublime work mirrors
Soviet corruption in its engaging prose
. . . a transcendent allegorical epic'
– *Big Issue*

Lily was a beautiful young prostitute recruited by the
Bolsheviks to service the Communist elite. As a result of a
fortuitous marriage to a famous poet, Futurist and artistic
associate of Malevich and Mayakovsky, her own verse is
delivered to the official Communist press, together with an
entirely invented revolutionary biography. Before long she is
made poet laureate and is being fêted as an idealized symbol
of the Soviet era, while her husband, after being incarcerated
in a mental hospital by Lily, disappears in the purges. After
the collapse of several more marriages – and the Soviet
Union – she leaves Russia for the United States. This is
where we meet her, still striking-looking, engaged to a naïve
American and starting out yet again at the age of ninety-six.
Following further bizarre and picaresque adventures, she
reaches for her greatest honour: to be made 'Queen Lily the
First' of the brand-new island state of Grande Bravo.

www.peterowen.com

Also by Yuri Druzhnikov

Passport to Yesterday

978 0 7206 1218 9 • cased • 204pp • £15.95
Translated from the Russian by Thomas Moore

'Slender, delicate and written in a voice that manages to combine plainness and poetry, horror and humour, in a quite extraordinary way' – *Literary Review*

'Druzhnikov, a 2001 Nobel Prize nominee, writes with vigorous, uncompromising prose, emitting flashes of cinematic brilliance.' – *Good Book Guide*

'People are badly put together. They remember everything. Remember even things that should have been scattered to the winds long before.' Gifted young Russian violinist Oleg Nemets' rural life is overturned in the storm of the Second World War and the repressive regime that succeeds it. Blown far away from home and a father who never returned from the front, Oleg lands in San Francico as a violinist in a symphony orchestra. But years later, when the orchestra tours the Soviet Union, a series of events and clues from his past lead him back to his old town, the story of his father's disappearance and the Russia he left behind . . .

www.peterowen.com